Ross D

They Die Alone
Sleep Not, My Child
For A Sin Offering
To Catch Is Not To Hold
Unto The Daughters Of Men
A Bullet To Dream Of
Every Secret Thing
Naked Shall I Return

NAKED SHALL I RETURN

A Ross Duncan Thriller

Christopher Bartley

PEACH PUBLISHING

Published by
Peach Publishing

Dedication

For my Karen, who grows pitaya – the "dragon fruit" cactus. Their blooms are bright and complex and they avoid the light. They only appear at night for a few hours, and only once in the life of the plant. If not pollinated in those hours the flower dies and the plant remains dormant for many more months. The flower, whether pollinated or not, is itself a part of the cosmos. It is ephemeral, fragile, beautiful, and precious, reaching up toward the brief, faint access to light – to starlight. I love to watch my Karen from the windows as she moves about in her garden-orchard.

Author's Note

This novel is a work of fiction set within a specific historical context. Although the principle characters in this story are fictional, the broader historical context, including the Chinese Six Companies, Adolf Sutro, and the magnificent Cliff House, are genuine. Apart from its fictional elements, I have done my best to ensure this novel is historically accurate to the period in which it is set. Similarities to people currently living or dead are purely coincidental. I apologize in advance for the inevitable historical mistakes and anachronistic inaccuracies, which are my fault alone.

"Naked came I out of my mother's womb, and naked shall I return thither: the LORD gave, and the LORD hath taken away; blessed be the name of the LORD."
(Job 1:21)

Prologue

Six of us entered the Illinois Trust and Savings Bank. The man Bendix had chosen to bring carried a double barrel sawed off shotgun beneath a folded raincoat over his left arm. The other four were carrying Thompson machine guns wrapped in brown packing paper. I carried my .45, a bag filled with handcuffs, and a diagram of the bank that Gordon had drawn on foolscap with a razor-sharpened charcoal pencil.

I was in the lead and held the wrought iron handle of a heavy door as the others went in before me. The brown packing paper was torn off quickly and discarded onto the floor of the foyer. I drew my .45 from its shoulder holster and thumbed off the safety.

Past the foyer there was an old duffer in a camel hair jacket. There was a green-blue-red peacock feather positioned carefully in his hatband. "So what's this?" he asked, as the others filed past him. Wide blunt fingers of one hand came forward slowly, as though he might place the entire hand on my chest. I didn't let him.

I showed him my pistol and held a finger to my lips. "Take it easy, pop. This will be quick and then you'll be on your way home as though it never happened. Stand over there, please."

"I've never seen —"

"Well, now you have. Over there."

We worked quickly with an efficiency of sound and motion. With information provided by our inside man we caught the armed guards flat-footed at the change of their shift. Gordon took the one coming down the ladder from the cage and got the cuffs on him quietly while Bendix and Willie Shears got the other guards herded together against the inside wall.

One of them thought about mounting a protest and took his palms off the wall. The spot he had vacated glistened momentarily with a sweat-laden imprint of his hand that shone in the light and then shrank quickly until it disappeared on itself. I noticed he wore a wedding ring.

"Forget it, grandpa," Bendix said, dangling a pair of handcuffs in front of his face. "These are yours. You know what to do with them."

The man snatched them angrily and fastened them onto himself without saying another word. The others cuffed themselves, hands in front, and then they all followed the next directive to face the wall.

"It's the best view today," Bendix offered cheerfully. "Study it with care. The less you see of us the better for you."

I directed traffic in the primary chamber of the bank, pacing down the long open room, pushing the customers back into a section of the bank shielded from view of the street, just under the light of a high transom that left me standing in a square pane of warm sunlight. Everything was quiet for the longest while.

Bendix's man with the sawed off shotgun positioned himself by the window looking over La Salle. There was a squinting apprehension over his face that hadn't been there earlier. Gordon and a man called Fingers Pete, who had come out from the east coast with Willie Shears, waited patiently against an interior wall deep in the bank with their Thompson guns pointed toward the ceiling. Bendix, Shears, and I roamed behind the cashier's station scooping piles of cash and bonds into our large leather valises.

The money had been laid out in neat piles of green, as if someone had anticipated our visit in advance – which perhaps they had. It was a lush emerald field that hypnotized. Momentarily I paused, taken by a dream, a reverie, a delusion of the seemingly infinite possibilities it represented.

Then the nagging drummer in my skull beat his snare and I turned back to the blood work at hand.

*

I was packing cash and humming a jaunty version of "Skip to my Lou" inside my head when I heard the gunshot. It was the crack of a low caliber pistol, not the sound a Thompson makes.

Ducking instinctively down below the counter where I stood, I came carefully around the corner towards the vault with my .45 in front of me. What I saw there was Willie Shears standing over a man, one of the bank employees I presumed, who was now down on the ground. I couldn't see his face well, but the man was of middle build with smooth, hairless hands and a recent haircut. From what I could see I placed him somewhere in his mid - to late-thirties. He was dressed in an expensive pinstripe suit and shoes that had been polished recently.

Shears had shot him in the head.

Without any sense of urgency the contract killer from New York stood there with a .22 pistol in his right hand and the Thompson cradled in his left, staring calmly down over the form below him as though he were studying a rare flower in a field. The toe of his wingtip shoe came forward and nudged the man gently. That didn't lead to anything. Satisfied, Shears put the pistol

2

into his back right pocket and shifted the Thompson gun to his right hand again, with the barrel now steadied again by his left.

I kept my .45 on alert in front of my body as I straightened up. "This has an explanation?"

"I told him to get out of my way. He reached for a pistol in the desk drawer. What else could I have done?"

"Nuts." There weren't any open desk drawers to be seen, but this wasn't the right moment for a discussion on the matter. Bendix came up beside me, furious and swearing. He carried his own Thompson pointed tightly in front of him.

"Shhhh, it's okay," I said to him without taking my eyes off Shears. "The man reached. Shears didn't have a choice."

I made a face that Shears couldn't see and Bendix nodded. He let loose with some more swearing, but Shears shrugged it off and moved toward the vault, kicking his valise across the floor in front of him. I glanced back at Bendix and swiped the first knuckle of my left forefinger down along the side of my nose.

"Don't turn your back on anyone from New York today," I told him in a low voice.

Bendix nodded again, quiet now, and then he picked up his own valise and moved toward the vault with it. I headed back to check on Gordon.

*

The pistol shot was soft enough that I doubted anyone outside the bank would have heard it. Still, it seemed likely to have narrowed our timeframe.

I whispered quietly in Gordon's ear to tell him the score. Then I hurried over to the front door for a look out at Jackson Boulevard. Nothing showed there. I glanced over at Bendix's man and made a circular hand motion with two fingers and a thumb in the air. His squint deepened. After a pause, he nodded, turned, and swept his gaze down the view along La Salle. With a tight grimace holding his ears forward he shrugged in an exaggerated fashion and shook his head. Nothing. He turned back to study the wide-open street again.

I didn't wait around for his next report. We had the valises filled and Bendix and Shears were coming out from the vault area now, walking fast, but not quite running. Their leather shoes seemed to skitter and scrape as they moved.

"Anything?" Bendix asked curtly, when he came up beside me. He'd held back just enough so that Shears got there first. He wasn't going to let the man have his back.

"It's quiet as a Sunday," I said. "Nothing to see out there at all."

3

"Those federal trucks might even help us out. They block the view and slow the traffic."

I nodded. "Unless there're snipers waiting on the roof across the way."

"You worry too much."

"Is there such a thing in this line?"

"Pshaww!"

"Let's go," Shears interjected loudly, pushing past us toward the foyer with disregard. When he got there he paused and looked through the window momentarily before he stooped at the knees to set his machine gun on the floor. Then he opened the heavy door and moved right through it in one long looping motion.

Fingers Pete was hurrying to catch up with him and almost forgot to leave his Thompson behind. As he leaned over to set it down, he gave a quick distrusting glance back at us. His dark eyes scanned the room in a fluid and experienced motion, pausing for an instant as they met mine. A flash of mutual recognition passed between us: two enemies sighting each other for the first time.

"Got to love Shears' confidence," Bendix said.

"Or wonder about it," I replied.

Bendix set his machine gun on the floor where he stood, readjusted his grip on the valise, and gave me a glance. "Let's hit sunlight."

*

Our plan called for us to split up at that point. Shears and his partner were to catch the Rock Island out of town from the La Salle Passenger Station that was a block south of us on Van Buren. I didn't know where they were headed, but I assumed it was back to New York. The rest of us were to head east for a block on Quincy Street and catch an 'L' train at the station there. In the planning meeting there'd been some discussion about who would take which station, but the New Yorkers were leaving town and we were not. That dictated the station assignments.

We stepped out, past the Doric columns of the bank and started toward Quincy, four of us with our valises and the handguns we carried inside our jackets. Gordon and I each wore a bulletproof vest. I wasn't sure about the other two, but I doubted they did. Neither of them looked bulkier than they should have, or moved with the leaden weight around them that a vest gave.

The sky above burned a blue flame that seared the back of the eyes. The wind had died and seabirds flew over in a loose formation.

We walked fast.

The gunners were waiting for us in an old Dodge sedan illegally parked by

The Rookery. There were four of them and the barrel of an overeager machine gun was visible as we neared. If we'd turned down Quincy as planned, they would have taken us from behind and made quick sport of filling us with lead. I saw them first, and then Bendix reacted too by drawing a .38 Colt revolver.

The sedan came at us with a roar. Slugs from a machine gun rattled the street around us, ricocheting up and away, sending chips of concrete into the air. A second machine gun came alive. A slug tore through my jacket below my hip, pulling it off-center. We returned fire on the move, staying low, not rooted to any one spot. My first two shots punched out a back window that hadn't been rolled all the way down and silenced one of the machine guns.

All guns blazed now. There was a cry at my elbow. Bendix's partner, a man whose name I'd never learned, fell over backwards with blood pumping fast from wounds in his neck and chest. He'd be dead in seconds.

I knelt beside my valise and steadied my .45 with both hands to fire rapidly, a tight arc across the front windshield, ending at the driver's side window. The pace of firing around me had slowed. When my magazine was empty I ejected it with my thumb and shoved in another one.

A new gun, a large caliber pistol fired at us from the Dodge now. It was the other man in the back seat of the sedan, leaning across to fire through the smashed window. Gordon was hit. He took a bullet somewhere to his torso and grunted hard as it pushed him backwards. He landed flat on his back and stayed there.

There wasn't time for me to attend to him. Bendix called out that he was reloading. I reentered the fight, squeezing off three shots, quickly paced, each with an intentional aim. More glass exploded from the Dodge and suddenly there was a lull in the fire. No one was shooting back at us.

I felt the motion coming up from behind us more than I heard it. The Buick pulled in fast and hit the curb at an angle, with a screech of breaks. Gordon was in first. He jumped into the back seat and all the way across so that he could fire out the far side window at the Dodge. The sound of his reports split the air.

Delilah had all the windows rolled down as I'd instructed her. Bendix was in next. I got off three more shots, dropped my empty magazine to the concrete and hopped into the front seat.

I was still pulling the door shut beside me as we made thirty miles an hour, tooling north up La Salle, right past the shooters in the Dodge who were now trying to keep up with us by moving in reverse. It was a losing proposition for them and they were slowed by the film of red that now covered the back window. In the instant as we went by them I counted only two heads upright and they were both ducking as Gordon took one last shot at them.

"Hit this right, darling!" Bendix encouraged Delilah as we approached the second intersection.

The Buick cornered smartly onto Monroe, flattened out and then slowed as we caught up to the traffic flow in front of us. There were two blocks of that and then she took a left on Dearborn, another quick left on Madison, and sailed that for all it was worth out past Union Park.

"You should get your ticket punched for this one, sweetheart," Bendix exclaimed, congratulating Delilah. "Nice to see you again. First time it was a boxing spectacle, and now the Indianapolis 500."

"I'm a regular sports fan," she replied. Her breathing was calm, but her fingers gripped the wheel tight enough to crack a walnut.

"Enough of that," I chimed in. "We've got other worries."

"We're lucky to have them," Bendix said. "That trap was meant to finish us. Glad you enlisted your own driver."

"Are you okay?" I asked Gordon, looking back over the seat at him.

He nodded. There was a little blood at his collar, but not enough to suggest a major wound. "Two shots," he said, "direct hits to the center of my chest."

"You wearing a vest?" Bendix asked, with some surprise.

Gordon nodded again, with the same fatigued expression. "Lucky for me, but there's going to be a hell of a bruise in the morning."

"Better than a funeral," Bendix replied seriously.

"Are we clear yet?" Delilah asked into the next quiet space.

"I believe so," I told her. "They expected to catch us on foot down Quincy, an alley that dead ended at the station. They might have had a second team waiting down that way for us, but they couldn't have scrambled in time to keep up with us."

Gordon said: "Nice driving, best I've seen yet."

I smiled back at him and then patted Delilah on the lap with my left hand.

"Now where?" she asked with a sigh. She swiped the hair from her forehead with the back of her hand, keeping the wheel straight with her other hand balanced at twelve o'clock.

"We have to ditch the Buick."

"Why?" she exclaimed. "I like this machine. It cost real money."

"I know it. We have a better one waiting for us."

"So we just ditch this, give it up for nothing in return?"

"If you're going to be a moll, you have to learn about these things. Once you use an auto on a job, you can't continue to drive it around town like nothing happened. You have to give it up. We switch them out all the time; there's a small industry of people who help us, for a nice profit. Think of it as a trade. They trick up the next one, and collect this one. They break it down so no one can recognize it and we don't have to worry about it."

"Yeah? What else do you know?"

"Plenty. Maybe I'll write a book."

"Maybe you ought to. What're we driving next?"

"A Ford: simple, non-descript, roomy. It's all but bullet proof and it has a V8 engine that doesn't wait for anyone."

"Sounds just like the old jalopy I traded for this swell Buick."

"See the pole? The left right after it is ours."

Chapter One

November 1934

From the window I looked out over the bay. Directly overhead the sky rippled blue, though it was darkening farther out in the direction where I looked. The wide end of a tapered rainbow landed heavily in the water, splashing the air with red, yellow, and blue colors.

I'd arrived in San Francisco a week before with three suitcases and a large satchel. Collectively they held my personal belongings, a lot of cash, several small bags of hot jewels, and twenty thousand dollars worth of narcotics that had been stolen from Detroit.

The only other thing of note that I'd brought with me was a woman. Her name was Harley Nevers and she'd brought everything she'd wanted to bring with her in a paper bag that had a string tied around it. It had been a nice week, but now she was gone – off to try her luck with the other doomed hopefuls in Hollywood. I didn't hold that against her. She was young and beautiful and didn't yet know that a lot of other people were too.

As the morning drew late, I was down to my last Chesterfield and I had to make some decisions. I stood up and went out onto the balcony, into the early afternoon sunlight, to light the cigarette. Alcatraz was out there, resting in the bay, anchored hard amid the swift currents. While I smoked, I stared at it and thought about the men I knew who were out there. There were several.

The wind picked up and brought a seabird with it. He fluttered in and landed on the rail. It occurred to me he could have been out to Alcatraz and back many times in his life. I wondered if he'd met Al Capone or Machinegun Kelly out in the yard. I asked him out loud, but he didn't answer me. A moment later he gave a mysterious screech and took off again into the air.

I finished the cigarette all by myself.

*

At the Hyde Street Pier I bought a couple packages of Chesterfields and caught the auto ferry across the bay to Sausalito. As we passed Alcatraz, I sat on the opposite side of the ferry so I wouldn't have to see the penal island up close. I didn't want to think about it.

After we docked, I fell in with a long line of automobiles and worked my way down the main street of Sausalito until I connected onto Highway 101.

A short time later I veered off at Route One, the Shoreline Highway. The traffic quickly fell away and I followed the road up through the curves into the densely wooded hills.

I drove slowly. It would have been easy to get lost. Eventually I took a series of turns and then a private road took me up to the house. It was one lane until very close and then it opened up to offer a brick-paved parking apron.

The sky floated expansively above. I checked inside the satchel I'd brought with me and then latched it again. After I climbed out of the Ford, I glanced back over the bay toward the city of towers on the other side, now partially submerged in a low-lying fog. As I drew a long breath a prayer floated through my mind and then I remembered why I was there.

The house was a tall structure, at least three stories, layered in the style of an oversized Italian villa. Built solidly of large stones, I could see it was L-shaped and a part of the drive passed through a pair of wide doors, below a windowed room that looked out over the front of the house.

The doors had been left open, reminding me of a lowered castle drawbridge, though I was unsure which approach I should take. I opted for the formal route and went up to the massive front door and clattered the knocker about. Nothing happened for a moment and then I heard the muffled sound of a woman's voice.

"Around here," it called.

I came off the front steps and retraced my path back to the parking apron and driveway to peer through the wide doors that had been left open. From that angle, I could see a parked automobile on the other side – a well cared for black Auburn V-12 Boattail Speedster with white-walled tires.

It was parked deep in on the lawn at a stylish angle with its tapered back end and silver accent lines pointing toward the house. It was a two-seater with a long front end and a lot of power – the type of automobile that only someone who really liked to drive would have.

I tamped down my envy and walked through the opening into the private courtyard. There was a long gentle pool with black tile on the bottom and a fountain with a Cupid-like figure spitting a steady stream of water into the air. A large pool house – built in the same style as the main house – waited at the other end of the pool. It was dark and closed up in a way that was not inviting.

An attractive blonde haired woman, who appeared to be in her mid-forties, rose up from beyond a bed of dead marigolds, Mexican or African I wasn't sure. Her eyes were encircled heavily with dark mascara as if to represent a thousand sorrows she had borne witness to in her life.

"You must be Mr. Duncan," she said, coming towards me with her hands dirty and full of clipped stalks and leaves. "I understand you have a special

9

relationship to the men that Mr. Hoover directs."

With the scratch in her voice and the markings on the back of her hands, I realized she was a little older than I had initially thought. I liked her immediately and felt at home with someone who could be so earnest with a stranger she had only just met.

"Call me Ross, please," I told her. "I'm not sure the relationship is so special. We don't exchange cards at Christmas time."

Ignoring my quip, she held out her hands to me. "This is Tiburon Indian paintbrush," she said to me, holding up the clippings she recently cut. "It's an herb and it peaks with bracts of pink, yellow, and reddish orange. However, I can't get it to thrive up here at this elevation. Every year I plant it, and every year just when I think it's going to make it, it fails. They say it does better at lower altitudes, and I guess they must be right. I've also tried to grow Tiburon Jewel flower, but with even worse success."

"I'm sure your garden is lovely in the springtime."
"Do you mind frogs?"

"They've never done anything wrong to me."

She looked at me earnestly. "We have a lot of the California red-legged frogs up here. When my grandchildren come to visit we catch them and keep them in small aquarium we have inside the house. We also have a turtle."

"You hardly look old enough to have grandchildren, let alone grandchildren old enough to chase frogs and turtles."

"I'm seventy-two, a year younger than my husband. You didn't come all this way to talk frogs and Tiburon plants with me. Let me find my husband. He's around here somewhere." She made a quarter turn toward the spur-end of the house, searching with her eyes, focusing her gaze past the Auburn Boattail Speedster. "Randolph!" she called, though not too loudly.

A moment later a very fit man emerged from behind a hedge with a large pair of clippers in his right hand. Above a pair of dark slacks, he wore a well-tailored blue shirt with a white collar. The shirt was stained faintly with his sweat in the areas where it clung to his body. The ample gray hair on his chest showed through at the unbuttoned V of his neck.

"Hello, you must be Ross Duncan," he said enthusiastically. "You have good references. I'm Dr. Randolph Orion; this is my wife, Susan."

He smiled genuinely, showing a lot of white teeth as he shook my hand firmly. His other hand rested on his wife's shoulder.

"Dr. Orion, I'm pleased to meet you," I said.

"We'll sit over there, by the pool." He pointed toward a round iron table with a quartet of chairs drawn up around it. It waited in the shade of a tall tree and was covered with fallen leaves and clipped shrubs that had been laid on top of it.

"Oh, Randolph, that's too dirty," Susan Orion complained.

"It's perfectly fine, dear. You don't mind sitting outside do you, Mr. Duncan?"

"Call me, Ross, please."

We crossed the yard together, kicking through the leaves and grass clippings on the ground. Dr. Orion gestured toward a chair for his wife and one for me, and then sat down in one himself once we were seated. I placed my satchel on the table and unlocked it, but did not open it.

"Where are my manners," Susan Orion exclaimed suddenly, sitting forward with her hands clapped in front of her. "What would you like to drink?"

"Nothing at all, thank you," I said to her.

"Not even coffee or tea?" she asked anxiously. "I can offer you something stronger if you would like that."

"We have a bottle of Champagne chilled," Dr. Orion said. "Do you like champagne?" he said to me.

Before I had a chance to answer the question, Susan Orion had jumped up from her chair and was moving quickly back across the lawn toward a door at the side of the house. I relaxed back in my chair and lighted a cigarette.

Dr. Orion leaned forward with his arms on the iron table and smiled at me. It was a reassuring smile that he shared over his dirty hands. It made me like him. "I've been out here for almost seven hours today, working on those hedges. They require a lot of clipping. You don't mind if Susan joins us, I hope. After a lifetime of a surgeon's hours, now that I'm retired we try to spend as much time together as we can."

"It must be nice to have had that shared intimacy over all those years."

He nodded and his smile broadened. "We've been married fifty-two years, but we go back farther then that. We come from neighboring small towns, so we've known of each other since high school. She was the most beautiful woman in the county then – and would be still if we went back there. I've been fortunate to have her at my side all these years, though I'm not sure how she's put up with me or my work hours all these years."

I almost blushed on her behalf. "Would you like to see the jewels?" I asked.

"Sure, but I'd like to have Susan's input too. She has an artistic eye and I rely on her judgment." As if reading something in my face, he continued. "You can trust her as you trust me."

"I have no problem with that."

"Some men do. Forgive me for acting defensively. It was needless. I can see that now." He gestured with his open hands.

I opened the satchel. There were ten felt bags and a black felt lining on each side of the case. One by one I released the drawstring of each small bag and emptied its contents out onto the lining of the satchel. I used the back of the fingernail on my forefinger to separate the gems from each other and arrange them in lines on the black felt.

Susan Orion returned while I was doing that and handed a bottle of cold French champagne to her husband. He twisted off the wire that secured the cork and then eased the cork out with his thumb, pointing the bottle out over the pool. When it popped, the cork sailed in a soft arc and landed in the middle of the pool with a light splash.

Randolph Orion chuckled and poured champagne into the three flutes that his wife had arranged on a tray in the center of the table. She busied herself by sweeping off leaves and debris from the surface of the table with the palm of her hand.

"To *this* life," Orion announced as he held his glass aloft.

We clinked our glasses and then drank. Orion drank most of his; I tried to keep up. Susan Orion took only a small sip and set her glass down and frowned at it.

I stared at the bottle, trying to read it.

"It's Pommery & Greno; a nice French wine," Randolph Orion explained as he poured more champagne into my glass and then his own. "Do you like it?"

"I do," I said. "Mrs. Orion, you're frowning."

"There's a funny taste."

"Is something wrong?" her husband asked.

"I can't put my finger on it. It tastes off to me, but that's probably just me."

"How well do you know French champagne?" Orion inquired, looking in my direction.

"Not well at all," I confessed. "I've only had it on a few occasions. I only know I like it when it's cold."

"That's all that ever matters," he replied, smiling. "If you enjoy a drink, it doesn't matter if it cost one dollar a bottle or fifty. We're not highfalutin here, never have been."

I smiled at him and nodded.

Susan Orion interjected: "I always think the best wines are the ones you can drink and enjoy without having to be self-conscious about what they cost."

I drank off the top half of my refreshed glass of champagne. "Mrs. Orion -"

"Call me Susan, please," she interjected.

"Susan, would you like to look at the jewels I brought before I show them to your husband?"

She smiled at me and received the open case as I slid it her way on the iron table. Dr. Orion watched her happily, without showing any actual interest in the jewels that I had arranged for display.

"They're very beautiful," she said. "Where were they cut?"

I shrugged. "I believe some were cut in Amsterdam; others were cut in Egypt or Iran. At least that's what I was told."

"Do you trust the one who told you this?"

I had to laugh. I finished my cigarette and ground it into an ashtray that was on the champagne tray. "I don't know. I don't know what difference it makes. I heard it several times from seemingly independent people. Once when I went into the store, the salesman explained it to me that way. The man who planned the robbery also assured me that they were all cut in the Netherlands or the Middle East. These are supposed to be high quality stones."

"Do you believe they are?"

"For my money, we're all robbers in this business."

Orion's expression became intrigued. "What do you mean by that?"

I ran my tongue along my lower lip and looked at her very clearly in the eyes. "As you can see, I'm no expert in jewels. I'm a thief, and I was persuaded to take them. So, I did. The man who hired me died a few hours later. Someone I trust gave your name to me. He said I could trust you. I'm at your mercy."

"Thank you for being honest with us," Dr. Orion said earnestly. "Its commendable of you to take the straight approach."

"What do you think of them?"

Susan Orion held a glass eyepiece in one hand. Slowly, she went over each line of stones, occasionally stopping to pick up a gem with a special pair of tweezers so that she could study it in more detail. Once she did that and held it up toward the sky to catch more light. It took her almost fifteen minutes to go through the entire batch. We didn't speak while she continued her inspection. Occasionally Dr. Orion glanced at me and smiled reassuringly as he sipped his champagne patiently.

When she finished, without comment Susan Orion handed the eyepiece to her husband and carefully pushed the entire satchel over to him so that he could inspect the jewels too. With the back of the case opened at a 90-degree angle, it essentially formed a shield that prevented me from observing his study of the stones.

It would have been a simple matter for him to make substitutions that favored him. I didn't worry that he would do that. I barely even watched him. After less than two minutes he set the eyepiece down and stretched back in his chair with his arms behind his head, smiling. He had barely looked at the gems.

"What do you think?" I asked.

Dr. Orion answered. "I think we can do business if you're willing to accept our commission." He named a percentage.

I nodded my agreement. "How much do you value the stones at?"

Susan Orion cleared her throat and responded by naming a rather high figure. "At least it should be somewhere in that neighborhood, give or take a few thousand."

I whistled. It was a quite bit more than I expected she would say.

"I take that to mean we have an understanding," Orion asked.

I nodded. "We do."

"Have a little more champagne?" he offered.

"Thank you," I said. "How long will it take you to move the stones?"

"For something like this, seven to twelve days. Is that fast enough?"

"That's plenty fast."

"Where are you staying?" he asked.

"Do you need to know?"

"We have to find you somehow. Do you have an answering service?"

I considered it and then said: "I'm at the Fairmont right now, under the name of Richard Huddleston. Sometimes I move around a bit, so if I'm not there when you look for me, post a letter to me, San Francisco, General Delivery. If I move out before I hear from you, I'll check every morning starting the day after tomorrow."

Dr. Orion smiled mysteriously and nodded his head as he reached for the bottle that now had condensation dripping down the sides of it. "That's fine. I'm going to change the topic because I think there might be something *you* can do for us," he said.

"It's getting chilly out here, Randolph" Susan Orion stated, as if to move her husband along.

He nodded to placate her. "What do you think about immortality?" he asked me as he poured out the rest of the bottle into the three glasses. "Are we more than mere shadows on the wall of a cave?"

Chapter Two

The temperature in the air was beginning to drop as the sky moved over and the shadows lengthened. I finished the champagne in my glass before responding to Dr. Orion's question.

"I thought *immortality* was a dream from the middle-ages, a fantasy, something that unscrupulous con men sold to the gullible in the form of elixirs, bathes, potions, spells, quests. Now modern medicine offers a new twist on it? I don't think so. It's a cruel impossibility."

"Is it?" Orion asked cryptically. His eyes were sharp as he watched me.

"You're the surgeon," I said. "You tell me, Dr. Orion. I'm sure we've both seen plenty of death in all its ugly forms. Maybe I've got it wrong."

Orion's face twisted seriously. He nodded in agreement to acknowledge my experience, glancing at his wife. "Susan, what are your thoughts?"

The Orions spoke to each other as though I were already adopted into the family. Susan Orion shrugged and looked off to one side and then stared back at me. "I think the longevity of human life is only just beginning to expand. Right now, we can only speculate about its limits."

"What do you mean by that?" I asked.

Her eyes didn't so much as blink before she responded: "Last year the life expectancy for a man in America was sixty-two years, and for a woman sixty-five years. Randolph and I are already well beyond that ourselves. Thirty-one years ago, in 1903 – the year my grandmother died in her late fifties – life expectancy was forty-nine and fifty-two, for men and women respectively. That was not much different from the years after the Civil War. There was very little change over the forty years to that point. White people could expect to live about forty-eight years, and poor colored folks could expect to live for thirty-three. Who knows where expectancy will be when our grandchildren grow up."

"You've studied the topic," I said.

"I like to read."

"It seems there's a rising trend," I offered.

"There is and it's going to rise more over the next fifty years, and perhaps not in tiny steps, but in large leaps. I think by the end of this century, many people will be living well into the hundreds."

"Medical advances and science," I replied. "Maybe they'll help people live longer. That's not the same thing as living forever."

"No, it's not," Dr. Orion interjected. "However, I think the upward trend can

15

be accelerated. If people today live into their sixties, we can project younger people living into their seventies, eighties, and nineties. Right? Where does that end? Who is to say that humans can't reasonably live to be one hundred on a frequent basis?"

I thought about all the bullets that had missed me to that point, and grinned. "Why stop there?" I queried.

"Exactly," Dr. Orion responded loudly, slapping his hand down on the iron table between us. He grinned at me with his lips fixed back. I nodded as he leaned forward with his elbows on the table close to me. "That is *exactly* the point! If humans can live to be a hundred, why not a hundred and ten; and if that, why not a hundred and fifty; and if that, why not more? We won't get there unless we can imagine it."

The light in his eye could have been the glow of madness, but I found myself nodding in agreement as I heard a chorus of '*amen*'s' singing in the deep recesses of my mind.

*

"I mentioned there is something you can do for us," Dr. Orion reminded me.

"You didn't mention what it was."

"There is a package of great value that we would like you to recover for us. We cannot entrust anyone else with this."

"Why me?"

"Because you have special talents, and because I believe you have the right heart. They say you are a very serious man, a determined man when you are convinced of the cause – even if the cause is merely business or loyalty to others."

It was an unusual statement. "Whatever gave you that idea?"

"Everyone agrees you have special talents."

"What about the rest of it?"

"Some have described it to us before you arrived. I can see it for myself. I would be surprised if Susan did not also see it too. Susan?"

Susan Orion stared at her husband for a moment, and then turned toward me and nodded in agreement with what he had said. She did not speak.

"What is it?" I inquired. "What is this package you want me to find and recover?"

"What is it not," Orion responded mysteriously.

I shook my head. "No riddles, please. I'll need to know what I'm looking for."

"I'll tell you this," Dr. Orion replied. "I believe its here, somewhere, in the area near San Francisco, where it arrived from far away and from long ago."

16

"How far?" I was stuck asking all the obvious questions.

Dr. Orion's eyes narrowed and became clever. He glanced over at his wife before responding to my question. "We do not know for sure, but almost certainly it passed through one of the Middle Eastern countries within the past century. It could be from Egypt or Persia, or possibly another country from that area, that Fertile Crescent. Before that, you might ask? It probably came from China. It may have originated there, or it may simply have passed through during one of the ancient dynasties. Nobody knows and there are many theories."

"Where and when was this package last seen?" I asked.

Dr. Orion tilted his head back and laughed heartily. "Where was it *not* seen? How many yesterdays can you count?"

"We're not making much progress," I sighed. "What do you reliably know about it?"

"Reliably? Virtually nothing. We believe it was stolen from Sutro's French Chalet Cliff House, the second version of it, just before or during the fire that burned it to its foundation."

"I don't know anything about that."

"There's no reason you should," Orion grinned. "I think the fire was set to divert attention or to hide the theft entirely."

"Why don't you back up and start at the beginning," I suggested.

"That," Orion said, with a quick glance at his wife, "is a very good idea."

*

Dr. Orion told the story in one fluid speech, without moving or shifting his gaze away from mine: "The origin is unknown. The scholars cannot agree among themselves on where it came from, or when, or how, or even what it is. There is evidence it came through Egypt or Persia during the previous century. Before that, probably China. It may go back to the age of the druids, or even farther.

"Since we are already deep into the afternoon, I'll bring the story forward to a point in time during the last century, when the evidence suggests that it arrived on these very shores – the shores of San Francisco Bay.

"You may not know this area well, but I'm sure you know that the second half of the Nineteenth Century was a boom area for coastal California in general and San Francisco specifically. First, there was the gold rush of 1849, which persisted for several years, and resulted in the arrival of men from all over the world – hungry men, desperate men, men willing to work and sacrifice for their dream of riches.

"Few of those men ever actually found the riches they dreamed of, but no

17

matter, the momentum of history and demographics surged inexorably. The people who came to this area brought things with them – valuable things. They brought their cultures, their cuisines, their skills – the same skills that were needed to build cities and ports and seafaring vessels once the absurd dream of gold riches had receded into memory.

"It was a land of enterprise. The eastern railroads were coming this way and the local entrepreneurs built the railroads out to meet them in the prairies. That meant a new type of gold rush – land, agriculture, cattle, and international commerce. People continued to arrive here from all over the world. They came from China, Japan, Persia, Egypt, the Philippines, Russia, South America, and even old Europe.

"Many artifacts from the old worlds arrived here only to be bought and sold for new dreams, new ventures, new hopes. These included things of great value – inestimable works of art, recipes, heirlooms, rare jewels of fathomless beauty and value, even diaries and writings passed down from generation to generation. It is nearly impossible to overstate the trove of treasure that found its way into this port, this bubbling cauldron of human enterprise.

"In 1863, the same year that General Robert E. Lee reached the high-water mark of the Confederacy at Gettysburg, a California State Senator named John Buckley financed a local real estate speculator's dream to build the very first Cliff House. It was to be a restaurant and balcony overlooking Seal Rocks, intended to serve the wealthiest residents of San Francisco.

"Despite its exorbitant prices, the place quickly became successful and business boomed. A man named Foster who ran the place expanded it in 1868, enlarging the building and the promenade over the dunes to attract larger crowds, who increasingly became less, ah, shall we say sophisticated.

"More and more, the clientele gravitated towards the corrupt politicians and the Barbary Coast rowdies searching for good times. These parties were less concerned about matters of class and dignity.

"It was not long before the entire Cliff House and promenade had a reputation for scandal and wickedness. That phase lasted for sixteen years and then changed rather suddenly when Adolph Sutro moved into the heights above the Cliff House.

"This man had his sleep disturbed by the party down below one too many times, and in 1883 he purchased the house for himself. Once he owned it, he promptly embarked on restoring it to its former status as a place for the dignified wealthy with genteel tastes.

"It all went fine until 1887 when a schooner laden with black powder, kerosene, and dynamite caps ran aground just below the north wing of the house. Legend has it they heard the explosion all the way down in San Jose. Every window of the Cliff House and many in Mr. Sutro's house above it were shattered.

"The explosion demolished the north wing of the house. It would be nice to think the story ends there, after that, but a rather dull and routine kitchen fire destroyed the rest of the house seven years later on Christmas Day, 1894.

"I know what you're thinking. What does any of this have to do with the 'package' we've talked about, and why on earth, given the obviously cursed luck of this Cliff House, would anyone try to rebuild something there? But Mr. Sutro was not to be deterred. In his inimitable way, he rebuilt the Cliff House into a magnificent eight-story, towered French chateau-style mansion – a palace really, that he opened in 1896.

"There are still photographs of this palace around. Occasionally you will see them in a private home or antique shop. In any case, this second version of Sutro's Cliff House, a French Chalet, was entirely beyond words.

"Thirty years ago, Susan and I had the good fortune of being invited to an elegant soirée there one evening. It was splendid beyond belief. Entering the building on the ground floor, one could visit the bar, the dining room, or the sitting room. On the second floor were more rooms to eat in, as well as an art gallery and rare gem exhibit.

"The higher you went in this palace, the more spectacular it became. On the third floor was a photographic gallery and viewing parlors. The panoramic views through the oceanfront windows were, of course, incredible, yet they paled in comparison to the views from the tower that went up five stories higher.

"There was a ballroom filled with dancers and performers, the most beautiful and talented people you can imagine, brought in from all over the world. Adolf Sutro, who was probably half-mad, had established a nickel streetcar line to compete with the Southern Pacific's exorbitant fares.

"His dream was that his cliff house and baths would become low-cost entertainments for working class people, as well as the upper classes. He was a true populist of his day. He even ran for mayor against an established railroad man – and he won!"

"Where did that lead?" I asked, speaking for the first time in a good while.

Dr. Orion laughed quietly, glanced at his wife and then back at me. "Adolph Sutro died in 1898, two years after finishing his mansion. Isn't that just sad? He was land rich, but cash poor following his frustrating tenure as Mayor of San Francisco. That entire experience never developed into anything he could be happy about.

"You are probably beginning to understand that the resentments building against him were significant. Men of means and power were shaking their heads with disbelief. They lined up against him.

"Perhaps it should have come as no surprise, but a mysterious and

19

spectacular fire in 1907 caused the Cliff House to burn to its foundation in less than one hour. Sutro's Cliff House was no more. It ceased to exist right then and there."

Dr. Orion's eyes were wide and angry at the thought. "Was it a horrible accident, an act of God, or was it the dirty hand of bitter resentment? What started the fire? No one ever knew. The newspapers hinted it had something to do with renovations after Mr. Sutro's daughter had leased the house to a restaurateur named John Tait and his partners, whoever they were. Not many people in San Francisco accepted that story. Susan and I certainly don't." He gestured toward his wife to include her in the opinion.

"What happened after that?" I asked, interrupting the reverie of Dr. Orion's monologue.

"John Tait rebuilt the Cliff House in 1909 in an extraordinarily modest way. His three-story building is still there. You could drive down to see it if you wanted to. It's a small cliff house restaurant guaranteed to provide an outstanding view and unexciting food to all who arrive. It's designed to draw the masses, and they do come."

"You don't think the fire was a mere accident," I suggested.

"After what I've just laid out, do you?" Dr. Orion asked, smiling broadly.

"The mathematicians would tell us that real life is chock full of random occurrences," I replied. "Personally, I've never found it useful to accept that anything important is a product of happenstance."

"Exactly," Orion exclaimed with a large smile. He sat back in his chair and clasped his hands together in front of his chest and beat a slow tattoo with his thumbs along his chest.

When I looked at Susan Orion, she lowered her chin and closed her mascara-wrapped eyes. "Everything happens for a reason," she said elusively.

Chapter Three

"Very well," I started, smiling, confident now that Dr. Orion had finished with his discourse. "Neither of you believe the fire was an accident. Maybe I don't either, not based on what little I know. If your package was there in 1907 when the fire occurred, it means it hasn't been seen in almost thirty years."

"That's right," Orion replied, moving his hand in the air as if to encourage me.

"What do you think happened to it?" I asked. "Where's it been all this time?"

Orion shook his head. "I don't know and maybe it doesn't matter. Many objects throughout history have been lost and then found again, often only to be lost again. Who knows where it's been or why? Perhaps sitting in a dusty attic or a moldy basement. Maybe its been sitting on someone desk or fireplace mantle. It could even be a prized possession that has been hoarded and kept secret for some reason. We don't know."

"That seems rather fantastic."

Orion nodded slowly, glanced at his wife, and then stared back at me. "I won't argue with you."

"Why do you think the trail is warm again?"

"Sometimes you simply have a sense about these things," Susan Orion said.

"My wife does have a good nose. We also study the movements of several other scholars and two of them have recently returned to San Francisco after some time away."

"That's a rather thin clue," I commented.

"Perhaps, but one of these other scholars has hired a man to help him, a man who does not come cheap or easy."

"Who might that be?"

"In time. Then there is this: One of my agents spotted an advertisement in a recent local newspaper that got our attention."

From his billfold Orion produced a folded piece of newsprint that had been carefully cut out of a daily. With great delicacy, he slowly unfolded it, studied it, and then reached across the table to hand it to me.

I accepted it from his hand. It was an unremarkable section from the classifieds that read: "*Thorough's Auction House, November 22, 1934. Lot #73 – rare items, antique furniture pieces, oil paintings, unusual furs, and a sealed trunk of unknown contents and origin. Crying to begin promptly at 2:30pm. Queries: Jameson Tucker, III.*"

"This auction is scheduled for tomorrow," I observed.

"Indeed, it is."

"What makes you think this has anything to do with your package?"

"We believe it is possible that our package may be inside the 'sealed trunk of unknown contents and origin,'" he explained.

"Why?"

"That would be a very long story indeed, and it does not matter in the end. I'm hoping you might show up and see what can be learned."

"You want me to bid on the trunk?"

"No, we want you to obtain the trunk – bid on it, win it, steal it – it does not matter to us how you obtain it."

"What if your package is not in the trunk?"

"That is a possibility. In any case, we believe there is a connection to this Lot seventy-three. You must see what you can learn at Thorough's."

I lighted a Chesterfield and smoked it while I considered the situation. "We've talked around the subject long enough," I said finally. "Exactly what is it that I'm looking for? What is this package?"

"What do you suppose it to be?"

I could see we were about to play Twenty Questions. "How large is it?" I asked. "I already told you I don't like riddles."

"It's not large. It would fit into the average lunch pail."

"How much does it weigh?"

"Oh, let's say it's not heavy either."

"Is it heavier than my sandwich?"

The frown I received in response told me something about the game and something about the person I was playing the game with.

"What's it worth?" I tried.

"Might as well ask what your dreams are worth."

"The dreams I have in my sleep are cold, dark, and frightening. I often awake in a cold sweat and decide not to go back to sleep. Those dreams aren't worth very much to me at all. In fact, I'd pay for better dreams."

"What about the dreams you have in your waking moments – the dreams that represent your hopes, your desires, your aspirations?"

"Those are worth everything," I conceded.

"Exactly," Orion replied most seriously.

"Does it have to be so mysterious?"

"I cannot tell you what is at stake. I fear you would not believe me and I hate to lose a man of your considerable talents – especially after I have so patiently waited for him to arrive."

For a moment I wondered what he meant by that. I glanced at Susan Orion. Her expression told me nothing and I decided not to pursue it. "What's in it for me, then?" I asked, trying to dampen my mounting annoyance.

Dr. Orion smiled and then he laughed all by himself. "Of course that is a very good question for you to ask. Young man, it would be a large service for me. My gratitude would be undying and could overwhelm you. I would repay you handsomely of course, but I also have something that might intrigue you." His voice had dropped to a near whisper by the time he got to the word "intrigue."

"What is that?" I asked impatiently.

"Have you heard of a man named 'Fingers Pete'?"

I had. I nodded my head without moving my lips.

"He is involved in this matter. I believe you have a standing interest in this man called 'Fingers Pete.' I do not know what his real name is. He is on the other side – hired by one of the other scholars, though we do not know which one. If you were to deliver the package to me successfully, it almost certainly means that you will have had an encounter with Mr. Pete. What you do with that encounter, of course, is your business. I don't intend to ask any questions. My only concern is the package in question. If you can find, retrieve, and bring it to me, I will be most grateful. You will find that I know how to express my gratitude in the most emphatic way."

"What if I cannot find it?"

"You are a resourceful man, sir!"

I lifted my chin slightly before responding: "The world over, resourceful men fail all the time."

Orion chuckled as though he knew lots of things I didn't, and he probably did. "In that case, my young friend, you'll be paid the handsome sum of nothing, plus any reasonable expenses that you have incurred in the course of the effort. That goes without saying."

"Of course," I said. My mind was already moving backward to another time in another city.

"You have the advertisement. Is that where you will start, with Thorough's?"

I smiled. Now it was my turn. "That's probably best left a secret that only I know the answer to."

Orion laughed and drank the last of his champagne. "Indeed, sir! You are a savvy operator and I respect any approach you may take toward addressing this matter."

*

Our meeting was almost concluded. "We might not meet again, Mr. Duncan," Orion suggested.

"What if I find your package?"

"I'm optimistic that you will. Here is a card with a telephone exchange on it. This is a service monitored twenty-four hours a day and it is the best way for you to communicate with me."

"I assume I should be careful about what I say?"

"One can never assume complete privacy. If you leave a message, my agent will get back to you."

"Does your agent have a name?"

"He works by the name of Beakman."

"How will I know Mr. Beakman if I should meet him?"

"That's a good question, because you might. He's very short and bald, heavy on his feet. There is nothing graceful about him."

"That's a little ambiguous for my liking."

Dr. Orion grinned as though he could read my mind, and nodded his head in agreement. He glanced at his wife and then turned his gaze slowly back toward me as if he were thinking. From his billfold he produced another piece of paper. This time it was a one hundred dollar bill.

"See it?" he asked, waving it between us.

"I do."

In a motion he tore it into two pieces at a diagonal, with the tear cutting through Ben Franklin's face. Solemnly he handed one half to me. "When you meet him, Mr. Beakman will have the other half of this bill to show you."

*

Together the Orions walked back to my automobile with me. As we passed the Auburn, I slowed to admire it. "It is sure a beauty," I said.

"Of course it is Susan's," Dr. Orion explained, "she is a highly skilled driver."

"Not really," Mrs. Orion replied. Then she hugged me to say good-bye, reminding me again that for some reason I didn't fully understand, I was being treated like family.

"Remember this," Dr. Orion said emphatically as he shook my hand. "Disease is chaos. That's what it is. If you can harmonize the brain – if you can harmonize the central nervous system – you will almost certainly eliminate disease entirely. I believe that is the secret to immortality."

I smiled into his eyes while our hands were still clasped.

Orion added one more thought before our hands released from each other: "I want you to understand that our objective is not about personal interest. If we are successful in bringing this package to light, the whole world will benefit. Good-bye and good luck."

I climbed into my Ford with that last intimation playing in my ears like a song, a tantalizing, but unresolved solo by Bix Beiderbecke. It was as strange and mysterious as the coronetist's death had been.

Chapter Four

I spotted the woman on the shoulder of the road as I reached the end of the long drive. Perched against the front hood of a DeSoto with a hand on either headlamp, she seemed to be waiting for me. I didn't see a flat tire or any other obvious sign of vehicle distress. Coasting in behind her I set my brake and climbed out onto the gravel.

The cool ocean breeze caught my hat and nearly sent it flying. The woman watched me calmly as I walked toward her. Angled to one side, she displayed ample hips and healthy legs that were crossed at the knees as she balanced with one foot over the other. She stared straight ahead, defiant and proud and confident, with her short black hair windblown across her face.

The shoulder strap of her dress on one shoulder was casually sliding down toward the elegant hand that supported part of her weight. Loose bracelets hung from each wrist. A lot of her skin was showing; all of it darkened by a combination of genetics and sun exposure. I didn't think she was the most beautiful woman I'd ever seen and I didn't think she thought she was either. She only carried herself as though she was.

When I was closer to her, I noticed other things: the small cleft in her chin, the fullness of her unsmiling mouth, and the dark, deep pools of her irises. I wondered if she was immune to everything.

"Are you okay, Miss?" I asked. "Do you need help?"

Her eyes focused on me, cool and evaluative. "I've been waiting for you. I need to talk to you. It's kind of important to me."

I glanced from her face to the DeSoto and back again.

"Oh, the automobile is working fine," she assured me without moving. "That's not my problem."

"What is?"

"We can't talk here. Can we go someplace?"

"What is the problem?" I asked.

"My husband has disappeared."

"I'm not the police. You should file a missing persons report."

Her calm exterior cracked a little, split narrowly by a hint of growing desperation that she'd been holding at bay for too long. "Please," she said. "It's urgent. There's a coffee house down the road, just before you reach Sausalito – 'The Hanging Moon.' It's less than ten minutes away. Meet me there. Please. I'll pay you a hundred dollars to hear me out. It won't take long and if you're not interested you can move on, no harm done."

"You've mistaken me for someone else."

"I haven't. Please, won't you?"

I studied her for a moment while the breeze swished her hair about over her face. "Okay, I'll follow you there."

*

The woman, whose name I didn't know, drove very fast down the hill and I decided not to keep up with her. There was no good reason to draw further attention to myself. Soon she was out of my sight.

The curved road drew me down through the hills, past glimpses of the bay and Angel Island off to one side. By the time The Hanging Moon came into sight a foggy dusk had begun to settle over. I pulled into the tiny parking lot and looked around. The DeSoto was parked carelessly at the far end, with its front tires almost hanging off an edge that dropped twenty feet to the rocks below. I pulled into the near end of the lot and squeezed in between a battered Dodge and a rusted Plymouth coupe.

I glanced at my watch. It was almost six o'clock, which explained why the air felt so heavy. The coffee house was actually a diner and it appeared to be popular with locals. I found the woman sitting anxiously in a booth at the back, staring at her watch.

"I hope you didn't think I'd stood you up," I said when I was standing over her.

Her lips tensed. "I worried I'd lost you."

"It wasn't for lack of trying," I suggested.

"I'm sorry about that. I always drive too fast when I'm anxious."

I took the seat across from her in the booth. "Am I buying you dinner?" I asked.

"That won't be necessary. I couldn't eat anyway – I'm too jittery."

"We never exchanged names. Mine's Huddleston. Who are you and what's your story?"

"I'm Mrs. Jennifer McPhael. I was born in Tehran and I have only lived in America for two years, since I came here with my husband."

"Your English is perfect."

"I've studied English ever since I can remember and I lived in Hong Kong for two years with my parents when I was fifteen. Even after that, we spoke only English in the house on Wednesdays."

"What brought you to America?"

"I came here after marrying a man that my parents chose for me."

"An arranged marriage?"

"Yes."

26

"We don't see many of those in this country."

"It is not your custom, though it is common in Persian culture. My parents were looking out for my interests, and also for their own."

"How so?"

Her tone was reflective. "My husband is Persian too, though a very successful business man in this country, with dealings and ventures back home as well. You must understand that in my country this is how families protect and further their interests."

"Your father wanted to do business with the man who is now your husband?"

Without quite appearing ashamed, Mrs. McPhael lowered her eyes. "Yes, that's right."

"You said your husband has disappeared. Why do you think I can help you? I'm no dick."

She smiled warmly. "I know that. Hear me out a little more and maybe it will be easier to understand."

"Okay, we'll come back to that. What can you tell me about your husband? Maybe you should start with his name."

"After he immigrated to America he adopted the name Walter McPhael. It is an Americanized version of his birth name. He is a good man, though often stubborn and hard in his manners. He developed a highly successful import-export business, trading valuable goods between Tehran and San Francisco. He owns several of his own ships."

"What's his birth name?"

She shook her head. I wasn't sure if that meant she didn't know, or she didn't want to reveal it. "That's irrelevant now," she said.

"May I ask what type of goods he trades in?"

"His business involves many types, mostly objects of rare value brought from Iran to America; and basic commodities from American to Iran."

"He makes money in both directions."

"Isn't that a sensible way to do business?"

I smiled and nodded. "What are the 'objects of rare value'?"

She paused before responding. I read her body language and the long moment of silence as the preparation for a lie. "He brings Persian rugs, jewels, incense, unusual medicinal compounds, and artifacts and works of art into his adopted country. Back to Iran, he ships many things, such as gold bullion, wheat, steel, cotton, medicines."

I raised my chin. My instincts told me she wasn't telling the truth about something, though I couldn't tell which part of her statement was false. "When did he disappear?"

"I haven't seen him in two weeks?"

"You don't look too worried. Has he ever disappeared before?"

"You must excuse my appearance. I'm very worried. Although he travels a lot, he always tells me where he is going and when he will return. He's never disappeared like this before."

"When did you start looking for him?"

"The day after he didn't come home."

"When was that?"

"Five days ago."

"What steps have you taken so far?"

"Everything I could think of. I called his office in San Francisco. His secretary didn't know anything. She was worried too. I called every one we know socially. No one has heard from him. I sent telegrams to people in Tehran. Nothing."

"What about the police?"

She glanced away, perhaps thinking of another lie or hoping to elicit my compassion. "I cannot approach them."

"We'll come back to that. Tell me: what do you think happened to your husband?"

The question caused her to close her eyes tightly for a moment. The thin, delicate skin around her eyes folded delicately. I realized she was probably even younger than I'd initially thought.

"I suspect he has been murdered," she said abruptly, opening her eyes suddenly as she spoke, as though she were emerging from a nightmare.

"Why didn't you go to the police?" I asked.

The nightmare caught up to her quickly and seemed to envelop and hold her, as its dark shadow spread across her face and contorted her expression.

Chapter Five

Jennifer's eyes dropped downward again, signaling the hot shame she wanted me to read in her face. I couldn't tell if it was an act or not. "I have reason to believe my husband's life was more complicated than I previously understood."

"Are you saying he led a double life?"

She stared at me for a long pause, then pursed her lips and glanced away, anxiously, without saying anything.

"Alright," I said. "What do you know or suspect about this other life?"

"I don't believe you could understand," she said quietly, still looking away from me.

"Don't be coy," I suggested. "If you want my help, you're going to have to explain."

"Mr. Huddleston, may I confide in you?"

"If we're to be confidante's you might as well call me Richard."

"Richard Huddleston," she mused, talking to herself for a moment. She turned her face back toward mine. "It's a strong name and I like it. Is it your real name?"

"Why not?"

"No reason, I guess, I just wondered. People do change their names."

"You must have a reason for your doubts."

"You'll have to pardon me. It's simply that, well, you don't look like a Richard Huddleston."

Wondering what she actually knew, I smiled and lighted a Chesterfield. I licked a bit of shredded tobacco off my lower lip. "Maybe you were expecting somebody else?"

"I want you to be who you are," she insisted awkwardly, trying to mother over the *faux pas* that she thought she had made.

"Huddleston's as good a name as any. Is Jennifer your real name? You already told me that your husband changed his?"

"You are very forward, Mr. Huddleston."

"That's why you're talking to me, right? You don't need a guy who isn't capable of being forward."

"It's true," she conceded.

"Anyway, I think I'm right and that's the beauty of America. We all get to be who we want to be. This is a country borne of personal reinvention. "

"I don't follow your meaning."

"What's in a name?"

29

"In my country – everything."

"Not in the U.S. In this country, it's very simple: Having trouble in your old country? Come to America and start over. You leave the past behind as though it never existed. Change your name to whatever you like. That's okay too, and if you don't change it, someone might change it for you, like a bureaucrat at Ellis Island. My grandfather was six years old when he arrived, and they changed the name of his entire family, keeping the first two letters and the last. They scrambled everything in between."

"Such ignorance!"

Smiling, I took a drag off my cigarette and exhaled. "I don't think so. I think it's brilliant. If you embrace it, you realize, suddenly, that it is liberating, that you are now a real American – as real as anyone else who is here. How many other countries have ever worked that way?"

Jennifer's smile was slow to develop, but once it did, it was alluring. "I think you have helped me understand something I didn't think about before," she conceded. "A fresh start is indeed what I came here for."

"And your name, before it was Jennifer?"

"Afsoon. It was my great-grandmother's name, passed down to me. I don't use it anymore, though I confess that at night when I can't sleep I whisper it to myself."

"It's beautiful. What does it mean?"

She clutched at her shoulders modestly and drew a deep breath. "Bewitchment, a magical spell."

As I looked into her large brown eyes, I began to think she was well named. "Let's go back to your husband," I suggested. "You were going to tell me about his double life."

She shook her head shortly. "I can't speak of it and I'm not sure of the facts, anyway. You must understand I cannot easily speak ill of my husband, and certainly not until I'm certain."

"How can I advise you if you won't share your suspicions?"

Her lonely eyes traveled down from mine to a spot on the table between us. They glowed reflexively as if she were watching the sails of a distant ship receding toward the horizon. "Please don't ask me to humiliate myself," she whispered. "I couldn't bear it."

I tried a different approach. "How did you come to be waiting in that spot for me? It seems you don't actually know who I am. So, of course I cannot see the connection between me and your husband."

Slowly she exhaled in a long sigh. "Mr. Huddleston, I do hope you will not be as cruel to me as that question seems to suggest you may be."

"Then you didn't do your homework, Mrs. McPhael. Nobody who knows me would ever expect anything other than cruelty from me in a situation like

30

this."

Jennifer McPhael blushed hard and fanned herself with the diner's cardboard menu.

That's when the waitress arrived to take our orders. She was a large jovial woman with a sunburned forehead and gray hair gathered in a netted bun at the top of her head. "Sorry for the wait, folks. We had a little fire in the kitchen that I had to help out, but everything's Jake now. What can I bring you?"

We ordered coffee and angel food cake with strawberry preserves.

When the waitress moved away from our table, I opened my hand toward my companion: "You know I have to ask this. Why were you waiting for me at that precise point this afternoon? How did you know I would be there and why did you think I might help you? If you can't give me a straight answer, there's nothing I can do for you." I allowed my voice to soften as I finished the sentence.

"Alright then: desperate as I was, I hired a private investigator to help me find my husband."

"Who is he and how did that lead you to me?"

"Why do you press me so?"

"Your P.I. has a name. What is it?"

"Johnny Drake."

"That's progress. How did you come to hire him?"

"He was in the book, and a friend of mine said he was pretty good, that he might be able to help."

"What did he suggest to you?"

"He thought the Orions might know something about my husband."

"Why?"

"I cannot tell you. Please don't press me."

"Is that all?"

"Will you help me?"

"I don't know if I can – you haven't given me much and I don't even know what you're asking of me. I need to know how were you waiting for me when I came out of the Orion's drive. If you can't answer that, then I can't help you."

The smile that formed on her face was private. "Dr. Orion enjoys a prominent reputation in this community – everyone who matters knows him and his wife. I've even met them myself on several occasions. They are delightful people."

I played with my cigarette, rolling it between my fingers. "I admit that they are, but that still doesn't address my question. Why were you waiting for me there?"

"Johnny Drake said you were the person I should talk to."

31

"Why?"

"He wouldn't say."

"I don't know him from Adam."

"He seems to know you."

I stubbed out my cigarette. "What do you want from me?"

"I had hoped you would know something that would help lead me to my husband."

"I never heard of your husband before this afternoon."

"There must be a reason Johnny Drake sent me to you. Will you help me? Please. Oh, you must."

"How can I answer that? I don't know what you're asking of me."

She took a deep breath and sighed, turning her head to face out toward the bay below. "I'm not sure what I'm asking either, other than you were identified to me as someone who might be able to help."

"Alright," I said. "Maybe I can help, but I need to know a lot more. Where can I find Johnny Drake?"

Her lips formed a spontaneous smile as she realized I was hooked. "You can't find him; even I can't find him. All I have is the number to his service. He calls me back after I leave a message and we communicate by telephone and letter. I write to him care of General Delivery, San Francisco."

"In other words, you've never met him in person."

She nodded her head. "I should leave now," she replied.

"Are we finished then?"

Jennifer McPhael nodded rapidly as she arranged items within her purse. "Please don't follow me," she said, with anxiety filling her eyes. "I'm so frightened."

"How will I communicate with you?"

"Forgive me for being so fearful. On the advice of Mr. Drake, I have begun to use an answering service myself."

"That's fine," I replied. Apparently everyone in San Francisco used an answering service.

From her purse she found a small gray notebook and scribbled something. Then she tore the page out, folded it in half, and tucked it under the saltshaker. After that she dug around inside her purse a little more and came out with a few bills. "I promised you a hundred dollars for talking with me. Thank you."

"Forget about that."

She tucked the bills in under the peppershaker. "If you don't want it, you can leave it as a tip for that hardworking waitress."

*

I finished my cigarette and had another cup of coffee inside The Hanging Moon, though I left the angel food cake – when it arrived – untouched. Then I drove back into Sausalito and caught the *Eureka*, a side-wheel paddle steamboat, for the trip back across the bay.

On the return, with the sun going down, I forced myself to stare toward the lights of Alcatraz in the distance and allowed a bootblack to shine my shoes while we churned across the water. It was easy for me to imagine the indignities and lack of ordinary freedoms the men in the cellblocks endured. I'd been in a place like that before. Relative to the boundless possibilities that surrounded me in every moment that I wasn't a federal prisoner, it nearly broke my heart.

The cold spray of salt-water in the air braced me. I breathed deeply of it, letting the lights of Alcatraz fall behind in the foggy night air along with the broken, lonely sighs of a woman-child named Afsoon.

Chapter Six

The Fairmont Hotel was rather fancy for my tastes, but they had a side door I could use and I enjoyed the view from my high balcony. As I stepped off the elevator I smelled the cigarette smoke. It was heavy in the hallway. I peeked around the corner carefully and saw the man sitting at the end of the hall in a chair by the window with a newspaper open on his lap. He didn't appear to be reading it. There was no one else in the hallway.

I drew my gun and went around the corner fast.

"Remain still," I told him. "Especially the hands."

Slowly, his face turned from the window toward me. The eyes that looked up at me were bright blue and sincere, framed by sun-bronzed skin that was stretched smoothly over high cheekbones and a wide, block chin. When he smiled, his white, even-rowed teeth caught the light perfectly.

I knew I was supposed to swoon to the floor, but somehow I managed not to. He was the most handsome man I'd ever seen – right out of central casting, and he knew it. Clark Gable would have trembled if he knew this man walked the earth. His clothing and shoes were expensive and fit perfectly to accentuate his broad shoulders. On his wrist, carefully visible, was an understated gold watch. Everything about him was carefully designed to announce that he was a man of breeding and taste.

"My name's Tucker," he explained in a thin, reedy voice. "Jameson Tucker, the Third. I've been waiting to talk with you, Mr. Huddleston. I think we might have some business to conduct."

I smiled at him and used my thumb to push the fedora back on my head so the light could hit my eyes more fully. "As you seem to know," I said, "my door's right here. If you'll hold up your hands, we'll go on in. When you raise them, make sure they're empty."

*

As soon as we were through the door, I frisked Jameson Tucker carefully in the foyer. He wasn't carrying anything stronger than a small pocket nail file. I took it away from him anyway just to seem as though I were playing it safe and dropped it on the parquet floor. After I holstered the .45 under my shoulder, I studied at him. "So, I know your name. What do you want?" I asked.

"Gosh, it's lovely here," Tucker said genuinely, looking around. "I've never been inside the Fairmont, though everyone says it's wonderful. You've got practically an entire library in here." He waved toward the shelves of books that lined the far end of the wood-paneled parlor, walking past me to approach them.

"Are you a reader? Help yourself."

Tucker made a show of studying the titles for a long moment before turning ninety degrees toward the long wall of windows. "Do you mind if I step out onto the balcony? I'd like to see the view from up here."

I shrugged. "Don't get any bright ideas," I replied and followed him out into the brisk night air. The lights spread out below us, ending abruptly at the water line. Suddenly, the divide between the brilliant lights of modern urban humanity and the dark mystery of the watery unknown had never been starker for me.

Tucker made another show of seeming to appreciate the view. Small sighs and exclamations escaped his throat for the next two minutes. I wondered if that was habitual for him – how he made friends and ingratiated himself with others – or if he was simply prone to the experience of awe.

During that time we didn't speak. I watched a steamer making its way under the long bridge they were building out there on its way out to sea and I wondered where it was going.

"Do you mind if I smoke?" Tucker asked presently, breaking the reverie.

"Since I don't know you, I do mind. We can take it inside if you must." I didn't want to allow him the chance to signal anyone who might be watching from below or from another building.

Tucker nodded absently and in the darkness I was unable to read his expression. "Let's go get a drink in the Cirque Room?"

"We can talk right here. What's your business?"

"Maybe we could sit down for a few minutes and I can explain it to you before we leave?"

"Where is it that you think we're going?"

"Well, that's what I was hoping to talk to you about. There's something I'd like to show you. It's at my office, only ten minutes from here by taxi. First, maybe we could sit for a few minutes? The city lights really are marvelous."

There was a wrought iron table with four matching chairs, a chaise lounge, and two wicker chairs with upholstered cushions. I gestured and let him make his choice. Tucker chose the chaise lounge, and I pulled one of the wicker chairs over so that I could sit with my face close to his.

When his shoes were crossed over one another at the ankles and his head rested back on the folded elbow of one arm, he smiled up at the night sky and drew a breath in through his nostrils as though he were experiencing the scent of the universe.

"Its really quite wonderful up here," he said. "You can smell the bay with accents of Chinatown, but without any of the unpleasant odors that ordinarily accompany the Chinese sector."

I didn't know what he was talking about, so I didn't say anything.

As if sensing my ambivalence, Tucker qualified his previous statement. "Forgive me. I was an actor some years ago and I still carry the instinct for the dramatic moment."

I realized I was supposed to be impressed and to ask him to tell me about his career. Before I got the chance to, he continued. "You probably didn't see any of the movies I was in, and even if you did, I doubt you would recognize me now, all these years later – without all the pancake we wore back then. I was something of a star in the 'silent movie era' you know, before the 'talkies' came on the scene. According to some people I could have been as big as Valentino, only everything was up-ended before I had the chance."

"The price of progress," I suggested.

"United Artists signed me shortly after they worked things out with Valentino.... Then he died suddenly – mysterious circumstances."

"I thought it was pneumonia."

"That's what they said," Tucker sighed, running a comb-hand through the top of the hair on his head.

"You don't believe it?"

"Nobody did."

"Why?"

"It was the era – it was changing fast. What were they going to do with him?"

"Murder?"

Tucker shrugged and appeared to lose interest. "Not necessarily... I don't know... you hear different rumors. It might have been murder, suicide, narcotics. I don't know. The mystery underlies the man's legend. He couldn't have scripted it better if he had tried."

"What happened to your career?" I asked, though I already knew the answer.

He formed a pallid smile in the faint light and started to chuckle to himself. It seemed a well-rehearsed response, one he'd made many times before. "I didn't have the voice for it. Producers said it didn't translate well onto the screen – it wasn't deep enough, strong enough." He sank into the gloom of his own self-pity as he reflected on the glory that had been snatched away from him. "I guess we all come from nothing and we return to nothing. In the end its all the same."

"Job said it better."

"Huh?"

I continued on. "So you played a few small roles in the silent picture era and thought you would hit it big. How does that make you any different from the thousands of other disappointed Hollywood stars who were unable to survive the transition? At least you got onto the screen. Most don't – not in any era."

"Do you know something about the acting game?"

"Only that it's ruthlessly selective."

"That's right. People come to Hollywood from all over the world, hoping to come for a star. If they can't manage to be one themselves, they hope to find one – a lover or a friend – who will remember them after they reach the neon lights." He'd spent his life too far removed from the messy side of life.

"There's no need to sell it in such ugly style. Anyway, we're not in Hollywood – we're in San Francisco, and you made a decision to be here instead of there."

Tucker's smile stretched the shadows that surrounded his face. "It's been swell sitting here with you on this balcony. It really is marvelous out here under the stars with the city lights strewn out before us."

"Sure," I said. "Now that we're pals, maybe you could tell me what it is that you actually want."

Tucker continued with the same smile and stroked his chin between his thumb and forefinger. "I've got something to show you and I think you'll want to see it."

"What it is?"

"Come with me and see for yourself."

"Do you know who I am?" I asked.

"Not exactly, but I have a faint idea you're someone who doesn't want to be found."

"Then, how did you find me?"

Tucker reached into his breast pocket and found a folded piece of yellow paper that he handed me. I unfolded it and read the telegram: "POTENTIAL BUYER LOT 73 STOP MR HUDDLESTON STOP FAIRMONT BUCKINGHAM SUITE TONIGHT RUSH STOP."

"Who sent it?"

"I don't know."

"Are you going to show me something related to this lot?"

He nodded. His face was entirely serious now, the shadows encroaching upon his silent expression again. He pantomimed something with his hands in the dark. I crumpled the telegram slowly into a ball in one hand and let if fall to my feet.

"Let's go," I said.

Chapter Seven

At my insistence, we walked a block before catching a cab near Huntington Park and took it a long way down California Street until we reached Fillmore. The ride was less then ten minutes and then we walked the last few blocks – again at my insistence. Though it was well after dark now, I wanted to see what I could of the neighborhood before we arrived wherever it was he was taking me.

"Fillmore tips at a twenty-five percent grade down there," Tucker informed me, pointing with a strong finger along the center of the street. "The cable cars moving along here are counterbalanced with a steel line, linking the one going uphill with the going down."

"Which is your house?"

"A little farther down. We'll turn left at Broadway and then head over to Steiner."

I saw no reason to mention that I wasn't familiar with streets of San Francisco. Tucker kept up a jaunty pace and he had his keys in his hand when we reached a house on the corner that was his. It was a three-story brick house with a gabled arch over the front entrance.

No lights were on inside, though there was enough light from the sky and streetlamps to outline the series of dormer windows that lined two sides of the roof and the conical turret over the protruding tubular corner of the house.

"I thought we were going to your office?"

"This is my home, but a lot of my work is here also," Tucker explained as he worked the key in the lock. "Come on inside."

He began pushing buttons and turning on lights all throughout the house. I stepped inside and moved sideways to stand just to the right of the door after it was closed. I wanted a solid wall behind me in case anyone was watching us from the street.

"Do you live here alone?" I asked, looking around at the grandeur of the interior finishing's. Every inch of the house was polished to a high shine.

"I do," Tucker sighed, glancing over sheepishly at me. "I bought the house six years ago after giving up in Hollywood. I inherited well and my business has thrived since then. Please don't ask if I'm lonely here all by myself. I've had plenty of girlfriends over the years, but never quite found the right one. Maybe you can advise me."

"No man can ever advise another on that subject," I told him.

Tucker smiled as he removed his jacket, which he threw over a banister leading upstairs. "I guess we might as well try to explain the pyramids or the secret lives of bees to each other."

"I'm not sure it's so mysterious. People can be selfish creatures. Until they're ready to put another's needs above their own, they have little hope of finding a love that will last them."

His lips curled in a half-smile. "I thought you couldn't advise another man on the subject."

I smiled myself in response: he almost had me there. "I didn't mean it as advice, so much as an observation."

"It may be spot on, though," he mused. "In my case at least, it probably is. The thing I fear most is the sadness of another human being, especially a woman. I'm weak that way, so I avoid it all costs. It means I never engage deeply, and I run away from them before I ever have to face the emotional aspect of their company."

"You must already know what Shakespeare said about that."

He ignored my comment and continued with his self-pity. "Some women have called me a cold fish, but in fact, it is never so much about them. It's the sad eyes, the tears, and the hurt moments that I'm unable to tolerate. I've protected myself by closing myself off before those moments are ever reached. I've tried everything: Christianity, ancient meditation practices, alcohol, even the occasional night in an opium den. Psychoanalysis led me nowhere. Nothing has worked."

I wasn't sure whether to feel sorry for him or despise him. "You ensure your own loneliness to protect yourself from what it means to be human."

Tucker nodded glumly, glancing down at his checkered tie.

"If you have no argument to refute that, then perhaps you should let it go," I said, coldly. "You get exactly what you want."

"Maybe I do," he conceded and his eyes moved about anxiously. "Come on back to the kitchen. Let's have drink and see what there is there to eat. You must be hungry."

I followed him deeper into the house, treading carefully, listening for sounds that weren't supposed to be there.

*

Jameson Tucker's kitchen was entirely white – white tile floors, white tile countertops, and white cabinets – and it was spotlessly clean. I imagined the taste of bleach in my mouth. Without a word Tucker went to a cupboard and found a bottle of something European. As he brought it down, he studied the label, uncorked it, and then brought it to his nose with uncertainty.

"Would you like a little Claret?" he asked, squinting at me.

39

"Do you have any American whiskey?"

"I might be able to pour you a drop of bourbon."

"I'll take that, neat, if it's allowed."

Tucker smiled with relief. "I'll join you."

He returned the Claret to its cupboard and then moved to the far end of the kitchen where he had to stand on his toes to find a bottle of the stuff. From a stainless steel tray in the middle of the counter he picked out two highball glasses. He poured out a generous measure of bourbon into one, and a very tentative measure into the other. He handed me the glass with the generous measure. We clinked glasses and drank a little.

"You don't mind if I smoke *now*, do you," he inquired, showing off a charming smile.

"I'll join you."

Tucker reached into his jacket and came out with silver cigarette case. He opened it with one hand and extended it to me. "I smoke Gauloises. Will you try one?"

I picked out one of the wide, short cigarettes and inspected it. "I usually smoke Chesterfields," I said.

"No shame in that, but give this a try. You might like it. The Syrian tobacco the French use is quite good."

We each lighted up off of our own lighters and stood there, leaning against the counter with our bourbon and our burning Gauloises. The bourbon was the good stuff, aged longer than the usual juice. The tobacco had a harsh, unfamiliar accent to it. I liked it a lot and held it inside for a while, feeling the burn down into my lungs and not minding that at all.

"What do you think?" Tucker asked presently.

"I like it," I admitted. "These are usually hard to get though, in this country – right?"

Tucker shrugged. "In my business, its no trouble to get them at all."

He didn't explain further and I didn't ask. We smoked in silence for a while and I finished my drink. Tucker refreshed both our glasses and when we finished the cigarettes, he said: "Are you hungry? I've got some nice sliced smoked ham, caviar, Gouda, salt crackers. Its no trouble – my house lady prepares it for me every evening."

Although I was hungry, I shook my head. "Let's get to the business."

"We'll go up to my office then," Tucker replied with his most charming smile.

Chapter Eight

At the top of the stairs on the second floor, Jameson Tucker led me down a short hallway, past an open bedroom door and a bathroom to a room at the end of the hall. When we got there and he turned on the lights, I realized we were in the tubular corner room of the house that extended from the front all the way to the back.

Given the steep grade of the street, I realized there must have been expansive bay views from the back of the house. The large room was magnificent and would have been more magnificent still in the light of day.

Tucker moved about, lighting every lamp in the room in order to give me the full effect. "It's not the Buckingham Suite at the Fairmont," he said quietly, entirely full of his own false modesty. "But it does serve its purpose for me."

I laughed, not because I was expected to, but because his artifice was so transparent. "We can trade homes any time you want to stay at the Buckingham Suite," I challenged him.

"I'm glad you like it," he said. "Feel free to look around. I have many of my own favorites displayed in here. There's a rather humble Degas over there in the corner."

The artist's name didn't mean anything to me. When I followed the direction of his finger I saw a spindly sculpture of a ballerina balanced on a small corner table. I moved about the room examining the walls. They were covered with all manners of artistic pieces.

There were oil paintings, watercolors, framed photographs, and mounted sculptures. Many of them were from the Orient; others were of European origin. I paced slowly down one wall of the room and then turned and came back up the other. I had little appreciation for what I was looking at, but I assumed they were rare and valuable. Most of them had been hanging where they were for a good while as evidenced by a thin film of dust along the lower horizontal surface of the frames. Idly I wondered how many of them had been stolen.

"Any of these beauties hot?" I asked.

Tucker chuckled at the question. "In my game, nobody ever asks that question."

When I looked over at him, he was seated with his elbow on a wide, ancient desk that overlooked the front of the house. He had his sleeves rolled down.

I walked over to him, still scanning the walls as I moved. On the wall to the side of his desk was a framed photograph of what could only be described

41

as a palace balanced delicately on a cliff. The sheet of glass over it reflected the light in the room and gave me the feeling that I was looking through a window into the past.

It drew me toward it, though it took me a long moment to realize I was looking at Sutro's lost Cliff House. I moved closer to study the photograph.

Taken from a spot on the flat beach below, a rippled reflection of the house in the wet sand drew my eye upward through a small crowd of tiny well-dressed people walking into the surf with their feet bared and their pants and skirts hiked up to their knees.

From there, a sharp crop of rocks formed an abrupt cliff that jutted out into the water. The enormous house was tenuously planted on these rocks, looming out over them on angled struts that appeared impossibly too fragile to hold.

The first three stories formed a solid rectangular structure, with an even row of windows stretching across and around the beveled corner toward the side of the palace that faced the water. Above that were more stories, rounded corner turrets, dormer windows set into the roofline, and a high Victorian tower in the center that rose up into the white empty sky. I wondered if the sky that day had really been so ghostlike or if the photographer had worked a clever trick with exposures or chemicals to wash it out.

"Incredible isn't," Tucker said quietly. "Sadly it burned to the foundation in 1907."

"What's your connection to it?" I asked, still staring at the photograph.

"No connection," he answered evenly. "I found the photograph framed like that at an auction several years ago and I liked it, so I bought it and its been hanging there ever since. I keep it there as a reminder to me of how incredibly temporary our existence is: from nothing to nothing. I'll look for the Job quote you mention. Men like to think of their accomplishments as permanent fixtures, records of their accomplishments. Its how we deceive ourselves into believing we have some warped chance at immortality. But of course we don't – we have no chance at it, no chance at all."

I turned from the photograph to look into Tucker's eyes. It was the first sign of depth I'd detected in the man. Maybe he had center after all. "I hadn't taken you for a theorist," I said.

"As magnificent as that house on the cliff was in its day, there's almost no one alive now who remembers it ever even existed."

"Does anyone know what happened to it?"

Tucker shrugged enigmatically. "Somebody does – or did. They've never stepped forward, though. I once saw another a photograph of the house. It was taken from almost the same vantage point on the beach as the one on the wall there. It might have been a little bit closer to the house.

"In it you could see the entire structure of the house, except that there were high flames licking out of every window on the third floor. The floors below were dark and calm; the rising smoke smothers the floors above.

"On the beach is a gathering of local citizens, mostly men, though there is one woman off in the distance, well down the back toward the rocks, staring up toward the fire. She seems to be separate from the others. You couldn't see her face, but I've always imagined that it was filled with stunned grief at the destruction that was occurring suddenly up on those rocks.

"The men on the beach appear to be calm, merely curious about the dramatic moment. Three or four of them stand hat in hand facing back toward the photographer."

I made a mental note of the photograph he described; layering it over the one I had just studied. "Are there any fireman to be seen in that photograph?"

"Do you have any experience with house fires, Mr. Huddleston?"

"None," I said.

"Twenty-five years ago there was very little anyone could have done to save that house. There was a coastal road, a dirt road, really, that fire trucks and such could have reached the house, but nobody believes they could have saved it. From all accounts, the fire spread quickly and engulfed everything. There were no hydrants and no pumps available to bring the seawater up in sufficient volume to put out the fire. I've heard it burned to the ground in less than one hour."

"It's unknown what caused the fire to start in the first place?"

"Correct."

"Was there not an investigation?"

Tucker's face slowly lost its enthusiasm and became pale again. There was a wounded look in his eyes as he remembered fully that something had been lost and never found again. "I'm sure there was, but almost surely it's been lost to time. Maybe there are records that still exist. I don't know. It's beyond my talents to understand – or even care too much for something like that, so long ago."

"Twenty-seven years," I said, chewing a match between my teeth. "It's not really so long ago at all, when you view that way."

"It really isn't," he conceded. "I guess I keep that photograph there to remind me of it."

"How long did you say its been hanging here?"

"Oh, for years, I don't even remember exactly where or when I found it."

"Its not connected to Lot seventy-three?"

"I don't follow."

From where I stood in front of the photograph, I made a quarter turn to study him. "There's no dust on the frame as there is on the other frames in this

43

room. That leaves me to think maybe you hung it very recently."

Caught in a lie, Tucker blushed red and busied himself with his hands. "I never really know what my housekeeper does. She cleans this house at her own rhythm, and I've not had reason to complain or question her before."

"Of course," I replied.

"Would you like to see something else now?" he asked.

I nodded and sat down in a wide chair at the end of the desk, kitty-corner to where Tucker sat. I let my wrists hang loosely over the armrests while I watched him. "Let's see what you've got."

Chapter Nine

Tucker removed a chain from around his neck that had been tucked inside his undershirt. A tiny silver key dangled at the end of it. With a serious expression on his face, he quickly wrapped the chain around the open palm of his right hand, with one end of it looped over his thumb.

Then he leaned over and dropped to one knee, reaching under his desk to feel along the interior surface, searching for something. When he found it, he appeared to insert the key and turn it once. Then he sat up again in his chair and opened the third drawer down from the top on the same side of the desk. He pulled the drawer all the way out and set it aside on the surface of the desk.

Without speaking a word to me, Tucker stood up and pushed his chair back. He knelt down again to reach into the empty cavity where the drawer had been, leading with the same key. Silently he groped around at the back of the cavity until he found what he was looking for.

I could hear the key scrapping, and then it fit into a hole and turned against a small bolt. A moment later, his hand emerged from the mysterious back of the desk, holding a small covered sub-drawer that he laid over his knees.

"This is it," he said quietly. His expression was placid rather than triumphant.

We weren't through yet, however. Tucker looped the chain and key back over his head and let it fall down beneath his shirt. Then he found a second key that was in the top narrow drawer of his desk. It was taped to a postcard that waited near the bottom of a stack of postcards. It appeared to have been sent from Hong Kong.

This key he used to unlock the covered sub-drawer, as though he were opening a tiny treasure chest of immeasurable value. His hands trembled noticeably. When he lifted the lid, he broke into a smile and glanced at me to see if I approved of the precautions he had taken. I nodded my encouragement. The upturned lid hid the item of interest from my view.

"What is it?" I had to ask.

"This," he replied. What he set in front of me was a small rectangular box, upholstered in red and black silk with gold threading. There was a prominent Chinese symbol on the top of the box. I lacked the education to describe it. To me it looked like a partial circle with several slanting lines through it and accent marks over one of the lines. I didn't know what it meant or even what language it might have represented. To my ignorant eye, it seemed likely to be Chinese.

"Go on," Tucker encouraged, "open it."

I picked it up and positioned it on my lap to study it. There was a tiny ivory clasp that I had to work to unlatch, and then I raised the cover to look inside. My nostrils were filled with the powerful musky scent of ancient incense. I wondered when the box had last been opened.

"What do you see?" Tucker inquired.

Inside the box was a large circular piece of black metal that carried the same Chinese symbol that adorned the top of the box. Extending from it was a small, odd extension – a piece of polished brass, which I realized formed a strange key. It had a V-shaped end and a series of slanted gradations along the length of it. I picked up the entire piece and held it up toward the light. The base was quite heavy, possibly lead-based, while the key itself felt nearly weightless.

"What does it open?" I asked.

"What would you wish for?" Tucker asked in return, reminding me of Dr. Orion's mysterious manners.

I replaced the piece back into it's fitted slot in the red and black silk upholstered box, closed the lid, and refastened the ivory clasp. Without any dramatic motion, I rested my hands on top of the closed box and replied to Jameson Tucker the Third: "It's not about what I would wish for. Let's be practical. As you already seem to know, I'm looking for a package that may be connected to Lot seventy-three. Is it there? Does this key open something that gets me closer to that package?"

"It might," Tucker replied, leaning forward in his chair so that his face was as close as possible to mine. "It's obviously a valuable, important key. The thing is, I don't know what it is a key to. I cannot figure out what it opens."

"Tell me about Lot seventy-three."

Greed and uncertainty combined to fill Tucker's eyes with a slow-burning anxiety. "Even if we assume the key opens something important in Lot seventy-three, we don't know what."

"You have the Lot under your control?"

"No. I – we – only oversee the auction. That gives me advance information about some of the pieces; sometimes I'm allowed to view them in advance. However, this lot is a little different. Another vendor physically holds it. All I've seen is the manifest, a list of items."

I nodded as I began to understand. "So, you know the list of items, but you do not know which items are important?"

"Correct."

"So it would be impossible to know which items to bid for?"

"Also correct."

"This key opens something that matters, something pertaining to Lot seventy-three, but we cannot know what? Is that what you are telling me?"

"Yes, that is correct," he replied, nodded rapidly.

"Where did you obtain the key from?"

"I'm not at liberty to say."

"How are you so certain that the key relates to Lot seventy-three?"

"If I were to explain that, it would reveal too much."

"How long have you had the key?"

"This is not Twenty-One questions, Mr. Huddleston."

"You don't seem concerned that I'm holding the key in my possession right now. What's to stop me from taking it?"

Tucker shrugged and leaned back in his chair, allowing his shoulders to relax. "The key won't help you unless you know what to do with it. It's my hope that we can work together. I believe that you might be able to learn which specific parcel the key relates to."

"What's in it for you?"

"Certain promises have been made to me about what I might expect to receive if I can help you successfully recover what it is they are looking for."

"But of course, you cannot tell me who made these promises."

"That is correct, though even if I wanted to tell you, I would not be able to because I simply do not know."

I grinned. "Do you have another one of those Gauloises handy?"

"I never smoke in this room because of the valuable pieces of art that are here." Tucker extended his silver cigarette case all the same, and I selected one of the French cigarettes.

"I understand," I said as I lighted it. "Where does this leave us?"

"Are you prepared to visit Chinatown tonight?" Tucker asked.

I lighted the Gauloises and exhaled toward him. "Tell me where to start."

Before answering, Tucker leaned forward to pick up the red and black silk upholstered box off my lap. I allowed him to. Working silently, he reversed the process to return the box to its secret hiding place in the dark interior mechanisms of the ancient desk.

When he finished with that, he stood up and looped the chain around his neck again and dropped the silver key down inside his shirt. Then he searched around on the desk and found a piece of yellowed paper, which he handed to me. There was an address scribbled on it in dark ink.

With his million-dollar smile and frank charm on full display, Jameson Tucker escorted me back to the front door and shook my hand earnestly.

"Come by at mid-day tomorrow," he suggested. "I always take my lunch at home."

"Depending on what I find…" I replied.

"Say twelve o'clock?"

"We'll see."

I stepped out into the bathing night. A light, cold rain was falling now at long intervals. Above me the lights of the city reflected off the white mirror clouds that hovered, curious, overhead. I was well down the twenty-five percent grade of Fillmore Street before a hack stopped for me. The driver wasn't enthusiastic about venturing into Chinatown after dark, but he liked the sawbuck I waved at him.

Chapter Ten

"Chinatown's right ahead," the cabbie exclaimed crossly, as though I had asked to be dropped inside the middle of a penitentiary. "You can smell it coming. Are you sure you really want to go there? It's a savage corner of this city. The people there aren't like you and I."

I flashed the sawbuck at him again and he quieted down. "I've never found people from one group to be so different from the people of another," I told him. "I find people to be far more similar to each other than they are different. They want the same things; they have the same dreams, the same problems."

We were halted at an intersection. The driver turned in his seat to glare at me with his wide face. Pink flesh bunched around his eye sockets as he squinted against the hot night-lights of the street.

His response wasn't pleasant. "You're paying for this ride, pal, so I won't tell you how wrong I think you are," he snarled before he proceeded to do just that. "There are people who are like you and me; and then there's a lower level. People aren't equal, if that's what you've been thinking. Too many of them have no Christian upbringing, no work ethic, no family history that means anything, and no principles to speak of. If you think you can change those people, you're more the fool. Chinatown is it's own. Just smell it out there. If you're not from here, you should never come here. That's what I think, anyway."

"What's your name?" I asked.

"Strickler, sir. William B. Strickler."

"What does the 'B' stand for?"

"Bassinette. It's an old family name. I don't know what it means or who it connects to anymore." The driver lowered his eyes, suddenly ashamed of something that only he knew about.

"Since I'm paying for this ride, Mr. Strickler, I'll offer my own, rather different opinion."

"Go ahead," Strickler allowed. He turned back to his job and eased the automobile forward through the intersection.

"It's this," I started. "There are mostly decent people and also a few crooked people everywhere. That's not determined by skin color or country. Most people are reasonably honest most of the time – even the crooks. All of them respond to sticks and carrots. That's what drives human behavior, right?"

The cabbie nodded reluctantly.

"From that angle, I think most of the people in Chinatown are no different

49

from you and I. They're trying to make a buck, trying to get along – just like you and I are."

"Mebbe you're right," Strickler acknowledged in a mumble. "No matter how you frame it, though, it still stinks bad down here."

I cracked my window down an inch and sat quietly for a few minutes, allowing his bigoted ideology to flow past me with the bracing air. "We're close," I said, eventually.

"Yes, sir, there's your address down there, a block off."

"You can let me out right here."

I climbed out at the corner of Grant and California, under the night shadow of Sing Chong's Bazaar, a four-story building with a pagoda tower built on top.

*

After William B. Strickler had snatched the sawbuck from my hand, he didn't wait around. I watched as he accelerated down the avenue, taking the shortest route out of Chinatown.

When he was out of sight, I crossed the street with its many bright, blinking neon lights, dipping my head under a banner that ran from one of the shops to a streetlamp at the curb. The writing on the banner was large, slashing red Chinese letters that meant nothing to me. I headed down Grant a few blocks and then turned back up towards Nob Hill, climbing slowly away from Grant Street.

A short, hooded woman working from a sidewalk cart offered me a bowl of dumplings. The hood was tight around her face, squeezing her wrinkled cheeks and forehead outward. She released a rapid torrent of verbiage at me.

Though I had a general idea of what she wanted, I could only shrug with incomprehension. The odor of fresh ginger, frying oil, boiled cabbage, spices, and cooked meats sat heavy in the air. I found the heady mixture both enticing and sickening at the same time. She offered me a roasted duck, glazed with a salty wax. It was flattened as if it had been starched and ironed. I shook my head and kept going.

I moved on by and found the address I was looking for. The door was recessed, with a frosted transom over it and a large brass door handle with a thumb-operated bolt release. Its surface was painted red and decorated with black symbols at the top and bottom and the painted outlines of a white flower blooming in the middle of it.

It was past nine o'clock in the evening, though the street around me was bustling with motion: peddlers, fortune tellers, herbalists, shoppers, delivery boys, street performers, hustlers, walkers, barking dogs, working girls, beat cops, and seemingly everything else imaginable. The spectrum of human variation was represented in other ways too – young and old, men and women, poor and wealthy, happy and sad.

The balconies above it all were full of flowerpots and red lanterns hung from canopies all down the street. An older woman was selling vegetables that I could only marvel at. There were long string beans slender as blades of grass, candied lychee nuts and ginger, bitter melons, bamboo shoots, and colorful lotus roots.

Near where I stood, a group of old men smoked and played some type of card game at a table they had set up on the sidewalk. Most of them wore loose dark jackets and black skullcaps. One of them used an abacus to calculate wagers. A very skinny, dark-marbled cat prowled around their feet underneath the table. He was the talkative type, though no one paid any attention to his hungry yowls.

Nobody paid any attention to me either. I knocked on the red door and stepped back from it to wait. After a moment, I heard an internal bolt drawn back. I moved around a little bit on my feet at that point, shifting my weight.

The little girl who opened the door for me was impossibly small. The skin on her face was without blemish – it was pure and soft, a creamy light brown color. She peered at me with the lower half of her face hidden behind the door. Her eyes were green and luminous, darting about earnestly, like the eyes of a Thai cat. It didn't seem possible that a Chinese girl could have green eyes, but there she was. Her age was somewhere between twelve and thirty-five and I had no confidence about guessing which end of that range she was closer to.

"I'm looking for Master Khai Chi," I told her.

She blinked at me without moving any other part of her body. There was no way for me to know if she understood what I had said.

"My name's Huddleston," I continued. "I'm looking for Master Khai Chi. Is he here?"

The girl blinked again and closed the door. I didn't know what that meant, so I waited and about a minute later she opened the door again – all the way this time and waved me inside quickly, with rapid squeezing motions of her delicate hand.

I crossed the threshold in the darkened interior and waited while she reset the bolts that held the door. As my eyes adapted to the light, I glanced about the room, realizing I was standing in the middle of a family business – probably a Chinese pharmacy.

The long, narrow room was filled with tables and shelves lined with jars of different sizes and they appeared to contain a variety of different mysterious things. On one shelf there were dark powders, light powders, tiny red objects, large yellow objects, and medium-sized green objects. On another shelf were jars holding green straws, yellow hair, pills of different shapes and colors, and milky liquids with gruesome dark shapes floating in them.

At the far end of the room behind a counter was a wall of unmarked drawers that I assumed held varieties of herbs, ointments, barks, roots, nuts, and flowers imported from China. I couldn't have described, let alone named the odor that floated in the air. It was a musty combination of primordial extractions held together by recent infusions of dried floral scents.

I didn't like it because it reminded me of my grandmother's apartment on Hennepin Avenue. She'd been a short, tight, unhappy woman who had treated her family poorly and then died after a protracted illness while I was still a child.

The young girl stared at me defiantly. I had the thought that she was utterly clean and untouched by the odiferous things that surrounded her.

Chapter Eleven

"Would Master Khai Chi see me?" I asked the girl.

Still she gave no sign that she understood the language I used. Her lips pressed together tightly as she stared up into my eyes, blinking. Eventually I stopped asking questions and stood waiting with my hands at my sides, watching her as she watched me back.

"Would you like a cigarette?" I asked her, offering her one from a package of Chesterfields.

She shook her head quickly and waved two flat palms in front of her chest. I got the message and pulled back the offer. I returned the package of cigarettes to my breast pocket without selecting one for myself, though I wanted to light one.

"How old are you?" I asked.

The response that came out of her mouth was not well formed in English, but at least she answered. She bowed after she gave her answer, which I did not understand. I interpreted her response to indicate she was either thirteen or nineteen or twenty-nine, and I couldn't tell which one it was. Maybe she hadn't even answered the question I had asked. I bowed myself and asked again about Master Khai Chi.

That elicited a nod and a tentative smile. She waved at me with her delicate hands again and indicated I was to follow her. So I did. I followed her into the dim interior of the building. When she reached a table with a flickering lantern on it, she leaned over to light a pair of candles. In the yellow glow, before she could straighten up, I realized her eyes no longer appeared green.

In the new light, with the shadows of the room dancing about on the walls, her eyes appeared to be a pale gray, possibly even a blue. She handed one of the candles to me and beckoned for me to follow her as she took the other candle and led the way down a short hallway.

There were no sounds. The walls on either side of me emanated a moist odor of incense and cooking oil. The scent was pleasing to my nostrils and possibly hypnotic in effect. At the first door she stopped and gestured with her hand near her mouth for me to be quiet. So far, she had not uttered a single word I could understand and again I wondered if she was bashful or simply spoke no English.

She knocked quietly on the door. If there was a response from within, I didn't hear it, but she opened the door anyway and gestured for me to enter. She took the candle from me before I realized how dark it was going to be.

I moved into a room that was blacker even than the rest of the house. It took my eyes a while to adapt. While they were doing that, I had a vague awareness that the girl had closed the door silently behind me and left me there alone. Stock still, I remained by the door, until my dark-adapted eyes permitted me to take the first step.

"Hello," I said quietly as I took two short-shuffle steps forward.

The room was silent, shielded somehow from the noise of the street. One corner of the room was especially dark, though I sensed a motion from within it. I watched it patiently, with my eyes focused slightly off point.

"Is somebody here?" I asked, standing still again.

"Here," came a raspy voice from the dark corner of the room.

I took two more careful steps in that direction and then stopped again. "My name is Huddleston," I said, keeping my voice low. "Are you Master Khai Chi."

There was a long pause. "Who gave you my name?" the voice rasped eventually.

"A man named Jameson Tucker," I replied. "He's with Thorough's Auction House."

My explanation was followed by a long silence. Then, the voice commanded: "Come forward."

I took several short, careful steps towards it and stopped again. The darkness gave me pause. What man could easily step onto ground where he could not see where his foot would land? "Are you Khai Chi?" I asked.

Again there was a pause. "I am," the voice finally responded.

"I mean you no harm. I'm here with a few questions. That's all. Would it be possible to provide a little light?"

"Who are you?"

It occurred that honesty might be the best approach. "I am a thief, though I am not here to steal from you. I've been sent to learn something about Lot seventy-three, an Oriental key that Jameson Tucker holds, and a package that went missing after the Sutro house fire of 1907."

There was a small noise ahead of me in the dark, toward the corner where the raspy voice came from. "You may step forward," it said. At the same time, a tiny lamp was lighted and pushed out toward the center of a low table that was on the floor between us.

A little wisp of a man peered out at me from the shadows behind the lamp. They wrapped around him like a protective cloak, depicting a mystery. The darkness of the room was oppressively claustrophobic, more oscuro than chiaroscuro in the mingling of light and darkness.

Nothing meaningful about the man was visible straight on. I couldn't see his eyes, only the outline of a mustache hanging over taught lips. The sense of foreboding caught hold of me. I thought about the dark horror of the moment when Judas announced: *"Whomsoever I shall kiss..."* and then the explosive sorrow of John the Evangelist.

I moved toward the light and when I was close, I realized I was supposed sit on the floor. A flat, round cushion waited there and I sat down on it, sweeping my jacket out behind me so that it did not bunch up tightly around my shoulders. If I needed to draw, I didn't want anything to hinder my motion.

"What do you seek?" the quiet voice in the shadows asked.

"Something of great value, believed to have disappeared from Sutro's Cliff house before the fire."

"What is it?"

"I do not know," I replied, feeling foolish as I said the words out loud.

There was no immediate response. I waited without moving.

"Why do you believe *I* can help you?" he asked.

"Jameson Tucker directed me to you. He thought you might have some connection to Sutro's house before the fire."

"Indeed, as a much younger man, I *was* employed there."

I held my breath and did not move.

"Very well," he said presently. "Let me ask you this question: Have you been shown a key?"

"I have."

"Describe it for me, please."

I did as he asked.

"Is the key in your possession now?"

"No." I shook my head.

"Do you know where to find it?"

"I do," I said. "Though I would not steal it, if that's what you're wondering. Jameson Tucker trusted me when he brought it out to show me."

"Very good. I would show you something myself," Khai Chi said. For a moment his hand was visible as he gestured toward something he wanted me to see.

In that instant, I saw the pale, wrinkled knuckles, with long slender fingers. His nails were dirty and overgrown. Then the hand disappeared beneath a sleeve and back into the shadow.

I turned to see what he had pointed at. Beside where I sat there was a small lacquered shelf attached to the wall. Small objects – boxes, carvings, ivory talismans, small bells, framed photographs little bigger than a postage stamp, pieces of jewelry – filled every surface of its six shelves. If I had been unprepared I would not have known which object he had intended to indicate, but I knew it immediately when I saw it.

"May I?" I asked.

"You may."

Stretching only slightly from my seated position, I was able to reach the red and black embroidered box. I brought it down to my lap and unfastened the ivory clasp. Inside was a key quite like the one Tucker had shown me. I lifted it up and held it toward the light thrown by the lamp. It looked and felt identical to the one I'd held only an hour before in the Pacific Heights.

The question was on my lips before I could inhibit it: "How many of these keys are there?"

"There are only two, and you've seen them both tonight."

"What do they open?"

"That is the right question. Although they appear to be the same key, I believe – I expect they open two different locks."

"What does that mean?" I asked.

"It is not something I know with certainty, but something I suspect. Ancient Chinese Kings often produced more than one treasure, with more than one key. Usually only one key opened the real treasure. The others were decoys. You are young enough and you must think about that as you plan your moves."

The house was dark and silent. None of the noises from the street filtered in. From somewhere deep in the structure came the soft sound of water dripping onto water. Every third drop was louder than the two that preceded it – drip, drip, drop; drip, drip, drop – forming an inexorable pattern that seemed capable of driving a man into madness.

I drew a long, tired breath to keep from losing myself, even as I wondered about the hypnotic effect of the incense I'd been breathing.

Chapter Twelve

Khai Chi's voice, when he spoke again, was a murmur torn from the bottom of his larynx. "Have you seen the yellow bloom of a dragon fruit at night?" His long fingers reappeared momentarily to make a small spherical gesture before they disappeared again beneath his robe.

I shook my head.

"The bloom is bright and complex, though it is rare and it avoids the light. It only appears at night for a few hours, and only once in the life of the flower. If it is not pollinated the flower dies and plant remains dormant for many more months."

When he finished speaking I asked my question. "What happens if it *is* pollinated?"

"If there are moths or bats available and ready to pollinate it during the few hours that it is receptive, the fruit that results is a brilliant red, scaled delicacy. It has special properties for the man that eats it."

"Is there a trick to getting past the scales?" I asked.

He shook his head. "You cut it in half and eat its sweet, juicy pulp with a spoon – like eating a dish of custard. To eat it, is to know you are blessed."

"I've never tasted it," I admitted.

"Few men have," and he stopped talking here for a moment to emphasize the importance of what he was about to say. "The bloom, whether pollinated or not, is a part of the cosmos. It is ephemeral, fragile, beautiful, and precious, reaching up toward the brief, faint access to light – to starlight. It is of importance by itself even if the fruit never develops."

Although my crossed legs were starting to fall asleep, I didn't move. He was the master. I was to listen.

He coughed several times to clear his raspy voice. "The interior of the bloom is a complex natural mystery. It is a bloom within a bloom within a bloom of tight, controlling, beautiful lips like those of a woman's. The exterior flower opens to reveal an interior flower, as well as a separate internal eager stem. There is only a short time before the outer lips close together and the entire bloom sinks in upon itself. Once that happens it disappears quickly."

I sat very still.

After a pause, Khai Chi continued. "It is much like a human life. We too are ephemeral, fleeting, fragile. Our opportunities to reveal ourselves, to mate, to accomplish what we are here for is as limited as the night-blooming flower. Our time is short. We can be beautiful in our own right; and we can reproduce and be productive. None of that is assured, however. We too bloom only at night when nobody is paying attention. You remain quiet?"

"I'm listening."

Khai Chi then leaned forward onto the table with his elbows near mine. "My sense tells me you have killed men?" he stated gently.

I nodded. "When it was necessary, I have done so."

"How has it affected you?"

"A thoughtful man cannot kill another without dying a little himself."

Khai Chi nodded slowly and brought a slender, pale finger to his lips, which he pursed against it. "Why do you continue to kill?" he inquired.

"I hope I never have to kill another man again, though I expect I will."

"If that is your hope, you could make it so."

I nodded. "At what cost, though?"

"The ethical man realizes that every decision carries a weight. To *do* something carries one measure; to *not* do something carries another. Often, the difference is in the intent. There is, I think, a difference between doing something – or not doing it – out of fear rather than duty, out of self-service rather than self-sacrifice, out of anger rather than kindness, out of hate rather than love."

I nodded and remained quiet.

"You said you seek something of great value, something you believe may have disappeared from Mr. Sutro's house on the cliff shortly before the fire."

I nodded and lowered my eyes and then my face. "I would be grateful for anything you can tell me."

"I am curious," Khai Chi confessed. "In my youth I worked for Mr. Sutro in his house. I lived in a small apartment on the lowest floor, along with seven other Chinese men. Together we ran the lower jobs of the house. We did the cleaning, laundry, gardening, unloading deliveries by both ship and truck, and any other unskilled work that needed to be done on the grounds.

"We also helped prepare food for the lavish dinners Mr. Sutro threw for the wealthy people of San Francisco. The chef instructed us. We chopped vegetable for hours and butchered and cleaned the livestock for the meals. Have you ever butchered a calf or a lamb or any other animal?"

"No," I replied. "I grew up in a city. Those chores were not something city-children were tasked with."

"You're no longer a child."

"True, but I still live in cities and I take most of my meals in restaurants or from a grocer's bag. I've never butchered an animal."

"Yet, you've killed humans."

"I have," I nodded. "With respect, I'd like to ask about the fire that destroyed Sutro's house twenty-seven years ago. The important men who visited Sutro's house then are almost all dead now. His home is a memory to only a very few who are living now."

Khai Chi nodded. "It is more then that to me. There were rumors for months before the fire occurred. They implied the end of the house – and the disappearance of something of immeasurable power. It was inconceivable to me then, as a young man, that such a magnificent house of a rich man could burn to the ground and cease to exist within an hour of time – as it did."

"Did the rumors suggest what the item was?"

He withdrew into the shadows that engulfed him and became imperceptible to me. "They offered fantastic possibilities."

"What were they?"

"One said there was an elixir that offered immortality to the few. Another claimed it was a gem of such density the entire universe would be drawn into it and destroyed. Still another suggested a vial holding a disease that could spread and wipe out humanity within a fortnight. One rumor held there was a jar of powder that could be sprinkled over common stones to produce solid gold.

"Each of these theories suggested a transformative power, but whether it was for evil or for good was not clear. Dark forces exist, and I became persuaded that it was a force for evil."

"Are you aware of the auction at Thorough's House tomorrow afternoon?"

He bent his head slowly in affirmation.

"What are the keys for?"

"I cannot say."

"Cannot or will not?"

"Cannot."

I wasn't sure if he understood the difference in the same way I did. "Do you know which item within the auction parcel is the one I should bid on?"

Khai Chi rose up as straight and tall as his spine would allow. "You wish to know how to identify the larger item that may contain the smaller item of your interest?"

I nodded.

"There is no guarantee I can offer, but I am willing to accompany you to the auction."

"You are willing to do that?"

"I am, with a condition."

"Go on."

"I want to be there when it is opened."

"Is that all?"

"I may be asking a lot."

"Do you know what it is?" I asked.

Khai Chi leaned forward into the light so that I could see his face. He pursed his lips and closed his eyes. "I have heard only stories, which are the ancient whispers of Chinese warriors long dead. They are not something I could easily explain to you or any other man – especially a Western man."

I pressed him: "What do they suggest?"

He drew a long breath and exhaled slowly, fatalistically. "The end of everything," he sighed, and then withdrew back into his long robe and the penumbral shadows that engulfed him. The room was entirely silent apart from the interior dripping sounds that began to emerge again to my ears.

Chapter Thirteen

The next morning I was awake early with a poorly remembered dream niggling at me. I had a quiet breakfast alone on the balcony. The newspaper had an editorial titled "Indiscriminate Sale of Firearms Should be Prohibited" by Dr. T. B. W. Leland, Coroner, City and County of San Francisco. I read the editorial with some interest, though I couldn't see how the proposed solution solved the problem:

"The promiscuous sale of firearms should be prohibited. We have had ample opportunity to realize the dangers that arise from the use of the death-dealing instruments. When are we going to awaken? We must treat the men who carry guns as potential murderers. Be done with the sentimentalistic foolery. We have got to realize that a man who wields a gun does not do so with any sympathetic object. He is out of his game just the same as a hunter on the steppes.

It is unfortunate that a police officer, or for that matter, any other man should die the victim of a bullet which civilization, common decency and the inherent law to protect, should not allow. We may awaken sometime but it looks as if we are extremely indifferent, diffident and negligent.

We cannot pardon ourselves as murderers. We are assassins, cold in fact as this may appear to be, because we not only allow such a situation to prevail but we do nothing to prevent it. Some day we are going to elect judges who are going to impose the penalty which should be inflicted upon those who carry guns. We have had enough molly-coddling of the criminal. We demand not only that the criminal be punished but that judges will see the advisability of meting out the penalty that common sense dictates."

I set the newspaper aside and drank the last of my coffee while I thought about it. With a Chesterfield smoldering between my lips, I looked out across the city, toward the bay. Early seagulls filled the lower part of the sky; the upper heavens were an mélange of clouds catching the first rays of the sun and splitting them into crimson-inflected primary colors.

For much of the past week my challenge had been one I hadn't faced too often before. Business had been good lately and I'd had a lot to dispose of. The cash I had secured in a variety of places. Much of it I'd sent to Jimmy in Chicago and some of it to trusted connections in Cleveland, Reno, St. Paul, New York, Chicago, and Kansas City.

The Federal Reserve Bank of San Francisco had been happy enough to receive me. They helped me open my own account. I deposited two thousand dollars and leased a safe deposit box, which I filled with stacks of loose bills. I stitched five thousand dollars into the sides of a couple old suit jackets, mailed ten thousand to Delilah in Des Moines, and kept five thousand with me for walking around money.

The Dodge was a liability, so I had traded it along with some cash for a V8 Ford with bulletproof panels on the sides and back. There was also a suitcase of narcotics to deal with. Using an alias I left it for myself with "left luggage" at the Market Street Railway substation at the corner of Fillmore Street and Turk.

Now there was a new challenge to think about. My contemplation was interrupted by a sharp knock at the door. I glanced at my watch. It was early still, not quite seven o'clock.

I got up and went to the door. The man I saw through the peephole was short and bald, and I guessed he would be heavy on his feet. As Orion had promised, there was nothing graceful about him.

"Are you Beakman?" I inquired through the door.

"I am he. Are you Huddleston?"

"Is there something you'd like to show me?"

Without a word, he dug something out of his front breast pocket and waved it in front of the peephole. I opened the door and took it from him. It was the other half of the hundred-dollar bill that Dr. Orion had torn apart. After I matched it to my half just to be sure, I stepped back into the foyer and let him in.

"What can I do for you?" I asked.

"Can we sit down?"

"I don't see a reason to. You have a message for me. Deliver it and let's get on with the show."

Beakman was sweating heavily, as short, bald men, who are heavy on their feet are prone to. He'd spend a lot of time out in the sun recently. A red tautness captured his face and framed it. The suit he wore was off-white and at least a size too large for him. His appearance and his lilting accent led me to wonder if he was of Egyptian descent. "It's important that I know. Have you had any visitors over the past day or two?"

"Do you think I should have?"

"That's why I'm asking."

"You're asking, but you're not telling anything."

"Maybe if you share a little with me, I can share a little back with you." He spoke with the tone of a scolding minister.

"How did you find me?"

"I was given your room number."

"By whom?"

62

"It's complicated."

I didn't like that at all and said so.

"Sorry," he replied. "Nothing I can do about that. The underworld of this town has many eyes."

"I am under the assumption that you work for Dr. Orion. Have I got it wrong?"

"I work for Orion, but I also work for others, on other projects. Orion didn't give me your address. I doubt he even knows it – he set up an answering service rigmarole for us to connect."

"I guess you're smarter than he is?"

"We'll see. Have you had any visitors other than me? It's imperative that I know. Who has been here before me? Anyone?"

"Information usually flows best when it flows two ways," I reminded him.

"Meaning what, exactly?"

"Meaning, I'd be more inclined to tell you about any visitors I might have had, if you were more willing to tell me how you found me."

"Can't we sit down?" he asked again.

I relented and we went into the parlor. Beakman sat in the plushest chair there was and sank into it deeply, which he seemed to relish. A lavender handkerchief appeared in his hand and made a slow pass over his forehead.

Aware of my own impatience, I took a breath before I spoke: "I'll ask one more time and if you don't answer you'll be on your feet again. How did you find me?"

"A man named Travers told me you were here. Does this name mean anything to you?"

"Never heard it before."

"How about Josephine?"

"I don't know her either."

"Josephine is a mister – Mr. Josephine." Beakman watched me very carefully through narrowed eyes.

I shook my head and thought I saw the stifled signs of relief sticking out through his expression. "Who are they, why do they matter, and how did this Travers come to know where to find me. Moreover, how did he know to tell you about me?"

"Samuel Travers is a gunman for Mr. Josephine, who in turn is a leader of an association in Chinatown."

"One of the Tongs?"

Beakman shrugged and glanced out the window toward the sky over the bay. "There are many words that lose their value when translated between Chinese and English. Mr. Josephine is an important man in his community."

"Of Chinatown?"

"Yes."

"Go on. How did Travers locate me, and how did he know you might want to speak with me?"

"As I said, the underworld of this town has many eyes. Someone was looking for you and when they found you, Mr. Josephine was among those who knew about it. I assume he passed this information on to Travers, though possibly Travers is the one who passed it to him. Either way, once Travers understood the importance of it, he shared it with me."

"Why?"

"That's harder for me to say. We've cooperated in the past. Sometimes we help each other."

"Do you know my name?"

"I know you as Mr. Huddleston."

"How did Travers know you might have an interest in me?"

Beakman sighed and the lavender handkerchief reappeared. "He and I are birds of a feather – independent operators, if you understand my meaning. We both have our regular clients, though neither of us have pledged loyalty to any particular association."

I nodded to indicate that I understood what he meant.

"Travers heard I was consulting to Dr. Orion -"

"Because you told him that you were," I interrupted.

"We compare notes on occasion."

I shook my head. "That doesn't ring true. You and Travers are loose operators, each looking for a break. Tell it to me like it is. It'll go better for you."

Beakman sighed and tried his best to appear non-reactive. "Alright, maybe it played that way. Samuel Travers and I have been around this town a lot of years and we compare notes every now and then. He helps me when he can, and I help him now and again. What harm is there in that?"

"Continue with your story," I said. "I find it to be almost amusing. So, Travers heard what you were looking for and he shared a tip with you. Then what?"

"Then nothing. I've answered your questions. Is it my turn now?"

"Go ahead," I replied, curious to see what he would ask. Sometimes questioners revealed more than the people they questioned.

"Have you had any visitors here?"

"Only one until you showed up: Jameson Tucker, the Third."

"The auctioneer?"

I nodded.

"How did *he* find you?"

I grinned at the irony. "I don't know. He wouldn't say and it bothered me.

Now I think I have an idea."

"What's that?"

"The underworld of this town has many eyes," I replied.

"Don't kid around."

I frowned and reached for a cigarette. "I'm doing nothing of the sort, Beakman. If Travers heard I was here, why wouldn't others? On that point, if Travers heard and told you, why wouldn't he tell ten other mugs?"

"Things aren't that loose."

"Aren't they?"

"What did Tucker want? Did he try to sell you something?"

I smiled, figuring it would be disconcerting to my visitor. "Sure," I said. "He had a key that he offered me. It was exotic."

Beakman's face was a blank slate – no reaction at all. "A key to what? Nothing more?"

I shook my head. "Never mind, that was probably a diversion. The real deal was the address he gave me. It led me to a character in Chinatown."

"Whose address?"

"Does the name Khai Chi mean anything to you?"

Beakman thought about it for a moment and then shook his head. His lips purpled out a bit as he pursed them for my benefit. "Should it?"

"I paid him a visit last night, wandering deep into Chinatown."

Beakman exhaled. "You need to be careful there. You don't know what you're getting yourself into."

"Explain that to me."

"Chinatown is its own place," he began. "Its one thing during daylight, another entirely after dark. You cannot trust a Chinaman. Who do you think betrayed old Sutro at the end? I'm sure it was a Chinaman that lighted the match that burned his cliff house down."

"Why are you so sure of that?" I asked.

"Who else would do a thing like that?" Beakman asked indignantly. "They were traitors in the house and they stole the treasure."

"What treasure?"

"Don't kid me. You know what I'm talking about, though you have a lot to learn about this town and about Chinatown."

"Your pal Travers apparently works for a Chinatown big-shot. What does that say?"

"He works for him; doesn't mean he respects him. Mr. Josephine has a lot of power over there – but its limited to a twelve-block area. A man with slanted eyes can never move beyond that."

I found his attitude to be depressing. Without a word I stubbed out my cigarette and stood up. The balcony door was still partially open and as refreshing as the breeze had been, I couldn't take it anymore. I closed and locked the sliding glass door. When I turned around, Beakman had crossed his legs, indicating his determination to settle in.

"Anything else?" I asked him, still standing.

"No one else has approached you?"

"What are you fishing for, Beakman?"

"I'm trying to help you."

"Do you know a woman named Jennifer McPhael or a private investigator named Johnny Drake?"

Beakman's face involuntarily broke pale beneath the sun-hardened crimson and he squirmed a little in the plush chair he was deep into. "I'm afraid not," he replied, though his voice had a weird dip to it. "I don't know those names." Sweat formed along his brow again and rolled down his face. Willfully, he ignored it, holding back the urge to appeal to the lavender handkerchief.

"Too bad," I suggested. "She is a looker. From what you've told me, I would have thought you might have known or heard of Drake."

"Drake? His name doesn't ring a bell."

"Could be he's new in this town."

"Sure, that could be it."

I let my lips curl to show I didn't buy what he was selling me. "Are we finished?"

Beakman leaned forward in his seat – as far as he possibly could, given his girth. "There's something you need to see. I'd like to take you for a short ride around town if you'll permit me."

"What is it?"

"I'll show you," he said, "if you'll come with me."

As I followed him out, I notice a white line that looped around the back of his neck and disappeared from my view as it wrapped around to the front of his throat. Before I could figure out what it was and how it got there, he tilted his head back a half-inch and the line disappeared into a fold in his thick flesh, engulfed by the copper skin on either side of it. I was reminded that we all carry a hidden part of ourselves that rarely sees the light of day.

Chapter Fourteen

We left the Fairmont Hotel through the side door – bypassing the lobby and its large columns with Corinthian capitals, Persian rugs, gilded mirrors, egg and dart cornices, and laurel garland moldings – to catch a taxicab going down the hill. The door we stepped out of was quite ordinary, but it worked just as any fancier door would have.

Beakman gave a few directions to the driver and then sat back beside me and fiddled with a new cigar. The cabbie slalomed down the steep grade haphazardly and suddenly hung a hard, fast left that threw my shoulder against the door.

A few blocks later we were heading north on Grant Street, past the multi-story Bazaars on either side of us with their pseudo-Chinese facades, dragon motifs, and pagoda towers. The streets were crowded with people shopping, and the taxi worked it's way carefully now, slowly through the throngs. The cabbie used the horn judiciously.

"What do you know about the history of Chinatown?" Beakman asked me.

"Almost nothing," I replied, reading little into his question.

"You seem like an educated man, would you like to hear a little history of the neighborhood?"

"Sure, fill me in."

Beakman's smile revealed his pleasure. "The Chinese came for the gold rush in the early 1850s, along with other people from all over the world. Since they were different from the others, they stuck together in groups and clans and formed their own enclaves wherever they were. That's how this neighborhood started. When the rush faded, as it did quickly, they continued to come. There was money to be made working for the railroads and in commerce, and many men came over by themselves in order to work and send money back to their families in China."

"Like every other immigrant group that came to America."

"Yes, though the Chinese men were less likely to bring their wives and children and elders. They were hard workers and they kept coming until the Chinese Exclusion Act was passed in 1882. There was a lot of anti-Chinese animosity encouraged by the labor leaders and professional guilds. There were race riots in the years leading up the Act. The Act posed severe restrictions on immigration from China and it forbid the men who were already here from sending for their families. You can probably guess what that led to – all those lonely men with time and money on their hands and no female companionship."

I well knew what he meant. I'd seen a form of it in prison.

"Right," Beakman confirmed, as if I'd answered his question out loud. "Prostitution, gambling, alcohol, opium, thievery – the usual escapes that lonely men seek. Human smuggling became a thriving business – bringing families in, as well as slave girls to work in the brothels. Graft was rampant, along with segregation and overcrowding. Something else developed, though too: The Chinese Consolidated Benevolent Association, otherwise known as the Chinese Six Companies."

"Similar to the Unione Siciliana?" I referenced the Italian fraternal organization that involved itself heavily in labor matters. It was controlled by the Chicago Outfit and was influenced the Italian-American vote through the entire country.

Beakman shrugged. "The Six Companies were actually benevolent in their efforts and not controlled by crime lords. From what I understand, not only did they try to improve business conditions for Chinese, but also they made attempts to close down the prostitution that was rampant before the turn of the century. They were resourceful and they also provided a model of diplomacy for China. The Qing government turned to the Six Companies for help, and then adopted their techniques and arguments in dealing with the U.S. government. Its unfortunate, but the power of the Six Companies began to fall apart in the early eighteen-nineties. I believe that was a loss for the people living here, though they continue on and may someday regain their former position."

I glanced out the window to look at the scene. The taxi driver was taking us on a full tour of the area. "Go on," I encouraged Beakman, without looking at him. "You're about up to nineteen hundred with your history. Where do things go from there?"

"After the earthquake of 1906 the birth records of city hall were destroyed. That allowed Chinese immigrants to claim U.S. citizenship and then send for their wives and relatives still in China. The male to female ratio began to level out and the number of native-born Chinese rose dramatically. That's to tell you something about the people of this community."

"It seems some people still don't like the Chinese, including you."

Beakman nodded without seeming to make any particular commitment. "There are traits to every nationality that are natural and inherent in their blood. I prefer not to demean any group of people, but there are realities and it does one no good to pretend they do not exist."

"How well do you understand them? Do you speak their language?"

"Have you heard it? Its an impossible language to comprehend."

I noted the sudden turn in his voice that revealed him. "Where are we

68

going?"

"Ever been inside a Chinese opium den?"

I'd seen opium smoked in late night joints and private parties in Chicago and New York City, but I'd never been inside a Chinese den and I said so.

"That's where we're going," Beakman explained. "The local police used to burn opium publicly in the streets of Chinatown. It was their way of appearing to do something about a problem that was politically visible at the time. Of course, they only burned a small percentage of what was on the market at any given time, and they continued to take their graft."

I nodded. I'd grown up in the Twin Cities, which had operated under the O'Conner System. John J. O'Connor had been Chief of Police in St. Paul until his retirement in 1920. All criminal operations in the city had run through him. He and his men had received a cut of everything and the corruption was systemic. From top to bottom, most of the city police and politicians were in on it. I was reminded constantly that every large city in America worked in a similar way. Now, I could add San Francisco to that list.

"It's the Chinese secret societies and so called 'highbinders' that make Chinatown work. They control the labor, the opium dens, prostitution, gambling – even the laundries, grocers, and funeral parlors."

"Every town has its graft system and it's mobsters," I observed.

Beakman replied philosophically as though he had given the matter a lot of thought. "I think every town has ruthless business men who are willing to fill the vacuum that human nature and the government inevitably leave open. In Chinatown they're known as the Tongs."

"Anything else?"

"Yeah, there's a zealous police sergeant named Jack Manion. He heads the so-called 'Chinatown Squad.' You might watch out for him. The Chinese do. He's a head-breaker with a badge."

I knew the type well.

*

The taxi had snaked around slowly and finally dropped us at the entrance to a dirty, unmarked alley. We walked past a row of overflowing garbage pails and took long strides over dirty pools of water that collected around the sewer grates. I counted three brazen rats that didn't seem to mind our presence in the least.

The establishment that Beakman led me into was an old garment factory that was partially operational. The odor of lye, burnt oil, and wool was heavy in the air. We walked down an alley of ancient sewing machines that clicked away with their large spools of colored thread unwinding slowly.

An army of small hunched-over men tended to the machines. They ignored us entirely as we went by. We jumped the stairs up to the third floor and took a long hallway that led over to the building next door.

Beakman knocked on a steel door and leaned against it until the slot in front of his face was opened. He breathed heavily from the exertion to get there and it took him a moment to respond. When he did, he made an odd sign with the fingers of both hands. A moment later the door was opened and we were admitted into what could have been a banquet hall.

The room was filled with heavy smoke and Chinese men, probably at least a hundred of them, gathered around small tables. They stood bent over the tables in simple browns and blues. There was an audible buzz in the room made up of all those sharp, quick, hustling voices.

"Ever been in a fan-tan gambling hall?" Beakman asked, grinning.

I told him I'd never heard of fan-tan.

"It's the most popular game in this neighborhood – the 'ruling passion' of the Chinese," he explained. "It's a simple game: A square is marked in the centre of a table and the sides are marked one, two, three, four. The house banker puts on the table a double handful of small buttons, beads, or coins, which he covers with a metal bowl, or *tan koi*, as they call it.

"The players then bet on the numbers, setting their stakes on the side of the square that bears the number selected. Players can also bet on the corners. When all bets are placed, the bowl is removed and the *tan kun*, as the dealer is known, uses a small bamboo stick to remove the buttons from the heap, four at a time, until the final batch is reached.

"If it contains four buttons, the backer of number four wins; if three, the backer of number three wins; and so on, down to one. All winning wagers are paid the correct odds, less a five percent commission."

"Nice odds for the house."

As Beakman grinned, his jowls expanded into his neck. "Like any lottery or roulette game, like most other casino games, Fan-tan is a house game. It depends entirely upon the poor understanding of mathematics and statistical odds among those who play it. Follow me, now."

We crossed the room. Nobody gave us a second look, let alone a first. At the far end of the banquet hall we went through a door, past a couple of Chinese hard guys, and took a flight of stairs up a level and then crossed over to another building.

By that time I had lost track of where we were or even what building we were in. After we reached the next building, we descended a flight of stairs. By my estimate that brought us to the second level of a building, though I wasn't too confident of my estimate.

"Are you carrying a gun?" Beakman asked as we paused in front of a heavy door.

"Of course, I am," I replied. "Why?"

"They may frisk us here," Beakman explained.

"I'm not giving up my .45," I warned him. "I've already done that too many times in this life."

Beakman nodded politely. "Our hosts may be impressed. The Chinese are partial to our Government model 1911's. It's been a favorite weapon of the Tongs over the past twenty years."

The door opened suddenly and we were beckoned inside. Beakman handed a folded bill to the older Chinese man at the door and whispered something in his ear. The man nodded and pointed toward a nearby chamber room. We went into the room and sat down on a teak bench and waited.

Several minutes went by. Presently, a young woman came to us and beckoned. She was dressed in a silk kimono that did little to hide the shape of her body. She was tall and lean, with very little development where Western woman tended to have it.

Beakman stood up. "Han," he said to her.

The young woman nodded and bowed her head slightly, keeping her eyes on the floor in front of us the entire time. Her kimono followed the movements of her body as she bowed and gestured us to follow her with a pair of slim, delicate hands.

"It's an opium den," Beakman counseled me. "Don't ask what *she* costs."

"Why are we here?" I asked instead.

"Stay patient."

"For how long?"

"This den is operated by a man named Han. I think he might know something about what we're interested in. He's old enough to have seen many things and he's knowledgeable. Also, I believe he may be inclined to talk with us."

A slow-writhing layer of elderly men covered the floor of the room we passed through. They lay on small, ragged cots close to the floor. We passed into another room, which I assumed had higher paying customers. Nicer beds were arranged in slanting rows that drew inward. At each bed was a small table with a hookah, a candle, and a pitcher of water.

Most of the beds were occupied by older Chinese men whose vacant eyes reflected the bright visions of foreigners who had arrived, but had never been received, on the strange shores of their new land.

Chapter Fifteen

We made our way silently among the afflicted and were led into a small, private room that was sparsely furnished. There was a low, Teak bedframe close to the floor with a thin mattress on it. Beside it were a simple wooden chair, a low wooden table adorned with a candle and a book, and a small Teak dresser.

A floor lamp in one corner was the only light in the room, though an incense coil hanging from the middle of the ceiling emitted a low glow, as well as an odor that I could not identify, but associated with very old rooms and very old things.

Also in the room in waiting for us was an older man who was lucid and grandiose with his hands. It was his opium den we were in. His hands revealed a story as they moved rapidly in front of my face, gesturing and shaping the idea of what his establishment was about. I didn't understand the Mandarin he spoke, but I watched him carefully without reaction.

Eventually, Beakman interrupted him to make the introduction. "This is Han. He has lived in Chinatown most of his life and he now occupies a different role from past days. Many years ago, he was *boo how doy*, a soldier of the Tongs, a hatchet wielder. He fought in the Tong wars and he identifies Mr. Josephine as his mortal enemy. This is something we can count on."

"Why are they enemies?" I asked, looking at Beakman.

The heavy-set Egyptian smiled and bowed his head diplomatically. "It is probably wise to let Han explain that to you himself."

I turned my head to look at the man. Han's eyes did not avoid mine. "You don't know me. Why are you willing to talk to me?" I asked him.

Han spoke slowly, uncertainly. His command of English was poor, but his communication was effective all the same. "Josephine is enemy."

"Why?"

"Thirty-six years ago I pay him money. He make promise, bring my wife, child, here to San Francisco. I pay money, much money."

I nodded to encourage him.

Han's eyes were clear, though abruptly empty of any meaning. "They never arrive. They die in ocean, boat sink, all drown."

"You must have been heartbroken," I told him.

Han bowed his head, re-experiencing the sorrow again. Tears filled his eyes and flooded his cheeks, rolling down inside his collar. He raised his head to look at me. Staunchly, he did not wipe at the tears. He let them flow and his eyes struggled not to blink against them as he stared back at me with determination.

We waited quietly until Han was ready to speak again.

"Did you ever work at Sutro's Cliff House?" Beakman asked.

Han listened closely, considered the question, and then nodded his head. His hands were active, compulsively rubbing against each other, the fingers twitching and clicking involuntarily.

"What years were you there?" Beakman asked.

Han responded slowly: "Nineteen oh five, to nineteen oh seven. Until the fire."

Beakman smiled and touched him on the shoulder. "Were you there that day?"

Han nodded.

"What do you know about the fire?"

"I believe it started in kitchen. It moved fast, we ran from house."

"Of course you did. Do you know how it started?"

Han shook his head.

"Did anyone try to put the fire out?"

Han shrugged. "Fire moved fast. We ran out of house."

Beakman nodded and glanced at me, then back at Han. "You know what we seek. Tell us what you can. I heard you had a client who spoke about it to you recently."

Han nodded again, smiling grimly. His speech was halting. "Man here five days ago, deep into his pipe. The girl heard him. She called me. I sat with him several hours. He have dreams, described ancient box. He say it from burned Sutro house, hold something of great value. What it is – he did not say. I remember rumors from before, many past years."

"What do you think happened?" Beakman asked.

Han shrugged and said something rapidly in Chinese.

"English, please," Beakman encouraged him.

Han bowed, ashamed. "There is a box. It survived fire, very valuable. Who knows?"

"What was in it?"

"Who knows? I don't. Something ancient, something valuable. It is dangerous."

"How large is the box?"

Han gestured with his hands moving in space to describe something about the shape and size of a one-foot square cube.

"Where is it now?" Beakman asked forcefully.

"I don't know. Somewhere in city, available for sale, I think."

"Perhaps an auction?" Beakman suggested.

With his palms open at chest-level, Han shrugged again. Then he nodded reluctantly. The folds around his eyes creased delicately as he studied me earnestly, trying to read my reaction to what he had told us. "Window of time is narrow," he said, speaking directly to me for the first time.

Beakman nodded and patted Han on the shoulder again. He glanced at me. "Any questions?"

I watched Han, studying his face in return. I read him as a man who had seen most everything in his life and no longer cared about anything other than living long enough to see the ruin of his enemies. "This man who was in here five days ago: Had you ever seen him before?"

Han shook his head.

"So, you don't know who he was?"

Han paused before he answered. "I recognized him from newspaper," he conceded.

"Who was he?"

"Local businessman, merchant, very important in Chinatown." Han waved his hand and pointed off in the distance to indicate something that I could not understand.

"Do you know his name?"

Han nodded without speaking.

I waited, staring at him.

"Willie Fung," he said eventually.

"Why does he matter? Why is he important in Chinatown? Why did you sit with him?"

Han's eyes widened initially and then closed in upon themselves, reminding me of butterfly wings that closed partially when under threat. "Mr. Fung important Chinatown business man." From the corner of my eye I could see Beakman nodding in agreement. "His dreams distressed him so much," Han continued. "I very worried, sat with him to ensure his health. I place cool wet towels on his forehead, give him herbs to sleep, soothe him for hours."

"Was he soothed, did he sleep then?"

Han bowed his head. "Yes, he was quiet after that."

"What were these dreams about? Why did they distress him so much?"

"I don't know. He say many times: 'Whispers Pete, don't take me, Whispers Pete.' He was crying out from beyond the river. Sometimes he cried: 'Fingers Pete, please don't take me. Please, Fingers Pete.' Don't ask me who Pete is. I don't know. He cause fear." As if exhausted now, Han dropped his hands to his sides and buried them in the folds of his robe.

"Where can I find Mr. Willie Fung?"

"Nowhere," Han replied flatly. His expression was blank as he looked back at me and I knew that our conversation was over. "He is gone. The sewers of Chinatown are final resting place for so many. They are filled with ghosts now."

As we reached the bottom of the stairs, Beakman stopped me before I could open the exterior door. With his large hand resting gently upon my arm he looked at me, and his face was gray with worry. "Who is this Whispers Pete or Fingers Pete or whatever his name is? Does the appellation mean anything to you?

"Han seems to think he's a bogyman of sorts."

"The Chinese are a superstitious race," Beakman replied.

"What about you, are you superstitious?"

"Me? Never. It's the Twentieth Century now. We don't have bogymen any more. We left them behind in our distant past. That's what civilization means. Do you know who this Pete character is?"

Grimly, I patted the gun in my shoulder holster and nodded. "He's no bogyman, though he is a killer. We crossed trails once in Chicago. He's a part-time gunman for Lepke's mob – though he's mostly independent."

Beakman whistled through his teeth. "I wonder who he's working for now."

"He's elusive. For what he did to me and some people I cared about, I'd like to find him." I thought about a woman I'd shared an elevator with and a bank job in Chicago that had gone down the wrong way. Adrenaline surged within me and I squeezed my left hand hard upon itself to help control it. "What can you tell me about Willie Fung?"

"As Han said, Fung is an important business man in the Chinese community. I'm surprised to learn he was here in Han's den. I would not have thought him the type. That means something in itself."

"What happened to him?"

"Nobody knows. He disappeared several days ago."

"Before or after he visited Han's den?"

"I don't know."

"What do you think about it?"

Beakman's complexion took on the shade of blackened silver. "I expect Han probably called it right."

I exhaled slowly. "What's this place, Chinatown, all about anyway?"

"You're too young and too white to understand it. You and I will always be strangers here. The Tong wars prior to the earthquake of nineteen-oh-six were fought over two things – the failure to make full payment for a slave girl or insults to a Tong member's honor. Most of the power held by the Tongs as well as the violence between them ended after the earthquake. It destroyed the opium dens, brothels, and gambling houses and it brought about a new order."

"What replaced them?"

"Some think it is the Triads, which are led from the Chinese mainland."

"Are you telling me that Mr. Josephine is affiliated with the Chinese Triads?"

Beakman frowned and his hand fell off my arm. "I don't know, but he could be. There are rumors to that effect."

I found a Chesterfield and stuck it, unlighted, into a corner of my mouth. "It would be good to know for certain," I replied before pushing the door open to face the outside world.

In the blinding sunlight of the street, an old, stooped peddler offered to sell us a string of dried chicken claws. The word *no* was not something he seemed to understand and he followed us for half a block. His smiling mouthful of broken, yellowed teeth struck me as a metaphor for all the blight in the world around me.

Chapter Sixteen

I didn't spot the ambush until I had already walked into it.

Puffing with exertion as I strode up Nob Hill, I was almost even with the automobile before I saw it. It was a non-descript blue Dodge sedan parked on the other side of California street from me, across from the Fairmont, facing downslope. Something about the movement of the two men in fedoras sitting in the front seat caught my attention.

The driver pretended to read a newspaper, while the passenger strained to look back over his shoulder at something. As my gaze followed his, I realized what he was looking at. There was a man standing at the top of the hill at the corner of Mason Street, in the turn-around of the Mark Hopkins Hotel, partially concealed behind the front hood of a truck. A pair of binoculars was attached to his eyes. He was watching the entrance to the Fairmont Hotel.

They were Federal agents and they had found me.

I might have reached the side door of the Fairmont without being seen, but that was risky and in any case there were certain to be more G-men inside. They were probably already on my hallway, in the stairwells, around the elevator, and possibly even in my own room waiting for me.

I had only seconds before the driver of the Dodge would glance up from his newspaper and see me. There was no time to backtrack. I made my decision quickly and drew my pistol as I moved across the street toward him.

A black Ford Model-T braked in order not to hit me. The driver hit the horn and leaned on it, startling the driver of the Dodge. I was already on his running board with my pistol by his ear before he had his bearings.

"Hands on the wheel. You don't want a .45 slug through your brain. Go on and release the brake. Let's see how fast you can coast down California Street." I switched the aim of my pistol to his partner. "You have a gun. Drop it out the window on your side. Carefully." The man pushed a shotgun and then a .38 service revolver out the window. I heard the hard double clatter on the concrete as we began to move.

Up the hill there was a shout and then two rapid pistol shots, probably fired to alert others. I'd been spotted. By then we were rolling downhill. I had my right arm inside the Dodge, holding on tightly as we moved down the street. The .45 was in my left hand. I'd ridden a few running boards in my time, but with the hill extended below us, this promised to be something different.

There was another shot, almost certainly from a rifle, fired from behind us. It hit the back panel of the sedan. The vibration of the chassis rattled my arm and shoulder that were in contact with it. I knew the agent driving the Dodge was as motivated to avoid the fire coming from behind us, as he was by the pistol I held next to his head.

Sweet gravity pulled us immediately, drawing us fast down the hill.

"Give it a little gas and keep your foot off the brake," I shouted as I crouched down on the running board. We were already at fifty miles an hour. I hung on tight. Air rushed past my face and I lost my hat. It flipped back off my head and flew into the street we'd left behind. "Faster," I shouted, tapping my pistol against the frightened driver's cheek.

Looking back over my shoulder, I could see pursuit had not yet been organized.

"Right there," I shouted at the driver. "Pull over there, before that light!"

Fear had made the man a skilled motorist. "Please, mister, I have a wife and two children," he told me as he braked hard and came up right beside the curb at an intersection that was thick with pedestrians.

"Nuts," I said loudly into his ear.

I stepped off the running board onto the hard, steady surface of the street, still pointing my pistol at his face. I snatched the hat off his head and put it on mine, beaming at him. It wasn't a perfect fit, but it was close enough.

"Give me your wallet and your badge, as well," I demanded. With his eyes lowered, he complied. "You too," I shouted at his partner, who also complied. I put the wallets and badges into the breast pocket of my jacket.

"Now, let's make sure all the guns are out of this Dodge." I was looking at the driver who I had not yet disarmed. "Maybe you have something to drop out the window?"

With his eyes focused ahead, and with one hand still on the wheel, he used his right hand to draw the .38 revolver he carried in a shoulder holster. Without a word or a glance at me, he dropped it upside-down out the window. It landed at my feet and I kicked it lightly with my toe so that it skittered under the Dodge.

"Anything else?" I asked.

The driver shook his head, and his partner shook his head too a moment later when I looked at him.

"Who you boys looking for?" I asked. I didn't have much time to go down that line, but I wanted to be sure. Maybe it was vanity.

"Ross Duncan," the driver said. "We got a tip he was here."

"Give my regards to Special Agent Trestleman," I said. "Now, continue on down California as fast as you can. You should be fine. If you fly fast enough I won't be able to shoot you, even if I want to."

Nodding his head frantically, the driver engaged the clutch and eased forward as far as he could. We were at the corner of Kearny Street and the light was red, but he wasn't going to let that stop him. "Federal officers coming through," he shouted out the window. The sea of people in his way began to part. I moved along with it.

The Dodge accelerated through the intersection and disappeared. As I crossed Kearny, blending in with the crowd, I glanced up the hill. There were two vehicles just starting down from Mason Street. I guessed they were the Federals in pursuit.

I took my eyes off them and walked along normally with the crowd for two blocks to Portsmouth Square. There I found a cabbie napping behind the wheel and offered him a sawbuck to drive me out toward The Presidio. "No need to be slow about it either," I advised him.

That woke him. He headed off fast for a few blocks, ran a yellow light, and hung a right onto Broadway narrowly missing two pedestrians who were in the middle of crossing. I told him he could relax a bit and it was easy after that. When he caught Van Ness Avenue and turned right, I asked him to slow down, the race was over. I let him have the sawbuck to prove the point.

When he straightened out onto Lombard Street I told him to let me out at the next corner. Still moving, he turned to stare at me, as if trying to memorize my face. I gave him the gunner's salute with the full sneer. He left me at the spot I requested. From there, I walked a block to Greenwich, bought a newspaper and caught another cab.

*

With the classifieds open on my lap I let the cabbie drive me all the way out Geary Avenue to the ocean. I needed time to think and I had to find a new place to lay my head at night. I glanced at my watch to see how much time I had. Then I sat back in the seat and closed my eyes.

It had not been my intention, but when we ended up there, it didn't surprise me. At the Cliff House I climbed out to breathe the salt air and stare past the sun-reflected whitecaps and rising rocks toward the blinding horizon of the Pacific. The sunlight slanted in over my shoulder, reaching the ocean at an angle that cast the water in lovely light blue and green colors. It also warmed my neck and the air allowed me to breath fully.

The building that stood there now was a flat, square neo-classical block devoid of any character or intrigue. It was about as different from old Sutro's taste as one possibly could have achieved. Perhaps that had been the point. Sutro's daughter had commissioned the building. I wondered what had occurred in their relationship that prompted the daughter to so blatantly reject her father's vision. I looked down at the beach, visualizing the crowd of onlookers who had gathered there in nineteen-oh-seven to watch the fire.

Now the air was chilly and the beach was empty.

"It holds you, doesn't it," the cabbie predicted. He'd come up behind me undetected to stand next to me. I didn't mind that.

I nodded, without looking at him. "It's nice to see the ocean and to breath it's fine air, even if only for just these few minutes." "I can wait if you like," he offered. "You could even sit down on those rocks over there and take a short nap."

I shook my head, still staring out toward the open expanse. "Thanks, but no. This is all I needed. We can head back into the city now."

"What do you really need?"

I didn't tell him – I didn't answer his question at all because I wasn't sure I knew the answer anymore myself. To my relief, he didn't seem to notice. Instead he chattered on about some of the other people he had brought out to the cliff house, which was now a Bohemian restaurant.

*

The cabbie dropped me at a lunch counter in the Fillmore District. Even with all the time I'd been afforded I still hadn't reached any conclusions. I wondered how the Federal agents had found me, and then I wondered how the underworld characters had.

Whatever it was, it was probably the same thing that had alerted Jennifer McPhael, Jameson Tucker, Beakman, and the Federal agents. A long list of people had suddenly found me.

It was only part mystery. I had my own carelessness to blame.

While I smoked a slew of Chesterfields, I wondered what had given me away. Maybe someone had betrayed me or maybe I'd simply been spotted by accident. It could have been a bell captain, a waiter, a clerk, a housekeeper a hotel dick, or even an off-duty police officer or federal agent.

With some self-recrimination, I knew I had been foolish and sloppy, violating my own unwritten rule to avoid the finest city hotels. The Fairmont had been nice, but it had been a mistake. I had underestimated the risk, wrongly believing I would be anonymous in the unfamiliar city of San Francisco, so far away from my usual haunts.

I didn't know if someone I knew had betrayed me, or if some stranger had simply noticed me since arriving in San Francisco. Since not many people who knew me knew where I was, I guessed it was probably the latter.

For the first time, I realized what it meant that Hoover's agents were part of a Federal agency: they were everywhere in the country. As long as I was anywhere in the continental USA, I was within their range. That was a lesson I could not forget again.

I lighted a Chesterfield and stared out at the traffic moving by. I'd left a few items in my suite at the Fairmont that were now in the hands of Hoover's boys. Mentally, I reviewed the list: some clothing, a few area maps, a shotgun, ammunition, and about eight thousand dollars in cash.

They were welcome to it. It was nothing I couldn't afford to walk away from. There was nothing incriminating in the room, nothing specific that would lead them to my pals or to me. All I'd lost was some cash – and I still had plenty of that.

When I viewed it from that perspective, I knew I'd been extremely lucky. I had played something else right. I still had an automobile in storage. I'd have to approach the garage carefully, but there was no reason to expect it had been comprised. I'd taken pains to establish it separate from my identity at the Fairmont Hotel.

In the V8 Ford, I had more guns and ammunition, some of the cash, maps, and other papers necessary for my trade. I needed to check it out, and then I needed to find a place to sleep for the night.

Chapter Seventeen

By eleven thirty in the morning, I had recovered the Ford from its private garage and found what seemed to be a good apartment situation in the Lower Pacific Heights. It was a third floor overlook, with the first two floors occupied by a family named Green.

The husband, who answered the door with an amiable smile, struck me as a man infatuated with his wine. His tired wife, who greeted me in the starched white uniform of a nurse, shooed her husband away and whispered that he was a weary veteran, still struggling to find peace since the Great War. Her tone and expression suggested she was worried that might scare me off. Without saying so, I managed to assure her it wouldn't. From the kitchen came the light sounds of children throwing food about.

After a short discussion, we agreed on a two-month lease and I paid the entire amount in advance. For an extra six dollars a month she agreed to let me park my Ford in their garage, off the street. She seemed quite relieved that I was willing to pay in advance and apparently had very few belongings to move into her house. I explained I was a traveling insurance salesman and did not carry many materials for my work.

This brought a wise nod from her as though she understood perfectly. It was about this time that she remembered to inform me of her house rules: no alcohol, no cursing, no chewing of tobacco, no late visitors, and positively no female guests. She had her children to think of.

I agreed to her rules and added that mothers should always think of their children. "Because of my work I keep odd hours and I endure occasional overnight trips," I warned her. She didn't like that, but with all the fresh cash in her pocket she nodded and sighed and pretended to believe my story about being a traveling insurance salesman.

"Some nights I travel to other cities. If I have to be away overnight, would you like me to call to let you know? It's likely to happen with some regularity."

She considered the question and then she shook her head and focused her tired eyes on me. "There's no need for that. Unless you're going to be away for more than three or four nights, don't feel an obligation. We'll understand that it's your work."

My room was at the top floor with a good view of the street and access to the roof. Under the placid supervision of a lumbering black lab named Timothy I moved in immediately with one suitcase and one duffel bag. Nurse Green helped me navigate past her small children as I carried my things up to the third floor.

Timothy came up the stairs behind me and watched with his head cocked to one side as I paced the room and investigated the closets, windows, fire escape, and roof access. By the time I was unpacking the suitcase he had settled down flat on his belly with his chin and jowls resting on his front paws.

For a while he watched me lazily with one eye open. When I heard a deep sigh, I knew my supervisor had found something better to do. I finished my work quietly so as not to wake him.

Once I was settled, I walked a few blocks to a neighborhood drugstore to place a telephone call. From a booth in the back, I called both numbers that Jennifer McPhael had given me – one to her answering service, one to Johnny Drake's. Thirty-seven minutes later I was still nursing an egg cream at the soda fountain when Jennifer McPhael returned my call.

*

"Mr. Huddleston –"

"Richard."

"Richard, I am so relieved to hear from you. I have been very frightened – you cannot imagine. I must see you as soon as possible."

"Let's start at the top, Mrs. McPhael."

"If I am to call you Richard, you *must* call me Jennifer, please."

"Jennifer, have you heard any news on your husband?"

"Nothing. I'm afraid for him."

"Is your investigator, Johnny Drake, still working for you?"

"Yes, he is."

"What has he learned?"

"Nothing more," she replied, with a full layer of hopelessness laid over her shrinking voice.

"What kind of efforts is he making?"

"He said he's doing everything he can. Beyond that, I don't know. What am I to do?"

"How comfortable are you with him?"

"I don't know. I don't know what to think or expect. I've never hired an investigator before. Maybe you could talk with him for me?"

She was quick to invite me to be her knight in shining armor. I noted that, but I let it pass. I wondered if that was how she interacted with every man she knew. "Any word from Dr. Orion?" I asked.

"No, should I have expected there would be?"

I cleared my throat. "Not necessarily. I was only asking in case you had heard from him, Jennifer. Is there any news on your end, anything you can tell me?"

"Oh, I *must* see you," she blurted emotionally. "I simply *must*, won't you please allow me to?"

"Why?"

"Because I am so frightened, Richard. I don't know who to turn to."

"What happened?"

"Men came to my house today."

"What sort of men? What did they want?"

There was a pause at the end of the line and her voice, when she spoke again, was an octave higher. "I think they were government men – police officers or Federal agents. They came to my house in force and rang the doorbell banged on the knocker. They were very aggressive and some of them carried rifles. One of them walked around the house, peering in the windows of the first floor. I felt so scared and so violated."

"What did you do?"

"Well, I didn't answer them, if that's what you're thinking. I don't know what they wanted. I hid upstairs and pretended nobody was home."

"You don't have house staff?"

Her voice rose hysterically. "Not for the past month. My husband let them all go. He said we couldn't afford them anymore."

"Why is that?" I asked, trying to conceal my alarm at that revelation.

Jennifer sighed and continued to breath heavily. "I don't know. I really don't. He said business was slower than usual; that it was a down cycle, and that we'd be back in the money soon enough and we could rehire everyone we wanted to."

I interrupted her to bring her back to the more immediate issue. "What did the government men do, the officers with rifles moving around your house?"

"They didn't *do* anything. After they rang the bell and waited for a while, they walked around the house and looked into a few windows. After that, they simply left."

"All of them?"

"I think so."

"Do you have any idea what they wanted?"

"No idea at all."

"Were they looking for your husband?"

Her answer was coy. "Why do you ask that?"

"Look, they came to your house for a reason. Men like that don't show up for nothing. You mentioned your husband might have been leading a double life. I wonder what it was and if it was something that would draw the attention of law enforcement officers?"

There was a sharp draw of breathe at the other end of the line. "Oh, you

84

mustn't ask me about that. It's too upsetting. I can't think of my husband that way."

"Come on, Jennifer. Obviously, I have to ask about this. We're well past the point of social decorum. I need to know what is going on, what your husband's double life might have been, and why law enforcement officers might be visiting your house with rifles? Is he a fugitive? If you can't talk about these matters, I don't see how I can possibly help you."

"I really don't know why they were here."

"They made no public announcements?"

"No."

"Left no notice on your door?"

"Not that I saw."

"What time was it?" I asked.

"Shortly after ten o'clock this morning."

"Are you still at the house?"

"No. I waited until things seemed quiet and then I left through a back door, cut through to a neighbor's house. She gave me a ride into town."

"Do you think they had the front of your house under surveillance?"

I could feel her shudder over the line. "I don't know, but I fear they did."

"Where are you now?"

"I have taken a hotel room."

I didn't ask where she was staying. "Are you using your own name?"

"Johnny Drake told me if this happened I should use a false name. Is that unwise?"

I smiled to myself. I wondered who was really advising her. "You've done just fine. What name are you using?"

"Sharon G. Petula."

I had to stifle the impulse to laugh out loud. "You've done well, kid," I told her. "What does the 'G' stand for?"

"I don't know," she replied. "I didn't consider it. Should I have a response to that question?"

I chuckled. "Not for me, but you better have a response for any one else who asks."

"What do you recommend?"

"How about 'Georgia'? You can claim to be a Granddaughter of the Confederacy. If anyone inquires, tell them your great grandfather fought at the Battle of Atlanta."

Jennifer McPhael laughed out loud for the first time since I had known her. "It's perfect," she exclaimed. "Thank you!"

"Alright then," I said. "Back to your husband. What is the double life you think he might be leading? This is probably the key to understanding his disappearance."

There was a long sigh at the end of the telephone line. "Must I go into this?"

"I'm not going to plead with or flirt around with you anymore," I told her. "Either you tell me or you don't. If you don't, then we're done – I can't help you."

"Are you really such a cold fish?"

"Yes," I said simply.

There was a long sigh at the other end of the line. She seemed to be thinking about it. Then: "I think my husband was transporting two things into this country that are illegal."

"I'm listening."

"First, he has been smuggling human refugees."

"From where?"

"Everywhere they wanted to come from: Iran, China, India, Egypt. These people had no good life waiting them in their home countries. They wanted to come to America for opportunity, even if it meant they were here illegally."

"I know that story," I told her over the telephone line. "What is the second thing your husband smuggles?"

"Antiquities."

"Such as what?"

"Must you ask?"

"Yes."

"Jewels, furniture, oil paintings, sculptures, and everything else that American markets will buy."

"I don't understand," I said. "Why might that lead him into trouble?"

"Because he was selling items desired by so many."

"It doesn't seem like much," I stated.

"Really, then why am I so unnerved?"

"Why are they illegal?"

"All the usual reasons."

"The usual reasons are that they are stolen or counterfeit"

The line went silent. Then I heard her draw a breath, and then a pained exhale. "Yes," she whispered.

"What else can you tell me about your husband?"

"Oh, don't make me…"

"I need something to work with."

"Can't you see how desperate I am? Won't you see me? I *must* see *you*."

"Sweetheart," I said, trying to soften my town. "I need you to tell me about your husband. You are the one who said he might be leading a double life. We can't pretend that idea doesn't exist. You have to talk to me. You have to

86

trust me."

Over the wire came the sounds of a woman's tears. She was crying and conspicuously so. I waited quietly, wanting to light a cigarette. When the heavy breathing at the other end of the line seemed to be under control again, I spoke. "There is no way around it," I half-whispered. "This is something you'll have to talk to me about if you want my help."

"I know."

"Can you do that now?"

"I'd rather talk to you in person. Will you meet me somewhere?"

"If I do, can you promise that you'll talk to me?"

"Yes."

"No more avoidance, no more deception?"

"I promise, if you'll meet me, I will tell you every thing."

"Jennifer," I started, picking the words carefully as I went. "Why did Johnny Drake direct you to me in the first place? You have to see this from my perspective. I don't know Drake and I don't know why he sent you to me. Why me?"

"I'm sure you have good reason to be cautious," she acknowledged. "Mr. Drake is convinced that you hold leads to the answers, are trustworthy, and can help us navigate this situation. How soon can we meet, and where?"

"Alright," I sighed. "I have several appointments yet this afternoon. How about if I find you early this evening at the Mechanics Monument, say ten minutes before five o'clock? I'll come by and pick you up."

"Four-fifty in the afternoon," she replied. "That will be perfect."

"Invite Johnny Drake if you can," I said to her. "I'd like to talk to him too."

"I'll do my best," she promised.

"I know," I replied before I hung up.

I waited at the counter for another forty minutes, but Drake never called back. Fortified by two egg creams and a grilled steak sandwich with horseradish, I headed out into the early afternoon to retrieve the automobile that I'd left in front of the Green's house.

From the second floor window I saw the wispy-haired head of the weary veteran. The sunlight was in his eyes as he smiled at me and waved, and then he brought a dark-colored bottle to his lips. As I drove off I wondered what he had seen in the war and whether it had been good fortune for him or not to find a wife who was a nurse.

Chapter Eighteen

In the daylight, viewed through a prism of soft mist, Jameson Tucker's three-story brick house was quite striking. With its gabled arch over the front entrance, dormer windows lining two sides of the roof, and conical turret over the protruding tubular corner of the house I was reminded of something from a fairy tale. Built on an elevated berm, it towered over the steeply graded street and seemed much bigger than it had in the dark.

If I had been a tourist walking by, I would have stopped to look at it and if I'd been camera-prone, I might have taken a few photographs from different angles. Since I wasn't a tourist, I followed the brick steps straight up to the door and rang the bell. There was no response.

I waited a decent interval and rang it again, wondering about the housekeeper that Tucker had mentioned. She never showed and the door was never answered.

I glanced around carefully. Nobody was watching, so I tried the door. It was locked. I tried it a different way, using a pick that I carried in my wallet. This time it opened quite easily and I was inside. I closed the door and locked it behind me, and then stood still for a minute listening for sounds in the house. I heard nothing.

"Hello?" I called in medium volume.

There was no response.

"Hello?" I called again, using a higher volume.

Still there was no response. I assumed the house was empty, but I moved carefully. With my .45 out, I went down the hall as quietly as I could into the white kitchen. In the ambient light of day it was even whiter than it had been at night. The pristine floors, walls, and countertops were all burnished to a full luster. I blinked so as not to go snow blind and retraced my steps back to the front hall.

I went up the stairs to investigate the tubular corner room of the house that extended from the front to the back of the house. At the top of the stairs I paused to listen and heard nothing. A light curtain of floating sunlight hung in the door to my left – the doorway of the master bedroom. It played easily along the hardwood flooring and brought an orange glow to the doorjamb. I peered behind it and there was nobody there.

The great bed was neatly made and empty. Perched on the outside windowsill overlooking the room was a large seagull who stared at me with his side-ways eye and then moved his head away in short, jerky movements.

88

He called once as if to announce my intrusion and then took flight.

Stepping back into the hallway again I looked about and paused once more to listen to the silence. It washed over me as a series of unrelenting waves that were hard to bear. The door I focused on was open on the other side of the landing and I moved toward it with my pistol held out in front of me.

As I had expected, the large room was even more magnificent in the light of day than it had been the night before. I looked around quickly and then again slowly, studying the details as though I were filming them for a cinematic documentary of eccentric art dealers. My eyeballs were the camera lenses; the back of my brain was the celluloid. I proceeded to record the scene slowly and carefully, as if the footage would somehow serve for posterity.

Degas' spindly ballerina sculpture drew my gaze and I moved toward it, slowly, focusing as I drew near. When I reached it, I rested the back of one hand on its base as my eyes moved up to the paintings along the wall of one side of the room. They appeared to be untouched. I turned my shoulder as I followed my gaze back across the other side of the room, still slowly trying to note faithfully all the details of the wall.

When the camera of my eyes had completed their circuit and focused again on the form at the end of the room. I found the motion picture director within me at a creative loss. How was I best to frame the scene? I moved in directly for a close-up.

He was on the floor by his desk. His feet and arms were stretched out as though he was napping, but he wasn't asleep. Jameson Tucker III was handsome and rich. He had a hard square chin, custom-tailored shirts, a gold watch, a fancy car, blondes waiting in every corner of the city, and a tan that caused the whites of his smile to glow in the dark. He had everything except a pulse now.

The bloodless hole in his forehead was small and precise – the kind of hole a .22 caliber bullet makes. I'd known it immediately when I'd entered the room, even before I'd started my slow tour.

He'd been shot dead and recently. As I stood over his body, looking down at him, I had the cold sense of a specter passing through the room, laughing at us both. So much had been dangled and now it had been snatched violently away.

Suppressing a shudder, I knelt beside Tucker's body to feel his neck with the back of my hand. It was still warm. Gently I tried his arm and it moved easily – the rigor process had only just begun. He had longed to be a star of the silent movie era. Now he was just silent and he would be for the rest of time.

Standing again, I holstered my pistol and looked around the room once more. The paintings along the walls appeared undisturbed. The killer had left alone a lot of valuable property. That could only mean he was after something more valuable still.

I studied Tucker's large, heavy desk. It had been carefully disassembled, exactly as he had done it himself the night before in my presence. The key he had worn around his neck was on the desk now, along with the removed drawer. Beside it was an ashtray with one half-smoked Gauloises with a long black ash trail. It had been set there and then burned out on its own.

The only thing missing from the scene was the small rectangular box, upholstered in red and black silk with gold threading. Without any real hope of finding anything meaningful, got down on one knee and peered under the desk, where I felt around a little with my hand. The interior cavity that I found there was empty, as I expected it would be. I drew a heavy breath and leaned back from it.

As I stood up, I noticed something else. There was something missing on the wall above me. The framed photograph of Sutro's Cliff House was gone. The spot where it had been was marked by a darkened rectangle – an area where the sun had not dulled the color of the wall. Standing now and leaning toward it, I studied the wall carefully and then moved back three steps to survey everything else once more. There was the desk, the body, the wall, and none of it made any particular sense to me.

I had nothing.

I lighted a Chesterfield while I stood there and contemplated the view. Nothing smart occurred to me other than I had to visit Chinatown again soon. I thought of the girl with the blue/green eyes. With a sick feeling in my stomach, I sighed quietly and allowed the cigarette to burn out at my side while I stood there for a while without moving. I didn't care that the spent ashes fell directly onto the floor at my feet. They landed silently and meant nothing to me at all.

Before I left the house, I wiped down the surfaces I might have touched with a white silk handkerchief, finishing with the exterior doorknob and lock on the main entrance. As I went down the brick steps to the street, the automobile of a policeman went flashing by me with his siren blaring, on his way to some other sad emergency.

I tapped my fedora respectfully and climbed once more behind the wheel of my Ford. I wasn't looking forward to what I thought lay ahead of me.

Chapter Nineteen

As I drove down Grant Avenue it started to rain a little. It was a gentle, friendly, watering sprinkle that must have projected another hopeful rainbow out over the bay. My wipers worked against it for almost two minutes and then it dissipated as quickly as it had come up. A song passed through my head, but I refrained from whistling it. There were serious matters at hand and a man was dead.

I found the red door in Chinatown easily enough. In the light and shadows of daytime, it seemed less mysterious than it had in the dark. Now it was just a mundane red door with Chinese symbols on it. There was nothing imposing about it at all. Several loose dogs frolicked around nearby on the sidewalk, nipping at pedestrians and barking half-heartedly at random passing automobiles.

A man with a basket on his head crossed in front of me and distracted the mutts. I knocked on the door and waited, and when no one answered, I tried the handle. It was unlocked, so I pushed my way inside and looked about, closing the door behind me. That shut out a lot of street sounds. The sudden contrast was marked.

Dark space engulfed me and held me still on the spot where I stood. Unfamiliar odors reached my nose – they were unpleasant. Cautiously, I waited, standing still with my hands by my sides as my eyes adapted slowly to the darkness. There were no human voices or other sounds, and I decided not to call out for attention.

The front room was empty and the girl who had greeted me the previous evening was nowhere to be seen. After a moment I whispered for her, but got no answer. When I could see well enough to move ahead, I retraced my steps through the building, working my way as best I could down the hallway toward Khai Chi's chambers.

It was an old building and there were no sounds of human activity. As reached what I estimated to be the mid-point of the hallway, I caught the faint leak of a water drop landing in a puddle of water. It made the darkness seem all the deeper still. I halted every few steps to listen and move my toe forward into the unseen space ahead of me. The dripping water, landing at intervals of about five seconds apart grew slightly louder as I moved ahead.

My nostrils picked up the scent of ancient incense and burnt offerings, odors that I could not identify with any specificity. I felt my way along until I found the door I was looking for. I pushed it open with the back of my hand

and moved inside cautiously. The room was dark and quiet, dancing with the silent shadows of unfinished business and a tortured past.

A faint wraith-like glow moved about on the ceiling and opposite wall, as though it were undulating behind a shroud of ancient smoke. It took me a moment to understand. Once I did, I closed the door behind me and took several steps into the room.

On a low table in the middle of the room was a large round bowl filled with sand. Pushed into the course silt and still burning were an array of long, thin Joss sticks that were colored yellow and red. I had only learned to recognize them recently. They were associated with ritual and religious devotion in China. Traditionally, they were burned before the threshold of a home, before an image of a spirit or god, or in a shrine located at the main entrance to a village.

The Chinese word "Joss" was derived from Latin, meaning "God." They were almost entirely without aroma, since it was the smoke, rather than the fragrance, that was important in conveying prayers up to heaven. Still, I caught the faint odor of a Rose fragrance in the air. It mixed with something else: the paired stench of blood and violent death. I stood still, looking past the burning Joss sticks while my eyes struggled to see through the dim light and floating smoke in the air.

Slowly, the inert form of Chi emerged on the other side of the table, forming a tangible, unmoving shape within my vision. He lay twisted on one side, with a leg bent back under his body and the knuckle of one hand flat on the floor beneath him, bruised and bleeding as though he had blocked a strike with it. Even in the darkness, I could see the black, shining hole in his forehead, centered just over his staring, but forever-unseeing eyes. His robe had been pulled open after death to reveal the pattern etched into his chest.

I lighted the same lamp Chi had struck for me the night before and held it out ahead of me as I moved to inspect his body. There was no need to check for a pulse. In death, his face had twisted in an angry grimace that spoke of his final seconds in life. I swayed the lamp over him slowly to see what his killer had been looking at.

On his chest was a colored tattoo – crimson and black it seemed, though it was hard to be certain because of the poor light. The pattern was familiar to me by now. It was the same Chinese symbol – the partial circle with slanting lines through it and accent marks over one of the lines – which I had seen on the two boxes and the two keys.

Swinging the lamp around, I turned to look back at the small lacquered shelf. It was there, still lined with many small oddities. Its six narrow shelves were filled with all the same things as before – ornate boxes, carvings, ivory talismans, small bells, tiny-framed photographs, and jewelry. There were no gaps to found on any of the shelves, but all the same, I spotted it right off. The red and black embroidered box with the ivory clasp was missing and the items that had been in place on either side of it had been pushed together to cover the gap. Someone was methodically collecting the keys. I wondered if there were others and who might have them.

I studied the bowl and the pattern of the burning Joss sticks, looking for clues to guide me. None were forthcoming and I drew a breath. I glanced about the room, looking for anything that might have seemed out of place. Nothing struck me. In fact, in a sense it was the same scene I had encountered at Jameson Tucker's home: a dead body with a small caliber hole in the center of the forehead and a key with Chinese letters on it missing. I had a sense about what that meant.

Moving the lamp about the room in a series of slow, easy arcs, I surveyed the area for something, anything that might guide me. I didn't find it. Eventually I blew out the lamp and set it on the floor by the door before I went out again into the hallway. The Joss sticks I left to burn as Chi had intended when he had lighted them. Now their smoke would accompany him up toward heaven.

From somewhere in the building, the water continued to drip slowly, deliberately.

*

Slowly, I retraced my steps to work my way out of the house. I almost reached the exterior door when I heard the sound. It was a low moan, a hopeless effort, probably not intended for me, but it stopped me. I listened for it and didn't hear it again.

The room was strange to me. It was filled with things I didn't understand. There was the wall of shelves lined with jars filled with different colored powders, straws, pills, and milky liquids. Somewhere in the room were unmarked drawers that held varieties of dried herbs, barks, roots, nuts, and flowers. It represented a mysterious other world to me.

I moved around the long butcher-block counter toward the far end of the room and then I heard it again. As I turned the corner of the long counter, I found a candle, positioned into a brass holder that had been burned half way down to its base. With my lighter I got it going again and held it up so I could look about.

The girl lay flat on her back, still breathing, with her eyes wide open, watching me as I came in through the darkness over her and knelt on the floor beside her. Blood had pooled beneath her shoulders, soaking her blouse and spreading out on the floor in a slow moving ooze.

I realized she must have been conscious when I'd first arrived. Fear had kept her from calling out to me.

"Shhh," I whispered, touching her arm gently with the tips of my fingers. "I'm here. Do you remember me from last night? I will help you."

With great effort she tried to sit up. All she managed was a groan. I place a hand beneath her head and carefully raised it a few inches so she could see me easier. I sensed the question in her mind.

"Shhh, child," I told her, shaking my head. "Khai Chi's gone, but you can be his voice. Stay with me."

Her head moved a little, becoming lighter in my hand. The skin on the back of her neck was hot and moist. Matted hair clung to my hand when I removed it due to a sticky mixture of sweat and blood. Tenderly, I laid her head back down on the floor. Quickly I moved across the room to grab a chair cushion, which I used to prop under her head. At least that took it off the hard, cold floor.

Next, I found a small towel and pitcher of water. With the towel whetted, I wiped off her forehead and brought some of the water to her lips.

"Would you like a little water?" I asked.

The girl didn't reply. Her eyes were on mine, urgently following my every movement. From the countertop I found a tablespoon. Using this, I was able to serve her a spoonful of water. She swallowed this and accepted several more, without ever removing her gaze from my eyes. After the fifth spoonful, she pursed her lips together in pain.

"Ohhoo," she sighed, as she turned her head and became less focused on my face. Her breathing was labored.

I couldn't tell where she was hurt or how badly, and she didn't speak to me. "Forgive me," I told her, doubting that she could understand my English. "I'm going to touch you, just enough to turn you a little. It's going to hurt. I'll do my best, but I have to find the wound."

With my hands beneath her shoulders, I lifted her gently a few inches off the floor, just enough so that I could feel beneath her with one hand. There was a small tear in the fabric of her blouse. A bullet hadn't caused it; it was a knife wound.

She had been stabbed in the back and the blade and been jerked vertically after it had gone in. From the location of the wound I knew the blade had probably cut into her lung. Her hands were cold. She had already lost a lot of blood. Suddenly, I knew I didn't have any hope of saving her. All I could do was stay with her until she was gone.

"I don't know your name," I whispered. "My name's Ross."

Her eyes continued to hold mine and one of her small hands came up to grip my upper arm weakly. Delicate fingers traced their lines down to my elbow and rested there. She seemed to be trying to pull me closer. I lowered my face toward hers until I could feel the warmth of her breath.

With my face so close to hers I could see she was very pretty, with a simple, clear face devoid of lines, make-up, or any of the detritus of civilization. Her eyes held no fear and no anger – only a remarkable endurance. Shifting my weight slightly, I cradled the side of her head in one hand so that I could whisper in her ear for a moment and then I moved again so that I could look into her eyes.

Her stoic gaze continued to hold mine. I rocked her gently. Her lips moved, but no words came out. The hand she'd placed on my arm moved lower to find my hand. Clasping it, she held it fiercely, gripping it tightly as her body spasmed with pain. I clutched back at her hand and kissed her on the cheek, laying my own cheek beside hers for a long moment while we waited together.

The tempest in her sighs died with her, as my arms folded helplessly around her upper body and hugged her to me. Tears burned hot trails down my skin and fell onto her unfeeling face. I held her far longer than it made any sense to.

Chapter Twenty

Eventually I went back out into the bright sunshine that filled the streets of San Francisco. Thorough's Auction House was a three-story brick structure in the Marina District with a view of the bay at the front balcony and the Fine Arts Palace from the windows in the back. I knew this because I got there early and walked the block, studying the House and the neighborhood as I circled it.

When I went into the building through the front door – still a good bit early – the first thing I encountered in the lobby was a large, black magnetized sign on a tripod filled with white letters that read: "The Auction of Lot Number 73 is cancelled." No explanation was provided.

I climbed the stairs to the third floor. At the top of the stairs I encountered a pair of heavy French doors with frosted glass and brass Art Deco lever door handles. Black letters had been stenciled on to the glass that read simply: "Thorough's Auctions."

I pushed both doors open simultaneously with an open palm on each door handle and found myself looking into a long, narrow rectangular room that was sunlit, with another set of French doors half-way down on the right and dramatic oil paintings of matadors and bulls on the sidewalls on both sides. They were positioned between the windows on my left and on either side of the French doors on my right. The artist had a fondness for strong red, orange, and black oils applied with flurried brushstrokes. I glanced to the floor quickly, before I fell dizzy from the intensity of color in motion.

The other aspects of the room were quite a bit more placid. The flooring was made up of six-inch wide, lightly stained oak slats. The effect was soothing. At the far end of the room was a simple writing desk. It held a telephone, a typewriter, and a stack of letter trays. Well behind the desk were three wood filing cabinets, each with four drawers. They lined up nicely. In between the desk and the filing cabinets sat an attractive woman who appeared to be in her early twenties.

She was a blonde with her hair piled in curls over her ears, held in place by white ivory clips on each side. White pearls circled her neck and provided stylish contrast to a push-out black blouse. From beneath the writing desk I caught a glimpse of a gray skirt and crossed slender ankles in black-stockings. Topping off the ensemble was a pair of owl-framed black glasses and pale red lipstick. All signs indicated she was an eye-catching young woman in a big city who had not yet experienced her first humbling in life.

"Can I help you?" she asked haughtily, looking up at me with her index finger along the side of her glasses.

I walked the gauntlet of matadors and bulls to stand in front of her writing desk. "Have you heard the news there's a depression going on out there? They say it's hit most of the country by now."

"Pardon me?"

"Most people who have jobs are happy to have them," I continued.

She blinked her eyes twice as she studied me. "I'm sorry? Did you mean to register a question or a complaint?"

"It's nothing," I said. "Except that most people who have a job in this country tend to appreciate the fact. It means they make an effort to be polite, even nice to the potential customers who walk through their door."

With barely concealed irritation, she adjusted the glasses over her nose by pushing the centerpiece up as far as it would go with her index finger. "I'm sorry, sir. I don't understand."

I smiled as nicely as I could in that moment. "I'm sure that's not your fault. Maybe you can tell me why the auction of Lot seventy-three was cancelled?"

"Oh, that I really don't know."

"Will it be rescheduled? Can I get a look at the objects in the Lot anyway?"

"Who are you?" she inquired, determined not to let my charm cause her officiousness to slip.

"Me? I'm nobody very important. You can call me Phisby," I said, pulling the pseudonym out of the air on the spot. "I represent a buyer who is *very* interested in the items included in the cancelled Lot."

"Exactly, whom do you represent?" she asked, softening just a little. She fidgeted with her fingertips together, indicating that a hint of uncertainty had crept into the back of her mind.

I smiled as though it was a question I received often and was never able to answer. "You must understand," I replied. "My employer is a very private man."

"Of course," she said, nodding seriously. "What kind of items is he most interested in?"

"Only the rarest items – antique furniture, oil painting, unusual furs. He was very interested in Lot seventy-three and the antiquities he believed it obtained. Your advertisement thoroughly captured his attention. I thought the crying was to begin this afternoon at two-thirty?"

"Yes, it was, but we had to cancel it because of unforeseen circumstances."

"What were those?"

"I can't tell you that."

"Are you sure you can't tell me why?"

The young woman shook her head, allowing her guard to drop a little

97

further. "They never explain those sorts of things to me."

"This has happened before?"

"Often enough. Lots go up for sale, sometimes they're pulled back; sometimes they're sold outright beforehand." Her eyes communicated little additional information.

I pursed my lips and clucked my tongue. "Mr. Tucker is usually so reliable about this sort of thing. He assured me the Lot would be available today. My employer is *very* interested in it. He will be *very* disappointed when he hears my report. Have you any idea when it might reappear?"

The young woman shook her head firmly. "I have no information to provide you about this Lot or about Mr. Tucker." After she spoke the words, she glanced down at a typewritten piece of paper on the desk in front of her. She picked up a pen as if to signal to me that she had plenty of other work to do and checked something on the piece of paper with it. I read it as another fidgeting gesture. She hadn't had time to read what she had just checked off.

I leaned across the desk a little ways. I was no longer smiling. "I understand you're busy," I told her in a quiet voice. "Indulge me, however. Let me ask you a few more questions and then I will be out of your way."

The woman laid down her pen in a ceremonious fashion and glanced up at me, biting her lips inwardly as though I were causing her physical pain. "What are your questions, Sir?"

"First, what is your name? I've already told you mine."

"Customers know me as Ms. Morris."

I grinned through my teeth at that answer. "I'm sure your customers are happy with that."

"Excuse me?"

"Never mind. Who communicated the decision to cancel the crying of the Lot?"

"Mr. Tucker himself."

By this time I had a small notebook out and was writing in it. "What time and how did he communicate the decision?"

Ms. Morris frowned and studied me. It seemed she was trying to make a read on how important I was, wondering if she might have underestimated me. I stared at her coldly, determined not to make the decision easy for her.

"It was shortly before eleven o'clock this morning," she said eventually.

I made a notation in my notebook. "Did you speak to him personally?"

"Yes."

"In person?"

"By telephone? Yes. He called me direct at this very desk." As if to prove her point, she gestured toward the telephone that sat on the table between us.

"How did he sound?" I asked.

"I don't follow your question."

"Were you able to read anything into his emotional state? Was his tone of voice cheerful, glum, worried, excited, or fearful? Did it sound different in any way from how he usually sounded?"

Ms. Morris thought about this for a moment seriously. Then she shook her head and removed the glasses that she wore and set them down on the blotter page before her. "None of those," she stated crisply. "He was quite matter of fact."

"Is that typical of him?"

"Yes."

"How well do you know him?"

Ms. Morris blushed suddenly and then went on the offensive. "Are you a policeman?"

"What if I were? Would it make you anxious? Do you have something to hide?"

"Of course not! Well... are you?"

I tried not to, but I smiled a little. "No, never have been, never will be. What about my question: How well do you know him?"

"I've worked for Mr. Tucker for almost two years. He treats me very well."

"That doesn't answer my question," I observed.

"Our relationship is strictly professional."

"I'm sure it is. Are you certain Mr. Tucker offered no reason for his decision to cancel the auction?"

"He said there might be a more profitable way to sell it. He did not elaborate."

"Has he ever cancelled an auction in this manner before?"

In a gesture that was intended to be a statement, she repositioned her glasses on her face and secured them over her nose with both hands. When she looked at me again, she was fully recovered and I knew I'd learned all I was likely to learn from her. "This is not the first time an auction has been cancelled based on a deal to sell an entire Lot ahead of time. I am not saying that is what will happen. I am only saying it is possible."

I nodded slowly as I began to think about the pieces that had been listed in the Lot. "Have you heard from Mr. Tucker since he called to cancel the crying of the lot?"

She shook her head shortly, leaving her blonde curls to quiver. "Is there a piece you were most interested in?" she inquired politely, ever the sales representative. "I can make a note of it."

"I am interested in several of the pieces, especially the furniture, such as the desks and armoires, and the sealed trunk."

"Perhaps I can learn more and keep you appraised when and if they come up for sale?"

I smiled at the ruse, staring into her aloof blue eyes. "Sure," I told her. "I know Mr. Tucker well enough. We had a long, intimate conversation about the properties in this Lot at his house last night. Maybe I'll call on him there later."

Her demeanor did not change. "I'll be happy to take your name and ask him to give you a call when he returns to the office."

I shrugged. "There's no need for that. I'm only here for a few more days, and then I fly to Paris. I'll try to check with him before I leave. If I miss him, there will be other Lots. France is teeming with lovely antiques and works of art these days and the man I work for is a sucker for the romantic notions that come from other parts of the world." I leaned away from her desk and straightened up to fix the knot of my tie as though I had lost interest in her business.

That proved to be the final prick in the bubble of her self-confidence. "What were you most interested in?" she asked, sitting up straighter, projecting her best impression of sincerity. "Mr. Tucker will be interested to know. Maybe he could call you later today or tomorrow. Would you be willing to provide a number where he could reach you?"

I leaned across the desk toward her, far enough so that I could smell her perfume. It was *Vol de Nuit* by Guerlain, an Oriental style formed with prominent notes of vanilla. I pictured the bottle, which was inspired by the image of a spinning propeller and was packaged in a box made in an exotic zebra print design that represented the opening of Africa and the trophies people brought back from safari.

With my knuckles on the desk, I leaned across it to put my face as close to hers as possible. "Which wild animal are you?"

Blushing deeply, her eyes nearly lost their focus before she responded. "I'm sorry?"

I tilted my face upward, as though I were sampling the scent that she wore. "You're wearing *Vol de Nuit*. I'm wondering which of the African animal species you identify with. Forgive me; I've taken this crumb of silliness a bit too far. The fragrance is very nice on you."

Ms. Morris blushed deeply and lowered her chin. With her right hand, she moved the hair about over her bangs and around her neck, fluffing it out from her collar. "You may have some ideas about how we work here at Thorough's. I did not intend to make this conversation so complicated, but Mr. Tucker is a complicated man to work for."

I nodded sympathetically. "I understand." I suggested it with as much genuine warmth as I could muster. As I straightened up to move away from her desk, I turned slightly toward the interior of the long rectangular room.

100

From the corner of my eye I caught a movement near the French door at the side of the room. My impression was that it had been opened slightly and there had been a shadow inside, as if someone were eavesdropping on my conversation with Ms. Morris. I turned the other way and pretended that I was only interested in the waterfront.

*

Glancing out the window at the front of the building, I could see the bay clearly with the sunlight skimming across the tops of the whitecaps. It was virtually empty, though a quartet of single-mast Star boats ran before a light wind with their sails full.

The room behind me with Ms. Morris at her desk and the matador paintings on the wall seemed dim and quiet when I turned back toward it. With the bright images of the bay burned into my retina, the room was a mere rectangular box, filled with the obscure shadows of human activity and the flight of life, including the human failings of nightly dreams and hopes as rendered by some artist I would never know.

I spoke to Ms. Morris one last time: "The newspaper ad mentioned a sealed trunk of unknown contents and origin. That's what I was most curious about, what my employer is most interested in. We wondered what they might hold. Do you have any idea, any idea at all?"

The attractive blonde started to say something and then she bit off her answer before the first word could escape. I could hear the grating within her jaw. While I waited, she drew a breath and stared at a point well behind me. When she had recovered sufficiently, she shrugged to indicate she did not know anything at all and our conversation was over.

With that she glanced down at a piece of paper that was flat before her on the desk. As I turned away and moved toward the stairway, I wondered what the facts really were and whether Ms. Morris would be heartbroken when she learned that Jameson Tucker had been murdered.

Chapter Twenty-One

When I reached the bottom of the stairs I heard a noise on the landing behind me. I turned quickly with a hand inside my jacket. It was not the threat I expected, but a man with a badly gnarled hand gesturing for me to climb the stairs back to him. Standing within a shadow, the features of his face were indiscernible. The form of his bent shoulders and the awkward motion of his misshapen hand, which reached out into the light, made for an eerie presence.

My .45 was already drawn and pointed at him. "Who are you?"

"I'm the one you want to talk to," he replied quietly. His voice floated toward me like a burning whisper in the air. He pulled back further into the shadows and the hand disappeared entirely. I didn't lower my gun.

"How is that?" I demanded.

"Forgive me. I overheard your conversation. I might know something you would want to hear."

"That was your shadow I saw prowling behind the French door?"

"Perhaps," he replied. "There are many shadows about these days."

I couldn't disagree with him. I retraced my path up the stairs to the landing and followed him through a door on the second floor that he held open for me. More layers of shadows waited there. I found myself standing in a large, rectangular open room without any walls or windows.

Rows of high-backed benches were planted meticulously all the way to the other end of the room where there was a raised platform with a pulpit on it. The only lights were tiny bulbs mounted in the ceiling over the platform at the other end of the room. For the barest part of a moment I thought I had stepped into a church.

"Who are you?" I asked, forcing my voice through the layers of shadows. I still could not see the man's face.

"Do you know me?" he asked in a slight voice with a high Chinese accent.

"Have we met before?"

"Never."

"Why then should I know you?"

"Perhaps you should not," he replied. "Let's move to the other end of the room where there is more light." Without waiting for my reply, he turned away.

I followed him down the center aisle with my .45 held at my side. He moved slowly, with a notable limp on one side and several times he paused to balance his weight on the back of one of the benches. Each time his body

102

appeared to shudder in pain.

As we neared the raised platform, he hesitated and then turned left to find a seat in the first row bench. I sat next to him with three feet of space between us and looked into his ancient face. He talked to me in the same burning whisper. I had to lean close to hear his words.

"I was an actor once," he said. "I was a minor player in the silent movie era." He straightened his shoulders as though he wanted me to see him as he had been fifteen or twenty years before. The light bulbs in the ceiling above us were not focused, but they shed enough diffuse light to allow me to study him.

What I saw in the dimness was a short, slender man with narrow, stooped shoulders. Entirely bald at the top of his head, his eyebrows were shaved close and wisps of a long mustache drooped over his mouth and expanded the sides of his face. His down-slanting lips were thin and bloodless. He was dressed in a traditional Western suit – either black or charcoal – with a narrow burgundy tie knotted tightly at his throat.

"I am Chinese," he said, as if reading my mind. "Some of us dress as you do."

"Will you answer my questions?" I asked.

He nodded and waited. Without seeming to be aware of it, his small hands rose up and formed a large round chapel in front his chest. A murmured purr sounded deep in his lungs each time he breathed in.

"Why would you talk to me when Ms. Morris would not?"

"She is very young and inexperienced, and she has certain ideas that she thinks will help her find the life she desires."

"She's fond of money."

"She's young still. I cannot begrudge her that, though she has much yet to learn." His English syntax was perfect and his pronunciation was clear, though his Chinese accent was prominent. I wondered about his education and where he had received it.

"Who are you and what is your role here at Thorough's?" I asked.

"Lin is my name. I could tell you more about my family, by way of traditional introduction. Or I could give you the Westernized name I have taken. None of that would mean much to you right now, or to the cause I believe you pursue."

I shook my head in disagreement. "Names mean a lot to me," I said. "They tell you a lot about a man."

"I agree with that."

"What is your name, then?" I asked.

"Lin is my family name, the name I was born with. In America I go by the name Charlie Wong."

"Where did that name come from?"

"Hollywood." He grinned with his lips parted after he spoke the word, revealing rows of crooked and blackened teeth. "What is your name?" he asked.

"May name is Ross Duncan."

Lin sat still as he considered this. "Is that the name you were born with?"

I shook my head, and as I did, I realized the truth was hard to admit – even to a stranger. "No," I said. "I don't use that name anymore."

"You wish not to shame your parents?"

That stopped me cold.

Lin smiled patiently and bent his face toward mine in a manner that was conspiratorial. "You were right, of course," he whispered. "Names do tell you something about a man."

*

Aware of the time passing, I glanced at my watch. "What can you tell me about the crying of Lot number seventy-three, and why it was cancelled?"

Lin frowned and the expression on his face flattened. He shrugged and gestured with his bad hand as though he sympathized with my question, but his eyes had a second life of their own, and they were searching for a simple answer that would allow me to go my way.

Although he was two or three times my age, he seemed to me like a child weary from bad behavior and parental punishment. His hand looked like it had once been crushed. To compensate, he retreated to a time far in the past. Somewhat guilelessly, he brought the hand to hold against the side of his face before he began to speak.

"I came to America when I was twelve. That year was 1878. I was an orphan in my kingdom, and the village I lived in sent me to join an uncle who was already here and established in this country. No one knew what I would encounter when I reached the shores of this country. By the time I arrived, the revered uncle, who I had never known in the flesh, had already died of the fever. Many Chinese men had died of the fever by then. No one wanted *me* on either continent."

The bench we sat on was hard. I nodded and murmured encouragement to keep him talking.

Lin smiled now to indicate that I could relax and not be horrified by his childhood experiences. "By your interest in the specified lot I infer several things."

"Such as?"

"First," he started. "You are a man of taste and high connections. You know the important men of this society, and they place a high value on you.

104

This says something about a man that he cannot read for himself."

That response caused me to purse me lips. "What else do you infer?"

"You have a gun and dangerous eyes. Any man could infer many things from that."

I looked down at the pistol in my hand and without saying anything I returned it to the holster under my arm. "What else?"

"You're here, asking questions, when no other bidder has had any. That means you're determined. I suspect you know something about this lot that other people do not know."

"What do I know?"

"You know, or you believe, there is something of great worth hidden in it."

"Which is it?"

"Unless a man has the facts, he cannot know."

"Do you have the facts to support my belief?"

"I have only belief myself."

"Tell me then what *you* believe."

Lin smiled privately. His thin lips pursed and nearly disappeared in the process. "I am an old man. Plenty of people think I am not in my right head. They say this to me; they say it to others around me. I hear it and it has an effect."

"Who are these people?" I asked. "Do they know it, or do they merely believe it to be so?"

Lin's smile widened enough to show his teeth again. We sat with our faces close enough that I could feel his breath and smell the ancient, rotten odors it carried. The thought occurred to me that death was waiting for him very nearby. I could smell it when he exhaled and I could hear it in his lungs.

As if reading my mind again, he responded: "At my age, having heard it long and often enough, I can only wonder and doubt myself. Soon, I will find out, I think."

"How long have you heard these beliefs about yourself?"

"I reach my seventieth birthday early next year. When I look back, I realize that I have heard them all my life. As a child, when I arrived in this country they thought I was strange and they jeered me. In my early adulthood I did not wear the same clothing as my countrymen. Because of that, I traveled across the United States. When I was in my twenties – my youth – I worked for the railroad and then I took other jobs that brought me to other places."

"Where have you traveled?" I asked.

Lin's shoulders pulled back again and he smiled proudly. "I have been to New York City, Baltimore, and Detroit. I lived for two years in Chicago, and then traveled south to Atlanta, Houston, and then to Santa Fe. All this was before the century turned. In 1893 I came back to San Francisco. I was twenty-seven years old at that time. Even then, my own people told me I was 'not in my right head'. They still did not want me to be among them. I have thought long about this and I have decided that I believe the truth is very few people are in their right head. Why should they be?"

I smiled, nodded. "That's a philosophical point we can discuss another time," I replied. "I'd like to know if you recognize the difference between imagination and reality."

Lin nodded politely. "Sure, I do understand. You are busy and you have important business, and you do not want to be distracted by a man who has a poor grasp on what is real and what is not. Do you find me to be crazy?"

"Not so far," I replied softly, matching my voice to his, "though we only just met. Let's go back to my questions. Maybe the position of your sanity will be revealed in your answers. I'm interested in Sutro's Cliff House, prior to the fire of 1907 that destroyed it. Do you know anything about it? Was Lot seventy-three connected to it, and if so, how? What did the items represent?"

"I was there," Lin said, "when the fire broke out in 1907."

That startled me. "You were at Sutro's House?"

Lin nodded. "Oh yes, I worked there for many years."

"Before the fire?"

He nodded again to confirm.

"How long did you work there?"

"From the very beginning through its end, almost fourteen years."

"What did you do?"

"Almost everything during that time. I was hired to work on the grounds during its construction, which included heavy labor and many odd jobs. Later I performed all manner of maintenance on the building, inside and outside. Also, I worked on the lawn and plants and trees when that was required. As they came to trust me, I had more and more responsibilities to oversee things in those areas."

"You did many things, performed many duties. You must have known the house inside and out?"

Lin nodded gravely. His eyes softened as he remembered the past. "Until the fire, which of course changed everything for all of us."

"What happened? Tell me about it, about the fire, about the aftermath."

Lin shrugged his shoulders and looked about, and then stared back at me as though he had made a decision of great importance. "Again, you should know something," he said.

"Know what?"

"No one believes me when I speak of these things. They say I'm out of my head."

I used the pause to light a Chesterfield and exhale smoke toward the ceiling.

106

"Before we get too far into it," I started, tapping cigarette ashes into a small tray that was embedded into the back of the pew, "tell me this: If you are considered to be out of your head, then why does Thorough's employ you?"

"Only through the kindness of Master Tucker."

"How do you know him?"

Lin smiled wistfully as his eyes drifted away from mine before he replied. "For a few years I was a minor actor in the silent movie era. That's where we met."

"Tucker was a minor actor as well," I reminded him.

Lin nodded. "He was, but he had white skin and plenty of money in his wallet. I believe he inherited money. We met one day on the set of a melodrama and he befriended me. After that, we were in several movies together over the course of three years. We helped each obtain parts when we could."

"You were celluloid brothers?" I suggested.

Lin shrugged carefully, unsure if my question had been intended to provoke him.

"How many films were you in together?" I asked, more out of curiosity than any real need to know.

"At least five, and one or both of us were cut out of several others that we each performed in. I have lost track of the precise number that reached the theaters."

"The silent movie era ended abruptly."

"It did. Most of us were out of work very soon after the talkies arrived. The acting skills and voice qualities required in talkies were different from those that were valued during the silent movie era."

"Is that when Tucker hired you to work at Thorough's?"

"Yes," he nodded.

"What is your relationship to Mr. Tucker?"

Lin's eyes softened to indicate one answer. "We have never engaged socially," he said to indicate another. "His skin is lighter than mine; his world is entirely different."

"I understand." Somewhat ruthlessly, I decided not to tell him that Jameson Tucker was dead.

Chapter Twenty-Two

In a room without windows time seems to progress differently. I smoked quietly until I finished the cigarette. "Tell me about Sutro's Cliff House and Lot seventy-three."

Lin continued his gentle wheezing for a while longer and then spoke in his burning whisper of a voice. I listened with my head bent close to his so that I could catch every word.

"Mr. Sutro was mayor of San Francisco when I was hired on to work for him. He was a man of good cheer. Most men in his position would never have walked among the men he employed, but Mr. Sutro did. He knew our names and he was not afraid to get his own hands dirty with hard work.

"Once I saw him standing knee-deep in a *binjo* ditch with a shovel in his hands, shouting encouragement to others. A golden tie around his throat had been loosened and thrown over his shoulder as he plumbed the bottom sludge with a shovel. An ocean breeze was blowing that day, but it must have been over eighty-five degrees in the sunlight. Mr. Sutro was like that. Everyone noticed his effort that day, but no one was surprised by it.

"Later his foreman, a dark-skinned man, came over and they shook hands and shared a cigarette. We liked Mr. Sutro; we worked hard for him. I believe his daughter was less well liked – though I did not know her and rarely saw her. I think that was a preamble to the future.

"It is difficult to understand now what the house meant to those who lived and worked in it. Many of us were loyal to Mr. Sutro – loyal to him alone and willing to overlook other aspects of our work. The day he passed away, men I worked with cried."

Lin's facial expression changed from nostalgic to contemporary as he remembered that I was sitting there. With his head tilted back to catch the light, he raised his shaved eyebrows. "Forgive my assumption, but I believe you are far too young to have ever met Mr. Sutro."

I nodded.

Lin allowed himself a very short smile of conceit before he continued. "Mr. Sutro was an engineer, with an engineer's mind, though he liked people and he wanted to help them. He wanted to make their lives better. My impression is that when he died he was tired and defeated by his own failures. Many people would have thought his failures were not his own, and some would have laughed at him for his hubris in assuming the blame."

I had another Chesterfield out and toyed with it, rolling it between my fingers. I didn't light it, though I wanted to. I'd realized the smoke from the first one had bothered Lin's eyes. "Sutro's house did not stand long after his death," I said hesitantly.

"About ten years. You are interested in the fire of 1907?"

I nodded.

"You believe there is a connection between the fire and Lot seventy-three?"

I nodded again. "I believe it is possible."

"I will tell you what I can, though I will not be able to answer many of the questions you must have. The year before the fire was a good year. There were many parties, and many dignitaries were entertained at the house. Of course, Mr. Sutro was dead by then. We still remembered him. I personally light a Joss stick for him every year on the anniversary of his death. Even to this day – every year on the eighth of August.

"When the fire started, there were screams and people rushed about with buckets of water, but it was too late already. The house filled with smoke quickly and we had to hurry out of it. It burned rapidly and it was over within an hour. Nothing was left but the foundation and the haunted empty air where the structure had been.

"For a while, those of us who stood there felt we could see it: a ghost of a house now set against the hot painted streaks in the sky. Soon the authorities herded us off the premises. I've never back there, not once in all the years. Sometimes I wonder if I were to go back, whether I would see the ghost house standing there still. I've never seen the building that was erected there by Sutro's daughter. Have you seen it?"

I nodded slightly. "I went out there today."

Lin smiled and closed his eyes, tilting his head toward me. "What did you think?" he asked seriously, holding his eyes closed as I worked through my response to his question.

I whet my lips before I answered his question. "It's a beautiful place on the cliff overlooking the ocean. I didn't think much of the building that is there now," I confessed. "It struck me as an ordinary roadside diner, a mediocre destination, fulfilling none of the aspirations that Adolph Sutro would have had for it. It made me wonder what his daughter intended, who had advised her, and whether she hated her father so much that she chose intentionally to reject his vision."

Lin bowed ceremoniously toward me as if to vindicate my response. "Yes," he said, in his falsetto whisper. "Yes," he said again, louder.

"More cynically," I continued. "I wondered if this is part of the larger generic movement in America, the watering down of everything that could be excellent to the lowest common denominator that will sell, a denominator that assumes people will buy anything if others buy it too."

"Possibly, it is so," Lin responded with a short nod. He opened his eyes again to look at me.

"Do you have any ideas regarding Sutro's daughter?"

"I cannot speak ill of her," Lin explained. "That should, of course, be obvious to you. I was devoted to her father. No matter what disappointments I might feel, I cannot speak against her. That is what I owe to Mr. Sutro."

"Understood."

"She was not interested in her father's work. She did not speak much to those of us who worked the house and its grounds. So, though I have seen her, I never knew her."

I squinted in the low light. "What does that suggest to you?"

Lin pursed his lips and then glanced away from me.

"What do you think?" I asked again.

Lin smiled and then laughed a quiet, private sort of laugh. "I wanted to keep an open mind, to give Ms. Sutro the benefit of the doubt. I thought she would keep her father's memory close to her."

"Were you wrong about that?"

Lin's expression was grave and he shrugged. "It is not for me to say."

"At least you tried," I suggested.

"Trying and failing mean nothing to me, or to my ancestors. If it was a failure, it was mine and I was responsible." Lin bowed his head suddenly, deeply, and I realized he was feeling and expressing a personal shame related to the matter. "I must own this failure," he said quietly. "It is mine."

"I don't understand," I sighed. "What is the recourse?"

"Hard to explain, hard to know," Lin replied, holding his face and gaze down in supplication. "Where can you begin? You have a question – you may ask it of me. I am ashamed of where we have arrived with this conversation."

I asked the question that had bothered me from the beginning. "Do you know how the fire started?"

Lin paused before responding. His eyes were small dark spots surrounded by sick, yellowed swirls that bulged slightly from the blood vessels inside. "It was an unsolved mystery," he said in a soft breath that did not engage his vocal cords.

"I know the official story," I replied in my own form of a whisper back to him. "What I am interested in, what I want to know is this: Do *you* know how it was started? You were there. Do you know what happened?"

*

It took Lin a long time to answer my question. Rigidly he sat there with his hands folded in his lap, staring straight ahead as though I were not present.

"If you go back before the fire, there were many rumors, of course," he said eventually. "You may have heard stories, perhaps, about the underground tunnels that existed?"

"Tell me," I replied simply, refusing to reveal what I might have known or not known.

"According to the rumors, small boats were used to ferry goods between freighters in the ocean and the house on the cliff. They said this went on for many years. One rumor suggested this began shortly after the gold rush waned as a way to move contraband – gold and war materials to China; opium and valuables from China. How do you question that?"

"You don't, unless you have the evidence."

"Then we are back to belief. Here is what I believe: I believe there was a tunnel through the cliff even before the house was completed."

"Go on," I said to encourage him.

"I knew men from a prior generation who talked about this tunnel. They claimed to have built it with hammers and spikes and dynamite. The house on that part of the cliff has had five incarnations dating back to 1858. The second was a house built there in 1863 during the war between the American states of the south and the north."

I smiled before I spoke. "I grew up in the northern Midwest – St. Paul, Minnesota," I said. "I've always heard the war referred to as the American Civil War." With significant effort I curtailed the grin that nearly formed on my face.

Mr. Lin shrugged studiously. "Wars always have many names – usually the victor's name is the one's that persists into history. The vanquished have their own name for their wars, of course, though these are usually lost when the war is lost."

I nodded. "As the Chinese Americans have experienced," I said. "The victors write the histories, but they don't always get the facts right."

Lin nodded and allowed himself another private smile. "According to one rumor, Mr. Sutro bought and developed the cliff site because the tunnel was already there. Maybe he did that and enhanced the tunnel, bringing it up into the bottom of his new house. Or possibly he created the tunnel himself from the beginning of his ownership in 1883, blasting it out with the same methods he had used in the gold mines that made him so rich."

"That's a lot of speculation," I observed. "Which story is the right one?"

"Perhaps none of them are right?" Lin said.

"Is that what you believe?"

"No," he replied flatly. "I believe the tunnel was there and that Mr. Sutro refined it for his own purposes. He had a vision and a genius for things like that."

111

"Why?" I asked quietly. "What was this tunnel intended for?"

Lin frowned, tightening his compressed lips so that the skin around them folded in accordion fashion with tight, delineated lines running north and south on his face. "You don't understand much about what was driving Mr. Sutro?"

"Educate me." I still fingered the Chesterfield, rolling one end of it across my lower lip.

"I believe the tunnel was used for a variety of purposes," Lin told me. "If you accept that the tunnel, which might have been a system of tunnels, dated to 1863, as I do, that is the place to start. Ships could arrive and anchor out a short ways, sending in their smaller boats to make deliveries. I think it was a secret way to move contraband – gold, war materials, opium, and many other things."

"To be clear," I assumed, "this was occurring before Mr. Sutro?"

"Yes."

"Then we are talking about history that occurred seventy years ago?"

"That is correct."

"Do you know of anyone who was around then and who is still alive today?"

"No."

"In your lifetime, if we go back to the early days of your involvement with Mr. Sutro and his Cliff House, did you ever know or speak to anyone who had been involved in the tunnel activity during the American Civil War?"

Lin smiled and leaned toward me. I met him part way, nodding my head forward so that we were almost touching. When he spoke, I could feel his breathe hot on my face. "There were several men – Chinese – who had been around since the 1860s and who talked about the war-time activity."

"According to them, who was involved in these activities?"

"Captain Junius Foster held the original lease on the house in those early years. Who was he? Presumably he sided with the Union Forces, based on his military appointment, but I am certain of nothing. Do you know of him?"

I shook my head. I had never heard of the man. "What transpired later?" I asked, working hard to maintain my quietest voice.

Lin pressed his time-ravaged lips together tightly. "I knew the house better than most and I knew of the rumors. That does not mean I knew the truth."

"I think you know more than anyone alive now does. Did you ever see the tunnels for yourself?"

Lin nodded. "One time. Mr. Sutro knew how to make tunnels through rock. He was very skilled at it from what I understand, and from what I saw."

"He was an engineer," I said quietly, nodding my head, working hard to hold back my own excitement.

Lin continued: "I do not know for a fact, because I was not supposed to go down low enough into the house to see them, but there was one time. I followed another man down there. I was trying to stop him. What we saw surprised and frightened us. Can you believe me?"

"Yes."

"You do not worry that I may not be in my right head?"

I shook my head. "I am not worried about that anymore. Tell me what you saw."

"This man opened a door in the floor of a storage room behind the kitchen. When the door opened, it triggered lights there and revealed a set of rough-hewn wooden steps that led down into a room beneath the floor. I followed him down these steps. Below the foundation of the house was a room carved into the rock."

"How large was this room? Was there anything in it?"

"It was about twenty feet by twenty feet, with heavy wood tables lining three walls. They were mostly empty apart from a few crates holding bottles of French wine. There were also three cots, several candles, tins of food, and bottles of water."

"What did that mean to you?"

Lin was silent and I asked the question again. He lowered his head in shame and remained quiet for a while. Eventually he spoke: "Men and women used that room as a resting place to be smuggled into or out of the house."

"For what purpose?"

"People have been smuggled for many purposes throughout history. I do not know why the tunnel beneath Mr. Sutro's house was used."

"What else did you find there?"

"A large door, that when opened led down to a deep shaft cut through the rock of the cliff. Wooden stairs were bolted into it. Electrical wires lighted small caged bulbs at intervals. The bottom of the shaft was not visible from the landing we discovered. There was a vast darkness far down below."

I was beginning to develop an idea in my head. "Did you climb down those stairs?"

Lin shook his head. "I was too frightened and I decided to turn away. However, my companion climbed down and I watched him for as long as I could until he was completely out of my sight. I waited in that room for as long as I dared to – almost an hour, but he did not return. Eventually I climbed back up into the house proper and resumed my duties."

"Did he ever come back?"

"I never saw him again. Neither did his wife. After three months she was declared a widow."

"Do you think the fire started in that tunnel?" I asked.

Lin nodded. "Desperate men used it and in the dark, they needed candles, lanterns, electric lights that were strung along bare rock walls. I do not know how the fire started, but I suspect it began deep in the rock beneath the house. I believe the men who started it by accident must surely have perished by asphyxiation. I do not think anyone lived to explain how it started."

Chapter Twenty-Three

"What else is there?" I asked once Lin's words had sunk in. Without realizing it, I had inclined away from him with my elbows rested over the back of the bench we sat on. He moved over toward me on the bench, closing the distance between us, and leaned in with his fetid breath close to my face.

"There were stories of a secret society, of passwords, of communications with ships out at sea – of nefarious reasons for intentionally burning the house down. We heard those tales. Do you want to know what I think of them?"

"Yes," I whispered.

"Then I will tell you," Lin whispered back. "I think they are false. I think there were tales of intrigue that were told to make sense of the facts afterward. I believe Mr. Sutro was a man who designed his cliff house, his baths, and his estate to help people. He was a man of the people – all people, no matter the color of their skin."

"In other words, he was a saintly man?"

"Do not mistake," Lin replied. He smiled as he paused to study my eyes and read me like I was his book. "I believe there was a tunnel through the cliff that came up under the house. I believe goods and people passed through that tunnel for many years, goods and people that would not have been legally delivered otherwise.

"I also believe Mr. Sutro knew about this tunnel and approved of the goods and people moving through. He saw himself as part of an 'underground railroad' for the Chinese. There were men who helped move African slaves from the American south to the north in the years before the American Civil War."

I bowed my head in sympathy with what he described.

"Occasionally I saw these men and women as they passed through. I did not speak to them, but I heard enough to know who they were and where they came from – and what types of things they might have brought with them. It is very hard for the Chinese to be displaced from their native land."

"What did they bring with them?"

"They were poor people. For any ocean voyage, they could not carry much, so they carried the smallest, most valuable things they owned – small jewels, family heirlooms, items of talismanic value. These items would rarely hold monetary value. To you and other white men they would be meaningless trinkets."

"They were reminders of home."

Lin nodded. "You must understand: for the Chinese, *the moon is rounder in the native place.*"

*

Eventually I drew a deep breath and exhaled. "These are the sought-after items of Lot seventy-three, the ones contained in the sealed trunk?"

"I believe it is possible. Grateful Chinese immigrants would have felt compelled to give a small gift to the man who helped them."

I nodded, thinking out loud now. "With many small, seemingly inexpensive gifts, it would be easy for something of greater value to get lost in the mix."

Lin nodded with finality.

I was beginning to understand where he was taking me. "If they were connected to the house, how is they did not burn with the house. Why are they on the market now after all these years?"

Lin's smile was polite. "Mr. Sutro had other holdings, other properties. He would not have kept everything he valued at the Cliff House. I can only state that I believe there are forces at work in Chinatown and beyond that have accelerated someone's plan. I do not know why."

"What does that mean?"

"Men will die searching for something they believe to be of great value."

I knew men already had and I said nothing.

Lin interpreted my silence accurately. "You know I am right and perhaps you know more than I do. For myself, I am not a part of this struggle. I am an old man and I am tired. I know nothing more than the rumors and the small bits I put together from what I hear on the streets and read in the newspapers."

"What have you heard on the streets?"

"I have heard there are men, serious men, converging on Chinatown with a purpose."

"They are looking for something."

Lin nodded. "They are."

"Do you know what it is?"

"Only what it is rumored to be: the secret to immortality."

"That's impossible," I said.

"Is it?"

"How can it not be?"

Lin shrugged philosophically and tilted his head back, closing his eyes again. "Who can say what the ancients might have discovered? Whether it is possible or not, the dreams of some men will cause them to be ruthless in their search. How many men have killed and died throughout history in search of this thing that would seem to be of great value if it existed?"

116

"You are a skeptic," I said, allowing my voice to rise.

Lin shrugged. "Who am I to say?"

"What men are converging on Chinatown?" I asked.

"Mr. Josephine, for one. There are others, though I do not know their names."

"How do you know this, if you do not know their names?"

"It is the word of the street."

I understood that. "Tell me about Josephine. I don't know him."

"You will soon enough. He is a Chinese leader here in the city, very dangerous, very powerful."

"You mentioned newspapers. What have you read?"

"An Iranian businessman has disappeared."

"Walter McPhael. He's been missing for two weeks."

Lin nodded and his lips curled appreciatively.

"What do you know about him?" I asked.

"Only that his disappearance has caused minor shockwaves throughout the Chinese community."

"Why is that?"

"He was closely aligned with Mr. Josephine's legitimate businesses. Mr. McPhael had a successful import-export business, trading valuable goods between Tehran and San Francisco – much of which involved goods moving in and out of Chinatown."

I thought this over and offered my own understanding. "I was told his business involved objects of rare value brought from Iran to America - Persian rugs, jewels, incense, unusual medicinal compounds, and unusual artifacts and works of art; and basic commodities from American to Iran, such as gold bullion, wheat, steel, cotton, medicines. What's the connection to Chinatown?"

"The items you mention on both sides of the ledger are relevant to the people and the commerce of Chinatown. Chinese artifacts are in demand here."

"Tell me more of what you know," I whispered.

"Have you seen the key?" Lin asked instead.

I nodded. "Mr. Tucker showed it to me at his home last night. Have you seen it also?"

"Yes."

"What did you make of it?"

Lin bowed his head. "This is a game being played out by people above us."

"No," I shook my head in disagreement. "There is no one above us. We are our own. What did you think of the key? Did you recognize it?"

Lin's expression was mysterious. "I did not recognize it. I venture that my reaction was the same as yours."

"What was that?"

Lin smiled. "You were awed by it's importance. I was too. I began to think it must unlock something very important."

"Where did you see it?" I asked.

"Also, in Mr. Tucker's home."

"I thought you didn't socialize with him." In that moment, I knew Tucker had shown the same key to many others. It was a fatal mistake.

"It was the only time I was there – six days ago. One day after our working hours ended, he invited me to his home to show me something. Alone in his house for the first time together he poured me a glass of white wine from Provence and we shared a plate of *foie gras* with small, thin white crackers his housemaid had baked. It was not a social visit. It was formal. He invited me to his study where he had something to show me: the key, which he extracted from a compartment hidden deep inside his desk."

I nodded slowly. "What did it mean to you?"

Lin shook his head slowly. "Unimportant curiosities are sometimes known for their complex access systems. Usually they come around in the end to mean nothing. If you want someone to believe in the value of an object, what better way than to cloak it in layers of mystery?"

I grinned because I had been affected by the complexity Tucker had used to hide his treasured key. "So, what do you think?"

"I think it is probably fake."

"Why?"

Lin shrugged. "What else could I think?"

"I don't understand?"

"In my life, I have found that complex mysteries of a man-made nature are rarely anything more than a portal to emptiness."

"Did he tell you what it might open?"

Lin's smile shaded toward sadness. "He did not, though he implied it was connected to Lot seventy-three."

"Nothing more?" I inquired.

"Nothing more."

"Do you know why the crying of Lot seventy-three was cancelled?"

"No."

"Is it stored here in this building?"

He shook his head.

"Do you know where it is stored?"

Lin lowered his face and stared down at the floor between us. I knew our conversation was over. Even though I didn't think it would surprise him, I didn't tell him that Tucker was dead or about the second key I had seen or about the fact that both keys were now missing and their owners murdered.

He would find out soon enough and there was no use worrying him about it now. With a little luck I told myself I might even have the entire affair sorted out before he learned of Tucker's death.

The emotion written on his face had coalesced into something profound, though I could not read what it indicated.

*

With my mind elsewhere, I took the stairs down to the first floor of Thorough's Auction House. In the lobby I paused with some relief to light the Chesterfield I had been fingering for the past twenty minutes. The hot, harsh smoke burned my lungs pleasantly and soothed me. I thought about the rumors, the stories, and the theories Mr. Lin had shared with me.

Some of his ideas were unusual and hard to believe. By his own admission there were plenty of people who thought he was not in his "right head." In Chinatown I knew that could have had many meanings. As I held the tobacco smoke deep in my lungs, I realized I didn't know what to believe about any of it. Maybe Lin was crazy, or maybe the tunnel was there and had played its role.

*

As I came out of Thorough's into the blinding sunlight of the late San Francisco waterfront afternoon I involuntarily squeezed my eyes shut. I'd spent too much time sitting in a windowless room. My pupils were still adjusting to the brightness when I felt the hard poke at my back, just below my shoulder blade. I half-turned and then stopped against the metallic finger that prodded me quite persuasively.

A hard, low voice I didn't recognize said quietly: "I'm guessing you know what a pistol barrel in your side feels like."

I dropped the cigarette butt I held between my fingers onto the sidewalk and stepped on it. "Don't tell me," I replied. "A .38 caliber?"

"Try a .32," the voice said. "It makes less noise and it's just as deadly at this range, which is no range at all." He pushed the muzzle into me harder, as if daring me to back away from its provocative tickle.

Chapter Twenty-Four

It was mid-afternoon and building shadows had shifted to the eastern sides of the street. With my hands flexed open beside me, I turned my head enough so that I could see the man out of the corner of my eye. "You have me at a disadvantage."

"We're going for a short ride," he said, forcing a grin that he didn't feel. He was a slight, nervous man with pinched jowls and a fedora slanted sideways over his eyes. "Don't get anxious about it. It's a round trip we have planned. My boss wants to talk to you – it'll be easy peasy."

A long automobile whisked up beside us on the street and a back door was opened from within. Another shining pistol barrel appeared, this one pointed at my chest. I raised my hands until they were even with my shoulders and climbed inside, as the man behind me suggested, prodding me some more with the .32 automatic.

We pulled away from the curb with a jolt. The long automobile became fast and heavy as it pushed through the streets. Curtains along the windows on both sides and the back were drawn. I looked around the obscured cab and saw the outlines of the two pistols still pointed at me. The odor of whiskey and stale tobacco floated on the breath of the two men who sandwiched me in the back seat. I couldn't see the driver very well and he did not speak. All I had was an impression of large shoulders and heavy hands.

"Wear this," the guy to my left proposed and a hood was pulled down over my eyes. Now it was pitch black for me.

Hands reached inside my jacket and found my .45. I sat back and relaxed into the ride, listening carefully to the external clues and counting the turns. Nobody spoke and I didn't ask any questions. We made three left turns in a row, followed by two right turns, a long straight away, two more right turns, another long straight away, and then two more lefts. I was almost dizzy by the time we came to a stop.

They pulled me out of the automobile, two hands holding each of my arms, and rushed me into a building. We took the stairs up to the third floor and then moved down a hallway to a room that was opened with a key. I was pushed down into a sofa. Two lamps were clicked on and the door was locked again before the hood was removed.

As my eyes adjusted I looked around the room, allowing the details to occur to me as they registered. The room was a modest parlor, with a pair of upholstered armchairs, three floor lamps, a corner cabinet, a bar cart, a large radio positioned strategically near one of the armchairs, and a large, low circular table placed in front of the sofa where I sat.

On the table was a pair of ashtrays, both empty, an assortment of ladies magazines laid out in accordion fashion, and a dish of small golden-wrapped candies. There were two windows with shades drawn and two other openings in the room. One led into what appeared to be an adjacent dining room and the other toward a darkened hallway that probably led to a bedroom or two.

The man who had approached me on the sidewalk and another man, presumably the other one who had been in the back seat of the automobile with me, stood in the middle of the room watching me. They both had guns out and pointed at me still.

"Cozy," I said. "What's the rumpus?"

"Easy," the first guy advised. "Don't get all excited. As I said before, boss wants to talk to you."

"About what?"

"He'll let you know when he gets here."

"After that?"

"We'll see. I imagine we'll drop you anywhere you like."

"You have a name?"

"Sure, I'm Travers."

"You probably have a first name too."

"Samuel."

"What about you?" I asked the other fellow. He was a tall, sallow faced man with a lot of grease holding the hair off his forehead.

"I guess you can call me 'gone'," he said to me. Then he addressed Travers: "You got this, Sam?"

Travers nodded and we both watched as the other man left the apartment, locking the door behind him.

"I guess it's just you and me now," I said to Travers when we were alone. "Why not sit down and take a load off your Buster Browns?"

"Don't get flippant."

"Why not?" I asked, allowing a natural grin to form. "You're only the hired help. It's your boss I may have to answer to, not you. Is this your apartment?"

"No."

"I thought maybe these were your magazines." I gestured to the ladies journals that were on the table between us.

"Are you mocking me?"

I laughed at that. "No, but I may yet," I replied. I reached into my pocket and found a Chesterfield. I lighted it with a match that I tossed into one of the ashtrays on the table.

"I didn't say you could smoke," Travers said. He was getting twitchy.

121

"You didn't say I couldn't, and anyway, I don't need your permission."

"I'm the one with the gun."

I blew a long thin stream of blue smoke toward the ceiling. "It's a .32. I thought only sissy's carried .32's."

"You know how many men I've killed with this, mister?"

"How could I possibly know that? You think I can see notches on that little toy all the way from over here? Not in this light. Why don't you open the shades?"

"I've killed plenty of men, mister. You best remember that."

I grinned and took another drag off my cigarette. "Why not open the shades and let a little sunlight in anyway?"

Travers shook his head. "Nope.

"Do you even know who I am?" I asked in my best idle tone.

"You're Huddleston. You're working for Johnny Drake, a private investigator we don't like."

"Who's the 'we'?"

"Me and my boss."

"I know your name, but who are you, and who is your boss?"

"Shut up and wait. You'll find out soon enough."

"I won't shut up," I replied. "I rather like talking right now and I'm starting to find you amusing. Does your boss know what he's doing? It's one thing to have sent three of you to pick me up. What I don't understand is why anyone thought it would be a good idea to leave you alone with me."

"That's rich, given you're the one staring down the barrel of a gun," Travers said.

"It would only be rich if I thought you were actually a menace with that toy."

"Boss knows I can kill a man if I have to."

I grinned harder. He was the type who was easily rattled. It was a shiny pistol that he held, but the way he held it made me doubt he'd fired it very often. "Call it however you like, but you have no character and your boss must see that."

That got to him and he set his jaw with his best sneer. "I think I've got plenty of character, more than enough to handle the likes of you."

I shook my head with certainty. "You haven't done anything yet."

"I have too," he boasted again. "I've done plenty. I told you, I've killed men. That means I've done something."

"You may have killed someone. Maybe you've done something, but nothing you've come to understand, and certainly nothing you've come to regret. Only when you realize that you've done something that you sincerely wish you hadn't, and that you cannot undo, will you have what anyone else would consider an element of real character. Until then you're just another empty suit with a slick haircut and a toy gun."

"Why are you riding me, mister?"

I grinned some more, knowing I was getting to him. "Because you're unformed and you don't know it. You wave that sissy gun around like it should mean something. Maybe it does. Are you a sissy? Maybe you are. In just a minute I'm going to take that pea-shooter away from you and pat you across the cheek with it."

"I'm not scared of you."

"Sure you are, kid. You're scared witless. You're trembling right down to your socks, and you don't know what to do about it. You just don't have enough character within you to recognize what would be so obvious to anybody else."

That was the final straw. He leapt across the room at me, tripping partially over the table between us. I caught the wrist of his gun hand and turned it, rolling with his body weight to bounce him off the sofa next to me.

When we came up again, I had the .32 in one hand and I slapped him hard on the face with the other. He buckled and brought both hands up over his face to cover it for subsequent blows. I didn't give him any. Instead I reached inside his jacket and found my .45.

"Sit up," I commanded, standing over him.

After he complied, I dropped his pistol into my pocket and then showed him mine. I pushed the .45 up under his chin to make the point. "Let's try it again. Who is your boss?"

"He'll be here soon enough."

"Fine, but you're going to tell me his name or I'm going to beat you silly and drop you out the window."

Travers glowered at me and rubbed the side of his cheek. It was starting to turn red where my hand had cuffed it. "Mr. Josephine."

"Does he have a first name?"

"Probably, but I wouldn't know it," he said resentfully. "Maybe you want to reconsider and hand the gat back to me? It will look better for you."

I stood over him still. He was a small and shrinking man. "I doubt it would, and anyway, that's not my style."

"Then you don't know much about Mr. Josephine."

"No," I corrected him. "Josephine doesn't know much about me, and neither do you."

"You're not so tough," he proclaimed, still rubbing the side of his face.

"Have a candy," I replied, plucking one from the bowl and dropping it in his lap.

The heavily shaded windows bothered me. A thin bright line of sunlight broke into the room at the bottom of each shade, accentuating the interior melancholy of the room. I wondered what there was to see on the outside.

Without taking my eyes off Travers, I crossed the room. With two quick motions I released each of the roller shades so that they snapped up instantly. The double flashbulb effect startled Travers and he gave a short cry and jerked his feet up off the floor.

"Easy," I said to him. "You've had too many dreams about the hangman's trapdoor."

Moving mostly my eyes, I took a quick glance out the window at the view that was afforded. The brightness that had crashed under the blinds was nothing more than the sun reflecting off the baking bricks of the windowless building eight feet over.

I still had no idea where I was, so I lowered the shades to wait for Mr. Josephine.

Chapter Twenty-Five

Fifteen minutes later a key was pushed into the door from the hallway and the door opened. Two men came in. One was the sallow faced man with an affinity for hair grease. He had a bowler hat in his hands. The other was a short, stocky Chinese man wearing an expensive silk pinstripe suit, dark blue tie, and a bowler hat. His face was clean-shaven and the strong scent of Bay Rum crossed the room to my nostrils the moment he entered.

"Welcome back Mr. Done," I said from a side of the room where they were not expecting to see me. Sam Travers was sitting where I had been when "Mr. Done" had left. I was now on the other side of the room, leaning against the wall toward the bedroom with my .45 out and pointed at them.

"What the –?" Done exclaimed, suddenly confused.

I smiled at him. "You should probably set the peashooter on the floor. Push it gently over here."

The words startled him until he realized that I was serious and I held the most important trump card in the room: a .45 automatic that was pointed at his chest.

"You must be Josephine," I said to the stocky Chinese man.

"I am he." His smile developed slowly and his hands came up wide and open, just as slowly.

"I assume this fellow is your employee. You might encourage him to follow my suggestion regarding the peashooter." I moved the barrel of my .45 around in a tight circle that focused on his chest.

Josephine clucked despondently, as a disappointed parent might have and he removed his hat carefully. Drops of sweat formed and stood out on his forehead, almost as though he had willed them to. His hands turned the hat around and around in counterclockwise circles, handling it by the inside of its brim.

After a heartbeat, he turned toward the sallow faced man. "'Mr. Done,' as he called you, or Jimmy Smitherton, as *I* call you, it seems this gentleman has obtained the jump on us. Maybe you should lay down your pistol as he suggests. I would hate for us to have an unfortunate misunderstanding at this early stage of our discussion."

Smitherton lowered his body slowly, bending at the knees while keeping his chin up. When he was close to the floor, he set the pistol – another .32 – on the area rug we stood upon. With the side of his foot he pushed if toward me. When it slowed to a stop near me, I put a foot over it and glanced around the room. "How many more of these .32s do I have to collect?"

"I believe you have all of the .32s in Chinatown now," Josephine replied in an agreeable voice. "We can dissect this later, but for the moment, its important we manage to have a productive conversation about the matter before us."

"What about guns of other calibers?" I asked.

"I am unarmed, of course," Josephine explained mildly. With his fingertips he opened his jacket wide to show he was not carrying a gun, and then he turned once, slowly, with the jacket raised high enough so that I could see his belt line was clear all the way around.

"That's fine," I said. "You can sit down. You too Jimmy Smitherton, but over there." I pointed with the barrel of my pistol where I wanted him.

With a begrudging sneer on his face Smitherton joined Travers on the sofa. Awkwardly, they each made an effort not to allow their eyes to meet.

Josephine planted himself comfortably in the armchair next to the large radio, where he proceeded to smooth out the lapels and breast panels of his jacket with the backs of his fingers. With his legs crossed, he set the bowler on the upper knee and clasped his hands together in front of his chest.

"Now what?" Josephine inquired cordially without any evident anxiety.

"I've got two .32s collected from the pair on the sofa. They're your boys, so I'll let you deal with them later. My concern is about a man with a pistol of a different caliber – a .22."

"A lady's gun," Josephine stated. The smile on his face was placid and revealed nothing to me.

"It is, unless a man is using it. Even a .22 slug can kill a person if it's put into the right spot."

"My, my," Josephine exclaimed pleasantly. "Is there such a person around?"

"There is. He's made a successful career as an assassin with a .22 pistol."

"Who is this man?"

"Maybe you've hired him already," I said.

Josephine smiled at me with his eyes and gave a slight shake of his head. "I don't think so. What is his name?"

"Fingers Pete." I said the name simply, hoping to rattle Josephine a little if he knew anything about him. His expression did not change. "Does the name mean anything to you?" I asked directly. "It seems he could be working for you."

Josephine glanced down at the bowler hat on his knee. His easy smile faded completely. "I have heard the name of this man. If I'm not mistaken, he is a contract killer out of New York. They say he works for Mr. Lepke. I don't know why he would be here in San Francisco – it seems awfully far afield from his usual haunts. I certainly did not employ him and I know nothing about his activities if he is here in our town. Maybe you know something I don't."

I didn't believe Josephine's amiable words, but there was nothing to be gained by saying so. I shrugged hard, and moved toward one of the chairs in the room.

"What do *you* know, then?" Josephine asked me. His eyes narrowed to thin slits, as if he were trying to hold in the force of vitality that suddenly exuded from behind them. "Do you have evidence this man is here in Chinatown, in my territory? If he is, I'd like to know."

Sitting now with my legs crossed, I held my eyes and my .45 steady, but my mind drifted toward the past, to a series of conversations I'd had while trying to locate the elusive killer.

*

"What about Fingers Pete from Atlantic City?" I asked Billie Preston.

Billie looked down at the drink in his hands and swirled the ice around slowly with a grim frown on his face. A curtain had fallen over it. His hands tightened. "I've heard of Fingers Pete from Atlantic City," he replied. "But I don't know who he is or where he comes from. Nobody does. I doubt the Atlantic City part is anything worth paying attention to. It's probably misdirection. If anybody does know, they ain't saying. Not on their life. He's one of those that people generally don't talk about much. Makes me sweat just to mention his name. He could be a ghost or something."

"Watch yourself," I said, pushing back from the bar.

*

"What about Fingers Pete?" I asked the supreme crime lord of New York City.

Lucky Luciano shook his head and set the burning cigarette down, balanced on the edge of the ashtray.

I stared back at him.

"Forget about him. He's gone."

"I need something."

"You really want it to be like that?"

"I do. Right now, yes. Do you know where they are?"

Luciano shook his head. "No, not like that. Fingers Pete is a difficult man to find. He's probably left town, and if he did, he's far away."

*

"Where's Fingers Pete?" I asked Willie Shears once we were alone.

"You don't know anything about him."

127

"I know his moniker. Where is he?"

"What do I know? He's special talent, and you don't know his real name."

"What's his real name?"

"It ain't 'Fingers Pete,' that's for sure."

"What then?"

"I don't know it myself. Who does? Around here, he's just a myth. People talk about Fingers Pete, they do it in a whisper."

"He's that scary?"

"He is."

"Who would know him?"

"I'm not gonna tell you that. I don't even know myself. Only people up the chain above me, way above me, and maybe not even them. You don't understand. Whyn't you take a hike, pal. Scoot back to Chicago and leave it alone. You've already made out lucky once. Lightning doesn't strike twice, you know."

*

Coming out of it, I focused on Josephine's words as he repeated himself. "The question I asked was: do you have evidence this man is here in Chinatown, in my territory?" His eyes were still narrowed slits. The dynamism behind them had been contained.

"I believe I do, and I think he is working for you. Do you employ killers from New York City?"

Josephine shook his head emphatically. "I have not, I would not, and why would I?"

"As we learned this afternoon, your own talent leaves something to be desired."

"That may be, though today is not over and in one sense, they have not failed me at all."

"How is that so?" I asked.

"My goal – my only goal – was to have a conversation with you. That has been achieved."

I played with this silently for a moment. "That might be true, but you intended for a gun to be pointed at me for this conversation, not the other way around as things stand."

"Perhaps," Josephine mused as he shifted in his chair. "You are young and brash, and I won't hold that against you. Why do you think this assassin from New York City is here in my town?"

"Where is 'here,' anyway?" I asked instead. "Where are we? I've opened the shades. There is nothing to be seen out there but the dull bricks of the

128

building next door."

"You're in Chinatown," he replied flatly.

"Am I?"

Josephine nodded as though he had lost interest in my curiosity. "Tell me about Fingers Pete."

"The man you claim not to employ?"

"That's right. Why do you believe he's come all the way out here?"

I drew breath. "It goes back to a rumor I heard in Kansas City last week."

"How did you hear this rumor?"

"It came to me by telegram from a man I know in Chicago."

"What man?"

"You must know I can't reveal his name."

Josephine nodded easily as though I had informed him what time the next bus would arrive. "What did the telegram say?" he questioned.

"Only that Fingers Pete was on a job in San Francisco and that if I hurried, I might catch up to him."

"Is that why you came out here?"

I smiled. "Its part of the reason."

"That seems a little thin. Do you have any more reason then that to believe he is here?"

With my .45 laid flat on my lap I nodded and lighted a Chesterfield while I watched Josephine's two boys closely. I didn't hurry and they didn't move. After I shook out the match, I exhaled and picked up the .45 again, leaning forward to drop the match into the nearest ashtray on the table between us. "I do," I said. "Several in fact. Would you care to hear them?"

"Most certainly, I care to hear them."

I counted the first reason with my thumb. "One is that I was told he was here by a man in Chicago. I've known this man a long time, and he's good with information. We've done favors for each other over the years, and I trust him."

"This is the man whose name you cannot reveal?"

"Exactly so."

Josephine smiled in a knowing way and nodded his salute of my concern. "Would it be fair to say that he's of Italian heritage?"

"In this country, we're all immigrants. I never asked where his grandparents came from."

"I understand, and my, you are an old fashioned man, one of the old-school champions – a gentleman even, and a real threat! I admire that, though you are sitting there with the gun. The way you handled my men was beautiful, the work of a matador. All of that is to say that I understand the code you work under requires that you would not reveal the source of your information."

129

I lowered my chin, waiting for him to finish, knowing he was building toward something.

His smile remained pleasant. "I admire the loyalty you show to the men you work for."

"I don't work for other men in quite the way you might think."

"An independent man, one who insists on going his own way," Josephine exclaimed. "I am not surprised and you have my respect for that. Continue at your own pace."

"What other pace would I ever continue at? Number two," I continued, flipping my index finger out beside my thumb, "there is another man who gave me similar information and he is much closer to local events than anyone in Chicago."

Josephine drew a gloating breath, so pleased that he could not contain his pleasure. "Fabulous! I can tell you that there are only four possibilities that characterize the man you describe."

"That's interesting to hear," I replied. "If you're right, it means you have a twenty-five percent chance of guessing his name. I'm curious to hear your entire list if you care to share it."

Josephine nodded confidently and held up four fat fingers, which he folded down one by one as he counted through his list. "The only possibilities I see are a Chinatown resident known locally as Master Khai Chi; a traveling surgeon named Orion; a local art dealer and impresario, Jameson Tucker; and an Iranian import-exporter named Walter McPhael. These are the men who are mostly likely to be involved in this little escapade."

"That's a remarkable list in many ways," I replied. "I won't reveal my source to you, but I can narrow your list. In the process of doing that, I'll reveal my three other reasons for believing that Fingers Pete is here in Chinatown." I closed the hand I had been counting on to form a fist.

"You have my undivided attention, sir," Josephine said, waving his left hand in the air with a flourish.

I drew a last drag from my cigarette before flipping it into the ashtray on the table. I glanced at Travers and Smitherton. They sat still, backs rigid, with their hands extended together between their knees. I wondered briefly if it was a pose that Josephine trained all his gunmen to adopt when they were compromised. I liked the idea at first. Then it occurred to me that it was a natural position for a disarmed gunman to assume while sitting with a man who waved a loaded pistol in his face.

They were afraid and taking pains to let me know they were not intending to rush me. Since they didn't know me, they had no read on whether I was angry, emotionally unstable, or simply ruthless. Up to a point that worked in my favor, as long as I didn't sell them the idea their position was hopeless. It

130

was important they believed they would be walking out of the room.

I smiled at them. "I hope you boys realize, this is just a pleasant conversation between your boss and myself. When we're finished, we all walk out of here and life goes on."

Two heads nodded in unison.

"You can smoke if you like. I've got Chesterfields if you're out." Leaning forward with my elbows on my knees and the .45 held down between them with my right hand, I spoke directly to Josephine now. "Two of the men on your list are already dead and a third is missing."

The stocky Chinese man's expression paled. Even in the low light of the apartment I could see the blood draining from his face. "Who are dead?" he inquired.

"Khai Chi and Jameson Tucker were both murdered during the night. I saw them each alive last night, before I saw them each dead this morning. The pattern was the same. They were both shot in the head with a .22 caliber gun."

Josephine drew a sharp breath as I finished the sentence. He glanced from me to his two men on the sofa. They indicated nothing apart from mirroring the surprise of their boss.

I paused a moment to let the news sink in before I continued. "A young Chinese woman was also murdered. She worked for Khai Chi."

"Are you certain they are all dead?" Josephine asked. His lips were grimly tight and the color drained from his face.

I nodded. "I found Tucker and Chi myself this morning – in their quarters. Each had a .22 caliber hole in his forehead – the signature of Fingers Pete. I found the young woman who worked for Chi on the floor of his shop. She was mortally wounded – stabbed in the back. There was no way to save her. I waited with her until she died."

Josephine lowered his head as though he was affected personally by what I had just told him. When he raised his gaze again, he had a question: "Did the girl identify her killer to you?"

My expression flattened. "Her last words were for my ears only."

"What am I supposed to think?" Josephine asked.

"Whatever you like. It was a private moment between us."

"We still have Orion and McPhael on my list."

"According to his wife, McPhael is missing – has been for about two weeks, but you probably already know that."

Josephine nodded grimly.

"Maybe you know something about it?" I asked.

"I don't," he said, and shrugged noncommittally and then stared down at his bowler. "Tell me more about the girl who worked for Khai Chi?"

"Why?" I inquired.

131

"Because she was my niece, Mei – *the red gem*. Now I have to inform her mother, my sister, that she has been murdered." Josephine sat quite still in his chair and his hands intertwined on his lap, though I could see they were squeezing each other hard, as though he was trying to bring the dead girl back to life.

Slowly his clenched knuckles began to assume a deepening shade of red.

Chapter Twenty-Six

The room was quiet. I felt the power of Josephine's words in my gut and as I looked around, and I realized the others did too. Suddenly we were not altogether on opposite sides of what mattered.

"I'm sorry about Mei," I said with an unintended hush in my own voice.

Josephine seemed to shrink inward for a moment and he was silent. His chin drooped almost to his chest. "I was so fond of her," he said eventually. His eyes had watered and he was blinking hard against them. "We were fond of each other. Even with nine uncles, everyone said I was her favorite. Every year on her birthday I took her out for rice pudding, just the two of us."

Smitherton's sallow face drew tight as he started to comfort his boss. "Mr. Josephine, I'm sor -"

Josephine held up a hand to cut his man off. "I know," he said quietly. He raised his head and pressed his lips together tightly, determined to resume his role. "There will be time for our tears later. Now, we must focus on the business we have chosen."

"Perhaps we can have that bigger picture discussion, if you like," I offered.

"The bigger picture? Yes, let's talk about that. You're starting to seem like a rather decent fellow, Huddleston."

I nodded and as a show of faith I holstered my pistol. I lighted another Chesterfield and tossed the pack over to the two boys on the sofa. "Help yourself, but don't get any cute ideas," I told them.

Josephine drew himself up and fashioned a smile. "That's what I hoped for. I think we might even be pals once we understand each other and the things that inspire us."

"I'm ready to listen," I said.

"That's all I can ask for," Josephine replied, smiling with his teeth – but not his eyes. He pumped a short, friendly laugh onto the end of his sentence. "Once we've talked it through you may see we are on the same side of the coin. Joining forces is what I hope to achieve. I believe we can help each other and I'm impressed with the skill you have shown."

"Perhaps there was no need for the dramatics outside Thorough's this afternoon. If a conversation was all you wanted, you might have sent me an invitation to tea."

Josephine laughed at this – his belly even heaved a little, and his shoulders moved. "I apologize," he said. "I see now it was misjudgment on my part. There will be no more gunplay among us tonight. That is over and we've moved on now. You can bank on that: no more curbside pickups at gunpoint. Now on to my question: With whom are you working for?"

I smiled and looked about the room, noting the relaxed position of Smitherton and Travers. "If you're asking the question it means you already know."

Josephine spoke into the pause that followed. "I think we have only Dr. Orion and his beautiful wife unaccounted for."

I shrugged without comment and took a drag off my cigarette, waiting for him to elaborate.

Josephine didn't leave me waiting long. "You must realize, of course, that Orion is a con man of the first order – a bilker, a fraudster, a charlatan, a scam artist – yes sir, a real smooth operator who would swindle his own grandchildren if there were a few dollars to be had."

"So you say."

"Yes, I do say!"

"What does Orion say about you?"

Josephine laughed again. It was a genuine laugh. "Bravo, sir! He might say the very same thing about me, and perhaps he would even be right." The rotund Chinaman hesitated for a moment to think it over. He turned his eyes up toward the ceiling, while a smile held his lips in place. "We are businessmen and competitors, and your point, is valid. We both aim to buy and sell objects of value at a profit. Yes, your point is valid."

"Fine, then I'll make a few more. Someone killed Tucker and Chi in their own homes. Why? Who would do that? Who would be *able* to do that? Not just any man can make his way into and out of a house without being noticed. Tucker, I'll grant was probably an easy target. He was naïve. Chi should have been more formidable."

"He was."

"Tell me about it," I suggested.

With his hands spread wide before him, Josephine spoke: "Chi was a warrior, a fighter, an acclaimed martial artist," he explained. "During his youth he won a championship bout in Beijing before he immigrated to the United States. It brought him great fame. Even in his later years, he was a skilled warrior and a mentor who helped train and develop younger fighters. That was why my niece, Mei, sought him out. The legend says he could throw a punch from three inches away from a man's chest that would crack open his breastplate."

I was taken by surprise. "You respected him?"

"I did."

"Yet, he was involved in this 'escapade,' as you called it."

"He was seeking the same thing I and the others are seeking, though I

134

believe he was seeking it for a different reason, perhaps a nobler reason."

"What reason is that?"

"National honor."

"*The moon is rounder in the native place,*" I murmured.

Josephine's eyes opened wide. "You are educated about the Chinese way in a manner that few white men are."

I played with my cigarette and shook my head. It had grown short and I could feel the heat encroaching toward my fingertips. "What exactly is it that you and the others seek?"

"Of course, Orion wouldn't have told you," Josephine replied. "He wouldn't want to risk having you steal it for yourself. I wonder what he did tell you?"

I shrugged. "Don't assume too much. I have some idea about what we are looking for. It's not large and it is rumored to be special, maybe even to have mystical qualities. Immortality has been mentioned, though I don't believe in magic of that sort. Perhaps its something related to chemistry or physics – or more likely, it's a hoax altogether that the lot of you are chasing after."

"What else do you think you know about it?"

"It may have originated in China. Perhaps it's even ancient, or at least rumored to be."

"What else?"

I smiled as I realized I had his interest piqued. "Men are willing to kill for it."

"Perhaps women too," Josephine added.

I nodded.

"I will tell you some of what I know," Josephine said. His voice had fallen into the lower register and he did not so much as glance at either of his own men as he spoke.

*

"The hunt is on to find a rare artifact. Some believe it came out of ancient China, possibly as far back as the Qin Dynasty. The story that accompanies it is a long one, with many variations and twists, depending on who is telling it – and who is hearing it. For our purposes, I will simplify the narrative as best I understand it.

"We could spend a long evening talking about the Qin Dynasty and the secret work of the monks who were devoted to the emperor. I will skip through that period, leaving that tale for another time. However, you must understand that something powerful came from it, something that held people in great awe throughout the Dynasty. From here forth, I will refer to this artifact as the 'Blue Orb.'

"Somewhere, and it is not recorded where or how, near the end of the Qin period, the Blue Orb disappeared and was then lost for many ages. It may have been lost and then found, or perhaps it was kept in hiding all this time. No one today knows. Most certainly it passed through many different hands through the years, and one must imagine that most of those who possessed it had no idea what it was or the power that it held.

"Now, I will advance the story to the year 1860, almost yesterday in the blink of an eye that human time is relative to the vastness of the universe. Many believed that the Orb came back into the possession of the royal family during a time of war and strife. It was smuggled out of China during the Second Opium War – or the Arrow War as some have called it, named for the pirate ship *Arrow* that the Chinese authorities seized, which inflamed the British war passions.

"Near the end of this war, which was virtually lost already, desperate measures were taken to secure the secrecy of the Blue Orb and to ensure that it did not fall into the hands of the invading forces. The mistress of one of the royal princes took it one night while her lover was sleeping. She managed to get it out of the Forbidden City before the English-French forces took control of the city. Disguised as a beggar child, she carried it to Tianjin."

I smoked quietly and nodded my head as Josephine continued to speak.

"From there she boarded a fishing vessel that managed to avoid the British flotilla and deliver her to one of the tiny atolls within the Japanese islands. Her journey lasted three more years as she traveled by steamer from Japan to the islands of the South China Sea. After a few hopeless, frightening weeks there, she crossed under the southern tip of India and spent several feverish months in Mumbai, before taking another ship to a port city in the south of Persia.

"All the while, she hid the Orb upon her person as though it were the most important thing she owned – which of course it most certainly was."

"Who was this mistress? Did she have a name?" I asked.

Josephine nodded and shifted uncomfortably in his seat, as though the burden of History weighed upon him. "Of course she did, though it has been lost to the ages by now?"

"What about the prince she stole Orb from? Do we know his name?"

"We might. However, we do not even know if she *stole* it from him. Some scholars believe that he *gave* it to her, along with a travel route and sufficient cash and jewels to help her escape with it."

"Why would this prince do that?"

"Because he knew the fall of the Forbidden City was inevitable, and he wanted to save the woman he loved and protect the Orb from falling into British hands."

I lit another cigarette while I considered these words.

I must have been frowning because Josephine commented on my expression. "You appear skeptical and I cannot blame you. I must rely on your trust that while the entire story is actually much longer than I have presented here, I have told you the parts of it that help explain why I believe the Blue Orb is now hidden somewhere in this city.

"I have spent much of my lifetime in private study regarding this matter. I have traveled extensively through the Orient and Persia. I have journeyed and read enough so that I am reasonably confident that I am right. It is here now and we must find it – this is our window of opportunity. You have more information about this than any white man has – including the esteemed Dr. Orion and wife."

"You've shared an entertaining tale," I replied, sitting back in my chair. "You're a good story-teller, I'll give you that, but is there any evidence to back any of what you claim?"

Josephine posed his fingertips together beneath his chin. "There is," he said quietly. "I have a letter written by the prince. Interpreted, it suggests that he helped his mistress to escape from the Forbidden City with the Orb in her possession."

"Where is this letter now?"

Josephine smiled grimly. "I have it hidden away, but I will read it to you."

Chapter Twenty-Seven

The silence between us was long. I began to imagine the gradual tapping of a drummer on a closed high-hat. "Maybe you should continue with the story of the Chinese mistress," I said before the high-hat reached a full-pedaled crescendo. "We can come back to the letter."

Josephine made a slight bow. "This brave mistress was sent forth by her Chinese prince. He was of the Qing Dynasty, which lasted only four years and ended in humiliation and death at the hands of the British Empire in 1860. While I believe my historical research has identified the prince, at least to my satisfaction, we do not know the name of his mistress. She is only a whisper amid the historical winds now. Somehow she managed to find her way to the Persian city of Tehran, which as you know, is a bustling city of enterprise since the end of the Great War."

"That brings us to Walter McPhael and his wife Jennifer."

"Well, sir, not quite, but I am getting there. There are a few more chapters to the story before we can bring it to present day."

"Continue then," I said.

"This Chinese mistress was a determined and resourceful woman. Her prince chose her well. When she arrived in Tehran she blended into the city, settled there, learned the language, and used the remaining wealth she had conserved to find herself a wealthy merchant for a husband. He married her because of her beauty and her dowry. She assumed his name, of course, and proceeded to bear him four children – all the while never telling him about her background or the Orb that she carried.

"We can only wonder where she kept it. Though it is tempting to believe she wore it as a jewel around her neck, most of us believe that is unlikely. The power of the Orb would have been too evident – too bright – to make that a reasonable option. Also, it is thought to be quite heavy. My own theory is that she wore it in a harness around her waist."

I interjected a thought: "I wonder why we don't know her name. If she settled in Tehran and married and had four children, how is it that we've lost her identity?"

"That is a reasonable question. I'll tell you honestly, the answer is so simple it will surprise you. She changed her name when she arrived in the city. So, while we can identify her by the name of her Persian husband, we have no information about who she was before she arrived in the city."

"What was the name of her husband?"

"Ehsan Rajavi. He was the son of a wealthy merchant and he built the family business that he inherited and developed it into an international firm, trading goods on four different continents. He had his own ships and offices in large cities around the world – Tokyo, Beijing, London, Amsterdam, New York, San Francisco, Paris, Rome, and many others.

"The Chinese mistress took his last name and adopted the first name Soraya. The last of her wealth – the precious jewels given to her by the Chinese prince, who was by now, long dead in the war, enabled her to assist her new husband's business with an infusion of capital derived from the sale of her jewels.

"By all accounts she loved her husband, and he loved her. They were a popular couple in the city, invited to many of the higher society functions – in part because of his extraordinary financial success, and in part because she was a delightful addition to any dinner party.

"She had that special glow that seduced both men and women to be her friends and confidants. Sadly, she fell ill. Before she died of fever in 1886, she passed the Orb along to her oldest child, a daughter named Yasmin, entrusting her with whatever secrets she knew."

"You seem sure of this," I interjected. "We're talking about a mother-daughter relationship and the handover of what was essentially a private family heirloom. How can *you* be so confident that you have it right?"

Josephine nodded patiently and posed his fingertips together again beneath his chin and rested his head on them. "The truth is we might never have known, except the daughter was not careful. She showed it to other people: siblings, friends, suitors, and even her father eventually. Without fully understanding – and perhaps he felt betrayed by his now deceased wife – Mr. Rajavi claimed the Orb from his daughter. She resisted him, but she was not able to prevent him from taking it.

"Initially, Rajavi's inclination was to sell the Orb. He had no idea what it was, but he smelled a profit and held no sensitivity toward his deceased wife's preferences. As a matter of record, he locked the older daughter in her room to keep her out of his way while he explored the market. One night she cut her wrists and bled out on the floor by her locked door so that her blood flowed beneath it and was discovered the next morning by one of the family maids – a Chinese woman loyal to Soraya.

"The family tragedies of history often end on a poignant note. One of the sons, the third child of Soraya, a large boy named Omid, who by now was sixteen, was defiant toward his father. He broke down the door that sequestered his older sister and held her lifeless body, crying over it while swearing his revenge. He stole the Orb from his father and went into hiding with it. He had little money and nowhere to go. In desperation he challenged his father to a duel with swords.

"The boy was strong, but inexperienced, emotional, and overly confident. His father defeated him easily and in the melee, which was over within a matter of minutes, the boy tripped and fell in such a way that he landed on the tip of his own blade and severed his carotid artery.

"Moments later the boy was dead and his father, almost apoplectic now was raging at the sky and the sun as the crowd that watched. He had lost everything that mattered to him – his wife, his eldest daughter, and his oldest son. There are accounts that say his fine black hair turned course and white that very night. Almost certainly these accounts are apocryphal, but they tell of the family tragedy."

"What about the Orb? Where was it?"

"No one knew for a while. In fact, most of the family who knew about it had given up hope it would ever be found or recovered."

"But of course it was," I projected easily.

Josephine shrugged. He didn't like having his story interrupted. "Three months later it showed up in the mail, a small package addressed to Leila, Soraya's second daughter, who was fifteen at the time. She took it and ran away from home herself.

"Like her brother, she didn't get far. When they found her nine days later the Orb was not with her, and she would not say where it was. Her father, tried to beat it out of her. When that did not work, he starved her in the same room where her older sister had been confined. On the twenty-third day, Leila passed away without revealing where she had hidden the great prize."

"Your unknown Chinese mistress raised children as tough as she was."

Josephine's nod was tight and grim. "I tip my hat as well. She did – though they paid a steep price for it."

"Where does the narrative flow next?"

"Into a dark hole for many years. Nobody knew where the Orb was. Nobody heard anything about it. For almost fifteen years, it was as though it had ceased to exist. Obviously someone must have had it in their possession. Most people eventually forgot about it.

"Ehsan Rajavi spent the rest of his life looking for it, though he was a broken man by then. His wife had died and he was directly responsible for the deaths of his three children. He was consumed by greed and obsessed by a desire to find the Orb, but he never did.

"Eventually, Rajavi died in 1894, succumbing to a fever similar to the one that claimed his wife eight years before. Some who knew him claimed he had succumbed to grief.

"I must say that seems a generous interpretation. I perceive him to have been a hard and brutal man. Essentially, he killed all three of his children in his pursuit of an artifact of which he knew nothing about, other than it might have been worth a few pennies."

"How many men through history," I asked, "have sacrificed everything they should have cared about – wives, children, lovers, parents, and siblings for some far-off, unobtainable goal?"

"Plenty," Josephine agreed. "Greed is a powerful force. It sweeps men along like a raging river."

"When does the Orb resurface again?" I asked.

"About twelve years ago an old man, a Chinese peasant, probably a former railroad laborer, returned home to his native province of Fujian in the south of China to die. That was not uncommon. Many Chinese laborers went home to die. The story this one told before he passed away garnered attention in his village, but it took a few years for it to circulate out of his province and reach the ears of a man in Hong Kong who had some inkling of what it might have meant."

"Another story then?"

Josephine smiled tolerantly at my unspoken frustration. "The Chinese are a patient people. The layers of rumor and myth that you have heard frustrate you, but this is how our history is formed and understood. We are an ancient culture. We have developed the forbearance to listen quietly and understand slowly as we piece together the clues of our past. Expectations are generally modest among my countrymen. We've learned to sift for years in order to arrive at some small truths about our past."

"What story did the man Fujian province tell before he died?"

"He said there had been an arrival of a succession of Chinese coming from Persia into the San Francisco area around the turn of the century – many of whom seemed to have connections to Adolf Sutro and his Cliff House. He had seen them and talked with them himself because he had worked for some years as a gardener at the Cliff House."

"What was so remarkable about this man's tale?"

"First, it was interesting to realize how many Chinese had immigrated to California via Tehran."

I brought the last of the cigarette to my lips while I thought this over. "What does that mean to you?"

"To me, it suggests the Chinese mistress was either following an established migration route; or she established it herself and others from her community followed her. Either way, it seems that someone from the Chinese community in Tehran acquired the artifact and traveled with it, very likely smuggling it into California via the tunnels under the Cliff House."

"Who could they have been, and how would they have come into possession of the Orb?"

"The Chinese mistress known as Soraya filled her household with loyal

141

Chinese house servants, most of them from her home region. One can only speculate, but after the deaths of her three natural born children, it seems likely the Orb fell into the possession of a maid. Loyal to her mistress and to China, this maid would have made a concerted effort to keep the artifact out of Ehsan Rajavi's hands and move it away to a receptive community of her native people."

"Do you know then when it arrived in the US?"

Josephine shook his head. "Not the year. After interviewing dozens of immigrants in this country and more in Persia, I estimate it arrived in the US through the Cliff House, perhaps two years, maybe three, before the fire occurred."

"Hmmm," I said, mulling it over. "I think that brings us right up to present day. Do you know where your artifact is now?"

Josephine smiled graciously. "I thought it might be in Lot seventy-three – and so did you. I'm not ready to give up on that notion."

I shrugged. "Do you know where Lot seventy-three is now?"

Josephine shook his head sadly.

"What do you know about Walter McPhael? What's his role?" I asked.

"He's my partner," Josephine confessed. "He's helped me at the Persian end of this adventure, opening doors there, obtaining information and government records for us to study. We cooperate on moving a variety of different goods – art works, antique furniture, heirloom jewels, and ancient manuscripts – between his city of Tehran and my cities of San Francisco and Shanghai. To explain: I was born in Shanghai. I came to San Francisco when I was twelve."

"McPhael is your partner? That's interesting," I said. "According to his wife, he's disappeared. She says she hasn't seen or heard from him in two weeks. Based on what she told me, neither his San Francisco office nor his Tehran office has heard from him recently. Nobody seems to know where he is."

"Does Mrs. McPhael have a theory about what happened to her husband?"

"She thinks he's been murdered."

"Based on what information?"

I shrugged tightly. "I couldn't say."

"Have the police been brought in? What do they think?"

"I don't know," I replied, taking advantage of the double question he asked me and the time since I had last spoken with Jennifer. I didn't see anything to be gained by mentioning her concern that her husband had been living a double life. "What do you think?" I asked. "He's your partner. Sometimes partners know more than wives do."

Josephine frowned and shook his head in an ambiguous response. "I can't say."

"When did you last hear from him?" I inquired."

"It's been awhile," Josephine conceded. "About eleven days, maybe twelve, I'd estimate. It could be more"

"Is that a long period given past experience?"

Josephine nodded. "I am worried. It is a long time for him to be out of touch."

"His wife estimated she hadn't heard from him in two weeks. That would be fourteen days. How does that strike you?"

"Was she precise about that?"

I shrugged and nodded at the same time.

"Some women are prone to hysteria. They might over estimate the time."

"Is that what she's done?"

"Perhaps," Josephine said with a sigh.

"Have you spoken with her in the past couple weeks?"

"No."

"Then your partner is missing. What have you done about it?"

"I am trying find him," Josephine claimed. He swept a hand toward the sofa. "My boys are looking high and low. We've got messages out to any place he might check, and our local network has been alerted in case anyone sees him."

"Then he's disappeared. Has he ever done that before?"

"No."

"That could mean something or not," I said. "Have you met his wife, Jennifer?"

"Yes, do you know her?"

I nodded.

"She is lovely, isn't she?"

"She is," I conceded.

"If I read your body language correctly, a beautiful woman does not impress you so much. Am I right about that?"

I finished my cigarette and leaned forward to mash it into the ashtray on the low table between us. "The world is full of beautiful women. Not all of them are anything special."

Chapter Twenty-Eight

"Tell me about Sutro and his Cliff House," I said once I had the next Chesterfield glowing. "It seems to be a centerpiece in this drama."

"Adolf Sutro was a genius," Josephine said. "He solved the problems of how to drain and ventilate the Comstock Lode, and it made him a very rich man, indeed. There are plenty of interesting stories about his house on the cliff. One version of the house was heavily damaged in 1887 by a dynamite explosion when the schooner *Parallel* ran aground and blew one wing of it to smithereens. They heard the blast a hundred miles away. The structure was repaired, but then completely destroyed later by a fire on Christmas night in 1894.

"Sutro was not to be deterred and he built a larger, grander house – a Victorian Chateau that some called the 'the Gingerbread Palace," which he opened in in 1896. That same year he opened the Baths nearby, just above it. Sutro was an engineer – and he was a tunneler. His solution for the Comestock Lode was the Sutro tunnel. You know what they work with?"

It dawned on me suddenly. "Dynamite," I whispered.

Josephine nodded evenly, smiling now. "That's exactly right. Dynamite. Makes you wonder what really happened with the schooner *Parallel*. Maybe it didn't run aground – maybe it was delivering something . . ."

I got there before he did: ". . . through a tunnel in the cliff."

"My, my!" Josephine exclaimed, grinning broadly at me.

"Easy," I soothed. "I haven't bought the automobile yet. I've only suggested an interest to test drive it."

"You know where this goes," Josephine stated.

"Convince me," I replied. "I'm a cynic."

"You *are* a shrewd man. I'll remind you of the letter that I have, a letter I think you will be interested to see. We should arrange a time for me to show it to you."

"What else is in this letter?"

"It's not without controversy, but some of us, including myself, believe it was written by the Chinese prince – a few days *after* he helped his mistress escape from the Forbidden City."

"After?"

"That's right. *After*. It was recovered *after* his death in the battle for the Forbidden City."

"How did it fall into your possession and why do you think it's meaningful?"

"It is meaningful because it followed his mistress out of China, through the route to Tehran, and from there, on to San Francisco – though it took many years, passing through many hands."

"Did it ever catch up to his mistress?"

Josephine pursed his lips and the dark of his eyes circumnavigated the room. "I don't believe it ever did."

"You hold it now?"

"I do."

"What is the Orb and what are its powers?" I asked.

"What did Dr. Orion tell you?"

I shook my head, smiling sadly. "I'm asking you."

Josephine smiled triumphantly. "I doubt Dr. Orion actually knows much about the Orb or it's nature."

"Are you so sure that you do?" I queried.

Josephine smiled softly and moved his jaw back and forth in a tired gesture that seemed to indicate his defenses were down. "The truth is, I do not entirely understand it myself. No living man does."

"Can you even describe it physically?"

"Depending on who you believe, it's a small polished blue sphere – about the size of a large marble – set tightly into a small gold base. Some writings say it glows at night, others say you can feel its heat if you hold your hand a foot away from it. One rumor holds that it comes in a small wooden box of ancient design. The box is lined with lead, which is said to contain its powers."

"Are we talking about magic?" I spit a small fragment of tobacco out of my mouth as I shook my head.

"You would be skeptical of that," Josephine observed, narrowing his eyes. "No, I think it's a matter of physics. There are rare elements in this universe that are not well understood, elements that are unknown to the Western chemists and physicists and natural scientists."

"Perhaps there is some coherence to this after all? The Orb is relatively small, and might be packed inside of a lead-encased wooden box?"

"Yes," Josephine replied.

"You mentioned it's heavy?"

Josephine nodded. "By reputation – at least heavy relative to its size."

"Have you an estimate?"

"I believe it probably weighs about twenty pounds."

"That's a dense bauble if it's really the size of a large marble."

"Indeed."

"Do you think it's in this city?"

"I do. What do you think?"

"Dr. Orion thinks it is. Mrs. Orion thinks it is. You think it is. Several others seemed to think it is. How could I say it is not?"

Josephine nodded.

"Maybe it is here," I said. "Maybe we can find it. Are we working together?"

"Would Dr. Orion agree to throw his lot in with me?"

"For equal shares?"

"You, me, and Dr. Orion?"

I wasn't in the game for a share, though there was no benefit to saying so. A man like Josephine would be inclined to mistrust another man who did not seem to be motivated by the same sort of greed that motivated him. "Jennifer McPhael might have a claim," I said instead.

"She might, but unless you speak for her, let's allow her to speak for herself."

"Fair enough. I'd like to see the evidence you have tonight. Meanwhile, I'll try to speak to Dr. Orion and also to Mrs. McPhael. I need to understand their views before I make commitments on their behalves."

"Understood," Josephine replied with a canny half-grin. He twirled his bowler hat off his knee and spun it around on a finger and then popped it on top of his head. "I keep a room at the Palace Hotel. Ask for me at the front desk and they will escort you up to me. Shall we say seven o'clock tonight?"

"Let's make it eight."

"I will have a light dinner available in case you might be hungry."

*

The plush Cadillac with the curtains still drawn moved a few blocks and took a few turns. Mr. Josephine distracted me the entire time with a flowing patter of praise, questions, and predictions.

When we finally came to a stop, he shook my hand vigorously and told me I was one in a million. He gave me to understand he was gravely concerned about my safety and if anything happened to me his life would be over. I didn't think that was the case, but didn't bother to contradict him.

After climbing out of the automobile, I took a moment to adjust to the bright, late afternoon sunlight. Directly across the street from where I stood was the Kong Chow Temple on Pine Street. It had a Victorian arch cornice crowning the top of the façade and a marble slab with gilt Chinese characters.

A small boy dressed in black robe and cap sat on the curb, staring absently at me. His fingers chattered absently to the rest of the world, sending a message I did not understand. I was in Chinatown. For some reason that fact had never seemed so comforting before.

I drew a breath, glanced at the sky, and tapped the loaded pistol beneath my arm just to be sure it was there. My head was spinning from all the old tales I'd spent the afternoon listening to.

Chapter Twenty-Nine

The sculptor Douglas Tilden had completed *The Mechanics* the year before the century turned. Built solidly, it survived the temblor of nineteen-oh-six. It had been commissioned by a man named James M. Donahue to commemorate the memory of his father who had opened, along with his two brothers, a blacksmith's shop in eighteen-forty-nine that later expanded into the foundry that became the Union Iron Works.

Thirty-five years after the sculpture had been completed, the ten-ton statue at the intersection of Battery, Bush, and Market Streets still showed the same four muscular ironworkers punching rivet holes in a piece of shipping plate. I circled it once and then drove a few blocks down Market and made a wide loop back around.

When I came by on the second pass Jennifer McPhael was there waiting for me, standing with her weight on her back foot and her front ankle partially turned while she calmly smoked a cigarette. She wore a long dark skirt with a charcoal sweater that had a long neck that had been folded over once below her chin. Her hair was neatly combed and arranged, pushed back behind an ear on one side.

When she saw me, she flicked the cigarette away and shifted her weight to lean toward the curb. I hadn't even reached a full stop before she opened the door and climbed in beside me.

I accelerated through the circle as the door closed heavily from the force of the automobile's motion. We didn't speak at first. I took the second right off the circle and worked my way around to slide down Hyde Street.

"Where's Johnny Drake?" I asked. "I was hoping to meet him."

"I left him a message, but I haven't heard from him since yesterday."

"Does that bother you?"

"It does," Jennifer replied calmly. "Where are we going?"

"Sausalito, back to the house where you found me."

"Why there?"

"I want to talk to the Orions and I don't want to do it over the telephone. I want to look them in the eye when they hear my questions. Anyway, it's not a bad idea to get us both out of the city for a few hours."

"You think one of us might be hot?"

"I think we're both hot, sweetheart."

"Men don't usually talk to me that way. I'm a married woman," she reminded me.

"You haven't heard from your investigator today," I reminded her.

Jennifer was quiet as she squirmed in her seat and sunk down in it a little. "I'm so frightened," she whispered without responding to my comment.

I glanced over at her. Influenced by the small cleft in her chin, the fullness of her lips, and the dark, deep pools of her irises that stared back at me, I'd formed the impression she was immune to everything. Now, I knew better. She was terrified, rattled to an extent that she never had been before. Her calm exterior was a willful projection, a veneer that covered the deep-seated vulnerabilities of a woman who saw everything that mattered to her crumbling away.

It wouldn't do either of us any good for me to pity her. "What happened?" I asked her, switching my eyes back to the road ahead.

"Do you mind if I smoke?"

"Go ahead."

With a pearl encased lighter that she flicked rapidly several times, she lighted a slender cigarette and exhaled a long thin stream of smoke toward the window that she cracked open for that purpose. After she dropped the lighter back into her purse, she squirmed over a little further on the seat so that her shoulder was against mine – though her face was turned to look out the passenger side window as she continued to smoke.

We traveled two blocks without speaking.

"What happened?" I eventually asked again.

"You really don't know?"

"Tell me."

"I'm not sure myself of the details."

"How can that be? Is there any word on your husband?"

"No."

"Nothing at all?"

"That's right. I'm so distracted; I don't know what to do. I'm beside myself. Don't you understand? I constantly check the mail, the messages. When the telephone rings I jump. I call his office every two hours and they never know anything. No one has seen or heard from him. No one knows where he is. There are no clues. I have a million thoughts dashing through my head."

"Is there more?" I asked, sensing there was.

She hesitated, as though telling me would somehow make the truth worse. "Two men were murdered last night. My husband knew both of them. I'm so worried about him and now I'm frightened for myself."

I was thinking about the two dead men I'd found that morning and the girl with the sigh on her lips as she died in arms. "I know about the murders," I said, without revealing any more then that.

Jennifer was too distracted by her own anxiety to notice my reaction. "They weren't bad men. They weren't cheats or anything. I don't know why anyone would kill them, but they were in the same business as my husband and I fear this *must* be related to his disappearance."

"Did they do business with your husband?"

"Jameson Tucker did. They worked together on deals, antique shipments on occasion. They were also competitors. I don't know any more then that. My husband rarely discusses his work with me. He only drops odd comments now and then about the people we meet socially."

"How well did you know Tucker?"

"Not well at all. He was a very handsome man, but his manners with woman were awkward, especially with married women."

"Did he make a pass at you?" I asked.

"Nothing like that," she replied with a hint of annoyance in her tone. "He was always a gentleman, though he was a bit eccentric."

"What about the other man who was murdered? Did your husband know him too?"

"I think so. At least he talked about him on occasion. Walter was very impressed by him and the skills that he had. Mr. Chi was Chinese, you know, and very well connected in the local community, revered actually."

"Did you ever meet him?"

"Mr. Chi? No, of course not. We never socialize with anyone from the Chinese business community. That isn't done."

"If you never met him and your husband never talks about work, how is it that you knew of him?"

"I said my husband *rarely* talks about his work, and the reason he talked about Mr. Chi was that he was hoping that Mr. Chi would help him obtain a very rare artifact. It was something uniquely valuable and of Chinese origin. Don't bother to ask me what it was – I don't know. All I know is that my husband thought highly of Mr. Chi and now both he and Jameson Tucker are dead – both murdered horribly in their own homes."

I glanced over at her, expecting to see her beginning to cry, but she wasn't. Her jaw was tight with determination. She sat up straighter than before, finishing her cigarette, which she stubbed delicately into the ashtray. "Your PI must have some thoughts about that," I said, bringing the conversation back around to my original question. "What does Drake think?"

My eyes were back on the road again, but from the corner of my eye I saw her turn her head to look at me. "I wouldn't know, would I? As I said, I haven't heard from Mr. Drake today. What do you suppose that means?"

"It could mean anything or nothing at all. Are you worried about him now too."

"He's a big boy and he is a professional," she replied. A trace of coolness had slipped back into her voice.

I glanced over at her quickly and then reset my eyes on the street. "Three men connected to you are now dead or missing and you're frightened for your own safety. It seems possible Drake could also be in some danger himself."

"He chose a dangerous profession. I'm paying him. I can't worry about him too."

"Is that what you'll say about me if I turn up missing?"

Jennifer drew a sharp breath, as if something heavy had just fallen into her lap. "I didn't mean it to sound so cold. Without you, I have nothing, and though I've only known you for a short time, I would be so very upset if *anything* happened to you. You must believe me."

"Shhhh. Let it go. Sometimes my sense of irony gets the better of me."

"You *must* know how grateful I am for your help. I would be lost without you."

"Shhhh," I hushed again. "Things aren't desperate. I have a few ideas."

"Please believe me. I am bitterly upset about the deaths of those two gentlemen."

"I do believe you," I replied quietly.

We drove without speaking for a while. The large bay ahead of us, at the far end of Hyde Street where the street lamps ended, appeared suddenly as a blackened area of depth and mystery.

"How can we ever understand the horrible things that men do?" Jennifer blurted.

"We have the philosophies to help with that."

She sighed and I turned to look at her. "Also religion," she said when our eyes met.

I nodded. "That too."

"There's something I've wondered about," she said in a rush. "This may sound strange coming from me at this moment. Although I am from Persia, I am Christian-born and I was raised to believe in Jesus. When I'm frightened or sorrowful, such as times like this, I have my Bible to turn to."

"What is it you've wondered about?"

"Why do you think Judas Iscariot hanged himself after he betrayed Jesus Christ?"

"That might depend on why he became Jesus' disciple in the first place."

"Why do you think he did that?"

I smiled grimly to myself inside the darkened automobile. "I think it was opportunity. He was a thief, a crook; he followed Jesus because he thought power and riches would follow. In truth, isn't that what most of history's prophets were after?"

"I wouldn't know."

"I think it is. I believe that's what motivated Judas. He was disappointed to learn that money and influence were not the plan for Jesus' ministry."

"Do you think he betrayed him for spite?"

I nodded. "Spite and thirty pieces of silver."

"That brings us back to my question: Why did he hang himself after the betrayal?"

I glanced over at her again. Twilight veiled her eyes. I said: "Some would say he hanged himself out of remorse for betraying Jesus once he realized what he had done."

"One reading of Matthew would imply that."

"Why are you bothered by it?" I asked.

"Because it means something changed. Judas was a thief. He betrayed Jesus Christ for thirty pieces of silver, but after the deed he gave the silver back to the centurions and then died by his own hand. Why would he do that? Why would any thief behave with such remorse?"

"I think that takes you back to the reason he was an apostle in the first place," I said. "He was chosen for a reason."

Jennifer remained silent for a while as we moved through the city. Presently she said: "The chief priests and ancients used Judas' returned blood money to buy a potters field – a barren field within which to bury paupers and strangers, people who had no one."

I thought she was going to say more, but she fell silent again and remained silent as we completed our long float down Hyde Street.

*

The last remnants of the sun dissolved as we reached the Pier. All that was left of it was a faint orange line in the sky with ever darkening shades of blue above it. Within minutes the orange had disappeared entirely and the blue was shading quickly to black.

The auto ferry carried us across the bay toward the Sausalito point. We remained in the Ford all the way across, aware of each other's heartbeat, though we did not speak while over the water. Once on Highway 101 we rolled the windows down to feel the racing air as I drove fast through the curves that led us along the Shoreline Highway and up into the forested hills.

Chapter Thirty

The grounds of the Orion's house were dreary and lifeless. At first I wondered if I had the right address as I curled up the shadowy drive. When I knew we were in the right place, I parked where I had the day before.

The house was the same tall structure, layered in the style of an oversized Italian villa. At night it appeared different. It had none of the exuberance of the afternoon I had sat drinking champagne with the Orions. The top floors were entirely dark, though curtained lights showed in several of the windows on the first floor. Something about it seemed off.

From the parking apron, I walked back to the driveway and found the wide courtyard doors were still partially open. A chain held them closed, but a slender man could push them apart far enough to slip in. I squeezed my way through.

By the light of the stars and half moon that filtered down through the trees I could see the long, rectangular pool was right where it had been. Its black tile glistened serenely at the bottom. Cupid still spouted a steady stream of water into the air.

The large pool house remained completely dark and uninviting. Missing was the black Auburn V-12 Boattail Speedster with its white-walled tires. It was nowhere to be seen and there were no lights showing at the back of the house.

Working my way back through the courtyard doors, I waved at Jennifer to wait in the Ford while I took the cobbled stones up to the massive front door of the house. There I moved the knocker around to make as much noise as I thought necessary. I stepped back from it and waited and a moment later the lamp beside the door was switched on and the door opened a crack.

"Hello?" a man I had never seen before answered. A black pipe was clamped between his teeth and he wore gold wire rim spectacles that amplified the shrunken pupils of his rectangular eyes.

"My name's Huddleston," I told him. "I'm here to see Dr. Orion."

"Hmmm, my name's Williams, Bert Williams. I don't know anyone named Orion. Are you sure you have the right house?"

I leaned back on my heels. "Dr. Randolph Orion and his wife Susan?"

Williams pursed his lips and shook his head. Confusion underlined the frown that creased his brow. Intrigued by the mystery, he allowed the door to open a little wider. "I'm afraid I don't know them. I think you're lost. Do you have a street address? Maybe I can help you."

I read off the address the Orion's had given me, knowing already that I was standing there.

William's expression moved from mild confusion to bewilderment. "That's this address, for sure, but it's our house and I never heard of anybody named Orion. Shall I ask my wife?"

"I don't want to trouble you," I said. "Apparently I got it wrong. I get numbers reversed sometimes, probably what happened this time. Would you mind if I asked one question?"

"Go ahead."

"Were you home yesterday afternoon?"

William's expression relaxed into a smile. "No, sir. The wife and I won a radio contest. We took the train down to Los Angeles to attend a dinner event with the Hollywood set honoring Myrna Loy for her latest movie. We only just returned home a short while ago. Imagine that! It was brilliant really – there must have been at least two hundred people in attendance and we were guests of honor, seated three tables away from Ms. Loy. William Powell wasn't there, of course."

"I thought he was terrific in *Manhattan Melodrama*," I added to keep the conversation going.

"Oh, yes, he was, he certainly was. Of course, they told us he was filming another movie and he was awfully sorry he couldn't be there to honor Miss Loy in her golden moment."

"That must have been an exciting evening."

"It surely was. The little dog, Asta, from the movie, you know, was there. She was a big hit and we took a photograph of her as they paraded her around on a leash. Have you seen the *The Thin Man* yet?"

"No, but I've read Hammett's book," I replied.

Williams nodded without sensing my irony. He was so pleased to have a chance to tell the story of his big adventure that he lost track of why I might have asked whether they had been home the previous afternoon. Privately, I wondered why wealthy people seemed to enjoy experiences that were designated as "free" when they could just as easily have purchased them at no sacrifice to themselves.

"I'm curious," I started. "I've never won anything like this myself. How did you enter the contest?"

"That's the beauty of it," Williams laughed, spreading his arms wide with the pipe in his left hand. "We didn't do *anything* to enter the contest – nothing at all. We don't even listen to the radio station that sponsored the award. Matter of fact, my wife and I almost never listen to any radio at all. We're readers, really. We prefer books. The Mrs. likes the classics – Shakespeare, Cooper, Poe, that sort of stuff. Myself, I like more contemporary writers.

Have you ever read James M. Cain? *The Postman Always Rings Twice* was my favorite novel this year."

I nodded, smiling. "I heard about it, though I haven't read it yet."

"It's something of a lark to have had an experience like this. I'm not as impressed by it as most other people would be, of course. As I said, the wife and I are readers. The movies are something we visit only on rare occasion, maybe four or five times a year. Its not the medium we hold with."

Williams smiled broadly and seemed to be pleased with himself, so I smiled too and nodded. "If I understand, you and your wife were away for the past two or three days on this trip that you won. That must have been terrific."

"Three days and two nights, all expenses paid. Say, if you had arrived here a couple hours ago, you'd be lost for the night. We only returned home an hour ago. Can't imagine what you would have done if I hadn't been home to answer the door!"

I grinned in false conspiracy with him. "I have good fortune once in a while. Congratulations on the radio prize. I'm sure it was an experience you'll never forget."

Williams had a sizeable grin on his face and he wanted to continue chatting. Expansively, he waved the pipe out in front of his chest, sweeping it in an oversized figure eight. I realized it was the first chance he'd had to tell his story to someone. "I can only begin to say how much."

"Thank you for your time," I said. "I hope Mrs. Williams enjoyed herself as well."

"She surely did and I can call her over if you want to hear her view of things."

I shook my head. "I'm already sorry to have bothered you tonight," I replied, tipping my fedora as I took a step back.

"Oh, no bother at all, sir. Good luck finding your address. It's probably several miles on down the road. The name Orion doesn't ring any bells with me, but they must be around here somewhere. A lot of new people have moved in the past couple of years and we haven't yet met them all. Keep going and I'm sure you'll find them."

"I'm sure I will," I said.

Williams closed the door behind me as I retraced my steps back to the Ford.

"Did you learn anything?" Jennifer asked me as I switched on the motor.

"I sure did. There are plenty of friendly, gullible people in this sweet old world of ours."

Chapter Thirty-One

The night was dark, though the shining stars above were unhampered by intervening cloud cover. Halfway across the bay, the water got a little choppy and the bite of the air was cold. We leaned against the rail on the right side of the ferry. Jennifer inclined her body toward me and shivered.

"I wish I could light a cigarette out here," she said.

"Not in this breeze. I'll go inside with you if you like. I bet we can find a cup of black coffee too."

She shook her head. "I want to stay out here. I love the feel of the howling wind blowing. It runs through my hair and makes me feel alive, like I might live forever. It takes my breath away."

"The stars up there aren't so bad either," I offered. The fog that encased the city lights ahead of us did not reach out over the water. Our shoulders were touching now and her hip was pressed up against mine.

"I do care for my husband, you know." She said it with her mouth close to my ear and her right finger tips on my chin. I felt the moisture on her lips, almost expecting a kiss.

"I wouldn't have thought otherwise," I replied.

"I'm a married woman and a Christian, but I'm cold and scared. Sometimes a woman needs someone to comfort her."

I put my arm around her shoulder and pulled her close so that more of her body was pressed against me. "Shhhh," I whispered, with my mouth close to her ear. "You don't have to explain."

She put a hand inside my jacket and brought it up over my shoulder to hold it behind my collar. Her dark eyes were bright as they looked into mine. "Please don't leave me alone," she whispered. "I've never been so afraid in my life and I feel safe when I'm with you."

"We'll get back to the city soon. I have an appointment tonight at eight o'clock. I have work to do."

"An appointment with who?"

I wasn't sure how much to tell her. "I'm seeing a guy who thinks he knows something about something. The way things are going he might be on your husband's list of connections."

"Do you think he knows something about my husband?"

I shrugged. It was dark, but we were close enough that I knew she could feel the motion of my answer. She also could probably sense my ambivalence.

"Who is he?" she asked.

I spoke the words easily, as though I didn't realize the importance of what I was saying. "A guy named Josephine. He's Chinese, though you might not know it by looking at him. Apparently, he's been successful in his business and now behaves as though he is westernized. Do you know him?"

She didn't say anything the English language would have recognized, but the response her body sent was palpable. A shiver that had nothing to do with the temperature of the air caught her and shook her fiercely. Her body moved away from mine and she pitched suddenly toward the rail as though she might jump over or wretch violently. I caught her a moment later and realized she wasn't going anywhere. With her palms on the rail she leaned over it as far as she could stretch.

"Nights like this, I like to stare down at the water as it's creased by the ferry's bow. Look how the churning turns the water into such bright white foam against the darkness down there. It's almost preternatural. If you were out here on deck by yourself and you were careful not to be spotted, you could easily climb over the edge and into the water and nobody would ever know what had happened to you. The current would take you and carry you out into the ocean. They would never find you."

"Why are you saying this?"

"It's a silly, desperate thought. It doesn't mean anything. Don't you ever have thoughts like that?"

I wasn't going to tell her what thoughts went through my head in my most desperate moments. Instead, I said: "It's cold out here. Let's go inside and get that cup of coffee now."

"You needn't worry," she said. "I wasn't really going to jump over."

*

With cups of hot coffee in our hands, we found a table toward the back of the cabin where few people sat. Jennifer sat down first and I took the seat next to her on the bench, leaving a few inches between us. She closed that gap almost immediately by moving her leg, though she didn't look at me or speak. The coffee was bitter, but it was steaming hot and it felt good going down, spreading its warmth into my chest and stomach.

"I suppose you must think I'm an awful silly fool," she said after we had been sitting quietly for a while. Well-dressed people moved around as they passed us, rolling unsteadily with the motion of the craft on the rough waters. Jennifer did not seem bothered by the motion of the boat or the people going by.

"I do," I told her. "I thought you should have out of the cold air the first time I suggested we seek coffee."

156

With a grudging smile, she nodded. "It is terrible coffee," she insisted.

"Tell me about Josephine," I said. I saw no need to mention that he'd already told me they had met and that he was doing business with her husband.

"Where are you meeting him?" she asked, evading my question again to buy for time.

"He keeps a 'possibility' at the Palace Hotel. He called it a 'room'; my guess is that it's more than that. Tell me what you know about him."

"I've heard of him," she admitted with a shrug. "My husband thought he was dangerous."

I didn't bite on that. "Based on what I was told, I thought maybe you had met him."

Jennifer bit her lip for theatrical effect and then, moving slowly, nodded at me and tilted her shoulders my way. "I may have. If he's the one I'm thinking of, I believe I did meet him once. Yes, I think I did. It was last summer, a short exchange. As I recall, he was arriving late, as Walter and I were leaving early. We met at the door, introductions were made, hands were shook, cheeks were kissed. You know the routine. I barely remember him. I doubt we would recognize one another if we passed on the street."

"Except that you would never pass on the street. You wouldn't be walking in the same neighborhood."

She pulled herself back from the rebuke. "Why must you be harsh with me?"

I took a sip of my coffee. "Why do you think I would believe what you just told me?" I asked.

"Oh, why wouldn't you? You must believe me."

It was my turn to have a reaction that had nothing to do with the temperature of the air. "Why must I?"

"Please?" Jennifer leaned close to me so that I could feel the warmth of her face and her breath, and catch the scent of her perfume, which smelled like burnt orange and vanilla. It was a scent designed to chemically break through a man's last defenses.

I smiled gently and falsely into it as though I were immune to it. "Why not come clean and tell me about it. Josephine already told me he knows you, that he is working with your husband, that he seems to have some ideas about our situation. I'd say he has a rather old-fashioned opinion about you."

"What did *that* man say about me?" she asked with an ambivalent mixture of anxiety and anger.

"He didn't say much about you at all. He didn't have to. He told me he's partnered with your husband and has met you a time or two. From what I understand, your husband is an important associate. It seems he helps Josephine at the Persian end of things, opening doors and obtaining information and government records. Josephine indicated that he and your husband have cooperated on shipping a variety of goods between Tehran, San Francisco, and Shanghai."

"I don't know anything about it –not at any detailed level. Walter doesn't tell me about things like this."

"You said your husband might be smuggling stolen and counterfeit antiquities into America."

Jennifer nodded without looking at me. She studied the coffee in the bottom of her cup intensely.

"You also mentioned he might be smuggling people from Iran, China, India, and Egypt as well."

She nodded again, and again her eyes didn't meet mine. I didn't think the coffee in the bottom of her cup could be that interesting.

"I'm not supposed to talk about my husband's business activities. He would be very angry with me."

"If he weren't missing. What else can you tell me about him?"

"Nothing. I shouldn't be talking about this."

"You already have."

"Please let it go. Let's change the subject."

"This is the only subject we have to talk about. You asked me – no, you begged me – to help you find your husband."

"I know I did, but I don't want to dwell on this part of his life and really – you must believe me – I don't know much about his business or the people he does business with. He does not talk about that with me. I'm a woman and I'm not allowed in."

I nodded and made patient noises in the back of my throat as though I were sympathetic. "Josephine was clear that he and your husband were partners, working together. He seems to be almost as distressed as you are about your husband's disappearance. I interpret that as concern about a lost investment on his part. If it's any comfort, he was explicit that he's looking for your husband too. His words were something to the effect that '*his boys are looking high and low.*'"

As if her past had slapped her on the cheek, Jennifer jerked her head around toward me and flinched when our eyes met. "That's fine," she managed to reply before she stared down again into the swirling mystery at the bottom of her coffee cup.

"Sure, unless your husband betrayed or cheated Josephine before he disappeared."

Jennifer's eyes expanded and she looked away from her cup, turning her head away from me, as if by instinct, sensing my gaze might have the power to read her thoughts. When she turned back to look at me, she shook her head

158

and tightened her lips. "I won't ever believe that about Walter."

"Your loyalty is commendable. Is it realistic?"

"I think it is."

"That leads me to a questions that have formed in my thoughts over the past few hours."

"What are they?" she asked anxiously, worrying her fingernails together.

"I hesitate to intrude, but I am curious to know more about your marriage. How was it arranged and by who?"

"My parents arranged it."

"How did they choose him?"

"We were born in the same town. His mother knew my mother; his older sister was in school with my older sister. My parents thought he was successful and on the right trajectory. He heard about me and approached my parents."

"Is that how it is commonly done?"

Jennifer nodded. "It is typical."

"How old were you at the time?"

"I was nineteen years old when we married; I'm twenty-two now. Walter was thirty-six then. He's thirty-eight now. That also is typical for arranged marriages in my country. They work by pairing financially successful business men – men who are in their thirties or forties, sometimes older – with younger, pliant wives."

"Are you *pliant*?" I asked.

Jennifer's eyes found mine. A spark of something appeared momentarily and then her eyes narrowed in telling fashion. "I've tried to be. It's what my parents wanted."

I drew a breath. "Surely you know this is quite unfamiliar to me. Has it been a happy marriage? Do you love your husband? I'm not talking about the polite mutual respect necessary to make things work on a daily basis. I'm wondering if you love your husband and if you do, what that means to you?"

She responded carefully, parsing her words as she spoke. "My marriage *is* very important to me. It's a sacred commitment, a responsibility, a duty that I committed to on behalf of my family."

I grinned at her. "You didn't answer even one of my questions."

"You asked if I have a happy marriage and if I love my husband."

I nodded. "That's right and you told me that your marriage is a sacred duty. I don't need a lecture in the Christian sacrament of marriage. I'm asking if you love your husband in a meaningful way."

"There is no such concept in my culture. It is irrelevant to my parents and to my broader family. It is irrelevant to my husband's family. My honor is based entirely on meeting the commitment my family has asked me to make to my husband. My personal feelings, my happiness, whether or not we are

159

in love with each other... These things do not matter. What matters is that I fulfill my duties as a wife and a daughter as they are written."

I drank the last of my coffee. "I'll accept that as part of your answer, but I'll also offer my own interpretation of your response. It is this: I think you have *not* found happiness in your marriage and you do *not* love your husband. You've told me it's a duty, and that's all right so far as it goes. It's a simple truth at one level to put it that way. If you did love your husband, it would have been very simple for you to have said so."

"You shame me."

I decided to let her know I wasn't so easily fooled. "No I don't. That's only what your culture requires you to say. You know as well as I do, that I'm right."

"Don't be so judgmental of me. I have my family in Tehran to think about."

Beneath us, the ferry shifted abruptly with a sudden swell and Jennifer slid from her seat to land against me hard. Instinctively I caught and held her close with one arm as the boat fiercely rocked to and fro for several minutes beneath us, shifting us about violently.

I braced a foot against the table legs and looped my other arm around a pole that ran between the floor and ceiling. Jennifer held on to me tightly, with both arms around my chest and her face pressed hard beneath my chin. Without intending to, I could feel both our hearts racing.

Chapter Thirty-Two

The ferry rocked about for several minutes. When it finally smoothed out, I glanced at my watch and saw we were within minutes of reaching the San Francisco pier. I eased my grip on the woman and separated myself from her. Jennifer leaned toward me, as if to resist my release. I put a palm on her shoulder and shook her a little.

"It's over," I reassured her.

"I think I'm going to be sick," she said in a hush. Her voice was as low as it could be.

"That's okay," I told her. "If you need to, it's best to do it straight away. No shame in it."

I put a hand beneath her forehead as she leaned over. When she was finished she sat up and wiped her mouth with a napkin and took a drink of water.

"It might be easier up on deck," I said.

"Why?"

"Most people find it to be. The fresh air helps and you can look off toward the lights on the horizon, which has a stabilizing effect on the gut."

"I don't want to go up there," she said. Then she was sick again. Afterward she agreed to go up on deck.

*

"Feeling any better?" I asked when we were standing at the rail again. The air was cold and blowing in quite a bit of spray. It tossed her hair around in a manner that she didn't seem to mind. The abrupt line of city lights at the wharf was close now and the dark surface of the water between us rippled mysteriously.

"I don't think so," she replied.

"I have a few more questions if you feel up to it, they're slightly less personal."

"Go ahead," she said.

"I'd like to know more about Walter's 'double life' as you called it. I assume you were referring to illegal smuggling operations."

She shrugged, as if even now she was reluctant to admit what she had already told me.

"Is there anything else you can tell me?"

She shook her head.

"How long has he been doing it? Who does he work with? Where does

161

he bank the proceeds?"

"No," she said stubbornly, shaking her head. "I don't know the answers to any of those questions, except that I venture Josephine is one of the people he works with."

"I've already given you that name and implied as much. Can't you tell me anything new?"

"I can't."

"Let's talk about Walter's cash flow problem."

"What do you want to know?"

"Everything. What can you tell me?"

She tilted her chin, stretching the cords of muscle beneath it taut. "This is agonizing for me."

I wasn't going to say anything to make it easier for her. I simply waited.

Eventually, she turned her entire upper body from the waist up toward me, squaring her shoulders as she leaned against me to place her chin on the back of my shoulder. Her arms were tight around my torso. Her voice when she spoke was muffled now behind me. "Why are doing this to me?"

"I'm trying to learn what I can about your husband and his situation. You told me that you had to let a housekeeper go, that money was tight, and that maybe Walter's business was in some type of trouble." I shifted so I could see her face.

She nodded to acknowledge my words. Viewed in semi-profile, the lights of the wharf reflected in the eye that was nearest to me – a miniature urban still life.

"Do you know why money is tight?" I asked.

"No," she said, absently.

"There are probably only a few possible explanations."

"I'm sure you'll tell me what they are."

I ignored the verbal sneer. "Let's go through them. One, maybe business is slower than before."

"I doubt it."

"Two, perhaps he made a large investment in some project or operation that required a cash infusion. In other word he is overextended, at least temporarily."

"Knowing my husband and his aversion to financial risk, I doubt it, but it's possible."

"Three, his financial investments have taken a sudden turn for the worse."

"Walter never dallies with the stock markets of any country. He doesn't trust them and he won't risk his money with them. He's very proud of the fact that this depression hasn't caught him in a bad position. What does that leave?"

162

"Three more possibilities. Number four, does he use narcotics?"

"Never."

"Five, does he gamble?"

That stopped her momentarily. "In truth, I do not know, though I cannot imagine he does. He is so controlled and so risk averse. I don't think he would ever risk money on a deal that he cannot control. What's the last possibility?"

I hesitated momentarily. "Does he have a mistress?"

Jennifer was silent for so long that we reached the pier and had to return to the Ford to begin the process of disembarking. I decided it was a question she didn't want to answer to me or to anyone, perhaps mostly to herself.

*

"Let me ask a different sort of question," I said when we were sitting in the automobile again, waiting for the line ahead of us to move forward. "Have you *ever* been in love?" I asked. "Have you ever even had the chance? I mean, real love. The kind of love that curls your toes and silences the narrative inside your head when you're laying in the dark with him."

Jennifer's initial response was soft, comfortable laughter that surprised me. "Yes," she said easily. "I have. Does that come as a shock to you?"

I smiled, unsure if the shadow of my fedora covered the lower part of my face. "Perhaps, though I'm glad to know you have it in you to be a part of the human race. I won't ask who he was."

"I've been careless. I beg you to hold my reply private."

"Of course."

"You don't understand what marriage means in my country."

"Maybe not, but you've only been married two years. In the US, that makes you practically newlyweds."

"You mock me."

"I don't," I replied. "If what you have in your marriage works for the two of you, then who am I to judge it. That's the usual American perspective on such things."

"Is it really?" Jennifer asked rhetorically. She didn't anticipate my next question.

"Does the name Willie Fung mean anything to you?" I asked casually.

Jennifer drew a slow deep breath before responding. "I never heard of him," she said.

I didn't believe her, but I moved on without saying so. "I've got a meeting with Josephine soon. Where can I drop you?"

"Drop me? Won't you bring me with you? I couldn't bear it if I had to be alone right now."

I glanced over at her in the reflected lights of the ferry landing. We were next in line to roll off. When the man directing automobiles circled his hand at me to move forward, I edged onto the road and accelerated enough to move up behind the Plymouth in front of us.

"I'm not sure about the set-up," I said. "He seems to always keep a number of his boys around. It could be dangerous."

"I won't be any trouble," she vowed. "I'm not afraid of him. Let me stay with you, please?"

I considered the various scenarios that would occur to any cynical mind.

*

Without speaking we drove through the lower part of town, climbing slowly up Montgomery Street as it angled across San Francisco. The city lights were in full blaze around us, though muted somewhat by the heavy condensation in the air.

I thought about the word "fog," which seemed like a euphemism for something I couldn't quite put my finger on. I could still taste the salty tang of the bay in my mouth. It mixed with the aftertaste of stale coffee and cigarettes. Shortly before we turned onto Market Street I had to engage the windshield wipers to clear the condensation off.

Jennifer hadn't uttered a word since we pulled off the ferry. Slunk down low in the front seat, she smoked one of her long, slender cigarettes absently without appearing to be looking at or thinking about anything at all.

I kept going forward. A moment later, she noticed. "Hey, you skipped by the Palace Hotel."

"I need to make a telephone call or two. So do you for that matter."

"Yeah? Who are you going to call?"

"A guy named Beakman. Know him?"

"Never heard of him. Who am I supposed to call?"

"We'll find a nice quiet drugstore with a telephone booth up ahead this way. You can try your P.I. again. Johnny Drake must be out there somewhere."

"He might be," she said, staring away from me with her face toward the window. "Anyway, I need an Alka-Seltzer right about now."

My focus was on the hard bumps in the road.

Chapter Thirty-Three

Several blocks later I parked at the curb near a drugstore. With the engine switched off I could feel the vibrating hum of the large city around us. It had a pulse and a presence as any living creature would.

Contrasted with that, I still felt the rolling sensation of the sea, a psychophysical illusion that began to fade as soon as I climbed out of the automobile. Standing on the sidewalk looking up into the bright neon lights, I felt the entire world sway until I began to walk.

Jennifer took my arm and we went inside the glittering store. They sold everything modern you could possibly need and they had soda fountain counter in the back that intersected a wall of telephone booths.

We started at the counter where a short near-sighted man in white apron and a white paper cap moved eagerly to serve us. "What'll it be?" he asked cheerfully. His voice was high-pitched and his eyes appeared to bobble somewhat behind their thick lenses.

I put a dollar bill on the counter. "We'll start with an Alka-Seltzer for the lady and change for the telephones."

The soda jerk moved quickly and soon Jennifer was watching the fizzy drink that he set in front of her. Once the tiny bubbles and their resulting spray settled a little, she picked it up and drank it in one motion, swallowing three times. She licked her lips after she finished and smiled wanly at the man behind the counter.

"Thank you," she said to him in a manner that – combined with her smile – must have made his night.

Now that I had a handful of change, I gave her a few nickels and said: "I'll meet you back here in a few minutes. See if you can get Drake to tell you something worth knowing."

Her smile, the fierce version now, practically burned me as she slid off the stool and sashayed toward the first telephone booth and closed the door behind her. Pretending indifference to it all, I stared down into my palm, studying the five-cent pieces that remained there.

Once I'd steadied myself I moved toward the booth that was farthest away from the one Jennifer had occupied. With an unlighted Chesterfield dangling from my lips, I closed the door behind me and weighed the nickels in my hand. I wondered if I had enough.

*

I left a message for Dr. Orion with his service. I hadn't expected to reach him on the first try.

For some reason, Beakman was easy to reach. "Of course, I know the Palace Hotel," he asserted over the wire. "I can meet you there. What time and where?"

"Let's make it ten o'clock?"

"How will I find you?"

"You won't. I'll find you."

"I'm not sure how that works."

"Have a drink in the Pied Piper – get there a little early just to make sure you can find a stool and a little elbowroom. If I'm a little late, don't get ancy. Order a second drink and relax. I'll come for you when the timing is right."

"Anything I need to know?"

"Nope. Everything's Jake."

"Maybe you should let me in on what's going on."

"See you at ten," I said and rang off. He would find out about Josephine and Travers in due time. I opened the door of the booth and returned to the counter of the soda fountain.

"Your girlfriend is still talking up a storm with someone," the near-sighted soda jerk informed me with his practiced grin. "Can I bring you anything?"

"Sure," I said. "I'll have a chocolate malt and the evening newspaper."

"Coming right up!"

*

The chocolate malt was perfect. It was thick and rich, chocolaty and malty. I ate the thickest part of it with a long spoon and then used the wide straw I'd been given to slowly work on the rest from the bottom up. I stirred it often.

Jennifer was still inside her booth. Of her face I couldn't see more than the tip of her nose, but her hands were well within my view. They chattered silently in the air. Periodically I glanced over and noticed the animation continued. She remained in there for over twenty minutes.

Idly I unfolded the newspaper, working my way across the top, above the fold. When I turned it over a story in the bottom left-hand corner caught my eye: "Local private investigator, Johnny Drake found dead."

According to the newsprint, Drake's body had been found at the bottom of a ravine. He'd either fallen or been pushed from the ledge of a building that looked out over a hill, a short distance from Coit Tower. The coroner thought he might have been dead for two days. The exact cause of death was not yet known, though the reporter hadn't let that hamper his wild speculation.

I folded the newspaper so the story did not show and set it on the counter beside my empty glass.

"Want another chocolate malted?" the eager soda jerk came over to inquire.

"No thanks," I said. "I'm just waiting for the lady." I pushed three quarters his way and smiled at him. "You're working late tonight," I said to make idle chatter.

"Till closing time."

"You probably started early too."

"These days a long shift beats no shift at all." Suddenly, the magnified crow's-feet at the corner of his eyes gave him away. He wasn't eager at all, just desperate and nervous like everyone else who had a job and knew how lucky they were to have it.

*

When she came out of the booth, Jennifer's eyes surveyed the room looking for something. I couldn't tell what she was looking for. The place was brightly lit, but almost empty.

As she moved up to the counter beside me, she fidgeted about and waved at the soda jerk to bring her another Alka-Seltzer. He didn't wait to be asked twice. When he brought her the glass of fizzy water, she drank it down in a series of steady gulps before turning her watery eyes on mine.

"How are you feeling?" I asked.

"Like I've been pressed through a laundry wringer," she replied. "Did you reach your man?"

"I did." I leaned an elbow on the counter and studied her face.

"That's fine. I was able to reach Johnny Drake finally."

"You were in there for a long while. I had a chocolate malt while I waited. Would you like one now?"

"My stomach is still trying to decide whether to forgive me or not. What did Beakman have to say?"

"Very little, though he agreed to meet me later this evening. What about Drake? Did he have anything interesting to sell you?"

"Only a lot of the usual," she sighed.

"In his case I wouldn't know what that is, I've never talked to him."

Jennifer smiled uneasily and leaned toward me a little, shifting partially off the soda fountain stool to lean her shoulder against mine. "I think Johnny Drake has seen too many movies. He tries too hard to sound like a tough guy, styles himself after James Cagney I think – a lot of short, clipped sentences and a lot of American slang that I cannot follow very well."

"What kind of slang?"

"You must know. A lot of words I don't remember. Sometimes with him, it's like another language that he's speaking."

I nodded encouragingly. "A unique American dialect. Apart from that, is he getting anywhere?"

She shrugged and peered down into the white foam at the bottom of her empty glass. "He's still working the case. That's something at least. He thinks he's got a lead on where Walter might have gone, might still be. He's going over to look at things tonight and may have some more information for me in the day or two. At least he's trying to sound optimistic."

"Are you feeling optimistic?"

"Me? I'm too tired to feel much of anything at all right now. I feel drained of everything."

"We'll get dinner at the Palace Hotel. That will pick you up. Did Drake say what his lead is?"

"He wouldn't tell me."

"Does he at least offer an opinion on whether Walter's alive?"

"He plays that one cautiously, though he makes optimistic noises when I ask, tossing out little slivers of hope here and there like confetti. It's never anything specific, nothing I can hold on to."

"It sounds like he told you nothing, essentially?"

Jennifer's lips pursed as she considered the question. "Drake plays his cards close. He always does. That's his style. I assume it's an American thing, something all you tough guys do."

"Do you think I'm a 'tough guy'?"

"Aren't you?"

I smiled into her eyes. "Maybe I am."

"Drake did tell me something I found to be interesting. He said he found something that referenced a pair of missing keys ... Does that mean anything to you?"

"What kind of keys?"

"Ancient keys, he said. There are two of them, both Chinese. Apparently they were stolen recently and are necessary to open some missing treasure, a sealed chest that is believed to contain ancient artifacts. Is that what this is all about?"

"Drake said all that to you just now?"

Jennifer nodded. Her eyes and lids were heavy and she waited on me with one shoulder turned against mine, as if that might protect her from everything.

"Did he say where this sealed chest might be found?"

"I don't think he knows."

"Why do you think that?"

"Because I asked him and he sputtered around for a moment and then said he's still looking for it. His behavior was a little strange. I wondered if

168

the lead he mentioned, the lead to Walter, had anything to do with the sealed chest."

"That is rather interesting," I told her.

"Is it?"

I unfolded the newspaper and smoothed it out onto the counter between us so that she could see the story of Johnny Drake's death. After she had studied it quietly for a moment, I helped her out: "The facts are pretty clear. It says they found his body this afternoon and he's been dead for about two days. It seems improbable that he spoke to you just now about missing keys or anything else."

Jennifer McPhael drew a breath, paused, and then she began to cry, softly at first and then harder as she turned away from me and buried her face in the crook of an elbow that she lay over the counter.

It was a good act.

"Come on," I said, drawing her up by the arm. "Let's take it out of here."

I left a bill on the counter for the soda jerk and directed her through the bright drugstore toward the neon lit sidewalk that was wet with a recent rain.

*

When we were inside the Ford I switched on the engine and engaged the wipers against the fog and the rain, but I didn't engage the clutch. We held tight to the curb with the city lights reflected in the moist windshield in front of us.

It was a yellow world. Everything was neon yellow and when it mixed with the fog and the slow drizzle it became more yellow still. The street was yellow, the sky was yellow, the city buildings were yellow. Yellow, yellow, yellow everywhere. I lighted a yellow Chesterfield and exhaled yellow smoke. The burnt tobacco even smelled yellow.

I didn't say anything. I didn't have to. I just waited. A minute went by, then two. The wipers continued their steady shifting arcs, with the notable bump at each end. I smoked my yellow cigarette and watched Jennifer's yellow face.

When she was ready, she opened her mouth. "You don't understand," she said quietly, her voice filled with a humble remorsefulness that I didn't buy into at all. "I didn't mean to deceive you, but I felt I had to tell you something or you would give up on me entirely. I couldn't bear the thought of that. You must understand that."

"Not a smart play given that Drake's been dead for two days."

"Obviously, I didn't know he was dead. If I had, do you think I would have made such a fool of myself just now?"

"That's hard to say," I said, focusing my vision on the burning yellow

169

cigarette that I twisted between my course yellow fingers.

"Is it really? You knew he was dead, and you continued to play me along like we were talking about the same thing? How dare *you*!"

I grinned what must have been a yellow grin. "Don't get all excited, sister. Of the two of us right now, I'm not the liar. Who were you talking to all that time?" I asked the question without looking up from the yellow Chesterfield.

"Don't change the subject," she retorted haughtily.

I looked into her yellowed eyes and continued to grin what must have been a yellow grin. "That *is* the subject, the *only* subject," I informed her coldly. "Who were you talking to? It had to be somebody."

"It's not what you think."

"How do you know what I think?"

"Whatever you're thinking, you're thinking the worst of me, and that's not fair."

I felt my yellow grin widen. "Convince me."

"If you must know, I was talking to a friend – a woman who I know from my home country. She is here, in San Francisco now, with her husband. We support each other, and I called her for that, but only after I tried to reach Johnny Drake and was unable to."

"You're telling me you didn't know Drake was dead, you tried to call him, and when you failed at that you spent twenty minutes talking to a friend."

"That is correct."

"You did all that, knowing that I was sitting out there at the counter waiting for you and then you came and told me a silly story about how you'd had a long chat with Drake. Have I got that right?"

"Why must you be so cruel?"

"Sister, you lied to me and I doubt it's the first time. Now I'm trying to line up the facts so that I can make some sense of all this salad you've tossed."

Jennifer bowed her head and nodded her acceptance. "I'm sorry," she said. "I suppose you must think I'm truly awful. I didn't mean to mislead you. It's just that I didn't want to lose you."

"Save it," I said. "Tell me this. How did you find me at the Orion's home the other day?"

"Johnny Drake sent me there. He really did."

"Maybe so, but there are problems with that story too. For one, the Orions don't actually live there. We learned that tonight."

Jennifer frowned and said: "It's possible the Orions wanted Drake to think they did – just as they wanted you to think so? Maybe they wanted me to find you there?"

"Really?" I questioned. "For what reason?"

"How can I know that?" she hissed and then immediately softened. "I'm sorry, I'm really sorry I lied to you about my telephone call." She hung her pretty yellowed face and it became brown again within the shadow that draped her. "I didn't know Johnny Drake was dead and I really did try to reach him first. I was afraid if I didn't have something to tell you, you would abandon me."

Jennifer glanced up at me from within the shadow around her face to see how I was reacting. Her eyes were watchful and solid; her hands were still on her lap. I didn't believe her and it must have showed on my face, which I didn't mind.

She started to protest again: "I hate to be embarrassed like this. I'm not used to being so vulnerable. The past few days have taken a toll on me. I've behaved in ways I'm not proud of. I said I am sorry, and I am. I mean it. Please say you believe me, even if you don't. This is so very hard for me. If you tell me to, I'll climb out of this automobile and you'll never have to see me again. Is that what you want from me? I can go back in to the drugstore and call a taxi."

"Forget about it," I said quietly. I'd finished my cigarette and now I rolled my window down just enough to toss it out. The air was cold and it felt good and it reminded me I had things to do. "We're going over to the Palace Hotel together."

I felt the air go out of her, though I didn't look at her again for a while. We drove down Market Street once more, through the rain that was falling steadily now. We were all talked out, so we didn't speak at all.

The silence was hard to endure. I'd become an intruder in the unfolding tragedy of her life as her world slowly spun its component parts out from the center, a widening gyre that appeared intent on returning everything that had ever mattered to her back to the chaos from where it had come.

As if in mournful sympathy, atmospheric conditions over the bay displayed a frenetic light show ahead of us. I couldn't tell if it was raining out there or not, but electricity filled the clouds and gave them an eerie glowing shape, causing them to appear as if they were otherworldly creatures approaching the city slowly with unknown intentions.

Jennifer and I watched them together without any further conversation until we reached the Palace Hotel. She exhaled a long breath as we arrived and began to slow toward a stop.

Chapter Thirty-Four

We pulled in at the Market Street entrance, finding ourselves in a line of unmoving automobiles. Flashbulbs popped from somewhere ahead of us. An attendant in a white coat was waiting for me and promised to park the Ford once the traffic jam ahead cleared. I press a tightly folded bill into his palm.

The lobby of the Palace Hotel was teeming with activity. A lot of young people dressed to the nines were lined up near the Palm Court. We detoured ourselves that way so that we could peer inside.

The Court was graced with a stained-glass ceiling that canopied over what was once the hotel's carriage entrance when it reopened after the earthquake of 1909. I knew by reputation that it was a popular spot for dinner dances, parties, and cotillions. Tea in The Court was a society tradition.

We moved past it. Raucous laughter reached us from the Pied Piper bar. We paused there next and peered in at the colorful mural of the piper that hung behind the bar. He practically climbed off the wall.

"There must be an event tonight," Jennifer said as we entered the polished marble lobby.

"Isn't there an event every night?"

"I wouldn't know."

Almost recovered now, Jennifer smiled at me and took my arm, pulling me assertively forward as we approached the front desk.

*

"We're guests of Mr. Josephine," I told the clerk behind the counter.

"Your name?" he responded curtly.

"Huddleston," I said. Behind us I heard the sound of flashbulbs. I willed myself not to turn around or show the anxiety I felt. If Josephine intended a betrayal, this wasn't where he would do it.

The clerk checked his list and then allowed a friendly smile to claim his face. "Of course sir, just a moment." He didn't ask for any identification, but immediately picked up a telephone and whispered a few words to somebody.

A moment later an attractive woman arrived beside us and invited us to accompany her to 'the party'. She was young and confident, with a dark complexion and a lot of skin showing on her arms and shoulders and neck. The white evening dress she wore was light and simple, with the shimmer that only silk threading provides. Her manners were smooth and remote, and she didn't allow herself to notice that we weren't wearing party clothing or party expressions on our tired faces.

An elevator took us up to the eighth floor of the hotel and we followed the hostess to the end of one hallway. When we reached the door she leaned her face near the peephole so that whoever was inside could identify her, as she knocked twice. The sound of piano music came faintly under the door.

The door didn't open, so the girl knocked again, harder this time. She glanced at us with an apologetic smile and explanation: "Mr. Josephine's parties are well known, sometimes even the security guards get into the fun a little too much."

"Is there a particular occasion for tonight's affair?"

"We never know," she replied with an exaggerated wide-eyed shrug. "He keeps the suite year round, and when he wants to throw a bash, he does. His guests come from all over. Often he's not even there himself."

"Have you met Mr. Josephine?" I asked.

"No," she admitted. Her confidence was slipping. She knocked again, several times, this time much harder than before.

Moments later the door opened and we were staring into the smirking face of Samuel Travers. Smitherton was behind him, peering over his shoulder at us. They both wore black bowlers and appeared as though they were having fun.

Travers smelled heavily of gin and Smitherton had a ladies scarf draped over his shoulder. The lady missing the scarf made her own appearance a moment later as she came up and cupped her hands over Smitherton's eyes. He swore and jerked his head away; she pulled the scarf off his shoulder and ran back into the room behind them with it, shrieking as she went.

Travers smirked at the hostess who had brought us to the door and said: "Yeah, they're with us. Come on in and get out of the draft."

We crossed the threshold into a small foyer. Travers closed the door behind us, locking the hostess out with a quarter turn of the bolt. Even through the door I imagined I could sense the girl's mixture of relief and disappointment.

*

"Welcome to the party," Travers said loudly, competing with the piano that was raking on the other side of the wall.

The fast music drew us in, with Jennifer tightly at my side. Her right arm was firmly locked around my left. It was a spacious, almost empty room, with a very high ceiling and a grand piano at the far end of it. A bar with two bartenders in service was set up along the interior wall and people congregated there as they do at such affairs.

At the piano a lanky man with his jacket off and his sleeves rolled up was bent over the keys intensely, pounding them with a rage that suggested they must have offended him in some deep manner. I recognized the tune, though only just barely. It was a raved up version of Hoagy Carmichael's "Georgia On My Mind." Played at a manic pace with widespread modal scales and without any vocals it took me a moment to recognize it.

Fifteen or twenty men and women dressed for a party stood around with drinks in their hands. Some of them loitered near the piano and several were actually dancing clumsily in the middle of the floor, trying to keep pace with the frenetic rhythm of the music.

I wasn't going to be the one to tell them this was not music to dance to. They so badly wanted it to be. I almost wondered if it was a scene staged for a B-movie. We weren't in New York or Kansas City, and I hadn't been expecting anything like it.

A tall Chinese woman in a long, black dress that swirled around her figure and crossed behind her at her left hip, approached us with a single martini in one hand. "Are you Mr. Huddleston?" she inquired.

When I accepted the name, she handed me the martini and then turned toward the bar to wave at someone there. "Follow me," she said with a wink in my direction. She ignored Jennifer McPhael entirely.

I downed half the martini before moving from the spot so that I could walk without spilling it. Jennifer and I followed the woman across the room, ducking past the inelegant dancers along the way. At the bar, a tray of fresh martinis was offered. Jennifer selected one.

"It's *very* good of you to come," the tall Chinese woman said to me with a smile that included her eyes. "Josi thought you would be here, though he wasn't sure. I understand a lot of people seek you."

I smiled and raised my glass toward the woman to acknowledge the veiled threat she had delivered on behalf of her boss. "I don't know your name," I said.

"I am Jingfei," she replied easily, almost as if I should have known that.

"That must mean something."

"*Still fragrance*," she replied and quickly turned away from me as though I had gotten too close to something personal. "Come with me," she said over her shoulder.

Long black hair hung down to her waist and she tossed it in a practiced manner. Without waiting for us, she moved briskly away from the bar and began to weave her way across the room through the crowd of dancers. Her hips swayed gently, effortlessly, as she walked.

Jennifer and I followed as best we could, but with drinks in our hands, we did not keep up well. By the time we had maneuvered past the gauntlet of dancers, Jingfei was across the room, waiting for us at a door that remained closed.

"Josi rarely joins his own parties," she explained when we reached her. "He is shy and self-conscious about these events. He draws pleasure knowing other people are having a good time."

"That is gracious," I said, though I didn't believe what she had just said about her boss.

Jingfei smile demurely and cast her gaze downward. "He instructed me that you would very likely be accompanied by a beautiful woman." Her eyes glanced at Jennifer for the first time as if she had only just noticed her. The smile on her lips was ice cold. "He also said you would appreciate a cold martini and a quiet room to have dinner with your friend before meeting with him." Again she glanced briefly at Jennifer before returning her gaze to my eyes.

*

Jingfei led us down a short hallway into an elongated dining room. With two doors closed behind us, the manic piano was relegated to pianissimo. That made it almost tolerable. I didn't mind fast jazz when someone who knew how to hit the right notes played it.

"I'll be serving you tonight," Jingfei explained. She gestured toward a table set for two. It was set on a raised floor by a low, wide window that looked out over the lights of San Francisco. "Please relax and enjoy the meal."

When Jennifer and I were seated, Jingfei lit three candles, each of different lengths. From a side bar she stirred a pitcher of martinis and poured two glasses. While we sipped them, she opened a bottle of red wine and poured two glasses and set them on the table as well. After that she made a show of arranging the bottle in a cloth-shrouded stand beside the table.

"Would you like time to enjoy your cocktails?"

"No," I said swirling my empty glass. "I'm hungry."

"You must be," she said, edging toward me. "You look exhausted." I thought she might place a palm on my forehead, but she held back from that.

I thought: *It was probably something I caught from one of the corpses I found this morning.* Instead, I said: "I haven't eaten much today."

"Our chef, Paolo, is from Naples," Jingfei said. "He's a drinker, but he is also the best Italian chef in the city. He has several courses to offer you tonight. The first is a Tuscan panzanella salad – tomato, bread and onions marinated for five days in balsamic vinegar, olive oil, herbs, and spices. After that, we have a platter of mussels stuffed with tomato and chopped fish. The pasta dish tonight is squid ink tagliatelle with fish and a light tomato sauce. The main course is ossobuccu with gremolata."

I lighted a Chesterfield and sat back in my chair to wait. My jacket was unbuttoned and I was aware of the shoulder holster chafing over my left arm. Jennifer watched me anxiously and smiled when I winked at her.

When Jingfei left the room, Jennifer leaned across the table toward me and showed her firm white teeth. "Little Miss Jing seems to think she's going to bed you."

I took a cool drag on my cigarette and was still exhaling when Jingfie came back into the room with a large plate of the panzanella salad.

*

During the final course, Chef Paolo appeared. He was a white-haired, sunburned man with a Roman hawk-nose and sharp blue eyes. His head was oversized for the short stature of his body.

"How was your dinner?" he asked lazily, in a thick Neapolitan accent.

"It was marvelous," Jennifer said.

"Yes, quite wonderful," I added.

Paolo's eyes didn't focus well. He might have been about to say something more, but as he was looking about, a small cat scattered by, disappearing through the door he had left partially open behind him. "Piccolo!" he called after it and left the room just as suddenly as the kitten had.

*

Presently Jingfei returned with a delicate bow and asked invited us to Mr. Josephine's quarters. The room she led us into was an oversized office that was already filled with other people. Mr. Josephine sat behind a large desk smoking a cigar, while his two gunners – Travers and Smitherton – in their bowler hats fanned out on either side of him. Two servants in white jackets loitered around a bar cart that had the usual assortment of wines and spirits, as well as a variety of baked sweets.

"Welcome to my city lodgings." Josephine stood up quickly and moved around his desk to extend a hand toward Jennifer McPhael. "Forgive me, Mrs. McPhael," he said, reaching his hands toward hers. "Your husband is very important to me and I share the distress you must feel. I hope truly that he will return to us shortly – in good health and spirits."

"Thank you," she replied without revealing anything. She pulled her hand back quickly as if he were a leper.

"I presume Paolo took superb care of you both," Josephine inquired, ignoring her discomfort. With an open palm he gestured toward two Barcelona chairs in the middle of the room, facing his desk.

"He did," I said. "You have an impressive get up here."

176

"It's a grand suite, isn't it?" Josephine grinned to encourage our admiration. "I like it. It suits my needs. Many U.S. presidents have stayed here over the years. President Warren G. Harding died just down the hall."

"Shall we talk business?" I said.

Josephine struck a pleasant and thoughtful pose. "Of course, it's late and you have both undoubtedly had a long day. Is there any news since we spoke this afternoon? Does Dr. Orion want to throw in?"

"No news," I said. "I haven't reached Orion yet. I do have an observation. In the day and a half that I've been looking at this puzzle, I've met three men who claimed to have worked at the Sutro Cliff House at the time of the fire."

"Three?" Josephine asked. "That's an impressive number given the small number of employees that Sutro kept and the many years that have since passed."

I smiled politely. "That is exactly what I would have thought."

"If I may ask," Josephine started, "what are their names?"

"Chi, Han, and Lin," I said. "Do you know of any connection between them?"

"I don't know Han or Lin. Who are they?"

I shrugged. "Two elderly men in the city who claim to have been there. Each of them told me a long and detailed story."

"I'm impressed. You've learned something about my people that I didn't know myself. What other connections have you found?"

Still smiling my politest smile, I lit a Chesterfield. When I had snapped the lighter closed and exhaled, I replied: "Orion told me he'd had dinner at Sutro's once himself before the fire. It seems we have a small legion of people who claim to have been there at a particular frozen point in time."

"Am I to take it that this has raised questions in your mind?" Josephine inquired. His eyes switched from mine to Jennifer McPhael's and back again. At the edge of my peripheral vision I was aware of Travers and Smitherton twitching beneath their bowlers.

I nodded silently.

Chapter Thirty-Five

Jennifer McPhael sat with her ample legs crossed over one another and her elbow perched on one knee. Her hand formed a fist that her chin fit nicely on top of. The bracelets around her browned arms shined artfully in the carefully arranged lighting of the room. Her large brown eyes didn't fare too badly either.

With careful intent Josephine paid no attention to her. Instead, he moved himself across the room toward a bar cart to play host. "What can I offer you to drink?" he asked, looking at me mildly with no particular worry about anything in his eyes.

I played along. "What are you having?"

"Like many people from the Orient, alcohol has never agreed with me. I don't drink it. I can't. Even one sip and I become a blushing, silly man who feels the heat of a raging furnace inside him. I don't dare touch the stuff. Nevertheless, I would not have my biological eccentricities give you pause. Will you have something?"

"By this time in the evening, I generally prefer whiskey," I told him. "What have you got in that category?"

That brought a smile to his face. He was oddly pleased with himself. "I've got spirits from Ireland, Scotland, Canada, and Kentucky, including several options in each category. It's popular stuff the world over now. Someday, I venture, there will be a Chinese corn mash. If you desire something I haven't got, we'll order it."

"No need for that, pour me a few drops of something from Kentucky," I replied. "Keep it neat."

"For the lady?"

"Nothing for me," Jennifer replied quietly.

Apparently I was the only one drinking. I took a ritual sip of the bourbon he handed me and set the glass down on the corner table near my elbow. "We have business to discuss."

"We do," Josephine replied, smiling as he sat down. "Where shall we begin?"

"I'd be curious to know one thing for starters," I said. "How did Jameson Tucker come to find me at the Fairmont Hotel? Or put another way, who set him onto me?"

Josephine cleared his throat as he paced the other side of the room. With his hands clasped behind his back he turned once on a heel and then stopped to face me. "I will confess," he said. "I had been in touch with Mr. Tucker myself in the days leading up to his death. However, I never mentioned you, didn't even know of your existence at that point. Thus, it could not have been *me* that sent him to you."

"Or so, you say."

"Yes. So I say."

I glanced at Jennifer with the same question in my eyes.

"Yes," she acknowledged. "I had also been in touch with Mr. Tucker several days before I met you. He knew my husband – remember? We'd talked socially on several previous occasions and so, yes, I called him the week my husband disappeared. I didn't 'set him' onto you, though."

"Someone sent him my way. Who might have done that?" I asked of nobody in particular.

"Perhaps, Dr. Orion did that himself," Josephine suggested.

"Why would he?" I inquired.

"Maybe it was his way of setting things into motion? Perhaps he thought Tucker had information that might be useful to you?"

"Perhaps," I said, musing into my bourbon. "It's plausible. I only met Orion once, though it seems he would have mentioned it to me. If his intent was as you describe, I can't see a reason why he wouldn't have. He told me about the operative he sent to me."

That captured Josephine's interest. "Who is this operative?"

"A man named Beakman," I replied. "Do you know him?"

Josephine's face registered something and quickly he looked away from me to busy himself by reaching into his jacket for a cigarette case. Once he had the cigarette going, he looked at me again. His eyes were relaxed and they revealed nothing. "Hmmm, that name is familiar," he mused. "I can't recall why, though. Has he been in San Francisco long?"

Travers started to speak, to say something, but Josephine cut him off aggressively with both a hand and vocal gesture. "Shhhh –" he exclaimed, with the open palm of one hand moving rapidly upward.

His eyes blazed at Travers momentarily. Then he turned his attention back to the burning tip of his cigarette while we were silent in the room. "I apologize," he offered after a moment. "It's been a while since I heard that name. Mr. Beakman – Mr. Gerald Beakman, of course. He was once one of my most trusted lieutenants until he chose to go his own way. While I could not begrudge him that, it was the manner in which he left me, and what he took with him when he left. Please forgive my outburst."

"Are you enemies now?" I asked.

"No," Josephine insisted, shaking his head so that his thick jowls wobbled. "I have no enemies. We declared a truce and he has respected it, as have I. It was years ago and bygones are bygones."

"That's fine," I said, "I like to hear things like that. It encourages my faith in Mankind. Let's move on. Beakman is a minor part of this. We've got larger mysteries to solve here together."

"Indeed, sir, we do," Josephine agreed. "What would you consider them to be?"

"I have a list in my head," I replied. "Do you want me to recite it out loud for everyone to contemplate?"

"Why not?" Josephine exclaimed. "Does that seem too clever?"

"Not by me."

"Sing to us, then."

I had five questions and five digits on my left hand. I listed them one by one, counting out a new finger for each one, starting with my thumb. "One: where is Lot seventy-three now and who has it? Two: who has had it's contents since 1907 and why are they bringing it to market now, why did they divert it from the auction scheduled for today, and did they set the Sutro house fire that set all this in motion? Three: what do the missing keys have to do with this, where did they come from, and who has them now?

"Four: who is murdering people in San Francisco and why? There are four men dead that I know of right now who are connected to this: Jameson Tucker, Khai Chi, Willie Fung, Johnny Drake. Walter McPhael has been missing for two weeks and we don't know his fate. He may be dead too.

"Five: why did Tucker's killer steal not only the key, but also the photograph of Sutro's Cliff House? Was it for the photograph itself? Was this a sentimental crime? Perhaps it was to mask something that was revealed in the picture so that others would not detect it. That's the explanation I like, though there is a third possibility. Was there something physically stored behind or within the photograph?"

Once my left-hand fingers were extended, I paused for a moment and then closed them all to form a tight fist as I looked about the room. It was a long speech by my standards. When I finished it, I took a pull of bourbon and lighted a Chesterfield.

There was silence for a moment, and then: "Bravo!" Josephine exclaimed. "Shall we start at the top?"

I nodded and glanced at Jennifer. She sat very still. I looked away from her and back to Josephine.

"Where is Lot seventy-three and who has it?" he started. "That is the central mystery we face. It may be the only question that really matters, though we may have to answer some of the other questions first to answer this one."

"What ideas do you have?" I asked.

"None, sir," Josephine answered firmly. "What about you?"

I shook my head slowly.

"Question number two then," Josephine said, directing the conversation now. "Who has controlled the Lot since 1907 – and did they set the house fire that set everything in motion? Again, I have no answers. You?"

Again I shook my head firmly.

"This is not progress," Josephine smiled, glancing around the room at the other faces. "Question number three: what do the missing keys have to do with this, where did they come from, and who has them now? For this, I may know something."

"I'm all ears," I said, quietly.

"I expect these keys, will open boxes contained within the sealed chest to reveal the treasure we seek. I have read an old document that speaks to this. It is authoritative. We must obtain the keys."

I glanced at Jennifer and noted that she had nothing to say. She sat well back in her chair with her eyes inspecting the ends of her fingernails.

"And question number four?" I prodded.

"Who is murdering people in San Francisco and why? While I don't know the answer to the first part of that question, the answer to the second part of it seems obvious. Someone seeking the Orb, our competition, in other words, killed those men. Tucker and Chi were killed for the keys they held. Fung was probably tortured to extract information and then killed to keep him quiet. Drake may have suffered the same fate."

"What about my husband?" Jennifer said angrily. It was her first contribution to the discussion. She looked up from her hands with small fires blazing in her irises. Her hair seemed to be in motion around her face.

Josephine took the question in stride. "Your husband has been missing for two weeks and the man you hired to find him has been murdered. I valued your husband myself and I don't mean to be unkind to you, but we must be practical. He is missing for a reason. Either he doesn't want to be found or he is unable to return to you."

Jennifer slumped visibly with her shoulders. "You think he's dead?" Her voice was small and remote.

I interjected: "It's no good to speculate. Let's work with the facts that we have, the ones we can be reasonably sure of."

"I agree," Josephine added. "Do you have any thoughts about who the killer might be?"

I was reasonably certain he was Fingers Pete, the contract killer from the east coast who preferred to use a .22 caliber pistol in his work. What I didn't know was who had hired him. "I don't have any facts," I said quietly.

Josephine nodded. I had given the response he'd expected. He was checking the questions off with his own fingers now, and he popped his thumb up last. "As for the last question regarding the disappearance of the photograph, I doubt there is any reason to it at all. Hanging on the wall in Tucker's office, it probably appealed to the irony of his murderer."

*

"What about the evidence that was promised?" I asked after a period of silence. "You mentioned an ancient letter, written in Chinese. It was something about a final command, a group of doomed men sacrificing themselves for the Orb and the glory of China."

"Did I say all that?" Josephine asked mildly.

I took my time lighting another Chesterfield. When the smoke was burning in my lungs and sifting upward from my hands, I blew the smoke away from me and said quietly: "You did and you promised to read it out loud. Do you have it with you?"

"I do," Josephine replied.

"How does it figure into our mystery?"

Josephine smiled cryptically and bit into his lower lip for effect. "You may find no point to it at all, but I will show it to you now. I believe it supports the point I've been trying to make."

He reached across his desk to hand me a large manila envelope. I accepted it and thumbed it open. The letter itself was written in charcoal on some type of natural grass paper. The lettering was Chinese. I counted the pages. There were six of them. They seemed very old and brittle. A tiny piece flaked off in my hand.

After I handed the letter back to Josephine he cleared his throat and began to read from it. The narrative told a story about the remnants of a dying army, fatally trapped by their own ambitions and hubris. Starving and low on gunpowder they wrote final letters as the bodies of their comrades piled around them day by day.

Josephine paused momentarily to regain his composure before he read the final paragraph:

"Yesterday our cannon burst upon an attacking company. From a wagon afterward hung a mangled body, his head down, his body burning slowly in the flames that consumed the wagon. The body of the man was still alive, moaning, the hands twitching desperately, helplessly. I shot him with my bow and my arrow pierced his neck. Tears then ran down my face. Why have I been crying for two days about a dead invader whose murderer I am? I am now without faith or hope. How will my wife and children ever know of these last few hours? All is lost. I am consigned to the lowest regions of hell for my failures and my sins."

When Josephine finished reading, I stood up.

"Where are you going?" he inquired.

"I have an appointment downstairs. It won't take long. I'll be back in fifteen minutes."

"What about this letter? Have you no reaction?"

"It's very touching. Though, I'm not sure its evidence of anything relevant to us."

"They were fighting for the Orb."

"I didn't hear anything about that in what you just read."

"Then you didn't understand the context."

"Perhaps you can explain it to me when I get back."

"You're not going anywhere," Travers said. He was already standing and moving sideways so that his body was between the door and me.

"Relax," Josephine instructed his man. "If Mr. Huddleston wants to leave, let him, but the girl stays behind. He will return. If we hold the girl, he'll come back for her. I believe that."

"That's right," I said to Travers. "I'll be back soon enough. You'll barely have time to miss me."

I glanced at Jennifer. Anxiety had captured the expression on her face and frozen the small lines around her eyes into a deep relief. I put a finger to my lips and whispered to her, though I knew everyone in the room could hear. "Shhh, I'll be back soon. I'm not leaving you behind and no one will hurt you."

"He's right," Josephine agreed. "Everything will be okay."

Jennifer nodded at me and lowered her face into her hands as though she would weep. Her body began to rock slowly from the waist up. I left the room without a backward glance.

Chapter Thirty-Six

I noticed the din of the Pied Piper Bar as soon as I entered the marble lobby. It was shortly after ten o'clock and the drinks had been flowing.

Beakman was waiting for me inside, nursing a gin cocktail of some sort. He had a stool at the farthest end of the bar and seemed to be contemplating the large colorful mural that hung behind it. I took the stool next to him and tapped the stem of his cocktail glass with a fingernail on my left hand to get his attention.

"I've heard the piper who took the children away was a disgruntled exterminator."

Beakman stared at me blankly. His eyes were tired and his lids were reddened. "It's late and I don't quite follow that."

"There are different versions of the tale," I explained. "The one I like has it the piper was a rat-catcher, hired to lure away all the rats from the city of Hamelin. After he did that successfully, the Hamelin mayor reneged on his promise to pay him. So, the piper extracted his revenge one day while the adults of the town were in church by piping and leading the town's children out to drown in the Weser River – the same river where he had drowned the rats. Only three of the town's children survived and they were in turn either: lame, deaf, or blind and unable to follow. Beautiful mural, though," I finished.

"You're a bowl of good cheer."

"I'm easily worried," I confessed, showing him my smile while I lit a cigarette.

The barman came over and asked about my taste in booze. I ordered an Old Fashioned and encouraged him to serve it as cold as he could. We made polite banter while he stirred the ice around in the rye.

"What types of things worry you?" Beakman asked eventually after the cocktail had been served and I'd sampled the first sip.

"Let's start with the fact that you haven't been terribly quick to return my calls."

Beakman stared at me with a hint of anger glowing in his eyes. "Maybe I didn't get your messages."

"Maybe you never checked for them."

"I sleep heavy," he informed me.

"Or lie heavy," I suggested.

Beakman snorted, climbed off his stool, and moved around on his feet as a boxer might have shifted weight in the ring. I thought he was about to take a swing at me, and I set myself for that, but instead he leaned back on his heels and showed me the palms of his hand.

"Never mind all that palaver," he sighed. "What are we doing tonight?"

"Sit down," I suggested. "I met your pal Travers this afternoon."

"And what of it?"

"I didn't like him very much."

"Why not?"

"If you have to ask, you probably can't understand."

Beakman allowed himself a grudging smile. "Maybe I don't have to ask, then. He's abrasive and awkward. Hard to imagine that even his own mother likes him."

"Good," I said. "Then we're talking about the guy. The gun muzzle he poked into my back didn't help. Maybe we can talk about other things now."

"Such as?"

"I have a few other concerns."

"Go on," Beakman suggested, trying to project a carefree spirit.

"Our glasses are empty. We should fix that."

"We should," Beakman agreed, nodding.

I nodded too and we waited without speaking while the barman mixed our drinks in two separate glass shakers, stirred them with ice, and poured them out simultaneously.

"Cheers, my friend," Beakman intoned grandly as he picked up his glass with his large, rough fingers.

I picked up my own glass and held it up to the waning light. "Back at you," I said and took a long pull. "This morning I told you about two men I visited last night – Tucker and Chi – and the interesting Chinese keys they each showed me."

"Yeah, I remember."

"So?"

"So, didn't you hear?"

Beakman shook his wide head. "I didn't hear anything. I've been working all day. What happened?"

"They were each shot dead in their homes and the keys they showed me were stolen."

"Did you do it?"

"No, but I found them."

"Was anything else missing?"

"As far as I can tell, only the Chinese keys were taken. Tucker had also had a photograph lifted off his wall."

"What kind of photograph?"

"An old portrait of Sutro's house."

"That's interesting." Beakman paused to clear out some of the gin in his glass. "Do you think I had something to do with the murders?"

I smiled. "I never said that, though it's a reasonable question. Maybe you can answer it?"

"No sir, I had nothing to do with either murder."

"That's a quick denial and it's good to know."

"Of course it is! You weren't expecting an admission. Do you really suspect me?"

I thought it over for a moment and then nodded slowly. "Sure, why not? You seem good for it. You had the knowledge. I'd just given it to you and hours later they were both dead and the keys were gone. Should I believe the timing was coincidental?"

Nervous now, Beakman shook his head furiously, flexing his open palms in front of him as if to show me how empty his hands were. "Listen, I had nothing to do with it and I can prove it. I have an alibi."

"Stop sweating for a moment and tell me what kind of pistol you carry."

"It's a .38," he said quickly, and then suddenly stopped short of saying more.

"I'll need to see it, but obviously not in here. Finish your drink and let's go."

"Where are we going?" Beakman asked nervously.

"Relax," I told him. "We'll finish our drinks, and there's no need to seem hurried about it. Then we'll find private spot to continue our discussion."

"I didn't shoot anyone."

"I'm glad to hear that," I told him. "This is an easy formality. We'll get it out of the way and then we'll be pals again."

Beakman raised his glass and swallowed down all of it as though it might be his last drink ever. I finished mine a little more slowly and looked at him. He was mopping his forehead anxiously with a bar napkin.

"Are you okay?"

"I will be," he assured me.

"Follow me out." I flipped a sawbuck onto the counter and climbed off my stool. I took a last drag at the Chesterfield and leaned over to stub it out in the stone ashtray on the bar as I exhaled.

*

Three minutes later we stood in the stairwell between the fourth and fifth floors.

"Show me," I demanded. "Just move really slowly with it." I didn't have my own gun out.

Beakman reached inside his jacket and pulled out a stainless steel .38 revolver, which he held carefully upside down by the trigger guard with two fingers. "Here, smell it," he said, offering the gun to me. "It hasn't been fired in a month or more."

I took the gun from him and held the barrel near my nose without taking my eyes off him. As I expected, there was no odor of gunpowder. Without saying a word, I popped out the cylinder and tapped out the cartridges into the palm of my hand. Beakman leaned away from me with his hands still held out from his body at chest level. He didn't want to risk giving me any impression of resistance.

"You could have cleaned it since this morning," I said, continuing my false line of patter.

"I didn't, and even if I did, you'd know it. You'd smell the solvent in the barrel."

"Are you carrying a second gun on you?"

"No."

"I have to pat you down just to be sure."

Beakman raised his arms as high as he could while I quickly felt around his shoulders, waist, and ankles. There wasn't a second gun to be found.

"You mentioned an alibi," I reminded him.

"I went down to Monterey today, met with a client, had lunch there in a Mexican cantina."

"Enjoyed a little sunshine?"

"It rained a little and there wasn't much sun to be enjoyed. I came back late this afternoon."

"I thought it was always sunny in Monterey."

"That's what they say in the songs. Don't ever believe it, though. You can read about it in the news if you don't believe me."

"Why should I believe *you*? Got anything to support your story?"

"I might have a parking ticket or something in my pockets I can show you."

"Let's see what you've got."

Beakman patted himself down and rummaged through several pockets. What he came up with was less than convincing. He had a matchbook from Damone's, which he could have been carrying around forever. He also found a receipt from Damone's that indicated he'd eaten a plate of mussels and risotto, and had two sherry cocktails.

The receipt wasn't folded too badly and the paper looked fresh, though it didn't mention a specific date when the mussels and cocktails had been consumed. It could have been as old as the matchbook.

He also had a parking stub dated for 11:06am through 1:27pm for the city of Monterey – right about the time he might have been eating lunch at Damone's – though it indicated today's month and date, it offered no information about what *year* the parking spot had been used.

187

"As alibi's go, these don't add up to air-tight," I pointed out.

"It wouldn't be hard for you to substantiate with a little leg work."

"You think I have time or personnel for leg work on something like this? Who was your client? Maybe I'll call him and get it over with quickly."

"He's a dame, and she would not appreciate a call from you."

"Why not?"

"Her husband is cheating on her and she wants to prove it, but she doesn't want the whole world to know about it."

"Sure. You're doing high-class P.I. work now? Why does that smell rotten to me?"

"Only helping out a friend," Beakman offered with a smile that was supposed to be conspiratorial and allay my suspicions.

"Who's the friend?" I asked. "Is it the lady, or someone else? Maybe you're reporting to the husband who's paying you not to find or not to notice the evidence against him."

It was a shot in the dark, but it hit flesh. Beakman recoiled from my casual accusation in the manner of a guilty man. "I didn't kill your boys," he insisted aggressively. "I couldn't have. I left for Monterey as soon as you and I parted this morning and I didn't return to Frisco until late this afternoon."

"Are you worried they were killed with a .38?" I asked.

Beakman frowned and produced his lavender handkerchief to mop at his forehead. "You implied it," he said. "Well, were they? Tell me, man!"

"No, I didn't imply it," I replied. "I merely asked to know the caliber of your pistol and then I asked to see it after you told me what it was. I think Khai Chi and Tucker were both killed with a .22 caliber pistol. Maybe you're off the hook, after all."

"I never used a .22 in my life. Why are you even badgering me about my alibi?"

I moved up close to Beakman's face with my best hard grin. "I wanted to hear what you would say about it. Even if you didn't gun them yourself, that doesn't entirely let you off the hook. You could have passed the information along to someone else who might have done the gunning. Monterey might be an alibi for where you were at the time of the murders, but it doesn't mean you don't have friends who did the job right here in Frisco for you."

"I don't know what you're talking about."

Still grinning, I handed his empty .38 revolver back to him. "Don't you? I think you know full-well what I'm talking about."

"How so?"

"We'll find out soon enough. Come with me. We're going upstairs."

"Where?"

"We're going to a suite up on the eighth floor, right here in the Palace."

Now my gun was out. I pushed the .45 up under his ribs to make the point and he nodded in easy agreement.

"Sure, friend," he breathed quietly. "We'll go up there together. I won't cause any trouble, none at all."

"I surely know that," I said, smiling into his frightened blue eyes.

Chapter Thirty-Seven

Travers opened the door to let us into Josephine's suite. I felt the abrupt silence in the room. It reverberated tightly: an angry, jealous, paranoid quiet that led me to wonder what might have transpired while I was gone.

"This is Beakman," I announced. "Meet Josephine, Travers, and Smitherton. The lady is Mrs. Jennifer McPhael. Go on, find a seat."

Jennifer was on one of the Barcelona's, exactly as she had been when I left. When she heard her name, she lifted her chin and formed a polite smile. It wasn't a real smile. It didn't involve her eyes, but it was polite enough that it made due.

Beakman held fast in the doorway as though he were stuck there and surveyed the room with a cold eye. I pulled him into the room far enough so that Travers could close the door behind him.

"We were just reading old letters when I left," I said.

"Mr. Beakman," Josephine greeted the new arrival. He came out from around his desk to offer his hand. "It's been many years and it is a pleasure to see you once again."

Beakman took the hand and shook it warily as if it might have exploded on him. His eyes never stopped moving. Once he had accepted a seat in the other Barcelona, he sat back cautiously with his hands on his knees. I was the only one who knew he was effectively disarmed and I didn't mention the fact.

"Where did we leave off?" I asked.

"I had just finished reading the letter," Josephine reminded me. "You went out in a hurry right after that."

"Don't get too excited," I replied. "Beakman, what time had you and I previously agreed to meet at the Pied Piper Bar?"

"Ten o'clock," he answered quickly. "You were a few minutes late."

"Okay, that's fine," Josephine acknowledged. "I retract the implication I left hanging. So, where did we leave off? We were considering the letter from the Chinese final command."

"I think I had raised the question of what it meant to us and whether it was relevant or not. You were going to convince me."

"Maybe I can," Josephine said with a smile. There was a twinkle in his eye that I didn't trust. "I think this mystery is one that goes in phases, like so many other aspects of our universe."

"Care to elaborate?" I lit a Chesterfield and set the match into the ashtray on the table between us.

Josephine's grin broadened. "Everything has phases – a woman's cycle, our seasons, our plants, our moon, the very planets in our solar system. Virtually all aspects of the natural world have their cycles. My point is simply this: We shouldn't assume we have all the information we need or that all the information we need will ever be available to us. Some information is hidden from us, and more than likely always will be."

"Hidden from us?" I asked. "Or seems to be so because we have not looked in the right place for it?"

"Is there a difference?" Josephine inquired.

"Certainly," I said emphatically, exercising my cruelest wit. I'd been drinking all night and now I wondered if it affected my thinking. I pushed on. "Think of our subject as a painting. Perhaps the painter took his revenge on the matter in advance. Perhaps he painted the blurred and swirling colors in an unfinished landscape – a seascape or a mountain scape – with a depth and meaning that only someone who had lived there could effectively instill. Would we care? Would we still study the work, looking for clues?"

"That's too intellectual for me," Josephine said, nodding. He poured another finger of bourbon into a glass, which he brought over to me. "However, it pleases me to know I am working with a man such as yourself. I had initially taken you for a man of action, but now I see you are far more then that. It's a marvelous point that you make."

"The point is easy to make," I said, sniffing the bourbon. "The reality of it is more complicated than you acknowledge."

"Maybe so," Josephine said with a quiet firmness. "What about you, Mr. Beakman. What do you think?"

"I think almost nothing," he replied. "I'm too newly introduced into this room to have any thoughts worth contributing."

"Surely that is not the case," Josephine said, narrowing his eyes. "Like myself and Travers, you are familiar with this city and its ways. I understand you are familiar with our quest and that you are seeking the same thing that we seek."

Beakman nodded carefully, not wanting to show too much commitment. "I am looking for something on behalf of another party – not for myself."

"Who is this other party?" Josephine asked with no attempt to be artful about it.

"I'll keep that to myself."

"We already know!" Josephine clucked. "You're working for Dr. Orion. Are you not his operative?"

Beakman looked around the room and when his eyes were settled resentfully on mine, he nodded. "What else did you give away?" he asked me. His tone dripped with ire.

"There's not a lot to be gained by going it alone anymore," I replied. "I think there were at least three, maybe four or five, strong parties all vying for the same treasure. Up to now, we've only been in each other's way and working toward cross-purposes. We might fare better if we work together, that is those of us who are willing to."

"What are you saying?" Josephine asked. He stood up with surprise and moved his short arms around about his torso as though he were warming up for an athletic event.

"Think about it," I said. I drew a picture in the air with my smoldering cigarette. "Once you do, it will seem clear and simple. We have several camps competing for this prize. I'm not sure exactly how many others are out there, but for the sake of this conversation we'll start right here in this room. I count three distinct interests: First, Mr. Josephine, assisted by Travers and Smitherton; second, Dr. and Mrs. Orion, assisted by Beakman and myself; and third, the McPhaels. From what I've heard and seen, I believe Walter McPhael was pursuing the Orb for himself – though he may have had a pact with you. Until we find him, his wife, Jennifer, should represent his interest. She hired the private investigator, Johnny Drake, who is now dead."

"You have presented us with an intriguing idea: an alliance," Josephine said. "Perhaps you could talk us through the advantages of this approach, as I'm sure you've already begun to think them through."

I shrugged and swirled the bourbon in my glass. "There are benefits and drawbacks to any alliance. In this case, the benefits are that we work together and we pool our knowledge. This increases our chance of finding the treasure. It also means we are not fighting amongst ourselves or killing each other. If we show that we are successful in our alliance, we may even draw others to us, growing our power and reach."

"I'm intrigued, but what about the disadvantages of such an alliance? What are the snares?" Josephine asked aggressively.

I smiled at him and took a pull on my cigarette. "There are several, obviously. Most notable is it means we have to divide or share the treasure among all parties if we recover it."

"Given the greed and avarice of Man, that may not be easy," Josephine pointed out.

I considered this. "It would be difficult to underestimate the greed of Man, but the value of this treasure, as I understand it, is so immeasurable, that there should be plenty to go around. If there are three interests and each receives a third, will anyone claim they are poor?"

Josephine laughed. His hands moved about in the air, near his face. Travers and Smitherton joined in, laughing along with their boss. Even Beakman broke a smile. Only Jennifer remained aloof from the laughter. She sat still on the couch with her gaze focused intently on her hands, which remained clasped together on her lap.

When the laughter stopped, Josephine cleared his throat and said: "You are a rascal, sir; by golly, you are a rascal and I respect you for it! You make a compelling case for our mutual self-interest. I for one am persuaded and I believe you have successfully made the important points that together we can do better and still also have plenty of treasure, as you call it, to divide among us. Even with a one-third share, a man – or woman – would have wealth and power beyond all needs."

"Are you for it?" I asked.

"There is one disadvantage that you have not mentioned," Josephine said in a quieter voice.

I knew what he was referring to. "There is," I admitted. "How do thieves work together and not fall out when the caper is done?"

"Ah, then you understand this point of contention."

I grinned at him. "The issue is as old as the Bible itself. As long as there have been thieves, there have been thieves falling out over the spoils. However, don't mistake this for a thieves' problem. Greed is a foundational motivation for humans everywhere, in every walk of life, throughout all time."

"What do we do about it?" Travers asked. He was nervous and edgy and he'd been touching the holster beneath his jacket all evening for reassurance.

"There are no guarantees," I replied. "You make your best arrangements and your best judgment calls. You don't make deals with people your instincts tell you not to trust, unless you build in contingencies. You develop confidence-building measures and checks and balances."

"What is a confidence-building measure?" Travers asked.

"This meeting right here is one," I told him. "We've spent much of the day together talking about our mutual interests and no one has shot anyone yet. Tomorrow, we'll all feel a little more confident about coming together."

"Assuming I buy that, what kind of checks and balances do you have in mind?" Travers pushed.

I smiled. I wasn't going to show him all my cards. Instead, I turned toward Josephine with a question of my own. "What do you think?"

Josephine offered his own response to Travers' question: "We don't let each other out of our sight, my boy! That's how we check and balance each other. We don't let each other out of our sight. It's simple and crude and it might even work for a short term arrangement, as we all hope this would be."

"Do we have the basis for an alliance then?" I asked.

"Maybe," Josephine replied. "I need to sleep on it, however. Shall we meet here tomorrow afternoon, say about four o'clock to discuss further? If we agree on the alliance, we can proceed with the pooling of our knowledge."

I glanced about the room, checking for reactions. Nobody said anything. "Alright then," I replied finally. "We'll meet back here tomorrow afternoon at four o'clock and we will continue the discussion of an alliance. If you're not here, it will be assumed that you're not in. Fair enough?"

All heads nodded.

"One other question," Josephine started, addressing his words to me. "If you don't mind my asking, exactly what is your real interest in this affair? You indicated that you are helping the Orions, but why? What did they promise you? What are you hoping to get out of this?"

I pushed my cigarette into an ashtray and glanced at Jennifer. She seemed tired and ready to leave, so I stood up and straightened my jacket. I pulled it down around my shoulders and aligned the cuffs. It was late and I'd been sitting for too long. I offered her my hand and she reached for it.

"Beyond fair cash payment, I only want one thing," I said.

"What is that?"

"The man who kills people with a .22 caliber pistol."

Chapter Thirty-Eight

While we waited for the elevator in the plush hallway, Jennifer looked at me with the kind of eyes I'd seen before. I knew what they meant. Primal emotions were stirring.

"It wasn't easy, was it?" I said to help her out.

She shrugged without removing her gaze from mine as if she were watching my expression for confirmation of something. "Where shall I stay tonight?" she asked. "I can't go home. I fear it's not safe. I don't want to go back to the Mark Hopkin's. There were men in the lobby this afternoon. I think they were the same men who came out to my house."

I nodded. "I saw Federal agents outside the Hopkin's this morning."

"Why didn't you warn me?" she asked in an accusatory tone.

"Because they were looking for me. Anyway, you were already registered there and you hadn't used your real name. I figured you were safe enough. If I'd said anything you might have panicked. The best thing you did was to not draw any attention to yourself."

"I can't go back there now, not tonight," she sighed anxiously. "Where am I to go?"

I fingered a Chesterfield as I thought about the options. "I can't bring you home with me. The landlady was very clear about her rules for that sort of thing. She has her morals – and her children to think of."

"I wouldn't want to be responsible for a child's moral downfall," Jennifer said with a suggestive sparkle. I was glad to see a little life appear in her eyes. "Do you think its safe for me to go home tonight?" she asked.

I considered the question. "Do you want me to be responsible for your decision?"

Her lips pouted out. "I hate to admit it – I really do – but I'm scared. I don't know what to do."

I decided to make it easy for her. "If I were you, I would *not* go home."

"Where would you go?"

"Why not stay right here at the Palace?"

"Really?" Jennifer smiled as though I were teasing her. I could see by the way she held her shoulders that she was very tired. "I almost think you're serious," she supposed.

I shrugged myself. "Why not?"

"It would be easy," she admitted. "Is there a risk?"

"There's a risk in crossing the street; in taking a bite of food; in not getting out of bed in the morning. There's a risk to anything you do – or don't do. That's the way it is in life and it's never been any other way. We live with that reality every moment that we breath."

Jennifer sighed and leaned against me with her palm on my chest. The scent of her lavender perfume reached my nostrils. "I'm afraid to be alone tonight," she told me in a half-whisper. "If I get the room, will you stay with me?"

"You're a married woman," I reminded her. "Are you asking me to sleep on the couch?"

She stared at me as though I might be the second catastrophe of her life. When she spoke her voice was thick with sorrow and bewilderment. Her eyes stared through me as though she were seeing the quiet swelling waves of eternity. "No. I'll take the couch. You've done enough for me today. I won't have you sleep on anything less than a real bed tonight."

The way she said it, I almost believed her.

*

While I waited in the Pied Piper Bar, Jennifer obtained a room under her sister's name. After a bellboy showed it to her, she came down and found me in the bar, sitting by myself with an Old Fashioned melting in front of me. My eyes were bleary now and my defenses were down.

"Would you like a drink?" I offered.

Her lips formed a half-smile as her eyes steadied themselves into a stare that might have been something close to pity. "I'd rather go back up to the room and get some sleep," she replied. "Wouldn't you?"

"I am pretty tired," I admitted.

"Let's go, big boy. Let's get you into bed."

We took the elevator up to the fifth floor and walked down the hall leaning against each other. As we reached the end of it, Jennifer caught me watching her face and movements, and she flinched from the expression that must have taken my face.

"Don't look at me that way," she implored. "I'm not half as bad as you must think I am. I'm afraid for my husband and I'm afraid to be alone tonight. I guess those must seem like conflicting fears to you."

I shook my head. "They don't," I said. "They make perfect sense to me."

"I'm sorry I lied to you earlier."

"I know."

"I didn't know Johnny was dead. I tried to call him and when I couldn't reach him, I called a friend to comfort me."

"You already told me that."

Jennifer started to cry a little as we reached the door to her room. I took the key from her and put it into the lock, opening the door for her.

She went in first, looked around, and then turned toward me with an expression of something that was close to lost hope in her eyes. I closed the door behind me and put my arms around her and together we swayed without speaking for several minutes.

*

An orchestral band played quietly on the radio for us. It was a low tempo piece, highly restrained, with low strings providing virtually all of the rhythm. We smoked cigarettes and sipped whiskey cocktails that I'd made from spirits and liqueurs I'd found in a cabinet beside a small kitchenette. With the cocktails in hand, we sat close to each other on the only sofa in the suite.

"Is this a Manhattan?" she asked.

"Something like that," I replied.

"Do you think an alliance with Josephine is a good idea?"

"Up to a point," I said. "What do you think?"

"I don't know, myself. In your mind, what is that point?" Jennifer was very close to me and her voice was muted. Her eyes, looking up into mine, were large.

I didn't exactly answer her question. "If we agree to work together, I think we can develop the parameters to do it right."

"Do you really think so?"

"If you have a different opinion I'll be happy to hear it."

"I have trouble seeing how we can trust Josephine to uphold his end and not turn on us once we have the treasure. He has a lot of gunmen, and he them all over the city."

"What do you suggest?"

"I don't suggest anything, but we need to be careful."

"I can't argue with that," I replied.

"I'm not sure you quite understand," Jennifer said. I could feel the warmth of her breath against my mouth.

"I'm listening."

"You can't trust Josephine. He'll make all the promises in the world and then he'll betray you when you blink. He has done it to too many others before."

"What do you advise?"

"Cut him first."

"Maybe we should have our own scheme, betray him before he can betray us?"

She lowered her eyes. "That did not come out the way I wanted it to. I should have left it alone. We will be careful and that must be enough."

But the suggestion was already there. It hung in the air as cheap cigar smoke did. "If you have ideas, feel free to share them," I said.

Jennifer shook her head slowly and haltingly, as if shuddering from the thought she had almost expressed. "Don't think too badly of me," she whispered. "I've never been in this position before and I am not used to feeling so vulnerable. I'm not as bad as you must think I am."

*

We finished our drinks without speaking. The distance between us on the sofa continued to close as the orchestra on radio played on as if only for us. I could feel the warmth of Jennifer's leg against mine. The scent of her perfume filled my nostrils. The lavender worked its way through my sensory systems and triggered ancient emotions processed deep within my brain.

With her lips close to mine she whispered now: "Only rarely in life does one recognize the special moments while one is actually still in them."

"Do you think this is one of those moments?"

She nodded and pressed closer against me. "You remember them later, often with sadness, as you realize you missed them at the time. I don't want to do that with this moment, not if I can help it."

I looked into her dark eyes and saw myself reflected there.

With her left hand, she reached up to my cheek. I could see her wedding ring glittering in the light that came in behind her. Also illuminated in that light were the faint, delicate hairs on the side of her cheek – those hairs that every woman has that don't show in normal lighting.

"Mrs. McPhael," I whispered.

"Shhhh," she whispered with her mouth against mine.

"Jennifer."

"I'm so lonely," she replied quietly with her eyes blinking large into mine.

She pulled my face to hers and I did nothing to stop her, nothing at all.

Chapter Thirty-Nine

The morning sunlight was clear and pure, parting the curtains over the windows to bring a swathe of warmth that lay itself gently across the bed at an angle. It showed up the paleness of the skin on my arms and shoulders set in contrast to Jennifer's much darker body. I pulled the sheet over her back and tucked it beneath her chin.

Dressing quietly, I scribbled a note for her and left the room while she was still asleep. It was a brisk, clear day and I decided to walk a few blocks to get my blood circulating again.

After twenty minutes on the hills, I caught a cab the rest of the way to the San Francisco Post Office. There I found a letter waiting for me at General Delivery from Dr. Orion. I found a quiet bench outside and tore it open. I read it quickly once, and then slower a second time through.

It was short. It informed me that positive steps had been made with the jewels and he expected an exchange to take place early the next morning. It also said he'd received a report of contact from Beakman and was glad that he and I had hit it off so well.

The letter offered no further information or clue as to where he and his wife were to be found. I refolded it and returned it to its envelope, which I pushed down in the bottom of my jacket's interior breast pocket.

A row of telephone booths was planted along one wall of the post office. I dug a card from my wallet and stared at it, thinking about the man who had given it to me. I had come to think of the entire affair as *Gentryville's Big Knockover*.

It was a grand title that could have filled a marquee for a movie starring George Raft or James Cagney. At the time, Hal Birch had been running for mayor of the small town and by now I knew he had been elected.

*

"Remind me what brought you to Gentryville," Hal Birch suggested.

"Two flats in one day."

"On your way to where?"

"San Francisco."

"What awaits you there?"

"A personal matter, something I've let linger for too long."

"Business then?"

I nodded.

"Dangerous business?"

"Is there any other kind?"

"Do you have friends there?"

"None that I've met yet."

"Here's one." Birch removed a card from his wallet and scrawled on the back of it with a short pencil he'd retrieved from a pocket.

I studied the card. It was a standard business card. The print side carried the moniker "William Q. McGreavy" and a telephone number, but no physical address. When I flipped it over, I saw Birch's signature.

"I never heard of McGreavy," I said.

"Put it in your wallet," Birch advised. "You may not need it, but if you find yourself wanting a friend, look him up and show him the card."

"Who is he?"

"I'll tell you who he's not. He's not the kind of guy anybody knows about unless they are very well connected or are in a lot of trouble. In the case of the latter, it's usually one of the last things they ever know."

I believed Birch was an honest man, but I realized he also had his own closeted history of arrangements. My sigh was weary. "Why do you give this to me?"

"I have a feeling that tomorrow you're going to save our town."

"Are you sure that's possible?"

Birch smiled mildly and nodded his head. With his thumb and forefinger he raised the front brim of his hat. Then he made a quick sign with the thumb and first two fingers of his right hand that I recognized. "I wouldn't be running for office if I didn't."

Suddenly I understood something I had missed before. I smiled and tipped my hat. When I glanced down at the street, the long sedan driven by Angel De Luca was nowhere to be seen. "Let's go inside and find that nurse."

*

It was time to give William Q. McGreavy a call.

Chapter Forty

McGreavy answered the telephone in a voice that floated in on a long slow undulating wave of a Texas drawl. I told him about the card I had from Birch and a little about the situation with the artifact. I also told him about the murders and the man with the .22.

"I've heard of Fingers Pete," he said calmly. "I thought he was strictly east coast."

"I thought so too, until recently."

"What do you make of it?"

I thought the question over. "Either he was brought out here for a special reason; or he was already here, seeking relief from the heat back east and he needed work."

"Which would you put your money on?"

"The latter," I said.

"Is either Smith or Huddleston your real name?" he asked casually.

"No," I replied.

"That's fine, don't tell me. I don't need to know it. Are you somewhere safe and private right now, at this moment?"

I said that I was.

"Tell me more about the situation. What are the names of the players and how do you read them with regard to this artifact."

I tore through it as concisely as I could. It took me less than three minutes of jaw work while McGreavy listened without comment.

When I finished, he cleared his throat. "I need to make a few telephone calls and then we should talk again."

"When?"

"What number are you at?"

I told him.

"I'll call you back within twenty minutes."

I hung up and waited, smoking one cigarette after another while I thought about nothing in particular and everything in general. Nineteen minutes later the telephone rang. "This is Smith," I said. "Or Huddleston. Take your pick."

"I think I've got something for you." McGreavy coughed hard a few times. Then it sounded like he set the receiver down to pour a glass of water, which he drank down in one draught. He coughed a few more times and then poured and drank more. I assumed it was water. It could just as easily have been gin he was drinking. When he came back on the line, his voice was

201

coarse and brittle.

"Don't die on me yet," I said. "I've got need of you."

"Its allergies."

"What are you allergic to?"

"City life. Back to business now. We should meet later today, once I've had a chance to look into this a bit more. It's interesting and it's more complicated than I guessed. I've got a few telephone calls yet to place, but I have some ideas already."

"When?" I asked.

"Let's meet at eleven o'clock this morning. That should give me enough time."

"Where?"

McGreavy gave the matter a little more thought and then instructed me to board a streetcar on the Market Street line near Fremont. I was to ride for five or six blocks standing in the back with my hat on. As we crossed past 4th Street I was to take a seat that would open up next to me and remove my hat. If we missed that, then I was to do the same after 5th Street.

"Is there a secret handshake I need to know about?" I asked after he reeled off his instructions.

"No, but just to be safe, tell me what you look like."

"Have you heard of Johnny Dillinger, know what he looked like?"

"Sure."

"That's close enough."

"Does it mean anything?"

I laughed. "Absolutely nothing at all."

"Bring the card Birch gave you. I'd like to see it – once. I'll give it back to you afterward."

"Understood."

*

The contact came off without a hitch. I boarded the streetcar at Fremont, as instructed. As we approached 4th Street a large middle-aged woman pulled the bell cord and climbed off after we crossed through the intersection. I sat down in the seat she had vacated and found myself looking at a broad-shouldered sunburned man. He had a large black mustache that covered his lips and made his jaw seem small. His hands were very large and scarred and they twirled a dirty white cowboy hat between his knees.

"Can I show you a card?" I asked.

The man nodded without seeming particularly interested.

I passed him the card Hal Birch had given me. He took it, glanced at the

202

front briefly, flipped it over, studied Birch's signature, and then almost smiled as he handed the card back to me.

"Nice to meet you, partner," he said stoically. He didn't extend a hand to shake. In person his drawl was richer and deeper than it had been on the telephone.

"Sorry to bother," I said. "Hal Birch said I might call you in a pinch. I'm in one now. Thanks for helping out."

"Any friend of Birch's is a friend of mine," he assured me with a wink. "You must have done something special for him. I gather it has something to do with all the fireworks I heard about out there in Gentryville a few days ago, must have been the day before Birch got himself re-elected Mayor. Did you have something to do with that fracas?"

I shrugged noncommittally. "How do you know Birch?"

"Ahh, it's a silly story not worth telling," he shrugged. "We were both part of the expeditionary force that landed in France a few years back. You might have heard of it. There was mud and forests and loud noises and a few nervous men telling us where to go and what to do at every moment. Birch and I met one night in the middle of everything. A cask of sour red wine, several curious school girls, and a deck of cards might have been involved. Come morning we found ourselves surrounded by a lot of guys who spoke nothing but German. Birch was a hero, I rode his coattails, and somehow we slipped under the fence alive."

I knew that sometimes men with guns formed lasting friendships. I didn't believe the modest, easy romanticism that underlay the story he told me, but I knew it was how men like McGreavy and Birch talked about their war experiences.

"This next stop is ours," he said eventually without looking at me. He reached up and pulled the bell cord.

We climbed off together and I followed McGreavy several blocks into a tavern on Polk Street. It took my eyes a few moments to adapt to the dim light. As I followed McGreavy past the bar and kitchen and through a room lined with long tables and into a back room, I realized he was very comfortable in the establishment.

Several men called out to him as we went by. McGreavy nodded back at them with a straight expression. I wondered what he did now, but I knew better than to ask.

A short, dimly lit hallway took us past a men's room and to a closed door at the end. McGreavy opened the door without slowing down and went into the room. I followed him. That put us in a small dark chamber with two other doors and a row of narrow windows near the ceiling.

One door obviously went through to the kitchen and the other I realized probably opened out into an alley. There was only one table in the room and it was already set for two. Behind it was a desk with a telephone and various papers spread across it. The morning's *Chronicle* had been set at an angle over everything, waiting to be picked up and read.

"Is this for us?" I asked gesturing at the table set-up.

"It is," McGreavy replied quietly. He looked at me and watched my movements as I pulled out a chair and sat down in it. "When our business is finished, I may stick around a little while longer, meeting with a few other people."

I nodded as I began to understand a little better what was going on. "Of course."

"You must be hungry," he guessed. "I know I am. How about lunch? Do you have time?"

"Sure," I said, nodding.

"What would you like?"

"You order for us. You must know what's good here."

McGreavy seemed pleased by that. With the wrist of one hand cupped in the palm of the other, he tapped his chin a few times with his forefinger. When a deferential man dressed as a waiter came to our table, the order he gave made my stomach growl.

Without so much as a blink to provide a cue for the transition he was about to make, McGreavy said: "I think its time you talked with Mrs. Hu."

"Who is she and do I really need another dame to fuss about with?"

"She's not to be taken lightly."

"Sorry, the remark wasn't worthy of me."

"Mrs. Hu is a local Chinese woman – very wealthy, very powerful. It doesn't take much more than a nod from her to get most things moving in certain parts of this city."

"Will she know where the Orb is?" I asked. "Or where I can find Fingers Pete?"

"Let me tell you something, son," McGreavy began. "When the land is parched, Mrs. Hu can really make it rain. That said, she's not going to get down in the weeds with you or anybody – and she's not an altruist by nature. Do you understand my meaning?"

I nodded.

"What have you got to trade with?" McGreavy asked in his slowest drawl yet.

I smiled because I had something.

It wasn't long before our meal arrived – two plates, each overflowing with meatloaf, sweet peas, green beans, mashed potatoes and gravy, buttered biscuits, and blueberry compote. A pitcher of lukewarm beer was set on the table as well. We ate hungrily without speaking. When our plates were empty, McGreavy looked at me with eyes that had already seen everything.

"Do you have any questions?" he asked.

"Just one," I said. "Because I'm the curious sort. What does the 'Q' stand for?"

McGreavy took a moment before he responded calmly. "I never knew. My father disappeared when I was two and my mother died when I was four. There wasn't anyone around to tell me once I was old enough to wonder myself."

Chapter Forty-One

When she personally opened the door to her very large home, Mrs. Hu stared at me as if I'd accused her of something heinous. Quickly her expression closed against that possibility as I studied her from beneath my hat brim. She was calm and quiet, though as I watched her, she seemed almost hyperactive at an internal level that I could not access. Some inner force rearranged her features, the shape of her lips, the angle of her eyebrows.

"You're the man McGreavy sent to me?" she asked directly.

I nodded.

"I don't want to know your name," she told me.

"That's fine."

"Come inside." She gestured for me to follow her and I closed the door and felt it lock behind me as I came into the large house.

"Were you followed here?" she asked.

"No," I replied.

"Are you good enough to know?"

"Yes," I said emphatically.

With that, she drew me past the sitting room and into small reading room that was off the kitchen at the back of the house. It was a narrow little room with a pair of stained-glass windows along the exterior.

There was only one comfortable chair in the room and it was clearly hers. A slim counter extended out from the wall on one side of the room and there were two simple wooden chairs pushed up under it. I couldn't tell if she was trying to keep my presence hidden from the house staff, or whether it was simply her preferred room to spend time in.

I'd learned long before that many wealthy people had favored chambers that were not the most ostentatious part of their house. It seemed as though they were privately uncomfortable with their own wealth and felt most relaxed in the more modest rooms of their large houses. It was a strange wealth effect that I'd noticed more than once.

"Would you like a cup of tea?" she offered.

"No, thank you."

"Where did you grow up?" she inquired. It was the type of question only a woman of her age would ask a younger man.

"In the Twin Cities," I replied simply, without going into detail.

That seemed enough for her. Mrs. Hu gestured toward one of the wooden chairs and I pulled it out from the counter and waited before sitting down in it. She positioned the other chair in front of a small writing desk that I had passed when we moved into the room.

She turned the chair toward me, and sat down in it with her eyes holding mine. Near her elbow on the writing desk was a red pincushion. I sat down slowly and spread my palms and fingers out on my knees.

Staring into my face, she took a deep, meditative breath and folded her hands together in her lap, waiting. I found her to be quite handsome in an aloof manner. She had silver strands in her long hair that stood out against the black ones, sharp parenthetical lines emanating from the corners of her mouth, and darkened circles that puffed out slightly under her eyes.

"I'm fifty-two years old and I have limited expectations for my own longevity – as should we all," she said. "It would behoove you to get straight to the point."

I got straight to it and gave her the same tale I'd given to McGreavy, in about the same manner and same length of time. I might have been a little faster through it now that I had practiced it once. When I finished, she looked at her watch and I realized she had been timing me.

She almost smiled. "I like it when a man can state his business as efficiently as you did." Habitually, she pushed her long hair back over her shoulder and stared at me with a passionate stare that didn't actually reveal any aspect of what she might have been thinking. An aura of ferocious and forsaken sexuality emanated from her eyes and mouth and her posture.

I nodded and waited without saying anything more. I wanted to light a Chesterfield, but I didn't dare.

"What do you want me to do for you?" she asked.

"You know the questions I have and I think you might be able to find some of the answers, if you don't already know them."

"Why should I help you?"

I was ready for that. "Three reasons. First, some of these rascals are likely to be in your way at some point, if they aren't already. If you help me, I expect I'll get some of them out of your way."

Mrs. Hu nodded, but she did not speak. She waited for me to continue.

"Two, because McGreavy said you owed him a favor."

She shrugged modestly. "I might at that."

"Three, because I have something to trade."

"What is it?" she asked without any apparent interest in what I might say.

After I told her, she nodded and leaned back in her chair. "I need to make one telephone call," she told me. "You should leave my home now, but provide me with an exchange where I can reach you this afternoon at two o'clock. I suggest you make it a public telephone. The only promise I make is that you won't be teased along. If you have not heard from my man, who will be calling on my behalf by five minutes after two o'clock, you may assume that I am unable to help you. Is that clear?"

"Perfectly so."

"You and I won't speak again. If I ever see you again, I won't know you."

"I understand."

"I didn't always have money, you know," she told me. "I certainly didn't come from money, though people often assume I did."

"Few people who have money came from it," I observed.

"You're right about that – it's a little known fact of life."

"Where *did* you come from?" I asked.

"Men don't usually ask a lady questions like that."

"I'm happy to withdraw it if you like. I don't mean to give offense."

"You first. You told me you grew up in the Twin Cities, but that is vague."

I told her the truth. "The dirty streets around Hennepin Avenue, Minneapolis. Nobody in my neighborhood had any money. As much as anything, I guess you could say I was raised in juvenile halls and prison farms."

"Why?"

"My role models were car thieves and robbers."

The shape of her lips didn't change, but a smile appeared deep within her eyes. "I was born in the 'Barbary Coast.' It's a neighborhood of San Francisco – the seediest part of this town. Fifty years ago it was filled with brothels, saloons, gambling parlors, opium dens, and not much else."

"Every big city has a neighborhood like that."

"My mother was a prostitute and a pickpocket; nobody could ever tell me who my father was. Now I live in a gilded mansion."

"That's America, for you."

"No," she chided me. "That is life on this earth."

I didn't respond right away.

Before I could think of the best response to make she rose, offered me her hand, and then she quoted scripture from the book of Zechariah: "*'Woe to the idol shepherd that leaveth the flock! the sword shall be upon his arm, and upon his right eye: his arm shall be clean and dried up, and his right eye shall be utterly darkened.'*"

I stood up.

She was a hard woman and she did not say another word as she showed me to the door and closed it behind me.

Chapter Forty-Two

Standing in the shadows of the clouds that passed over me on Market Street, I thought about my mother and the times she'd expressed hope that I would become a priest. Before her early death, she had been sure the calling would find me. There were times when I almost wished it had.

I had grown weary of other people's pain, hurt, deceit, and bad fortune, and I couldn't help but wonder if a white collar and a black suit might have provided an effective layer of armor against the tribulations of the world. I wondered if it would have shielded me or enhanced my sense of personal responsibility toward others. The idea didn't matter any more. It was too late now – I'd never find out.

One of the chores I completed whenever I arrived in a new town was to scout out a few neighborhood telephone booths and record their numbers in case I needed them. With no fanfare I arrived at the booth who's number I had given to Mrs. Hu about thirty minutes early.

When I reached it, I placed a call through to the switchboard of the Palace Hotel. I gave the operator the room I was trying to reach and waited a little longer. Eventually the call was answered by a voice I thought sounded like Smitherton's.

"Trying to reach Josephine," I said in my deepest, scratchiest, most disfigured voice.

"Who is this?"

"Put him on without a fuss," I said in the same voice. "You know I wouldn't have this number if I didn't know something worth knowing."

"Hang on."

I lighted a cigarette and whirred a few bars of the Hoagy Carmichael tune that still infected my mind.

"Was that 'Stardust' you were humming?" Josephine asked when he came on the line.

"You got the right composer at least. Try 'Georgia On My Mind.'" I said. "How much privacy do you have there?"

"Not enough," he replied, and then covered the receiver with a hand while he barked out commands at the people in the room with him. "Alright, I'm alone now," he said.

"What are the odds someone is in the other room listening on another extension?"

"I'd say low."

"Fine, let's drop them to down to zero. I think you should wander down to the lobby to buy a package of cigarettes and call me at this exchange."

Josephine murmured: "Everyone knows I don't smoke."

"Might be a good time to start," I said. "You got the number down?"

"Yes."

I rang off and sat back to wait.

*

Four minutes later the telephone in my booth rang and I picked it up.

Josephine chuckled with profane amusement. "You must be able to imagine the anxiety that created among my boys."

"It's good for them," I replied. "It will strengthen their hearts and purify their souls."

"If only that could be true."

"At least one of them has good reason to be anxious."

"Which one and why?"

"Easy, we'll get there."

"What have you got for me?"

"I've a proposition to make. It's between you and I, and nobody else. Once you hear it, I think you'll understand why I didn't want to risk having your boys listen in."

"A pact within an alliance is it?"

"Sure," I said. "I know it seems melodramatic, but let me explain."

"I'm eager to hear it."

I laid it out for Josephine quickly and then let him think about it for a moment. "I'm expecting another call in ten minutes," I told him. "You don't have to make a decision by then, but it would be nice if you would. I'll be sitting here until my two o'clock telephone call comes through. Do you want to call me back before or after that?"

"There's no need," Josephine said soberly. "I can agree to the pact you offer right now. I'll see you at four o'clock as we agreed last night with the entire group. This bit is between us, and I assure you I can deliver on my part of it."

"Since you've agreed to the pact, I'll tell you some more and then I have a few suggestions."

"Go ahead."

I told my story quickly and outlined a few steps that he should take. Josephine listened quietly and when I was finished speaking he made a series of clucking sounds with his tongue. "That's quite lovely," he said after a full pause.

"Are you still on board?"

"By all means."

"Do you see a problem with the approach I suggest?"

"It's bold, I'll give you that."

"Right, but do you see a problem with it? Can you manage your end?"

"Other than it might not work, I don't see any problem with it," Josephine replied emphatically. "I'm in. I will handle my end. You handle yours. Let's see if we can make it work."

"You can count on it," I said and rang off.

I sat back in the booth and lighted a cigarette while I waited for the next telephone call.

*

A few minutes later the telephone rang again.

"Are you McGreavy's friend?" a male voice of indeterminate age and race inquired.

"Yes," I said.

"Write down this address."

"Ready."

The voice spit out a number on Stockton Street. "How soon can you get here?"

"I can be there within ten minutes."

"Better make it twenty," the voice said and then the line went dead.

*

I found the address on Stockton Street easily enough and I checked my watch to be sure the requested twenty minutes had elapsed. When I arrived, I knocked hard on the exterior door and waited with the suitcase in my hand. It was a simple matchbox in my hand, and not especially heavy.

Eventually the door opened and a dark-skinned man with a serious expression on his face invited me inside. I didn't want to go in, but I didn't see an alternative. I smiled into his stoic face and handed him the matchbox that I carried. He took it from me and set it on the floor as though it didn't interest him at all.

He was a tall, dark-skinned man of slender build, with a short-trimmed black beard and mustache of uniform length. The gray suit he wore was conventional and tasteful, accented by a conservative charcoal tie. Wire-framed spectacles disguised his eyes and he had a long narrow nose that lent his face a powerful expression of dysphoria that I assumed he could never quite escape.

I wondered if he had internalized the exterior appearance of his face over

211

time or if it had worked the other way around. For all I knew his family thought he was a jolly old soul, quick with a joke and hearty laugh. It didn't seem likely, though.

"That's it," I told him. "As promised, it's all in there."

"Thank you," he said politely, bowing as he did so.

"Yes," I replied.

"You can wait over there," he told me in surprisingly facile English, pointing toward a long bench that was positioned just to the right of the entrance.

"It's a trade, though, right?" I said, as much to remind him, as to clarify my own understanding of the arrangement.

The dark-skinned man nodded slowly and looked over my shoulder as if he were bored already. I decided it was best not to remind him that Mrs. Hu had at least pretended to be on my side. I sat on the bench he'd pointed me to and lighted a cigarette and closed my eyes while I smoked it.

Time went by and my imagination worked itself through a number of unpleasant scenarios. I heard small sounds that worried me. As I looked around I realized I was sitting in the hallway of an old house that had been retrofit for a small business. It was no longer a residence.

I didn't know the man's name, but his features struck me as someone who might have come from Persia. I wondered if he was from Egypt or Tehran and if that meant anything I should be concerned about. Maybe it had nothing to do with anything; maybe I was imagining shadows where there weren't any.

The bench was hard and uncomfortable and I didn't feel like sitting there for long. The man had taken the suitcase into his office, which was on the other side of the wall behind me.

Halfway through the first Chesterfield, I decided I wasn't comfortable with that either and I stood up and moved to stand against the wall on the other side of the hallway, about ten feet down and just outside someone else's office door. My right hand rested easily inside the jacket I wore over the handle butt of my .45.

I finished the cigarette with my left hand. Ten minutes later the man came out of his office. A flat expression on his face told me nothing, and did not set me at ease. In his left hand he carried a large manila envelope.

"We have a deal," he announced. "The case of narcotics is exactly as you said it would be. I don't know where you got it, but we will take it. In exchange you get this."

He handed me the manila envelope and I took it from him and held it with my arm relaxed at my side without glancing at it.

"This concludes our transaction," the man said to me without emotion. "I wish you well. Might I suggest something?"

"Of course."

"Don't come back to this building. We only use our office sites once. We will never be here again."

"I understand."

"Do you?"

"Yes," I said, with a hard undercurrent to my voice that I was unable to stifle. "I don't know you. This meeting never happened. We never met. There was no suitcase, no manila envelope."

"Then, you understand perfectly," the man said to me with another slight bow.

I left the building with the envelope burning hot in my hand.

Chapter Forty-Three

In the early evening Jennifer McPhael and I rode the elevator together up to the eighth floor. With her hip lightly next to mine, I was aware of her body. I handed the man working the dials inside the car a folded dollar. I wanted him to look at the bill and not my face as we stepped out past him.

When the doors closed behind us Jennifer took my arm and leaned her head against my shoulder. The scent of her lavender perfume caught my nose and tickled some ancient part of my brain that knew only one way to respond. I leaned toward her and kissed her lightly on the forehead. She looked up at me with a smile in her brown eyes. In the dim light her pupils had expanded. Something else could have caused it.

As we moved down the hallway I thought she might take my hand, but she didn't go that far. I knocked on the door of Josephine's suite and Smitherton opened it a moment later.

He rubbed a spot beside his eye with the knuckle of his left hand. "You're kind of late," he said resentfully.

"Don't ride me," I replied. "We got here when we could."

Anxious electricity flowed between the people in the room. Smitherton joined Travers and Josephine to stand along the interior wall. They wore matching bowler hats.

Beakman was there too, nursing a foamy beer on the sofa. His jacket was laid over the armrest and his sleeves were rolled up past his thick elbows. He was sweating as if it were hot. It wasn't. A shoulder holster and harness was looped around his right shoulder and fat neck. The revolver under his left arm was a .32. I assumed he'd managed to find new bullets for it.

I didn't see anything to be gained from playing a stall, and I felt Josephine's studious gaze following me as I moved across the room. I struck a grin and found a spot on the exterior wall I could lean against. I left my hat on for no reason that I could have explained afterwards other than it would allow me get out of there faster if I needed to.

Jennifer sat down on the end of the sofa, near me. The way her hair fell down over her face, her eyes were veiled to my view.

"Interesting to note that most of us are standing," Josephine observed.

"Let's get on with it," I replied.

"Where shall we begin?" Josephine wasn't looking at me, though I knew he was expecting me to respond to his question.

"We are looking for a sealed chest," I started. "This afternoon I learned where it is. The chest was initially listed as part of Lot seventy-three, which was withdrawn from auction at Thorough's House yesterday. You all know what I'm referring to." I paused to glance around the room.

Nobody registered any particular reaction or said anything, though the anxiety index in the room ticked up a notch. I wondered if it could have been measured by mercury.

I continued: "The fact that it was withdrawn from auction almost certainly means something. Does anybody have an idea what?"

There was a silence until Josephine cleared his throat. "Perhaps the seller suspected the value of what he had. He might have withdrawn it in order to increase the mystery and raise the price. Possible?"

"That's a reasonable guess," I said. "However, it's not correct."

"What is it then?" Beakman demanded. His voice was irritable and I realized he looked like he hadn't slept the night before.

"Sentiment," I explained. "The owner of Lot seventy-three held on to this treasure for many years. Emotion, passion, and hunger have all intervened. How do you sell at auction that which is connected to your very ancestry? Its not an easy decision – even if you need the money."

"Do you know who the owner of Lot seventy-three is?" Beakman asked.

"I do now," I said, nodding.

"Who is it?"

"I doubt his name would mean anything to you."

"Try me," Beakman suggested.

I smiled and the smile must have seemed as tired as I was. "Not yet. I'll hold that close for the time being. I wouldn't want anyone to disappear from this conversation with an idea they might reach him. Anyway, it's not important right now. What is important is the location of the chest."

"Do you know where it is?" Josephine asked.

I nodded.

"Where?"

I held up the envelope. "It's right in here, all written down."

"You're certainly smug about it," Josephine declared. "What have you not told us yet?"

I smiled. "I have information about Walter McPhael. I know where he is now."

Jennifer gasped and buried her face quickly into her hands. Intentionally, I'd said nothing to her beforehand.

"Its hard for me to believe you have anything real," Travers scoffed loudly. He leaned off the wall and moved his hands around near his belt buckle.

"Why do you say that?" I challenged. I came off the wall myself and unfolded my arms. I held out the manila envelope in my left hand as though

I were holding a platter.

"I trust my instincts," was all Travers said. "You don't know where the chest or McPhael is right now. I think you're making it up as you go along."

I shrugged. "Maybe you're not interested in what I have in this envelope. Feel free to leave any time."

Travers reddened as if he'd been shamed. "I didn't say that. How did you get this information?"

"There are powerful people in this town. I had something to trade and one of them had the information I was looking for."

"Convince me," Travers said bitterly. He moved his body forward in a manner that was intended to be physically intimidating. He was a couple inches taller than me and had me by at least twenty-five pounds.

I smiled to offer him a little relief from his own anxiety. "It's right here in this envelope. Shall I open it and read it to everyone?"

"No," Josephine said loudly. "You don't have to read that for my boys."

"Doesn't he?" Travers asked. "I think he does, and I think he should do it right now."

"I don't answer to you," I told him curtly.

Suddenly Travers had his gun out and pointed at my face. It was a long-barrel .38. Steadying his gun hand over his opposite write, he aimed at me from across the small room.

From the corner of my eye, I saw Beakman pull his own pistol – the .32 revolver – and point it at Josephine and Smitherton who were standing close together, still against the wall. He moved it back and forth between them.

For a moment I watched them, studying the pistols and the odds. The only thing I was holding was a manila envelope.

Jennifer started to cry in a quiet, panicked sort of way. She shrunk inward, with her shoulders folding over her hands and face as though it might help her to become as small as she possibly could.

Travers took charge now. "You don't answer to me? I think you do now, and I'm not in a mood to compromise. You say you have an envelope with the information, well then hand it over because I'm your new boss." He took a few steps forward. Now he stood in the middle of the room.

I looked at Josephine and he pursed his lips in response to my gaze. "Is Travers acting on your behalf?" I asked.

Josephine shook his head tightly, without saying anything. His eyes were focused on the gun that Beakman pointed at his face. "No," he replied calmly. "Is Mr. Beakman acting on yours?"

"He's not," Travers volunteered for me. With his lips pressed tight together, he worked hard to push back the grin that was trying to form on his face. "Beakman and I decided to go into business for ourselves. There's no need for you to read the contents of your envelope. Toss it over here and I'll look at it myself."

"A Mexican standoff?" I suggested.

"Not at all," Travers laughed. "We have two guns drawn, to your none. Give me the envelope."

I flipped it to him and it sailed a bit.

When he reached out to grab it, I drew my .45 and shot Beakman in the side of the head. The heavy Egyptian died instantly. Carried by the force of my blast, parts of his face splattered against the wall. He had pretended to work for the Orions, but now he would never pretend to do anything again.

Travers jumped a bit, but he kept his calm. His pistol was still aimed at my head and he pulled the trigger with full intent.

He had me dead to rights, but for one thing: his pistol didn't fire. There was no rush. I aimed my .45 at him, but I didn't shoot. Puzzled and confused he shook his own pistol and turned in time to see Smitherton bearing down on him with his gun drawn.

"After all these years?" Travers sneered. "I don't think so. I don't think you could."

He was wrong: Smitherton did.

Chapter Forty-Four

As the cordite in the air settled, Jennifer McPhael fell back into the sofa and let her arms fall loosely at her sides. Her eyes were opaque with something I couldn't identify as she turned her head numbly about the room. I moved over to sit next to her on the sofa and placed my face close to hers.

"Shhh," I whispered. "We're okay." It wasn't wholly a lie that escaped my lips.

"Someone should call a priest," she spluttered, reaching out an open hand to me, as though offering me a portion of her sorrow.

I took the hand and pulled her toward me so that the warmth from her shoulder traveled through mine and then deeper inside me. She started to cry lightly, holding her head so that she wouldn't have to look at the bodies of the two dead men or their blood that was spread about.

From the desk Josephine made two brief telephone calls. "No one heard the shots, so we won't be bothered by the authorities," he said calmly after he replaced the receiver. He ignored Jennifer and the fact that she was weeping quietly into my shoulder. "My men will be here shortly to rearrange the room."

They must have been down the hall, because a minute later four men wearing bowlers came in without knocking. Setting to work quickly, they swung large canvas bags with zippers and began moving furniture out of their way. One of them pushed a cart of cleaning materials. They were careful not to look at us.

"Shall we move into the next room?" Josephine invited with an open palm held out to show the way.

I stood up and pulled Jennifer with me gently. She moved compliantly, an obedient rag doll, waiting to be tossed about or pushed in any direction.

We filed out of the room as Josephine's men were lifting Beakman's body and fitting it into a canvas bag. The grating sound of a zipper followed us out.

*

There were drumbeats in my temples. Josephine led us into a parlor that was a lot like the room we had just left. It was less cozy, but as dimly lit and devoid of character. I guided Jennifer toward a white chaise lounge that was printed with black zig-zag lines. The senseless thought that occurred to me was that the drumbeats and the zebra lines meant I was in a jungle. I pushed that away.

Jennifer dropped onto the chaise lounge and I sat down beside her. Immediately, she slumped against me and took one of my hands in two of hers. Vigorously, she rubbed it, massaging it with her thumbs and forefingers.

At least she wasn't crying any more. Her eyes had changed in some way that I couldn't identify. They were clear now and more focused. Still, she did not speak.

Josephine and Smitherton took high wingback chairs that were already positioned across from where we sat, and together we waited without speaking for while. Smitherton's expression was simultaneously anxious and triumphant. As though he was pleased with his accomplishment of removing a threat, he was unsure of what it meant he should do next.

I watched him carefully with my gaze moving between his eyes and Josephine's. They offered no clues.

*

Eventually, I lit a cigarette and passed it to Jennifer McPhael who took it and placed it between her lips as her own. I lighted a second one for myself. "I think we should explain things to Mrs. McPhael."

"We should," Josephine agreed seriously. "Our clever friend here," he said nodding at me, "uncovered a betrayal plot that Travers and Beakman planned to implement today. They were going to kill us all and pursue the treasure for themselves. Myself, I didn't want to die today. I assume you did not want to either?"

Jennifer managed to shake her head, but she didn't raise her tear-filled eyes to look at him.

"Of course you didn't," Josephine pronounced. "We prepared for it together. Mr. Smitherton has been close to Mr. Travers from some years, but he is loyal to me. He found a chance this afternoon to remove the firing pin from Mr. Travers pistol. From there it played out exactly as you saw. Mr. Beakman was the key, and our friend here took care of him."

"Those two men are dead," Jennifer said quietly. Tousled strands of hair hung down over her eyes on both sides of her face. "I've never seen a man killed before." Her eyes were small dots of horror and disbelief. I worried she was in shock and I knew what that could mean.

I felt her wrist, then I took her hand and patted it, but I didn't say anything.

"Killing is always regrettable," Josephine explained. His voice was gentle. "If there had been another way, we would have taken it."

Jennifer remained quiet. She watched my face intently as though searching for hidden answers there. I didn't think there were any to be found.

As I studied her in return, I sensed the internal workings of her mind. Her thoughts were racing and she played out one scenario after another, as though she were locked in on a game of chess and calculating the outcomes

219

of different possible moves.

I couldn't predict her next reaction, whether it would be offensive or defensive, but I knew she was working frantically to decide upon it before something else happened and stole the turn away from her. Her hands were actively worrying themselves on her lap and I reached over to place a hand over them.

"Try to stay calm," I suggested to her.

"Tell me about my husband," she replied. "What do you know about him?" Her voice achieved a level of determination that pleased me. I wanted to see her resolve.

"He's on his way to Tehran," I told her.

"Why?"

"I believe he is following a lead."

"Are you lying to me?"

I shook my head. "I wish I were."

"Why have I not heard anything from him?"

I paused before I answered. "I'm not sure. There are a number of possible reasons. If what I learned is correct, he was on a boat out of San Francisco harbor the very day you noted his disappearance. The steamer might have had several stops to make, and probably has not yet arrived in Persia."

"He would have sent me a note before he left. He would have arranged to wire a telegram."

I told my biggest lie of the night. "I believe he tried to, but his message didn't come through for one reason or another. One of his office assistants may have betrayed him. She may have intercepted a message that was meant for you."

"What is her name?"

"It doesn't matter now, she's disappeared. We can't trace her."

Jennifer was silent for a moment. I assumed she was reviewing the list of her husband's office staff. "Do you think my husband is alive?"

"I'm optimistic, though I can't know for sure." With that I surpassed my previous big lie of the evening.

Jennifer drew a deep breath and sighed. With one motion of her hand, she swept the hair back from her cheek to park it behind an ear. She repeated the motion with the other hand, the other side of her face. They were vulnerable gestures. I was close and tempted to kiss her on the first cheek she cleared, but I didn't.

Across from us, Josephine coughed politely to remind us of his presence and interjected: "Brass tacks now: Where is the sealed chest of Lot seventy-three? You told me you had a line on it."

I nodded slowly, still watching the woman. "Yes," I confirmed without saying anything more.

"Where is it?" Irritation crept into his tone. I wasn't sure if it was part of his act or not anymore.

I studied him now. "We have an understanding between us, right?"

"Of course. Where is it?"

"It will be arriving on a steamer in the morning, quite early." I opened the manila envelope and consulted a piece of paper that I removed from it. After studying it, I named an arrival time.

"That *is* early," Josephine observed. "Should we be there to meet it?"

"No point in that," I replied. "We don't know the pier yet, and even if we did they won't be unloading the moment it docks. They certainly won't be handing out parcels to rummies like us gathered around."

"Do you have the name of the steamer in that envelope?" he asked.

"I do, but I think it's a wrong play to be waiting for it when it comes in."

"That bothers me."

"It shouldn't."

"Tell me why you think this."

"It's too obvious, and anyway there won't be a good chance to intercept the chest at that point even if we know the right pier." I paused to look about and then spoke as firmly as I could. "Look: There is a specific delivery address for the shipment. They will be transporting it across town to a warehouse. It will be much easier to take it there."

"Do you have the address of this warehouse?"

"I do," I nodded.

"What is it, then?" he asked.

I didn't answer the question right away. I looked at the two other people in the room with us. Smitherton sat quietly with his hands relaxed on the armrests of the wingback chair he sat in. His eyes blinked as I stared at him.

Jennifer was watching me carefully. I drew a breath and found a pack of Chesterfields from a front shirt pocket and lighted one. The irate impatience in the room was palpable, though I didn't care about that. I shook out the match and placed it leisurely in the center of the nearest ashtray. It stuck up straight into the air, a miniature finger of god pointing at the ceiling.

"It's like this," I started slowly, and then paused to take a long drag on the cigarette and exhale. "Here is where trust comes in to play, where our alliance must be tested."

"Oh, come now," Josephine exclaimed. "Minutes ago we killed two men who plotted against us. Together, we outmaneuvered them, anticipated their play, and we took them down effectively – at considerable risk to each of us. Is that not a demonstration of a meaningful pledge between us? Have we not proven our bond through that baptism of fire?"

221

I smiled at Josephine and gestured with my hands as I worked on the Chesterfield. After another drag, I glanced at Jennifer and then back to Josephine. "You're perfectly right," I said. "I will tell you the address of the warehouse. However, first, I think we should agree on a plan. How are we going proceed?"

"What do you suggest?"

"I think we should send Mrs. McPhael to claim the chest," I said. "She'll have the credibility we need and no one will expect her to be anything other than what they think she is."

Jennifer moved her head around slowly and stared at me with surprise and fear in her expression. I leaned toward her with an understanding smile.

Josephine grinned hotly and clicked his teeth hard. "That could be just the right play," he cooed, grinning from ear to ear. "A female like her won't tip our mitt."

"It's going to be alright," I promised her. It was a lie, and I noticed the lying kept getting easier the more I did it.

She was already beginning to shake her head. "It's risky?"

"You can do this," I whispered. I patted her hand.

"What's the address of the warehouse?" Josephine asked greedily.

I opened the envelope, removed a sheet of paper, and read the address out loud. Then I handed the paper to Jennifer. Josephine stood up to read it over her shoulder as she studied it.

Smitherton began to cough. He coughed long and hard enough that eventually I got up to hand him a glass of water.

*

Jennifer and I didn't remain long in Josephine's suite after that. There was no reason to. We still had the room she had taken the night before.

We retired there together and ordered for two: rare steaks, baked potatoes, fried corn, half an apple pie, and two bottles of red wine to be brought up to us. I wasn't in a mood to talk much, and neither was she. We sat on the sofa together while we waited and I put an arm around her.

"He's an awful man, that Josephine," she said quietly, after awhile. Her mouth was tucked into my neck.

I couldn't disagree with her.

"He'd sacrifice his granddaughters for a few dollars," she whispered.

"Probably," I replied. "Though, remember he *did* have a reaction to the death of his niece."

"Was that genuine?"

I couldn't answer her question, so I remained silent.

"Why are we doing business with him?" she asked after a while. Then she pulled her face away from my neck so that she could look into my eyes.

"You already know why," I told her.

"Remind me."

"Because he has the connections, the guns, the information, and the understanding of Chinese history and culture that we need."

For a while we didn't talk. When the food arrived, we had them set it up at the dining table. After the server left, we ate in silence. Once all of the food and the first bottle of wine were finished, we returned to sit next to each other on the sofa with our private thoughts unspoken until the second bottle of wine was empty too.

It was almost late enough. Jennifer looked at me with large sad eyes as if she were about to erupt.

"Don't go all watery on me now," I said. "Please."

"I've had too much to drink."

I shook my head. "You need to sleep it off then."

"No. I need you, right now.... It's as simple as that, isn't it?"

I shook my head, but I didn't fight her.

Chapter Forty-Five

I left the Palace Hotel at seven o'clock in the morning after ordering room service: a pot of black coffee, three poached eggs over sourdough toast, beef hash, roasted tomatoes, and a bowl of canned peach slices.

Jennifer didn't stir while I dressed and ate, and she was still sleeping soundly as I watched her for a long moment from the doorway. A lock of hair was pasted hotly against her cheek and her mouth was open slightly. Her face was sunk so deeply into the pillow that I couldn't see her eyelids. The only movement I saw was a slight twitch in her left hand – the hand that wore her ring.

I closed the door quietly behind me. The long hallway was silent with muted lighting.

*

With Louis Armstrong's recording of 'Stardust' still playing in my mind I collected my Ford from parking and drove it around the block once. A Chinese man in a bowler hat joined me at the last corner and climbed into the passenger side seat beside me. I didn't know his name, though his face was familiar to me. We didn't speak.

From there we drove around the block again and found a good place to watch the exit I thought she would come out of. We didn't have to wait long, not more than fifteen minutes. When she appeared, Jennifer McPhael walked up the street a half block to get away from the hotel bellboys and hailed a taxicab on her own.

Traffic wasn't too heavy yet. I merged into it and followed the cab across Montgomery, up Pine Street, and then right on Mason to the Mark Hopkins, where Jennifer breezed out of the cab and into the hotel. I pulled to the curb at Mason, halfway between Pine and California Streets and nodded at the man beside me. Without a word he climbed out and disappeared into the crowd of pedestrians that moved along there.

The sun came out briefly to create long shadows of the city buildings. I drove back through the striping of the shadows to the Palace Hotel and let the valet take my automobile again. I tipped him well enough to hold it there for me because I would be coming back for it soon.

Josephine was waiting for me in long flannel pajamas when I reached his suite. His eyes were heavily crusted from a night of lousy sleep. It was the first time I noticed that he looked old, possibly even unwell. Dried age spots

224

dotted his cheeks and neck. His lips were parched and starting to crack at the corners.

"Coffee or tea?" he offered. "There are eggs, pastries, sausage, and fruit on the sideboard there. Also there's fresh orange juice if you like that sort of thing."

"Is that a Chinese breakfast?"

"I'm assimilated," Josephine replied with an easy yawn as he resumed his seat at a long dining room table. A half empty plate of food with a fork in the middle of it sat before him. He didn't pick up the fork or show any interest in the plate.

"I'm not hungry." I told him where I'd left Jennifer McPhael and his man, what I thought about it, and where I thought the entire show would lead.

With his eyes cast down toward his breakfast Josephine did not comment. His tired fingers picked up the fork from the plate and also a knife. It took him a moment to position them usefully within his grip.

"What have *you* got for *me*?" I inquired.

Josephine carved a browned sausage in half lengthwise, cut one of the lengths in half, speared one of the pieces, dragged it through syrup and placed it carefully into his mouth. I waited quietly while he chewed and swallowed. "The lady made a telephone call from the hotel after you left this morning."

"She pretended to be asleep. She must have moved quickly after I closed the door behind me."

"As you predicted, she called a guy she addressed as 'Mr. Pete.' How well do you know him?"

"Well enough," I said as I stood up.

"Don't forget to call."

I left the room and went down to collect my automobile. Something inside me ached and my mood was ugly and sour. The world was never quite the way I wanted it to be.

*

There was no particular hurry now. I made my way across town slowly, stopping three times to make telephone calls from different public booths. None of the people I spoke to seemed happy to hear from me, though each of them indicated an interest in what I had to say.

At the last stop I checked in with my answering service and then returned two telephone calls. After that I made a few more stops in the business district, spending money everywhere I went.

By noon I had bought, packaged, and shipped a few items, retrieved something I'd left at the train station, and purchased a ticket that would take

225

a man far away from San Francisco. I had one more call to make before the afternoon theatrics I expected.

*

When I arrived at the warehouse there was no particular commotion on site. I drove around to scout the area and then parked three blocks away and went back on foot, through an alley to the building next door. A fire escape took me up to the third floor roof.

The roof access door was unlocked and I took that down to the third floor, down a hallway and into an empty office overlooking the warehouse. I was pleased to find the window was already cracked open and a chair had been drawn over to it. I sat there and studied the street below from behind a thin blue curtain.

I checked my watch, saw I still had time, and lighted a cigarette. Smoking slowly as I leaned back in the chair, I thought through the things that were going to happen over the next few hours. I'd brought a pair of field glasses along and looped them over my neck for ready use. Every few minutes, I used them to survey the area quickly, and then I dropped them down to hang against my chest.

All I had to do now was wait and I did that easily. Over the years, I'd become good at it – the waiting. I sat quietly for over an hour until I heard sounds down on the street. Two trucks pulled up into the alley below me.

Men in suits climbed out and moved quickly into the warehouse from a side entrance. I watched them through the field glasses. Most of them carried shotguns or machine guns. After they were inside, the two trucks moved on through and disappeared out the other end of the alley.

Everything was quiet again. I lighted another cigarette and watched. During the next half hour nothing happened other than the cigarette burned down to the butt and became a pile of ash and a pleasant memory.

'Stardust' continued to play on inside my head, though the tempo picked up slowly as the hour approached. I pictured Armstrong's face and the grimace he made when he played the tune. How many real artists were there in the world, anyway? What did they have to endure, to sacrifice, in order to pursue their art?

Shortly before four o'clock a wide loading door that fronted the street was opened from the inside. An angular man in a white t-shirt stepped out onto the loading dock and glanced about. I could see the green tattoos flexing and moving on his massive biceps. With a thumb and forefinger placed in the front of his mouth, he loosed a loud, shrill whistle.

Immediately, a small line of trucks made their way up from along the

226

street and formed a line toward the loading dock. One by one, they pulled up, paperwork was exchanged and reviewed, and then goods were loaded. I smoked another Chesterfield while I watched the slow procession move through.

At some point near the end of that procession a low, black Dodge pickup truck appeared in the line. It was one of the smaller trucks that had come through to make a pick up.

I watched through the field glasses as paperwork was handed out through the window and several minutes later a small trunk was loaded into the back of the black Dodge. The driver had climbed out to supervise, though he didn't open the trunk that he received. He touched it with his fingers and ran a hand over the top of it – almost contemplatively.

I smiled to myself and kept my eyes focused on the glasses. It didn't take long. Within a moment, and before the man could climb back into the driver's seat of the truck, three men with Thompson guns appeared around him. Two of them stood on the loading dock pointing their muzzles down at him. Another had crept around the back of the truck and came up with his muzzle pointed at his back.

From the window where I sat, I watched as several other men in suits appeared and pulled the man down to the ground. There were curt shouts of instruction. Within seconds they had him flat on the ground beside his truck with his hands behind his neck, hand-cuffed. Badges were flashed at that point.

There was some discussion among the men standing around and then a black Ford sedan appeared suddenly. I knew it had left a little of its rubber on the road outside the loading dock.

The handcuffed man was hustled off the street and into the Ford. Two men climbed in after him and a third hopped into the Dodge truck. They pulled out behind the Ford and followed it down the avenue until it turned down a side street outside my field of vision.

With another Chesterfield burning between my lips I watched for another ten minutes, but nothing of any interest happened after that and I closed up shop.

Chapter Forty-Six

There was no reason to overthink it. I parked as close as I could and fixed my fedora squarely, pulling the brim down over my face. I walked in through the front door as though I were the boss of the joint.

Once inside, I closed the heavy front door behind me. The sounds of traffic diminished sharply, though I became aware of the immediate reverberations of the building I had entered. Somewhere ahead of me telephones rang, voices murmured, and a typewriter banged along at medium speed. Odors of old tobacco, sweat, urine, blood, and fear permeated the air. My own footsteps echoed below me on the hard floor.

An older man – sixty if he was a day – in regular shabby blues ambled out to meet me. The white shirt he wore beneath his jacket had come un-tucked over his belly and there was a mustard streak near his mouth and collar.

He conceded his authority quickly when I flipped open the shield I carried. It was the badge I'd taken from the federal special agent who had carried me down California Street two days before. At quarter to six o'clock in the evening, the office was emptying out fast. Two young ladies in cashmere sweaters and wool skirts went by us, whispering rapidly to each other as they passed.

"End of day shift," the old man in blues explained to me in an apologetic voice.

Clerks, stenos, administrative assistants, and special agents were heading home for the evening. There was a photograph of Edgar Hoover on one wall, over a desk. It was tilted noticeably to the right and covered in some dust. Someone had looped a piece of red yarn over the low corner at the top. It wavered in the steam of air cast by an electric desktop fan.

"How long have you worked out of this office, sergeant?" I inquired.

Bright hard lights shone through from the back of his eyes and then faded quickly. "Little over a year, sir. Before that I had a night desk at a county lock-up, and before that I walked a beat. This office was only established in the spring of thirty-three. I'm here because it beats lock-up and beat duty. I'm too old to have much pride left about this kind of soft work."

He had a thousand tight wrinkles around his eyes and he hadn't looked at my badge carefully or asked any questions. I hadn't expected him to. I wore a dark suit and walked like I knew what I was doing.

I stood tall above him and didn't make an effort to hide the .45 in my shoulder holster. "I'm T. A. Jackson, Special Agent in Charge, Sacramento.

Heard you had a prisoner I should talk to? He might be one of the boys we've been looking for."

"Yes, sir."

"Then you have the prisoner?"

"Yes, sir, I believe we do."

"Has he been fed yet?"

"Yes, sir."

"Caused any ruckus?"

"No, sir."

"Take me to his cell."

"You'll have to sign in here."

"Blazes, man!" I half-roared, cruelly in my best thespian voice. "Let's get to it!"

His hands trembled as he filled out a slip of paper and then pushed it over to me on a clipboard. I scrawled something vague that was illegible even to me.

The old man in blues led me through a short maze of hallways, offices, and small holding cells. A sign informed me when I had left the federal office building and entered a county building, even though it was the same building. We went down a narrow flight of stairs that hadn't been painted in about twenty years, turned a corner, and entered a long hallway with jail cells on both sides.

They all looked the same. The color of everything was a blinding flat gray – the floor, the ceiling, and the bars of the cells. We went all the way to the end, chased there by the echoes of our footsteps. The cell on the left was empty. The opposing cell had a body lying on a cot with a black hat over its face. The man's feet were crossed over one another at the ankles in a carefree manner.

"If you don't mind, you could wait down there," I said to my guide.

"Sure, boss," he replied quietly. He shuffled off and by the slump of his shoulders I took it he was gravely disappointed. When he was far enough away I banged my knuckles between the bars of the cell on my right.

*

The body sat up on its cot and removed the hat from over its face. When his eyes had adjusted to the light and identified my features, Fingers Pete stared at me. "You're darn good," he admitted flatly. "When they arrested me, they thought I was you. Matter of fact, I was arrested under a warrant with your name on it – 'Ross Duncan.'"

That pleased me and I said so.

"Just out of curiosity, what was in the chest?" he asked.

"A series of stolen bonds and certificates."

He whistled softly through his teeth. "That ought to work toward sending me away for a good spot. It means you've hooked *me* with your crimes, which clears *you* of them."

I shrugged. "Maybe."

"They have my gun too."

"Probably."

"It's covered in my finger prints and ballistics will no doubt link me to a few things."

"Like the young woman in Chicago?"

He shrugged. "They wouldn't have known where to look except for an anonymous tip that came in by telegram after I was pinched. One of the older blues got a lot of enjoyment out of telling me that. I wonder who sent it?"

I pursed my lips tightly and let him get whatever he could out of it.

"What do you really want?" he asked. "You didn't come in here at great risk to yourself simply to gloat."

"Didn't I?"

Fingers Pete pursed his lips and shook his head. "No," he said. "I don't think so. That's not your style."

I found a pack of Chesterfields and withdrew one. "You want this?" I asked, offering him the rest of the pack.

"No thanks."

I pushed the pack in through the bars of his cell anyway. It landed flat on the floor and sat there. Pete didn't look at it. "Where are you supposed to meet the lady?" I asked him.

"What lady?"

"You know who I'm talking about."

"Why would I give her up to you?"

"Why wouldn't you? You're finished."

Pete shook his head. "I don't go that way. I never have. Would you?"

Begrudgingly, I shrugged. "Maybe if I thought she had betrayed me."

"She didn't."

"Do you trust her that much?"

"I don't trust her at all, but she doesn't know enough to give me away. You conned her."

"Are you sure about that?"

"I'm sure enough."

"Where were you going to meet her?" I asked again. "Tell me where and when she'll be waiting for you."

Pete stared at me and his expression said nothing.

"Come on. Where?" I asked again.

He just shook his head and looked away.

"It might make things easier for you."

Pete shook his head again and leaned forward with his elbows on his knees as if he were about to be sick. Then he raised his chin and looked at me. His soft, feminine eyes were ice cold. I could feel the chill through the bars.

I drew my .45, snapped off the safety and pointed it at him. "Maybe I'll just shoot you right now."

While he thought about it, his expression didn't change. He played it straight the way he had lived. He was Fingers Pete who could take any hand the world dealt him without breaking a sweat, and he'd play out the string only one way and all the way to the very end. With that, he said: "Maybe you will and maybe I'd be better off if you did."

"Would you rather die now than spend the next thirty years in prison?" I asked.

"Go ahead," Pete encouraged, nodding. "Put one in me." He sat up straight and pulled his shoulders back to give me a fuller target.

I thought about it. "No, I guess not. You'd rather I did than let them send you away for a long stretch. I'll leave you to that fate instead."

"If they don't hang me, it surely means I'm for the Rock."

I considered this and then nodded. "Perhaps," I said.

"In that case, I might see you out there some day," Pete said without a smile.

"You might," I returned. "I have another question. Maybe you'll answer this one. After you killed Tucker, why did you take the photograph of Sutro's Cliff House from the wall?"

Pete's face remained still. "It was an interesting photograph. I liked it."

"There's more to it."

He shook his head and his lips clamped firm.

"Where is it now?"

"I posted it back to myself in New York City."

Then it struck me. "Do you collect souvenirs from all of your crimes?"

Pete stared at me with no expression on his face for a long time. Eventually I turned away.

*

Before I left the building, I spoke to the old man again: "When they picked him up, he had a few things with him. Where are his effects now?"

"Most of them are in the evidence room, sir."

"What do they have there?"

"For certain? I couldn't say. We'd have to look at it. What's not there is the .22 he used to kill those people, including that Chinaman. The gun is at

231

the lab now. They're running prints and ballistics. Ought to have something by tomorrow afternoon."

"Any doubt about it?"

"Not in my mind," he insisted. "What I hear, no one worried the prints and ballistics won't match him to the murders. It's the gas chamber for that dumb onion." He overheard the callousness of his own words and amended them on the spot: "Sometimes there are other considerations. He could get life instead. We have judges that lean that way. Myself, I don't know which is worse."

I didn't either. "Show me his personal effects," I said.

"They're back here in this old carton."

We moved around behind the counter where he showed me a cardboard box on a shelf that had once been used to hold a case of Schlitz beer. Now it held something else. After he lifted it down for me to see, I peered down into it.

There was a crumpled and half-empty package of Fatima's, two match books – one from the Sausalito ferry – a heavily worn leather wallet holding thirty-eight dollars, a key-ring with six keys on it, a folded napkin, a city street map, the card of a taxicab service, and the two Chinese keys that had been taken from Tucker and Chi.

I glanced at the officer who had showed me around. "You've been very cooperative. I suppose it causes you trouble if I take some of the items out of this carton?"

He smiled, squinted at me, and shrugged off-hand. "It's my job to catalogue them and I haven't had time to do it yet."

With my best smile I handed him a c-note and said. "You must have had a long day. Why not take a load off over there. I'll finish up here shortly and I can return this box to its shelf."

"Thank you, this is too much." He winked and shuffled away, already spending the money in his thoughts.

Once I was alone I peered back into the box and picked out the folded napkin, city street map, and the two Chinese keys. I ran my fingers over the keys, feeling the smooth, polished surface interrupted only by the indentation of the lettering. After a moment I slipped them into my pocket.

Next I unfolded the napkin and studied it. I put it in my pocket, along with the city map. Searching around in the box again, I examined the matchbooks, opening each of them and then closing them. They told me nothing other than he'd been on the same ferry I had taken at some point – though I had no way of knowing when.

I rifled the wallet and quickly lost interest in it. The key ring held nothing of any obvious value, but I pocketed it all the same. The last thing I did was to inspect the package of cigarettes. I examined the case and poked around inside with my fingers. All I found for my efforts were cigarettes, and not a brand I had any interest in. They went back into the box.

I didn't study the napkin or the city map until I was back in my Ford. The napkin had Jennifer's name written on it next to a time and date that added up to early the next morning.

The city map had a few spots circled on it – only one of which had not yet come into play. I struck a match to the napkin and city map, and once they were well aflame I dropped them out the window. I had just enough blaze left on the match to light a Chesterfield for myself.

I had to laugh out loud at that.

*

From a telephone booth near the corner of Van Ness and Bay Street I made the promised call to Josephine. Smitherton answered after the second ring and handed it to his boss immediately. He'd come to recognize my voice by now.

"What have you got?" Josephine's terse voice demanded.

"Federal agents picked up Fingers Pete at the warehouse this afternoon."

"Of all the lousy luck."

"What about the lady?" I asked.

"She gave my man the backdoor slip," he told me. "We lost her."

"Entirely?"

"Yes."

I thought about it for a moment. "I don't know where she is now, but I know where she'll be tomorrow."

"Where?"

I gave him a short answer that stopped him. He didn't like it, but there wasn't anything he could do about it. For a moment all I could hear on the line was the distant chatter of a million anxious whispers.

"What about the chest in Lot seventy-three?" Josephine asked eventually.

"It's gone," I said. "You'll have to look for it in China now if you still want to find it."

"*What?*" he responded anxiously.

"That's right," I said and hung up.

233

Chapter Forty-Seven

I was sitting at the bar counter of Bernstein's Fish Grotto on Powell Street with my second martini when the Orions arrived thirty minutes late and saw me through the large glass picture window of the bar. Susan Orion waved at me with a big smile on her face. It warmed me a little. I finished my drink quickly and climbed off my stool to join them in the dining room.

"Hello, young man," Dr. Orion exclaimed enthusiastically. He shook my hand and gestured toward his wife. I hugged her and kissed her on the cheek, self-conscious about the gin on my breath.

"Its very good to see you," Susan Orion said. "Have you learned anything?"

"Let's get our table and order some wine first," Dr. Orion suggested. "Then we can catch up on the things that connect us."

A moment later the host appeared and his face blossomed into a large grin when he identified the Orion's. "Doctor and Mrs. Orion!" he exclaimed loudly. "Welcome! It is so wonderful to see you both again! I have wondered where your world travels have taken you lately?"

"It's a pleasure to be back, Charles," Orion said with a beaming smile. "Our travels have been grand." He shook the host's hand and then hugged him. A moment later a waiter approached us, grinning. He was a short, dark fellow with thick, wavy hair and heavy glasses. He too shook Dr. Orion's hand and then gave him a sincere hug that he held for a ten-count.

"Freddie," Orion said as he came out of the mutual clinch. "How are your children?"

"They are well, Dr. Orion."

"I'm glad to hear."

"Allow me to introduce our friend. This is the famous Mr. Huddleston who comes here from the other end of the country."

I shook hands with Charles and Freddie and traded polite compliments with them.

"Follow me, if you will now," Freddie said with an exaggerated bow. "We have saved the best table in the house for you."

Mrs. Orion glanced at me and smiled as we were quickly shown to a table by a window that overlooked Powell Street and the faux bow of the ship that extended out over it.

"How does he know all these people?" I asked her in an aside as her husband continued to exchange pleasantries with Freddie.

"Randolph is *very* friendly," she said with a smile and a shrug.

Once we were seated and without looking at a wine list, Orion had a conversation with the sommelier about a suitable wine.

"Do you like white?" he asked me.

I told him I could live with it.

There was more discussion between them and Orion nodded emphatically and seemed to be approving something.

A moment later, Freddie reappeared. He shook Orion's hand again and they exchanged confidences. "Are you okay approving the chef to cook for us?" Orion asked both of us.

Susan nodded, though almost reluctantly. "He might want to see a menu," she said, nodding my way.

I shrugged and nodded too. I knew what she meant, but I'd already seen the menu and I was okay with following the chef's plan.

We made small talk while a bottle of French Chardonnay was opened, tested, and poured. Moments later a platter of baked oysters, still steaming, in spicy hot lime juice was set in the middle of the table. Someone set a cold martini in front of me. We ate the oysters quickly with tiny three-pronged silver forks.

The next course was a dish of mussels Bordelaise. By the time we finished them, the bottle of Chardonnay was empty – as was my martini glass. A plate of coo-coo clams appeared next. Before we went to work on them, Orion detained Freddie by the elbow and whispered into his ear.

Minutes later a bottle of Italian red appeared. By the time it was opened, tested, and poured, the clams were gone and we each stared down into a plate of carefully arranged abalone steaks. We ate the abalone while still exchanging only small talk. It was friendly and funny and even interesting. I didn't mention my visit to the Sausalito house they had led me to believe was theirs.

After the abalone there were two plates of rare New York strip steaks with mushrooms and port sauce. The Orion's split one between them. These were followed by small cheese plates, homemade biscuits, Bibb lettuce salads, and baked apple crisps. Along the way a third bottle of wine was delivered – this time a French Bordeaux – and then there was coffee and apricot liquor. After the plates had been cleared, we were served small fried dough pieces rolled in caramelized sugar.

"Now that we're well fed and happily inebriated, shall we talk about our mutual interests?"

I nodded.

Smiling, he reached under the table and handed me a small briefcase he had brought in with him. "We were fortunate in moving the stones you showed us. There were three buyers. Susan negotiated a very nice arrangement in each case. I think you will be pleased." He rattled off some numbers – the details of each sale, the total amount of all three sales together, their cut, and my end – and he invited me to peek inside the briefcase if I liked.

"I don't feel a need to do that," I replied.

"Thank you for that," Orion said. "It's wonderful to enjoy such trust as you show us. Fill us in on your adventures. Tell us what you have learned."

I sat back in my chair and lighted a Chesterfield, my first since we had been seated. "You aren't going to much like what I have to say," I promised.

"We are interested only in the truth, not in the fantasies that so many others would peddle. We've read about the murders in town. Tell us where things stand now. We only want to know the reality – whatever it is. You are not to blame for all that has gone wrong in this town."

I produced the envelope from Mrs. Hu and charged right into it. "The package you seek was shipped out to China yesterday morning."

I fished into my pocket and gave them the two Chinese keys. They each took one, smiling down upon them as though they were small mirrors.

"They're smooth," Mrs. Orion said.

"Smooth and heavy," Dr. Orion added.

"Keep them safe because they may prove valuable some day," I said. "Together these two keys would have opened a box inside the sealed chest. I'm told a similar pair of keys was shipped to an address in China many years ago. They are awaiting receipt of the sealed chest and the Blue Orb in a small town there that held it two or three centuries ago."

"The Blue Orb?" Orion exclaimed.

I smiled into his upraised eyebrows. "That is what you are seeking?"

After a moment he shrugged. "We can call it that if you like."

"I have encountered other mysteries," I responded. "The 'Blue Orb' is what others have called it."

"I think it's fine for what we seek. Proceed then."

"A woman named Jennifer McPhael says her husband is missing. She met me at the end of your property the other day, as I was leaving."

"Who is she?"

"She is married to a man named Walter McPhael, a successful Persian businessman who is also seeking the Orb. The story she told me is that she is looking for him because he disappeared two weeks ago."

"The poor woman! What happened to her husband?"

I finished my coffee and lighted another Chesterfield. I had to tell it straight. "Walter McPhael is also almost certainly on his way back to Persia – murdered and wrapped in one of his own expensive rugs, en route to Tehran. He won't be found for a while and when he is found, no one will be able to identify him."

"That will be very hard on his wife," Susan Orion assured me.

I shrugged.

"How did our package get routed back to China?" Orion asked pleasantly and with sincere interest.

I told him. "The man who's held it all these years, a quite elderly man, a frail man, a man who had thought he might put it on the local auction market decided he simply could not do that. Instead, he sent it back to his home town – the small town in rural China from where it came so many years, so many lives ago."

"Who is this man?" Orion asked, curious about the man himself, but not the least bit angry.

"His name is Lin. He was sent over from China as an orphan child almost sixty years ago. Once here in the U.S., he traveled the country as a young man, and then worked for Mr. Sutro over the years. After that he made a career in the silent movies until the talkies came along. I think he expected to finish his life here in San Francisco, though his sentiment remained focused on that faraway village in China."

"Where is he now?"

I smiled as I took one last drag from the cigarette I'd been working on. "This very morning he decided to return to China – to the village that rejected him so many years ago after his parents died."

"You helped him leave?"

I nodded. "A little spare cash was tickling my pocket. I used it to buy him fare on an ocean voyage and took him down to the dock to catch his ship."

"That was kind of you," Susan assured me.

"It was no sacrifice for me to help him."

Orion smiled warmly. "Maybe I should be angry with you."

I shrugged that off. "There's no point to that. Lin had already pulled Lot seventy-three from auction and sent it back to his distant home village in China. He did that on his own. All I did was help put him in position to catch up with it."

Dr. Orion smiled philosophically and nodded. He raised his glass of apricot liquor.

"Maybe I'm not as patient as you are," I said.

"That's because you're a young man. Patience comes only with time and perspective."

"That's why I'm impatient," I replied. "I don't expect I have much time."

"We never know. Do you have anything more to tell us?"

I didn't see a reason to bother them with all the details, but I gave them most of the broad strokes, including Josephine's interest in the Orb, Beakman's death, and the arrest of Fingers Pete. They both listened intently without comment or question. "What will you do now?" I asked when I was finished.

"What *can* we do?" Orion said mildly, glancing at his wife. She smiled and nodded easily at him. "We'll go to China," he said then. "We'll find the village and we'll talk to your Mr. Lin. He might be confused or he might see things the way we do. Perhaps we can negotiate with him."

I had the strong impression this was not an issue of greed, but an issue of concern for the human condition. The Orions would continue their pursuit, not to enrich themselves personally, but out of belief they could save their fellow man. It was a principled mission and one they had written for themselves. I could only tip my hat to them.

"After all is said and done, I believe it's about the connections," Orion explained. "At the molecular level, the cellular level, the structural level. If we can understand them, we can tune them, harmonize them. The human brain is an amazing machine – graced by God it is the most miraculous biophysics device in our universe."

"How so?" I had to ask.

He shrugged allowed his cryptic half-smile to appear. "Electricity."

"Electricity?"

"Electricity. That is where the answers lie."

I smiled, though I was puzzled. "Are humans really that simple? Do we come down to nothing more than a blueprint concocted by an electrical engineer?"

"Perhaps, though don't ever assume it is anything close to simple."

"You are serious?"

"Or maybe the answers are to be found in the stars?" Orion said. "Who knows if there is even a difference there?"

"What does that mean?"

"You've never thought about it?"

"Is that what we've been chasing after? A crystal ball to view the future with?"

Orion shook his head adamantly. "Nothing so puerile as that. This is about science and the scientific method – not magic."

"Come on," I exclaimed with confusion.

"Moses was probably an astrologer and Newton certainly believed in it."

"What does astrology have to do with anything?" I asked.

Orion turned his head upward, as if to look at the sky and his spread his hands out from one another: "Behold!"

"What are you saying?" I pressed.

"You have your Bible and that is a comfort. I would not strip it from you, but there are other things in this universe and they are all connected, though perhaps chaotically so. If we can bring order to the connections, we cans make a difference in the lives of everyone. Don't you want that? Who wouldn't want that? There is nothing more tangible I can say to explain it."

I sighed and lighted a third Chesterfield, fighting to hold out against the sense of deflation that was coming over me. "Will you really go to China now?" I asked.

Orion smiled brightly and glanced at his wife. She looked over at him expectantly, waiting, as I was to hear his response.

"I think we pretty much have to, don't you?"

I exhaled two slow streams of cigarette smoke through my nostrils. "I don't know myself," I said. "I will say this. I believe we all tap along to a remote and enigmatic rhythm played far away by some ancient force we can never see or know. I think we all believe in it, though we have different names for it and different understandings of what it means."

"Exactly," Orion whispered. For perhaps the first time all evening, his expression was dead serious as he leaned across the table toward me, nodding earnestly.

I took another drag on my cigarette and turned my face to look at Susan. She was staring at her husband with an expression I couldn't read. Goosebumps climbed my spine and caused me to shiver inside my clothing.

Chapter Forty-Eight

The frames fluttered silently through my mind, amber-tinted images of an elderly man in a tightly wrapped kimono stepping off a train at a rural village stop. Once he was standing on the station platform with only his rucksack, the train engine began to puff heavily and then moved on down the track. The inter-title card showed in white letters on a black background: *Mr. Lin returns to his childhood village.*

The camera returned to the scene on the station platform where the elderly man looked about in all directions. He saw nothing that he could recognize. A gradual close-up showed the lonely sorrow in his weeping eyes. *Mr. Lin has been away from home for 56 years.*

The man lowered his rucksack on the platform between his feet and glanced about hopefully as the passersby moved along in each direction on either side of him. *No one is there to greet Mr. Lin upon his return.* Orchestral strings inside my head stirred, easing into a sad lullaby that wound toward a high-pitched solo violin representation of heartache and sympathy.

The man looked around and the pupils of his eyes dilated. He did not recognize his old village or any of the people living in it now. A kettledrum began a low and building rumble, bringing to a head his anguished realization. *Mr. Lin's village was different. Changed forever from the image he'd held in his mind all those years he was away.* He cried openly, with a chin rested on one sleeve.

With a heavy heart, the man wandered the streets of his village, searching for someone, something familiar, though he finds no one, nothing. He continued to wander the streets alone, searching, a foreigner now, until well after dusk. *Mr. Lin is forlorn, recognizing nothing, recognized by no one.*

Suddenly, the amber tint of the film shaded to blue and then to black. The final scene was of the man, alone, broken and fatigued, sitting on a curb by himself. As the strings played, he reached inside the rucksack and his hand came out holding a small, dark, glowing sphere that he pressed to one cheek as his tears ran down over it.

The music resolved to a final low cello note, held until the screen went black. The only sound after that was the flapping of the projector as the end of the reel continued to spin.

*

When I awoke, I realized the black lab, Timothy, was on the bed with me, vigorously lapping the back of my hand with his tongue. His rhythm matched the empty sound of the spinning movie reel in my dream-state mind.

I patted his head and rolled off the bed with my gun in hand and clutching at my watch.

Chapter Forty-Nine

It was still early in the morning and the sky was bright with a tranquil silver rain over the bay, just off the waterfront, as I walked a quarter mile past the Hyde Street Pier. The tiny drops seemed to fall slowly, reflecting the eastern sunlight, prism-like, back over the still-awakening city.

As I neared Pier 26 I could see her standing in profile with her back to the skyscrapers, looking out toward the water with her hands deep in the pockets of her overcoat. I wondered what was in her thoughts. She didn't notice me until I was standing beside her. Her reaction was smooth. It took her only an instant to recover, though she didn't remove her hands from their pockets.

"You startled me," she said, unwrapping a nervous smile for me.

I accepted the gift. "I didn't mean to."

She turned away from me to look back out toward the wide expanse of water. "This spot makes me feel contemplative. They killed two men here last summer during the waterfront strike riots."

"Let's walk a little," I proposed.

She seemed to like that idea and we moved out along the pier, moving slowly together. With one hand out now, she tried to take one of mine. I didn't let her.

"I couldn't stay at the Palace," she started to explain.

"Why not?" I said.

"I didn't feel safe there. After you left yesterday morning, someone knocked on the door. A message was pushed under it saying men were in the lobby asking about me. I don't know who delivered the note or who the men were or if there even were any men."

"There could have been men looking for you."

"It spooked me. Of course, I was worried about *you*, but I couldn't stay there any longer."

We continued to walk slowly and I didn't look at her. "Where did you spend last night?" I asked casually.

"I took a room at the Clift," she said slowly after a slight pause.

I shrugged. I didn't know whether to believe her or not, but it didn't matter anymore.

"What about you?" she asked. "Where did you sleep?"

"Nowhere as fancy as the Clift. I slept in the room I rented a few days ago over in the Lower Pacific Heights."

"I hope that was tolerable."

I shrugged. "My landlady, Nurse Green, was glad to see me. So was her dog."

"Are you feeling okay?"

"No," I told her. "I'm not." I stopped walking and turned toward her as she came to a halt beside me. She moved toward me, as if to put her arms around me and I stopped her with the palm of my right hand on her shoulder.

"What's wrong, darling?" Her deep brown eyes were wide and worried, and they seemed to be probing my eyes, searching for some clue I was trying hard not to give her.

"It's no use to pretend," I said. "You haven't even asked how I found you here."

She pouted her lips. "How did you find me here?"

"Fingers Pete won't be meeting you this morning. He's locked-up. Federal agents arrested him at the warehouse yesterday. They have him now and he's got a long stretch ahead of him, if they don't hang him."

"I don't understand."

"You do. You hired him to kill your husband and the others."

"No..." Her mouth remained open, but she was unable to find any more words to utter through it.

I nodded with a certainty that I now felt for the first time as I studied her face. "The sealed chest is gone. You can forget about it. It's been sent back to China, and the Orb with it. It's a few thousand miles away by now."

"You misunderstand me."

"Do I? I don't think so. You brought Pete into this play. I don't know what you promised him or what you paid him, but he murdered five people – your husband, Drake, Tucker, Chi, and the young girl who died in my arms. Her name was Mei."

Jennifer was quiet for a moment, though her eyes and lips were in motion, as if she were swallowing her last lie and preparing the next one. "I never expected him to do any of that. He agreed to help me, but he never said anything about killing people. I needed help. I didn't realize what he intended to do. Surely, you can't blame me for that."

"Surely I can."

"Oh, you mustn't. I'm so lost right now."

I smiled at her in same way I assumed she had smiled at others. "You know better than I do, but I think you've used men all your life, including your husband, Johnny Drake, and that heedless Sam Travers. They all ended up dead. Sure, their own greed played a role, but you pulled the strings the whole time. You manipulated them. I won't be used, not by you, and especially not by you because you expected me to fall in line like the others did."

"You must help me," she pleaded. "Travers was a bad man. You saw that for

243

yourself. He threatened me if I didn't do what he said. You didn't even know my husband or Johnny Drake."

"Didn't I? We were on the same side of the gender line. That means something."

"How can that count for anything after what we've meant to each other?"

"What have we meant?"

"Don't you know?"

I shook my head. "Not any longer, I don't."

"I love you."

"Those are only words."

"Don't I mean anything to you?"

"It's rough justice, sister."

"You can't steer things this way," Jennifer cried, still almost sure of herself. "It's not right. You can't deny your feelings for me." She touched a palm to the side of her face as she smiled sadly at me with her tilted head and her hip cocked out with the other hand on it. Self-consciously, she brushed her hair back behind her ear on one side.

"Why? Because I'm supposed to be sentimental?" I queried. "That's what you've counted on all along, isn't it?"

She shook her head adamantly and moved the hand from her face to touch my sleeve with it. "I don't know what you're talking about. Why must you be so cruel?"

"I don't like it either, but the fact that you were counting on my romanticism this whole time is all I need to let it go."

"Can't you say my name?"

"Afsoon." I said it easily and without emotion. That shook her.

"I thought you loved me too," she complained bitterly, working intently to hold my gaze.

She was so beautiful I almost had to look away. "I know – you never lost a man before. They've always done your bidding, even when it killed them. Maybe I'm different. Maybe love doesn't affect me the same way it does other men. Maybe if it had only been the four men and not the girl that died, but we'll never know. If Josephine doesn't catch up with you too quickly you'll have some time to figure it out."

"Josephine?" Her confidence was slipping and now there was real fear in her eyes for the first time.

I tilted my head. "That's why you want me, isn't it – to take you away, to protect you from him?"

She stammered a little and her fear seemed genuine. "You don't think Josephine cares about me, do you? Why would he bother with me?"

I had to laugh. "You know as well as I do you're number one on his list after this Chinatown affair."

"He wouldn't hurt a woman? I'm not in the rackets. What have I done to him?"

Calmly, I lit a Chesterfield and exhaled before responding. "Let's review the list that I assume he's working off of. You lied to him and you cheated him, stringing him along the whole time."

"I didn't do that," she protested.

I continued: "You manipulated his man Travers into betraying him and then you set Travers up to be murdered when he didn't matter to you anymore."

"How can you believe that?"

"Believe me, it's easy. Then there's this: you brought in other men, dangerous men like Fingers Pete and myself, to disrupt his play."

"I needed a man to protect me, that's all."

I ignored her. "He probably thinks you're the reason he didn't obtain the artifact he's been looking for all these years. We'll leave out the fact that you made a fool of him in the process of it."

"How can you say all this about me. It's not true. None of it is true."

"Sweetheart, maybe those things aren't enough for him to care. Perhaps Josephine doesn't see things the way I would if I were in his shoes. Who knows? He might not come after you. What do you think? Would he hurt a woman who did all those things to him?"

Jennifer pressed her body close up to mine. "He mustn't think any of that. It's not true, not at all, not any of it! You can persuade him."

I stared into the dark, deep pools of her irises. For long moment I thought about the first time I'd seen her, how she had stared straight ahead, defiant and proud and confident, with her short black hair windblown across her face. I thought about the soft texture of her skin when I touched it, and the dark, sun-bronzed arms and legs that stood out in contrast to the white core of her lovely body in the night. With all that, I remembered how I had formed an impression that she was immune to everything.

All those thoughts went through my mind before I responded to her. "To the contrary. It is true, it's all true – every word of it. Anyway, his boys ought to be here shortly. Perhaps you'll have a chance to explain to them."

"What do you mean by that?" There was a look of alarm on her face now for the first time.

"Look over my shoulder. Are they back there waiting? You might be able to spot them. Do you see two or three men in black suits and bowler hats?"

"What?" she exclaimed, with rising hysteria in her voice. "You called them?"

I shrugged and then moved my chin about. "I wasn't going to be the one left hanging out on the line."

Jennifer was crying tears now. "If you walk away from me, I have no one,"

245

she pleaded. "I'm naked. I have nothing."

"That's right. That's how you shall return – naked. It's how we all return when it's our time."

"I thought you loved me."

I laughed again – a cold, abrasive laugh that hurt my throat badly and my soul even worse. "Whatever gave you that idea? Even if I did love you, or still do love you, what does that have to do with it, anyway? Should that make even one slender lick of a difference?"

The offshore rain had stopped. Seabirds were calling loudly from above us. I dropped my cigarette on the pier, ground it under my foot, and turned away from her. I could hear her crying my name as I walked the length of the pier back to the wharf.

The Jennifer McPhael I knew expected me to have a change of heart and come back to her, but I didn't so much as turn to look over my shoulder before I joined the crowd moving along the waterfront. From the corner of my eye, I saw the bowler hats going by in the opposite direction, three dark men with fierce intent written in their expressions.

I thought about something she had said to me once: *"The chief priests and ancients used Judas' returned blood money to buy a potters field – a barren field within which to bury paupers and strangers, people who had no one."* Of course she didn't understand why Judas Iscariot had hanged himself. She couldn't – it was simply too far beyond her to ever understand it.

I kept on walking, going up a very long hill into the heart of the city. Some part of me wanted to turn around and go back to her, but of course I didn't. I continued to go on, up that long, lonely hill. All the while the cold breeze blowing in through the tall buildings stung the tears in my eyes.

The End

Acknowledgements

I am grateful to my marvelous agent, Sonia Land, and her assistant, Gabrielle Hancock, for all they do. I am also appreciative of the scholarly writings, historical insights, and helpful feedback from the acclaimed Chinese historian, Dr. Yucheng Qin.

About the Author

*Photograph by Georgina Longoria at
Open Bubbles Studio, Houston, Texas.*

Christopher Bartley, a pen name, is an American behavioral scientist. He is a professor of psychology at the University of Hawaii in Hilo, Hawaii, and also McNair Scholar and Director of Clinical Research at The Menninger Clinic in Houston, Texas. He conducts clinical trial, epidemiology, and neuroscience research, primarily with psychiatric inpatients, prisoners, and combat veterans. He has authored over 250 scientific publications, including a recent graduate textbook on psychopathology. He has consulted to US Congress, Department of Defense, Veterans Affairs, and the National Board of Medical Examiners. He has also published commentaries in the *National Review, Huffington Post, New York Times,* and *Time.* For his scientific work he has been quoted in the *Wall Street Journal, The Economist, Washington Post, Scientific American, USA Today,* and *Los Angeles Times,* among others.

This is his eighth novel. He lives on the Big Island of Hawaii with his wife and their cats. His email address is rossduncan32@gmail.com. He can also be "liked" on Facebook (facebook.com/christobartley) and "followed" on Twitter (@christobartley).

23105536R00165

Made in the USA
Middletown, DE
22 August 2015